BROKEN DOLLS

With a Metropolitan Police career
spanning 35 years, SARAH FLINT has
spent her adulthood surrounded by
victims, criminals and police officers. She
continues to work and lives in London
with her partner and has three older
daughters.

D1471255

BROKEN DOLLS

Sarah Flint

First published in the United Kingdom in 2018 by Aria, an imprint of
Head of Zeus Ltd

9 7 5 3 1 2 4 6 8

A CIP catalogue record for this book is available from the British
Library.

ISBN 9781786690722

Aria
an imprint of Head of Zeus
First Floor East
5–8 Hardwick Street
London EC1R 4RG

Also by Sarah Flint

The Trophy Taker

Liar Liar

Mummy's Favourite

About *Broken Dolls*

A baby lies abandoned amongst the rubbish; her tiny
face as white as alabaster, her body as
stiff as a miniature doll.

A young prostitute lies beaten, her figure lying like a
mannequin on the frozen concrete, her
blood spilt, her life ebbing away.

As DC 'Charlie' Stafford and her boss DI Hunter
struggle to identify the victim from the violator their
hunt brings them to the crack houses of Lambeth,
littered with damaged people, their lives scarred by
tragedy and violence, most broken beyond repair.
As further lives hang in the balance Charlie must
empower the weak to speak out against those who
seek to cause harm.

But can a broken doll ever truly be
mended; or will the wounds of the past,
fashion the events of the future?

To a real broken doll whose sad life was the motivation for my initial storytelling.

I can never forget the sight of her lying on a hospital trolley at the age of thirteen, sucking on her thumb; so similar – yet so different – to my own daughter of the same age who still retained the habit. I watched her gradual decline over the years, powerless to do anything to help, until she was absorbed fully into the seedy drug culture of Lambeth and later sectioned into a psychiatric hospital. I know not what became of her, or even whether she is still alive, but I will always remember her.

<u>Chapter 1</u>

Sunday 10th December 2017

He picked the tiny scrap up, not yet full term and wrapped it in a towel. Although it was only a hand towel, the material covered its whole form, encircling it several times. Small patches of blood soaked through, red and mottled against the lightness of the fabric. The body was cooling now, its umbilical cord still attached, but it wouldn't take long for it to fully lose its heat. The night was cold and the soft, pink towelling would soon freeze.

He stared down into the baby girl's face and felt nothing, pushing it from his sight into the bottom of a plastic supermarket carrier bag. It would have to be disposed of and it was his job to do it.

He looked around the room to locate his coat. The lamps were on, the light from them subtle and low. The walls were a dusky pink, clean and smooth. The pine laminate flooring was covered with a large fake-fur cream rug, situated in front of a gas fire whose imitation flames flickered warm and yellow in the fireplace. Above the mantelpiece hung a large print of a naked woman and several smaller pictures around the walls featured partial nudes. A cabinet stood next to a large bed, neatly spread with massage oils, sex toys and a selection of condoms.

The bed took up most of the space.

He heard a cry and looked towards the centre of the bed to see the young girl's tear-stained face. She was barely seventeen years old, lying on the bed where he'd left her, her knees drawn loosely into her body. The covers were thrown to one side and she wore only a T-shirt that had ridden up, exposing a large, ugly bruise, extending across her midriff, discoloured and swollen. Her blonde hair fell across her eyes, plastered wet against her forehead. Blood spread out across the sheets under her body. He frowned at the sight.

'Clean this place up, Tatjana. It's disgusting. And get yourself sorted. When this week is finished you must be ready for our Christmas clients. You need to start earning your keep.'

He slipped his jacket on, tied a scarf around his neck and pulled it up over his nose. A woolly hat completed his camouflage, leaving only a small gap through which to see. What he had to do had to be done masked and under cover of darkness. It would not do to be seen. He picked the plastic bag up. There was no weight to it.

She sprang up suddenly, lunging towards the bag, her fingers grasping a corner of it. He pulled it away from her, shoving her roughly back across the bed. Striding to the open door, he checked that Albertas was sat at his station at the bottom of the stairs, noticing a slight movement as one of his other girls disappeared into a bedroom. He took hold of the handle, ready to pull the door shut behind him.

The girl cried out again, wiping the hair from her face and wincing as her body contorted in pain.

'Please, let me see my baby.'

He ignored her.

She pushed herself upwards with her arms, straining towards him.

'Please Dimitri, at least let me see if I have a girl or a boy.'

'She's dead anyway, so why should you care? You do not need to see her. We do not need her. She will be gone soon.'

'So, my baby's a girl.'

'Or was.' He laughed spitefully.

The girl wiped her arm across her eyes. Black mascara stained her cheeks. She sobbed out loud.

'Maybe she is lucky to escape this hell.'

Chapter 2

The bin storeroom lay open. Eight large grey wheelie bins stood within: filled with black rubbish sacks, white bin liners and numerous carrier bags, some tied at the top, many split down the sides, household waste and discarded rubbish spewing out across the concrete floor.

DC Charlie Stafford and her boss, DI Geoffrey Hunter, gazed at the door to the storeroom, the stench of the area filling their nostrils. All around them, the estate wore a cloak of darkness, the longest night being just a few days away. Colourful fairy lights blinked from windows, plastic wreaths hung from doors and a multitude of decorations bore the message of goodwill to all. Charlie's breath spread out in front of her, the arc lights at the crime scene making the cloud of moisture appear brilliant white, almost ethereal, but what she was about to see was as far removed from the spiritual story of Christmas as was possible. Charlie was aware of what had been found, but she didn't want to see it. How could you ever be prepared for a sight like this?

The cordon tape hung still. Charlie nodded towards the uniformed policeman standing guard, who scribbled down their details. He knew them. They all knew Hunter and Charlie at Lambeth HQ.

'How was the body found?' She tried to put the moment off.

'The owner of a dog called it in. The dog was paying too much attention to the rubbish. Its owner saw the little arm and called an ambulance. We were notified at the same time.'

She jotted down what he'd said, then stepped across the tape into the crime scene. To the side of the bins lay a bright orange carrier bag, split along the whole of one side. The glare of the arc lights made the brightness of the bag look obscene against what it contained. A pink towel spread out from the hole, unravelled on the floor and the body of the tiny baby lay partially exposed, each feature perfectly formed. One arm was outstretched, its minute fingers curled loosely into a perfect fist. A fine layer of blonde hair, almost invisible to the naked eye, covered its head, with traces of blood from the womb dried across its skull.

'Oh my God,' Charlie couldn't help herself. 'How can someone just throw their baby out with the rubbish?'

Hunter remained still, silently taking in the sight, before sighing loudly. 'No one knows what goes on behind closed doors.' He bent down and concentrated on the baby, clearly trying to control his emotion and remain pragmatic. 'Looks like it's premature. It's too small to be full term, but we'll have to establish just how premature it is.' He glanced up towards where Charlie stood. 'If it's over twenty-four weeks it would be considered legally viable and we might be looking at a case of child destruction, but if it's under that, then the offence would be procuring an abortion. Or, of course, it might just be the result of a miscarriage. Whatever the case though, the mother will almost certainly require medical help.'

Charlie squatted to join him, looking around at the surrounding area. Everywhere was squalor and decay.

'What a place to end up, whatever the reason... and before life has even begun.' She peered at the miniature face, its eyes closed as if in sleep. 'Do we know yet what sex it is?' Suddenly it was important she knew the answer; whether the life discarded in front of her was a boy or a girl. It seemed wrong not to call it by its gender.

'I can tell you in a minute, that is, if it's clear to do a preliminary examination of the body.'

Dr Rob Finch strode towards them. He was the police doctor who attended crime scenes most frequently. His job was to 'pronounce life extinct'. It was a peculiar phrase that always vaguely struck Charlie as being outdated and impersonal, especially if used to the relative of a recently dead loved one. Tonight though, it appeared that life might never have legally existed.

The doctor held out his hand and Hunter shook it firmly. He was similar to Hunter in nature; straight to the point and with no frills, but he was the exact opposite physically; tall, lean, fit and with a thick head of hair. Charlie had crossed paths with him both professionally and off-duty, whilst running, most recently in her first triathlon. She stood to one side, not quite sure whether to offer her hand but deciding in the end not to. They knew each other well enough to dispense with formalities.

'Hi, Dr Finch,' she said instead. 'It would be good to know if it was a boy or girl.'

Hunter nodded. 'We need life pronounced formally, but try not to move the body any more than is necessary. Photos have been taken, but the forensics team are yet to start. I'll arrange for the coroner's officer to sort out the removal once everything is concluded.'

Dr Finch dipped his head and pulled on his gloves. Carefully he peeled the towel back, completely exposing the tiny shape. It was a baby girl, clearly dead for some time; her body, just over twelve inches in length, silent and still like a fragile white doll. Gently he placed a stethoscope on her chest, the pad of the scope covering far too much of her little frame than seemed right. Charlie watched as the doctor completed his checks with a tenderness that moved her almost to tears. He needed to do the tests before formally pronouncing life extinct, but it was clear the job was difficult.

Finally Dr Finch straightened, looking at them both. 'Well it's female. Life pronounced extinct at 22.05. She is premature and I would estimate from her size that she's probably around the twenty-six to twenty-eight week mark of gestation, but that can be confirmed at the full examination. By this stage of pregnancy her lungs and digestive tract should be pretty much fully developed, but, in the absence of any medical assistance, she would have struggled to survive, if, indeed, she was able to breathe independently at all.'

'So could she have survived if the mother had been in hospital?' Charlie asked immediately.

He turned towards her. 'It's difficult to say. She's on the very limit of survival. If she was very lucky and had medical intervention straight away it's possible, but it's also likely that she would have had some pretty severe medical issues to contend with.'

'How long has she been dead?' Hunter stepped forward, peering towards the baby.

'I can't say, I'm afraid boss, much as I'd like to help.' He bent towards the body with a thermometer. 'Rigor mortis is difficult to assess in infants and children, and even though she looks fully formed she's still technically a foetus. Newborn or pre-term babies have very little muscle mass and as it's the amount of lactic acid in the muscles that cause rigor mortis, it'll be extremely difficult to determine when exactly she died. Judging by her appearance and temperature though, I would say that she's been here for some time.'

'Are we talking hours or days? Just so I know how long to go back for hospital checks. We need to find the mother.'

'More likely days, but I really can't say Hunter. What I can say is that the mother will have gone through full labour. The chances are, as you rightly intimate, she'll need medical assistance.'

He pulled the towel back over the tiny girl, gently covering her body, as if tucking her into a cot. Charlie was again touched by this small act of humanity. They started to walk back towards their cars, pausing briefly to leave their protective suits, overshoes and gloves with the uniformed officer at the cordon. Hunter stopped to issue further instructions, while Charlie and Rob Finch went ahead.

She waited while the doctor opened the boot of his car and placed his briefcase carefully beside a pair of running shoes and an overflowing holdall, from which a towel and pair of swimming goggles spilt.

'Dr Crane at the path lab should be able to tell you more when he's done the post-mortem, Charlie. Hopefully you'll get the identity of the mother from a DNA test on the dried blood on the baby's head. I'm presuming that must be the mother's as there are no obvious injuries to the baby.' He paused, before slamming the boot shut and explaining further. 'The mother's blood supply is totally separate to that of the foetus so it will have different DNA, although the blood type might be the same.'

Charlie watched as Rob Finch folded himself into the driver's seat, turning towards her with a frown.

'You need to find the mother, Charlie. We don't know as yet how this baby was miscarried and it's highly likely her life could be in danger if any kind of infection sets in.'

Charlie pursed her lips. It was a thought they'd acknowledged earlier, especially should the baby have been forcefully removed. If the mother wasn't tracked down swiftly, then potentially they could soon be investigating two deaths, rather than just the one.

Chapter 3

Charlie slept fitfully in the office that night. There were too many things to be done to waste time travelling to or from her flat. She woke after barely two hours disturbed sleep as Bet pushed open the door, her discordant singing signalling her arrival before the light flooded in.

Bet came across, peering over her shoulder at a précis of the night's incident.

'You OK?' she put a hand on Charlie's shoulder and gave it a squeeze. 'It's never easy dealing with that kind of call.'

'I have to admit I have felt better,' Charlie ran her hands through her hair. 'Oh Bet, you should have seen how tiny the little girl's body was. How could anybody do that?'

'I don't know. I ask myself how people do the things they do all the time, especially to children.' She squeezed Charlie's shoulder again. 'You'll never forget that sight. The memory will stay with you for the rest of your life... but what you need to do now is use the image to catch who did this. I dealt with a child abuse case, years ago. I can still picture the poor little kiddie, Bethany Soames was her name, her body black and blue from where she'd been beaten and kicked to death by her parents. She had twenty-three broken bones and over a hundred other separate injuries. I couldn't rest until I had both parents locked up behind bars, but eventually I did it. So, use the image in your head to focus on, but don't let it take over your thoughts.'

'I will.' She sat up, determining to do as Bet suggested. In that instant she realised that she too would not rest until the person who had done this to the baby was caught.

Quickly, she passed across a list of hospitals yet to be checked on for admissions, before grabbing her shampoo from underneath her desk and disappearing towards the showers.

Time to get clean and get going; she'd sleep properly later.

*

Fifteen minutes later, she returned to find the whole team squeezing their chairs into a semi-circle around Hunter, who was briefing them on the details of the crime scene. She pulled up a chair too, brushing her wet hair off her cheeks and blinking her eyes open. The team were listening to Hunter's description in silence, their expressions conveying their obvious shock and disbelief at the depths to which humanity could sink. The group determination to find the perpetrator was already etched in every crease of their brows and shake of their heads. Charlie had no doubt that the image now firmly implanted in their mind's eye would be all that was required. No stone would be left unturned until the right result was achieved. Hunter, Bet and Naz all had kids of their own, but she, Sabira and Paul would feel it just as acutely. In the Community Support Unit in which they worked, they had all dealt with children brutalised by the adults in whose care they were entrusted... and the adults themselves unable to rise above the damage inflicted on them as juveniles by their own parents. It was an endless, unremitting circle of abuse, the participants of which were bound tightly into each act of domestic violence.

'Right, gang,' Hunter broke into their thoughts. 'DCI O'Connor wants us to get on with the job from last night. The post-mortem has been pencilled in for Friday, so we should then know at what stage of development the foetus was. We're still awaiting a DNA result from the blood on the baby's head, so as yet, we have no idea of the identity of our mother.' He turned towards Bet. 'You mentioned you were checking local hospitals. Any possible patients attending A and E, who might fit the bill?'

Bet shook her head and glanced towards Charlie for confirmation.

Charlie sat up as Hunter fixed his gaze on her. 'I stayed on after you left to get a few phone calls made, but nothing so far. Bet's done a few more for me.' She shifted in her seat again and flicked an unruly wave of hair from her forehead. 'I was also thinking, boss, about who the mother might be. The chances are it was an unplanned pregnancy, so the mother might just be a frightened teenager or someone similar but...' She closed her eyes momentarily and the image of the orange plastic bag in the glare of the arc lights came immediately to mind. 'It just seemed so clinical, so callous. To my thinking, it would have to be someone who doesn't value life, someone for whom an unwanted pregnancy would be a real problem. Maybe it would prevent them earning a living.'

'Like a pimp, or a dealer, or someone involved in the vice trade,' Naz interrupted. 'Some bastard who needs his girl out working and sees any possible baby simply as a hindrance to him getting his money.'

Charlie glanced across as Naz swore silently under her breath and their eyes met. Her friend had a way with words that cut through the bullshit political correctness. She was no-nonsense and fiery and not afraid to tell it as it was, yet she spoke for them all. Sabira might be quieter; Paul more diplomatic; Bet wiser and more experienced, but, as a team, they were tuned automatically on to the same wavelength.

'Exactly what I thought,' she acknowledged, looking back towards Hunter. 'So, I was thinking boss, it might be good to speak to the Source Unit. They've been putting out more information recently about drug dealers, vice and crack houses. They must have a new informant on the books who's around that sort of clientele. It might be a long shot, but it's worth a try.'

Hunter pulled a handkerchief out from his pocket and wiped it across his forehead. The central heating had kicked in and his cheeks were suffused with a rosy hue that was creeping rash-like down his neck.

'I like your thinking. Charlie, pop up to their office and see what they have to say. In the absence of anything solid though, we'll still need to do all the usual routine enquiries. Paul and Sab, you go to the crime scene and do house-to-house enquiries for witnesses overlooking the bin shed. Bet, you get started on CCTV. Naz, you start collating any information on the system. See if there is anything on any of our prostitutes or addicts who might be pregnant, or any reports of unusual behaviour that might indicate possible new brothels setting up in the area. It might even be worth checking with our local children's homes for men acting suspiciously outside. We all know that dealers and pimps tend to target vulnerable girls. I'll see if I can find out anything more from the neighbourhood policing teams.'

He stuffed his hankie back in his pocket and clapped his hands.

As one, the team rose, lifting their chairs in a solid wave over the desks and back to their various workstations. Nobody spoke as they gathered their equipment and got ready to set out.

Wednesday morning had barely started and they were already at full stretch.

*

A few minutes later, Charlie was knocking on the door of the District Source Unit, or DSU. DSU recruited CHIS, or Covert Human Intelligence Sources as they were formally titled, although better known as police informers, or narks, grasses, snouts, snitches or rats. CHIS were loved by police and hated by criminals for exactly the same reason... they could squirrel themselves into organised crime networks and gangs where even the best undercover officer feared to tread, and with far fewer restrictions. They just had to keep their heads down, commit no crime, tell no one what they did and report back regularly to their police handlers.

Charlie was interested in the source world herself, her natural curiosity at what made criminals tick driving her wish to gain an insight into life looking out from the inside, rather than always being the law-enforcer looking in. This time she had a personal interest. The increase in intelligence had occurred directly after she'd referred a local prostitute to the unit and she was itching to know if it had come from the same young woman. She would never dream of asking though; every CHIS needed the full protection of the law, not loose lips... and the less people who knew their identity the better. Even police officers talked. Secretly however, Charlie hoped she was right. The vulnerable young prostitute might get a little help and protection. She might eventually even see her way out of the lifestyle.

A head appeared around the door and a cheery voice invited her in. Five of the team were already there, discussing the daily politics and traumas of their morning commute. The office was one of the smallest in Lambeth HQ, crammed with desks, each with monitors winking and hard drives whirring, piles of paperwork and mobile phones lying across every spare inch. Each wall was plastered with photos, and whiteboards with figures and appointments. Children and teenagers stared unblinking from their custody photos, arranged together in postcode gangs: Roadside G's, Gypset, Angell Town, SIRU, ABM, young faces bearing the scars of their street lives while hopelessness dulled their eyes. Adjacent to the youths were the haggard, hardened expressions of the burglars, drug dealers and sex offenders, battle-weary from a lifetime of crime and custody.

Charlie peered around the library of faces, committing each image to memory. As a super-recogniser, the nuances of each feature needed to be seared into her memory for when she was called upon to assist with CCTV identifications. The faces on the walls were the targets of the District Source Unit's secret army, the small minority of repeat offenders that wreaked havoc on their local communities.

'Hi, Charlie. Picked out any suspects recently?' The voice of Angie, the officer who'd ushered Charlie into the room, broke through her thoughts. 'What can we do for you?'

She turned towards Angie, a short, blonde, cockney with hair styled into a bob, a mouth shaped by a sharp wit and a turn of phrase that cut straight to the point. Charlie recognised Angie of old, knowing that she was endowed with a huge heart, battling to raise a young child single-handedly whilst juggling full-time hours.

'I was called to the body of a pre-term baby girl thrown out in the rubbish last night in the Ramilles Close area.' Charlie was blunt, knowing the story would bring out the bulldog spirit in Angie. She'd seen her react to a similar incident previously when her maternal instinct had kicked in.

'Guys,' Angie shouted. 'Listen in. Charlie got called out to a dead kid last night.'

The room silenced immediately.

'I need to find out who the mother is as a matter of urgency and the circumstances of how she lost her baby. I know you've been putting out some information around vice and drugs recently and wondered if you could task your CHIS to try and find out about any street girls or drug addicts who have been pregnant recently, or any brothels in the area.'

Angie looked towards a girl on the desk opposite and nodded. 'I might be able to help, and you've got some contacts around that area too, ain't you, Von?'

Von tossed her head, throwing her long, streaked hair over to one side, and pursed her lips. 'Yep, mate. Certainly have.' She checked her watch. 'They're probably just getting their heads down now though, after a busy night in the town centre, but I'll wake them up quick.' She picked up one of the phones on her desk and started to tap in a number, before stopping and placing her hand over the handset.

Angie turned back towards Charlie, picking up her own mobile. 'We'll give you a bell, if we get something, mate. I've got yer number.' Angie stood up and pulled at the door handle. She nodded towards the open door and Charlie could see by the set of her brows that she meant when, and not if. There was no way Angie Cunningham would rest until she had an answer.

Until then though, the conversations needed to be held covertly. It was time for her to leave.

*

Three hours later, Charlie was hard at work in the office with Hunter, Bet and Naz when she saw Angie's name flash up on the screen of her phone. She smiled, realising she had been spot on with her judgement.

'Just to let you know we're on it. One of our CHIS has got some intel' on a brothel set up in the back streets of Streatham High Road, but we don't know exactly where yet. It's being run by Eastern Europeans. Word is they like young flesh and the guy in charge is hanging round some of the local children's homes trying to recruit more vulnerable youngsters. Our girls don't like that. They think it's out of order, you know, against their moral code, bless 'em. We've tasked 'em to get the address ASAP, mate.'

Charlie understood Angie's words. Prostitution was tacitly accepted as a necessary evil, but forcing underage girls to submit to the whims of grown men was implicitly wrong. No prostitute in Lambeth would withhold that sort of information from police. In an occupation with few moral boundaries, it very much crossed every remaining line.

'That's great, Angie. It sounds like the sort of place where an unwanted pregnancy wouldn't be welcome. Come straight back to me if you find out anything further.'

'It might be nothin', of course, but it's not too far away from where the body was found and you've gotta' start somewhere. I'll give you a bell as soon as I get the venue and names.'

With that, she was gone.

Chapter 4

Dimitri stared down at the girl curled into a ball on the bed in front of him. Her skin was ashen, mottled in places and a film of sweat glistened across her whole body. Her breathing was slow, what breath there was coming in short gulps between the shaking of her limbs. Every now and again she would cry out, her eyes rolling, the sound pitiful in the small room.

Outside the window, the day was gloomy, the clouds casting shadows across the blood-speckled sheets on which Tatjana lay. They had not been changed.

Dimitri frowned. Leaning over, he grabbed her by the shoulders and shook her hard.

'Tatjana, wake up, you lazy bitch. You've had three days. You need to work. Wake up.'

The girl moaned, her eyes flicking open and shut as she tried to focus. He slapped her hard across the face several times before releasing her from his grip and watching as her semi-conscious body flopped limply back across the bed.

He pulled at her grubby T-shirt, his face contorted with rage. 'You cannot stay here if you do not work.

You understand me?'

'She is not in a fit state to leave.' A second girl entered the room, pulling the curtains shut and switching on a lamp to one side. The girl, whose name was Hanna, was tall and slender, her hips swaying languidly with each movement. A thin cotton blouse tucked loosely into a miniskirt accentuating the curve of her breasts and the fact that she wore no bra. The light glowed pink; casting a rosy hue across one of Tatjana's cheeks and making the comparison with the other girl even starker. 'You need to take her to hospital. She is not well.'

Dimitri shook his head angrily. 'You know I cannot do that. She will be fine. She is just lazy.' He raised his foot and pushed it against Tatjana. 'Get up!'

A third girl came in, sidling up behind the second. She was shorter than Hanna, darker skinned, with the plumpness of adolescence not yet finally gone.

'She looks like she is dying,' she said quietly, her eyes wide with fear.

Dimitri spun around. 'She is not dying. She is young. She will recover, but she needs to get up and clean herself.'

He pulled the sheet completely from Tatjana, throwing it towards the door. Hanna gasped at the sight of her friend's shrunken form, pulling a jumper out from a nearby wardrobe and laying it across the girl's body. Tatjana stayed still, her eyes motionless; even the slight flickering behind the lids halted. Her breath became shallower, barely registering.

'You need to get medical help for her now, before it is too late.' Hanna spoke authoritatively. 'I have seen this before when a child is lost. I have seen what happens when infection takes over. You should not have forced the child from her, Dimitri. She will die and then what will you do?'

The younger girl was crying, sobbing quietly behind the older.

Dimitri ran his hands over his shaven head, his finger tracing the jagged scar that ran across his scalp down to his right ear; the result of a bottle attack on the streets of St Petersburg, soon after it had changed its name in 1991 from Leningrad, the city of his birth. He had grown wiser since that time. The streets were no place to make a living. Better to earn it off the back of others, and how much easier in this quiet area of London. Now though, this stupid girl was threatening his way of life. Why had she not told him she was pregnant before he'd brought her to the country? Why leave it until she was here to show him her swollen belly? Of course he knew why... but she was still a lying bitch. And now he was trapped. Go to the hospital and he risked her blabbing about what he had done. Leave her and he risked everything.

The older girl was staring at him now, waiting to hear what he planned, but he didn't know.

'Get out!' he shouted eventually, in frustration. 'I can't think. Get on with your business and leave me to sort out mine. I don't want to see you in here again.'

Chapter 5

Charlie paced across the front room of her family home in Lingfield, her best friend Ben having driven them both there from his flat in Brixton earlier. The meal was over and Ben was ensconced on the big maroon family sofa, with his black Labrador, Casper, snoring contentedly at his feet and her mother Meg and two half-sisters, Lucy and Beth, talking animatedly about their plans for Christmas and the New Year.

Charlie had finally capitulated to Hunter's order to go home and get some sleep when the DNA search of the blood on the baby's head came back with no positive match against the police database. It was a particular blow to her, concentrating as she was on that aspect of the investigation, but messages had now been left at all the main hospitals, walk-in clinics and larger GP surgeries in the area and there was nothing further she could do. Much to their disappointment, the baby's mother remained unidentified.

Everything else was in hand. Paul and Sab were still at the crime scene, Bet was well underway with the CCTV and Naz was now concentrating her efforts on the area in Streatham highlighted by the District Source Unit, trying to pinpoint where the brothel might be. They would need to corroborate any intelligence the DSU provided. CHIS could not be compelled to give evidence at court, so information from them could provide only a suspicion that might help point police in the correct direction or assist to obtain a warrant. And, of course, they didn't know whether this particular brothel was connected to the baby's body. They might not even be on the right track.

Hunter himself had insisted on dropping her off at Ben's flat, his delight at seeing the young man plain to see in the warmth of their greeting. Ben had come to their notice after being violently robbed nearly two years before and since then had become known and loved by the whole team, but especially Charlie, whose determination and powers of recognition had brought Ben's attacker to justice. They all admired his stoic tenacity to conquer the post-traumatic stress disorder, which had blighted his life since leaving the army, and were always keen to enquire as to his welfare or help in any way they could. Ben himself was clearly touched by this support, responding positively to every interaction, his resolve to banish his demons more evident as every day went by. It was a testament to his doggedness, and Casper's loyal service, that Ben could now be looking with any optimism to the future, and it was as a result of his and Charlie's growing friendship that he often found himself invited to join her and her family for dinner.

While the food was being prepared, Charlie had slept, fatigue allowing her body to rest deeply and dreamlessly. Only the growing crescendo from the words to 'Happy Birthday' prompted her to wake, as Ben and her family brought in a cake burning brightly with thirty-one candles. It was the first time since her birthday at the end of November that they had all managed to get together and as she bent towards the cake, the heat from its flaming decoration almost singed her eyebrows, prompting laughter from them all at her mother's creation. Meg had not only baked the cake but ensured that every candle was blazing before her handiwork was revealed, in all its fiery glory.

Now though, with dinner and the birthday celebrations having been concluded, Charlie was impatient to get away from the house. The evening would soon draw to a close and with time ebbing away she wouldn't feel complete unless she paid her usual weekly visit.

She called across to Casper, pulling his lead off the banister in the hallway and jangling it in mid-air. The dog stirred immediately at the sound, whining his approval and slapping his tail enthusiastically against the door frame as she clipped the lead to his collar. Ben moved to stand, but she stilled him with her hand.

'It's Wednesday. Stay there. I'll be back soon and I have Casper with me.'

Ben slid back, his expression momentarily pained, before nodding in obvious appreciation of the warning. Both knew better than to push the point. The location was one which brought back bad memories for him and they both knew he was not yet ready to return.

Fifteen minutes later, Charlie walked into the graveyard where her brother, Jamie, was buried, a torch lighting her path to his tombstone. Casper paced slowly at her side, his head down, as if recognising the solemnity of the setting from his own experience. Ben still took him regularly to visit his previous master's place of rest in Balham, though these visits were becoming less frequent as time passed. The old dog panted quietly, his breath fanning out in the freezing air and Charlie breathed a sigh of relief as the hands of the church clock snapped upwards. It was almost ten o'clock. She'd got there in time.

Reaching into her pocket, she pulled out a lighter and two candles taken from her cake: one for each of them.

'You'd have been thirty on your next birthday, Jamie,' she whispered, switching off the torch and lighting the candles, before sitting down and placing the two tiny glowing flames in the soil at the base of his grave. 'Fancy that! We'll celebrate that properly in a few months' time.'

Casper turned a circle before sitting down next to her, the flickering of the candles dancing in his eyes. They sat watching on until the candles were finally extinguished by an icy breath of wind and the clearing was plunged into darkness. The image of the tiny baby girl shimmered into Charlie's mind, her life snuffed out before it started.

'At least we had some time together, Jamie.' She stood up as her mobile phone vibrated in her pocket. Angie's name flashed on and off the screen. She pressed the loudspeaker, listening as the line clicked in.

'Sorry to bother you at this time of night, mate, but I've got the address you were after. The place is being run by a Russian geezer, called Dimitri, who likes his girls young. Dirty bastard. Brings them in from across the Channel or recruits from nearby. You got a pen and I'll give you the venue?'

Charlie pressed the notebook icon on her phone and jotted down the address as Angie gave it. There was still nothing as yet to say it was linked to the baby's body, but it was a good enough lead. If they went in, they could compare DNA from any girl found in the brothel with the blood sample on the baby's head. It would be easy to confirm or eliminate the venue.

'I've got the Yard to break out this intel' and had them running some more checks on the location. There're a few other bits and pieces coming up. Should be enough for you to get a warrant, early doors.' She stopped talking and Charlie could hear a plaintive cry coming through the speaker. 'Fuck it. Think I've woken me boy up now, talking too loud. Gotta go, mate, it'll be carnage here otherwise. I'll try and get you more as I hear it.'

The line clicked off before Charlie could call out her thanks, but she couldn't help smiling. Angie was one of a kind, and her partnership with Von in the DSU always yielded results. What Von said in twenty words, Angie said in two and then cut you off before you could reply.

She keyed in Hunter's number and relayed the info'. If they were quick they could get a warrant application typed up, signed by the Magistrates and ready for action by nine the next morning. Tomorrow they would be entering the brothel at the start of their day. Hopefully, they'd catch the Russian guy, Dimitri, bagging up the takings at the end of his.

Chapter 6

Tatjana was dead.

Dimitri swore under his breath. The little bitch had fucked everything up. He stared down at the girl's body, still now, her skin perfectly white except for the dirty red patches of infection that stained her arms and legs. The bruise on her midriff was a dark purple, the shape of his boot accentuated in the colour of the contusion.

The younger girl had gone now. He had to tread carefully with her. She was not yet fully on board. She still needed more persuasion; a little more cash and attention. Dimitri had dropped her back to the children's home in Norbury promising to take Tatjana to hospital on his return... but it had been too late. By the time he had climbed the stairs to the top room, she was lifeless. All that remained was the smell of infection; the odours left by her lack of cleanliness, the stench of sickness.

That issue would be easily removed though. It was no worse than the smell of sex. A few deodorisers, some scented candles, fresh linen, nothing that he couldn't handle.

Tatjana would be more difficult. Now he had to get rid of her too, just as he'd disposed of her troublesome unborn brat, but unlike the baby, she couldn't be hidden in a bag and tossed away with the rubbish. Her disposal would take more planning. He glanced down the stairs at the minder he'd employed to guard his girls. Albertas would provide cover. No one dared argue with him. At the end of each night, Albertas had his pick of the girls, and while he was receiving his just rewards, those not chosen were locked away.

Tonight, nothing would change. The girls would be shut in their rooms and no one would see him carry Tatjana's dead body away. If any of them asked where she was, well, he would just tell them he'd taken her to the hospital... and if she never returned, so what? They'd just have to assume he'd replaced her with a healthier successor. They would never know any different because they were never allowed out.

But they'd all have to move on. He couldn't risk her being found and somehow traced back to the address. He swore again. How dare the bitch spoil all his plans!

Grabbing her body roughly, he pulled her down on to the rug, wrapping her round and round within the thick fur. He had some old plastic sheeting in the back of his van. By the time he was finished no one would find her, but even if they did, they would never find him.

He pulled a packet of cigarettes from his pocket, slipping one between his lips and drawing hard as the lighter gave it heat. Blowing the smoke out into the foetid air, he grinned. No one actually knew his true identity anyway.

*

The sound of Albertas' grunts stirred Dimitri into action. Albertas had chosen Hanna, the older, slimmer female who had questioned his treatment of Tatjana earlier. Albertas often chose her. She was the most striking and also the most experienced; two traits that paid well. She knew what to do and she did it expertly. More to the point, she played the games that Albertas liked to play. It was a trade-off. She fucked him as he desired and he gave her the best protection. Albertas took no shit. If the client didn't step straight into line, he'd leave with a bloody nose, or worse and never return.

The volume of his minder's groans was reaching a climax. It was time to get going. Muffled noises resonated from the other rooms, the sound of music being played, a DVD switched on, the distinct Romanian dialect of one of his newer arrivals, bunked up with one of the others. None had smartphones. None had contact with the outside world. They heard only what their customers told them, in a language that they didn't fully understand. It wouldn't do for any of his girls to get ideas. They needed to be kept in line.

They understood though. He knew their families.

Hoisting Tatjana up on to his shoulder, he staggered momentarily at the door. Although she was only slight, her body still weighed heavily wrapped in the rug. The stairs were narrow and by the time he'd reached the bottom, Dimitri was wet with sweat. He navigated his way through the kitchen and opened the back door, looking out to where he'd reversed his van earlier, as close as was possible to the rear exit prepared and ready. The doors were open, a tarpaulin spread out across its floor, the rope to bind it looped to one side. All around him was quiet. The area was residential and nothing much stirred between the hours of midnight and five, even less so during the winter months when curtains were drawn and windows kept tightly shut. He glanced around before lifting Tatjana's body down off his shoulders and sliding it into the base of the van.

The clouds were low, blotting out any remaining light from the last quarter of the waning crescent moon. It wouldn't be full again until early January. For a second, he stared skywards. He liked the moon; it reminded him of Russia, his home country, where the miles and miles of open plains and woodland allowed each waxing or waning phase of the moon to be seen in unobstructed splendour.

But this wasn't Russia. It was London and he had a job to do.

Quietly, he locked the kitchen door behind him, before closing the rear of the van. The last preparations before dumping the body would be made nearer the scene, away from any prying eyes. A small, derelict railway outhouse on the track nearby was perfect. Inaccessible, other than through a broken fence and an arduous walk along the railway line – only the most hardened graffiti artist ever ventured there. He had scoped it out himself because he liked to find places to hide things. People, drugs, documents, firearms... sometimes they needed to be kept far away from even the remotest possibility of discovery. Sometimes things had to disappear altogether.

He turned the ignition and held his breath as the diesel engine chugged into life. Hopefully nobody would be disturbed by the noise. He had further business to attend to when he returned.

Pressing the accelerator carefully, he eased the van out along the rear access road and smiled grimly to himself. Nobody would find Tatjana's body where he was heading, or at least not for a while.

Chapter 7

Redz pressed herself further back against the interior of the car door and prayed to the God she'd known as a child, seeking to distance herself from The Punter's relentless fists. But her God wasn't listening... and Razor, her pimp, was nowhere to be seen. Only The Punter could hear her pleas and he was revelling in every second of his assault. Another blow came into her stomach, forcing its contents up into her throat. Redz swallowed hard, feeling her rib cage creak under the pressure as he unleashed another punch, slightly higher this time, his mouth turned up in an ugly grin as he snarled aloud with pleasure.

She was trapped; her hair, the feature from which her street name derived, spread thickly against the glass of the window. Long, thick and a deep shade of glossy auburn, her 'crowning glory', so beloved by her father in her childhood, was now scraped back in a messy ponytail, held in place with a filthy elastic band. Her heart-shaped face appeared far older than her nineteen years, her skin displaying the sores, deep furrows and livid scars synonymous with a life shackled to hard drugs and the violence of prostitution.

Another blow came in, this time lower, forcing her guts to contract. Her breath bulleted up through her windpipe and out in a high-pitched guttural shriek. She sucked in another lungful of air, before spitting it out in angry terror, inwardly furious for allowing herself to be drawn into this situation. The sight of 'The Punter in the long black leather coat', perfectly described by her mates, should have prevented her mistake, but the lure of money for crack cocaine had taken precedence over her safety, drowning out the warning bells in her head.

She screamed again, this time louder and more urgently.

'Shut your mouth, you fucking bitch!' the man snarled. 'You're not leaving until I get what I want.'

He grabbed her by her hair, wrenching her head against the back of the seat, and clamped his mouth around her lips, the pressure of his weight blocking her airway.

Redz reacted instinctively, biting down hard on to the fleshy part of his lower lip.

The man also reacted instinctively. A fist exploded into her ribs, the impact crushing her lungs and sending her breath blasting upwards in a burst of energy that forced her teeth apart.

She screamed again, loudly and frenetically, the noise seeming to reverberate around the cramped interior before dissolving into the upholstery.

'I told you to shut your fucking mouth,' The Punter growled again, twisting her hair around his hand and jerking her head about. A pause and then she was rocketing forward, her neck powerless to stop the force from behind.

Her face slammed into the dashboard and she felt the resistance in her nose give way. Blood spurted from the open wound and an agonising pain filled her head.

She tried to scream again, but no sound came out.

Everything was in slow motion now. The sound of her bones cracking, the movement of her head catapulted backwards and forwards, her blood spraying into the air in front of her in a fine mist, her neck feeble, her body growing limp.

Then all of a sudden he stopped.

The only noise she could hear was The Punter's laboured breath and a low gurgling sound coming from between her ears.

Dreamily, she viewed her own body lying motionless against the seat and watched as the man leant towards her. He was stroking her hair; feeling it, examining it, playing with it. The door next to her opened; the interior light came on and the cold air roared in.

Then she was falling. Out on to the hard, icy pavement, her feet still trapped in the car. She heard the engine splutter into life and the car moved forward, freeing her legs from within. Through the haze she vaguely registered the sight and sound of the car, its tyres screeching on the tarmac as it hurriedly turned and departed, clipping a wheelie bin and sending its filthy contents out across the alleyway, before disappearing from her sight towards the road and away. The last thing she remembered before the darkness closed in was her laboured breath, throwing a cloud of wet humidity up into the air.

*

Maria Simpson sighed heavily. Unable to sleep in her freezing bedroom, she'd returned to the warmth of her electric fire in the lounge and was sitting in an armchair with a woollen blanket wrapped around her legs watching a repeat of that afternoon's quiz show. She often found it hard to sleep these days. Now, at almost one a.m., and fifteen minutes into the programme, the screaming had started.

Not for the first time, she cursed the position of her flat. One side looked out on to the busy, thronging Streatham Hill with its shops and late-night eateries; the other looked down on the seedier side of life. A potholed driveway snaked along the rear, with rows of dark garages ominous and threatening. Some stood upright and intact, their contents protected by heavy padlocks. Others lay voicelessly open, watching as the underbelly of society stumbled in blindly to service their needs.

Over the years, she'd watched the area grow, develop, change and ultimately self-destruct. This was where the stolen cars were dumped, stripped and left to rust. It was where the drug addicts shot up in the disused garages and the prostitutes came with their punters.

Maria heaved herself up from the chair and shuffled towards the window, intuitively knowing to which side of the flat she was needed. The screaming, which had become more intense for a few minutes, had almost stopped now, but she'd promised herself a long time ago that she would never ignore it, as most of the other residents in the block seemed to be able to do. Humanity dictated that to close her ears to a cry for help and do nothing was wrong.

As she reached the window, the screaming stopped completely and she saw a small dark car standing at an angle below. Although its lights were off, her attention was drawn to the position in which it was parked. As she looked towards it, she saw the passenger door open, the interior light come on and a shape fall out on to the pavement. She squinted to see better, but the dirt on the outside of her sixth-floor window made it difficult to distinguish details accurately. As she watched, the car moved away with the passenger door still open and she realised that the shape was a person. Its legs lay outstretched into a square of lamplight shining down between the angled silhouettes of the overhanging garage roofs. She heard the sound of a car door slam. The interior light in the car was extinguished and the vehicle moved rapidly away. Before the light was snuffed out, Maria could just make out the shape of a large, well-built man in the driving seat, facing in her direction. A glint of metal on his right hand gripped on to the steering wheel caught her eye before he turned the car and disappeared.

She looked at the prone figure and saw it was a female with bare legs and knee-length boots. The girl lay still momentarily, before slowly moving up into a sitting position against the wall, her legs pulled up towards her body.

Maria moved back across the room to the table where her telephone stood and carefully pressed the emergency number, waiting impatiently for the operator to go through a seemingly endless list of questions.

'Ambulance and police, please,' she said eventually. 'A girl's been attacked and she looks in a bad way. Send someone quickly.'

After giving the relevant details to the operator she replaced the handset and shuffled back carefully to the window, wondering whether it was the same young girl who normally worked this patch.

Finding a tear in the curtains, she looked out again, her eyes adjusting slowly to the dim light of the alleyway below. The figure was still there by the wall, but she'd slumped sideways, with her head facing the concrete. There was no movement and a dark pool of what appeared to be blood glistened on the ground beneath her forehead.

Hurry up, hurry up! Maria murmured to herself, willing the ambulance to arrive quicker. Why was it taking so long?

As she calculated the lengthening time on her watch, she heard the sound of sirens getting closer. The sight of the police car, with lights blazing, swinging into the driveway elicited a weary sigh of relief from Maria. As the blue lights snaked eerily around the garage area, the old woman relaxed, moving back to her armchair and the abandoned quiz show.

Plumping the cushions up, she eased herself down into its well-worn comfort, glad to hand the responsibility for the girl's well-being to someone else. She wrapped the blanket around her legs and stretched her feet towards the electric fire, sighing with relief. Duty done.

*

Razor swore silently as he pulled off the main road towards their agreed meeting place and checked his fake Rolex. Where was Redz, the bitch? She was supposed to be here now.

He frowned, glimpsing his own reflection in the rear-view mirror, his face set in its usual menacing scowl, his shaven black head and scarred forehead glistening with beads of sweat. A scar ran from the edge of his right eye down over pitted cheeks towards his mouth, a reminder of time served inside some of the hardest prisons in London.

He rubbed the back of his hand across his stubbly chin, his fingers retrieving the small bundle of tightly-wrapped drugs from his mouth and tucking them down inside his trousers under his ballsack, safe from the prying hands of cops should he be stopped. Business with DK, his dealer, had been conducted swiftly and silently, cash for crack exchanged proficiently and with no fuss. No other pleasantries were required.

It had been busy on the High Road, queues of drunken revellers writhing and pulsating towards the open doors of the local clubs. The night was shaping up perfectly and his three girls would bring in a fair wedge from their labours; enough to provide the crack cocaine they craved and to keep him supplied with a fridge full of beer and a wardrobe full of designer clothes.

His thoughts returned to Redz. Where was the slag?

She'd been mucking him around for some time now, taking the crack but not pulling in the punters... and complaining when he fucked her. His mind wandered to the memory of Redz' nubile young body spread out for his satisfaction, whether she liked it or not. Dutch and Caz too. All three of them. His girls, Razor's girls, just as he preferred them: young, weak and easily controlled.

He shifted his muscular frame in his seat and wound the window down, rolling himself a joint and reaching into the pocket of his jacket to locate his bulging wallet. A large wad of old business cards and rail tickets were kept in one side and he slid them out, thumbing carefully through the pile, locating several shiny razor blades hidden within slips of paper, their thin, delicate edges sharp enough to carve through hair, clothing and especially skin. These were his weapons of choice and the origin of his street name. He admired the way they scored through the flesh of his victims so easily. Many an adversary now sported his brand mark letter 'R'.

He ran his finger along the blade, feeling it slip easily between the layers of skin, sending droplets of blood speeding to the surface, the sweet, sticky redness reminding him of revenge he'd inflicted on his enemies. These days he preferred to save his violence for his girls. They didn't fight back.

Swiftly, he slid the blades back inside his wallet, taking care to ensure they were well hidden, but the cops were sloppy. They were only interested in stolen bank cards. They wouldn't bother to check through the pile of miscellaneous tickets for hidden perils. He smirked at the thought. He was wiser now and more careful. Forty-two years living in the slums and high-rises of South London had taught him well.

He glanced down at his watch again. Five more minutes had passed. Shit. Where the fuck was Redz? She was making him a laughing stock. Only the night before, he'd found her in another dealer's flat, virtually naked, freely flaunting herself... so he'd been forced to teach her a lesson. If she failed to turn up soon tonight and show some respect, he'd be teaching her another.

He turned the ignition key in its barrel and heard the engine roar to life, steering the car slowly along the back street to the patch where Redz worked. The wail of two-tones pierced the air as he neared. He clenched his fists subconsciously. He hated cops. A police car was speeding towards him, its headlights flashing crazily. The sound of its shrill siren intensified as the vehicle neared. He slowed to let it go by, but instead of passing him, he watched as the silver flash veered across his path into the alleyway. Redz' alleyway.

Sirens were beginning to converge from all directions and he sat momentarily mesmerised as the blue lights of an ambulance turned into the road and started making its way towards him.

Coming to his senses, he threw the car into gear and swung it around, instinctively aware that he would be better served well away from the area. With a slight screech of tyres, he barrelled away from the alleyway and out towards the main road, his sense of self-preservation kicking in.

His number one priority, before even worrying about Redz, was to get himself the fuck away.

Chapter 8

Dimitri climbed back into the van and pulled out on to the road spinning the wheels slightly in his haste. His had been the only vehicle in the small, dark clearing, more of a recess for council vehicles than a proper car park. Still, he had been relieved to be left to his own devices; no courting couples or prostitutes turning up to disturb him.

He wound the window down and gulped in the freezing air. Despite the grass being white with frost, he had built up quite a sweat hefting her body along the railway tracks. Carrying a human had taken more than he had expected, even one as diminutive as Tatjana. Tatjana now lay in a disused brick railway outhouse wrapped in the rug, trussed up tightly within the tarpaulin and bound round and round with rope. He wiped a sleeve over his shaven head, before pulling a cigarette from his jacket pocket and lighting up. He drew hard on it, calming instantly as the nicotine filled his lungs. Nobody had seen him. Nobody would have any idea what he had been doing. More importantly, by the time Tatjana was found, he and his girls would have moved on. Not far, but far enough. A new part of London, servicing a new list of customers. It wouldn't take long to build up the business. Word spread quickly and although the location might change, the same rules of supply and demand would never alter. Men demanded sex and their appetite for risky sex would soon bring them knocking at his door.

The reflection of blue lights flashed up on the interior mirror. He held his breath as a police car closed up behind him, before swinging out to pass. He exhaled in relief. Although he'd been extra careful, it had been hazardous. He would never know whether some busybody had been nosing around, watching his every move.

Another set of blue lights crossed the junction in front. An ambulance this time. There were a lot of emergency vehicles around tonight; more than usual. Something was happening nearby, on the streets of Streatham, and it was too close for comfort. He pressed a number on his hands-free. He couldn't afford to wait any longer, just in case he had been spotted.

Albertas came on the line.

'Tell the girls to pack up their belongings,' he instructed. 'They have fifteen minutes to get what they need. Otherwise it will be left. You too, Albertas. We are all moving out.'

Chapter 9

Ambulance P301 was nearly ready to go. The two paramedics working on Redz had done everything they could, but it wasn't looking good.

The younger of the crew, a thick-set woman with large watery eyes and only a few years' experience, was performing a rather lacklustre CPR. It never ceased to amaze her what mankind was capable of inflicting on its own.

A young cop came over. 'Does it look life-threatening?' he asked queasily.

She turned, slightly irritated, as he stood white-faced, staring at the smashed and bloody body in front of him.

'Yeah, almost certainly,' she replied tersely. 'It's only really me stopping her being pronounced.'

Her partner joined her and she paused fleetingly while they transferred their casualty on to a stretcher. As they did so, a large clump of hair fell down on to the ground, bloodied and wet.

'Christ,' the female paramedic muttered out loud as she was wheeled towards the ambulance, still performing CPR on their casualty. 'Whoever did this is sick. It looks like they've cut all her hair off. She's virtually been scalped.'

The cop radioed the information to the control room, following on and climbing up into the ambulance behind them.

'Apparently, I've got to accompany the victim to hospital for identification and continuity purposes. It's my first time,' he apologised.

The paramedic felt a twinge of sympathy for the new officer. She had never forgotten her first dead body and this sight would certainly be one he remembered.

The second paramedic slammed the back doors. The bright lights of the ambulance lit up the casualty's blank eyes. A deathly white pallor was already seeping across her skin.

'All set?' he shouted, climbing into the driver's seat and starting up the engine.

'Yep, let's go,' the female paramedic answered, pressing down on the prostitute's rib cage as they swung out from the police cordon. She stared down at the pulpy mess and grimaced. *Already gone!* she thought to herself.

*

The Punter drove towards King's Cross. He wouldn't be recognised up town and he needed another whore now. Adrenalin was still surging through his body and he was barely in control. His recently discovered penchant for violence had come as a surprise to him; an exciting, exhilarating surprise and one that he now needed to visit more often. It didn't matter how compliant the bitches were, he wanted to play rough. He craved the sight of blood, the smell of fear, the sound of desperation. In fact, he got more pleasure from the beating than from the sex itself.

He pressed down firmly on the accelerator, his whole body shaking with anticipation. The steering wheel spun through his hands, and he stared down at the sticky mess. Her blood and hair was plastered across the dashboard and footwell too and the sight of it sent shockwaves of delight... and rage racing to his fingertips.

How dare she deny him? He touched his swollen lip and was reminded of her obstinacy. Every second of their liaison played back in his mind; her blood, her screams, her hair, her lovely, long red hair, so easy to grab, so easy to utilise. Then there were the surges of pleasure escalating with every violent lunge, swelling and growing, making his head swim, until, just as he was about to climax, it had all ended. As she had gone limp, so too did his erection. The bitch had denied him his rightful gratification.

But he'd taught her, hadn't he? He'd humiliated her, and he'd teach the next one too. He closed his eyes and imagined the next bitch pinned up against a wall – the pain, the pleasure, the climax. A frisson of excitement shuddered up his spine as the image became clearer. Yes, he would drive to King's Cross and then he would get out on foot... and the next dirty prostitute would give him absolutely everything he demanded.

*

Razor drove straight to his favourite bar in Brixton Town Centre. He had to ensure he was seen and remembered by as many staff and clientele as possible. Not that he needed to worry. The venue catered for the type of customer who would swear to anything if it meant a few free rocks, especially if it included the chance to fuck up a police investigation.

The saloon was a particularly dingy affair. What lighting there was glowered dimly in the public areas, leaving dark recesses where pills were popped, powder sniffed and Spice zombies slumped, oblivious to anything and everything.

Razor strode straight to the bar, through groups of younger men shouting animatedly at one another. Every now and again, a jacket would be peeled back to reveal a handgun tucked into a belt or holster. If you owned a 'piece', you got respect. Until recently he hadn't seen the necessity for bullets, but with so many gang members and dealers having access to guns, he too was considering the possibility.

He was thinking about this when the barmaid came over. Viv had worked the bar forever. She was a curvaceous woman of about sixty. She wore her hair pinned back off her face, framing deep creases and furrows liberally covered in thick layers of foundation and blusher. Heavy gold earrings swung from each drooping earlobe and a solid gold chain encircled her neck, hanging loosely down into her ample cleavage. The top she wore strained to contain her massive breasts; being far too low and showy for a woman of her age... But still, Viv wore it with pride.

'You all right, love?' she shouted over the music towards Razor. 'You look as if you could do with a good drink.'

Razor brought his gaze up from her cleavage. 'Yeah, do us another pint, Viv. It's been a shit day.' He tried to make it sound as if he'd been there a while.

'What's up then?' Viv pulled a pint of draught beer and handed it across, leaning in to hear what Razor was saying.

'Just the usual. Redz has been misbehaving and now she ain't turned up where we was supposed to meet.'

Razor gulped the pint straight down, swilling the dregs around and banging his glass down on the counter.

Viv reached for the glass and held it under the pump again. 'She don't normally let you down though?'

'She don't normally dare,' he snarled. 'But she's out of control and needs sorting out. She's going to have to learn she can't screw around with me an' expect to get away with it.'

'Don't be too hard on her, love. She's only young and she's got a lot to learn.'

Razor frowned. Nobody else could tell him what to do, but Viv was different. Viv had always been there. She'd looked out for him ever since he was a kid, hanging round the streets, getting caught up in the inevitable low-level drug dealing, joyriding and the odd handbag snatch. She'd also understood how age and maturity had brought with it the necessary change to more violent crime and pimping. She might not have liked it, but she appreciated that reputation was everything on the streets. If you weren't the predator, then you were the prey.

'She certainly has got a lot to learn.' Razor narrowed his eyes, silencing Viv before she opened her mouth. She might be fond of his girls, maternal even, and he might listen to some of her opinions but… enough was enough. Redz and Caz were still under twenty and Dutch was only slightly older. He liked his girls young, malleable, addicted to crack and fully reliant on him. That was how it was. 'Any word on what's going on out there?' he tried to sound as casual as possible. 'There are fucking cops everywhere!'

Viv bent forward towards him conspiratorially, his rebuke forgotten in the chance to gossip. She placed the second heady pint down on the bar and leant in close enough for him to feel her warm, boozy breath on his cheek. 'Apparently a girl's been attacked behind the shops in Streatham Hill,' she whispered loudly in his ear. 'The rumour is it's bad. If she's not dead already, she soon will be.' As she said the words, Razor saw the colour drain from her face. 'Christ, Razor! You don't think it's your Redz, do you?'

The question caught him unawares, but he couldn't let her see his slight panic. Dead! Shit! He hadn't thought Redz might be dead! That would fuck everything up. Redz dead?! What the fuck?

He picked up the pint and sipped from it slowly, rallying as his instinct for self-preservation kicked in, over and above any vague sadness he felt for Redz. In his mind, she was gone and he needed to regroup immediately. Sorting out an alibi, for before and after the attack, would now be imperative. The cops would come after him. The bastards always did. And what about Caz and Dutch? They would have to be kept loyal. If Redz was indeed dead, he had failed with his protection. Now they might think he wasn't up to the job.

Then there was the bastard who had taken away his source of income, whoever he was. He'd have to be tracked down and made to pay.

Viv was still staring towards him white-faced.

He picked up the second pint, taking a few more sips, anxious to show he was still in control. 'I don't know, Viv.' He wiped his mouth on his sleeve slowly and shook his head calmly. 'But I intend to find out.'

Chapter 10

It was still dark when Charlie woke Ben the next morning. His immediate reaction was to reach out towards Casper, who lay half-asleep on the rug adjacent to the sofa, and stroke the dog fondly on the head. Casper stretched out his neck towards Ben, acknowledging the attention, before lolling back to his previous position, his eyes closed again. It was clearly far too early for a walk. Ben shut his own eyes and groaned.

'Come on sleepyheads,' Charlie whispered. 'Some of us have got work to do.'

She sat down next to Ben and ran her finger across his cheek to try to rouse him further, the heat from his body hot against her.

Ben reached out, wrapping an arm around her waist.

'Do you have to go in today?' he asked. 'Can't you stay with me a while?'

For a moment she imagined herself lying next to Ben, safe in his strong arms, their bodies entwined together. It was the first time he'd alluded to these sorts of thoughts for a long time, and then it had been she who had kept him at arm's length, wanting to put every scrap of energy into the job. Since then though she'd seen how fragile life could be. Maybe her priorities had changed ever so slightly and she was now ready. Maybe he was too.

'I wish,' she replied wistfully, not really quite sure whether that was actually the case, but not wanting to break the spell completely. 'But we've got an early warrant booked in.'

Ben shrugged his shoulders and hoisted himself upright. 'It's all right. I know my position in your list of priorities.' He let the duvet fall to the floor, revealing only a pair of boxer shorts covering his body, before flexing the muscles on his torso and grinning mischievously as he caught her expression. 'But I'm working hard on it.'

'So I can see,' she smiled up at him in appreciation. 'Let Anna know when it's safe for me to approach then and who knows what you might get for Christmas.'

She jumped up and patted her legs. Casper climbed to his feet and plonked his head on her knee, gazing up at her intently.

Ben shook his head at the pair of them, climbing into his jeans. 'Right, talking about Anna, can you drop me off at her office, rather than at my place on your way in? I'm due to see her this morning.'

'Are you now?' Charlie raised her eyebrows at him. 'Since when did you make appointments off your own back?'

'Since I started taking back control of my life.' He eased a sweatshirt over his head and pulled his trainers on, folding the duvet up on the sofa. Casper moved away, shaking his fur out as if to ready himself too. Ben dropped to one knee and petted the old dog, before stuffing his belongings into his bag and turning towards Charlie with a flourish. 'Right, DC Stafford, let's go.'

*

Charlie drove the car slowly alongside Tooting Bec Common towards Anna's office. Anna Christophe was Ben's psychologist and had been working with him over the last year. The transformation more recently had been remarkable and Charlie was full of admiration for her patience and support. She didn't, however, want to get too close herself. Anna had a disconcerting way of trying to get her to talk about Jamie's death and the ongoing issues she had with her mother. As far as Charlie was concerned, this subject was firmly off limits and would remain so, if only for her own sanity.

Anna's office was swathed in shadows as they approached, but silhouetted in the headlights was the outline of a woman sitting on the steps. The woman had her arms wrapped around her body and wore nothing on her legs apart from a pair of knee-length boots. A short skirt just about covered her dignity and a fake-fur jacket was pulled down across her midriff. The woman lifted her head as Charlie parked and she immediately recognised Caz, a prostitute she had worked with during a previous job. It had been Caz who she had referred to the District Source Unit and it was Caz who Charlie suspected was now providing vice and drugs information to Angie.

Caz squinted towards the car as Charlie got out, smiling towards her and looking questioningly towards Ben as he emerged from the passenger seat.

'Wotcha, Charlie.' Caz's voice wavered as she forced open her frozen mouth. She tried to lick her blistered lips but her tongue was dry and the effort seemed to start a series of tremors shuddering through her body. 'It's bin a while.'

'Caz, what are you doing here?' Charlie ran to the boot of her car and pulled out several blankets. 'You're freezing.' She wrapped the blankets around the shoulders of the young girl, who was by now shivering violently. 'Come into the warmth of my car.'

Caz nodded towards Ben, who, by now, had clearly realised that Charlie and the girl were known to each other and was in the process of tempting Casper out into the cold.

'Is this your fella?'

Charlie felt the heat rush to her cheeks, thankful it was still dark, as she remembered the sight of him dressed only in his boxers earlier that morning.

Ben grinned and waved towards them both, holding tightly to Casper, who was straining to chase a fox that had darted into the undergrowth on the common. 'I'd better give him a run before he changes his mind again. I'm not due to see Anna anyway for an hour or so.' He blew her a kiss and walked away, before turning one last time and winking. 'And there's a good cafe around the corner that does a wicked full English breakfast.'

She felt her stomach contract at the thought. What she wouldn't do for a plate of bacon and eggs right now, but she really needed to get into work. She turned back towards Caz. The girl looked as if she would benefit from some food too, anything warm and nutritious. She was skin and bones. Drugs had stripped her body of every semblance of health and vitality and the freezing air had sucked any last colour from her hands and face and frosted her lips with a tinge of blue.

'Well?' Caz asked again, pulling one of the blankets up over her head, leaving only a small hole from which she peeked, but keeping her eyes trained on Charlie's face.

'Well...' Charlie felt awkward giving away personal information to a prostitute so she smiled instead. 'Let's just say I'm working on it.'

Caz kept her gaze fixed on Charlie. 'I'm working on stuff too,' she said. 'In fact, I'm working a lot.'

Charlie met her gaze and nodded knowingly, suspecting what she meant. The urge to probe Caz further, however, was nullified as they were both lit up in the headlights of an approaching car. Caz turned towards it, sucking her breath in with a gasp, her eyes flying immediately to the registration number.

'It's only Anna,' she closed her eyes, expelling a cloud of condensation into the air. 'Thank God.'

Charlie had become quite friendly with Caz during their previous contacts and knew that she had been counselled by Anna since childhood, in fact it had been Caz who had given her the idea to recommend Anna to Ben.

'Were you expecting trouble then?' Charlie touched Caz's arm. 'You know we can help if you need it.'

Caz pulled the blanket round her even tighter. 'Yeah I know that Charlie, but I'm fine. I know where I can get 'elp if I needs it. There's a lot of 'elp around these days, if yer know what I mean.'

Charlie was amused at the blatancy of Caz's clues, now believing she was indeed correct in her suspicions. The prostitute shouldn't be making her new work status so obvious though and she knew Angie wouldn't be impressed if she found out. Any talk was dangerous, but maybe Caz knew that her secret was safe with Charlie.

Anna was walking towards them now, looking concerned. 'Are you both OK?' She checked her watch. 'What are you doing here so early?'

'Caz was here when I arrived,' Charlie explained. 'I was dropping Ben off on my way into work.' She paused, mirroring Anna and also checking the time. 'He's just walking Casper before his appointment. I don't know how long Caz has been here, but she's freezing, so I've wrapped her in some blankets.' She indicated towards where her car was parked, immediately in front of Anna's. 'I always keep them in my boot, in case of emergency, after watching a programme about people freezing to death in blizzards.' She smiled. 'I was just about to get her a coffee from the garage and get her warmed up in my car before heading in.'

Anna flicked the key fob and the locks to her car clicked shut. She chose another key and swiftly opened the door to her office. A warm waft of furniture polish fanned out into the cold air. 'Well it sounds like you're busy, so I'll look after Caz. You get on, but thanks.' She nodded to Charlie before putting an arm around Caz's shoulders and guiding her inside, her voice gentle and soothing. 'You go on up Caz and get comfortable and then we'll talk. I'm glad I decided to come in early. It must be your lucky day.'

*

Hunter was waiting for Charlie in the yard at Lambeth HQ when she arrived.

'No time to go in now,' he indicated an unmarked police vehicle positioned by the exit barrier, its engine running. Paul sat in the driver's seat. 'Let's go. We're needed at a crime scene. One of our local girls has been murdered.'

Charlie was about to remonstrate when he stopped her with his hand.

'I know what you're thinking, and we're still going to do the brothel. I spoke to the others last night, after you phoned, and asked them to come in early to help. Bet is searching the name Dimitri and has almost finished typing up the paperwork and Naz and Sabira will be going to court to get the warrant. We'll roll on to the brothel afterwards.' He blew on his hands as Charlie drew level with him, and shoved them deep in his pockets. 'DCI O'Connor asked for us specifically to attend this new case because you recognise most of our girls and the team all know their pimps and domestic arrangements.' He pulled his hands back out of his pockets and rubbed them together in anticipation, clearly raring to go. 'So he thinks we should be able to kick-start the initial enquiries. The poor girl was badly beaten and almost scalped.'

Hunter climbed into the passenger seat and indicated for her to get into the rear. 'As soon as we've finished at this crime scene though, we'll be in a position to move on to the brothel,' he shouted above the noise of Paul revving the engine. 'It won't be forgotten.'

She jumped into the back, trying her hardest not to look disappointed. Sometimes having the ability to recognise so many faces was a bonus, but occasionally, like now, it detracted from the work that she really wanted to do. She leant back against the headrest and closed her eyes, Bet's words about getting justice for the baby swirling about randomly.

In her head, Charlie knew that catching a prostitute's killer was as important as catching a baby killer, but in her heart...

Chapter 11

Anna Christophe gazed at the sleeping figure of Caz on her couch. The young girl had fallen asleep in the time it took for the kettle to boil. Now she lay curled up in a foetal position, her thumb in her mouth, her blonde hair damp from the frost, plastered against her head. Her expression was childlike, innocent even, despite the needle-track marks on her arms, the obvious signs of infection and the yellowy brown tinge around her left eye, the result, no doubt, of the last argument she'd lost with her violent pimp. Anna watched as the girl's pale green eyes flickered with a look of terror so animated that it made her want to lean forward and gently wake her from her nightmare.

The psychologist swallowed hard at the pitiful sight. It was only minutes earlier that she'd kissed the forehead of her eleven-year-old daughter, sleeping in her fresh-smelling duvet surrounded by soft toys and love. The child had also been sucking quietly on her thumb, a habit she'd retained and had failed to break before starting secondary school.

The two images were comparable and yet so devastatingly different.

A sudden sadness swept through her for the nineteen-year-old girl forced into such a brutal existence, an existence that she herself had experienced to a degree; one that time had locked away in the innermost sanctuary of her mind but was now seeping back excruciatingly into the present as she gazed down at her young client. She recognised in Caz the same hurt, pain and anger that she had known as a child when both parents were suddenly and tragically killed in a car accident.

She took a sip of her coffee and rubbed at her temples, trying to block the memories. With no other family, she had been forced into care and left to deal with her grief alone. The social workers had tried their best, but nothing and no one had been able to penetrate the awful black hole in which she found herself, a world where there was no love, only separation, injustice and despair. It was a world that, in many ways, mirrored that of the girl on her couch. She'd dealt with her issues gradually through counselling; her own recovery endowing her with the strength to help others, but the sight of Caz, or other similar souls, always gave the painful recollections room to stab at the wafer-thin protective layer behind which she hid.

Anna wondered whether to wake her, but at the same time she didn't want to disturb her from her slumber.

The girl was quiet now; a far cry from the screaming, spitting wildcat Anna had first met just over three years earlier. She flipped open the file in front of her and read through the details for the hundredth time.

Full Name: Charlene Zara PHILIPS
Date of birth: 28 January 1998
Sex: Female
Ethnic Origin: White/British
Address: NFA. Believed living at Flat 59, Milton House, Poets Estate, Tulse Hill, SW2
Next of kin: Mother – Dead/ Father – Unknown/ Brothers – Joseph aged 28 years, Michael aged 26 years, Edward aged 23 years.
Brief History: Family chaotic – Mother – alcoholic until death. History of abusive relationships. Brothers taken into care for long periods and now involved in crime. Contact details unknown.

Transferred to Davis Trust from Lower Addisley Care Home after displaying self-harming and mildly violent tendencies. Threatened another girl with a pair of scissors and involved in numerous fights. Taken to hospital twice after self-harming – Cut her left wrist with scissors. Took an overdose of aspirin and vodka. Neither attempts life-threatening.

Anna remembered her first NHS referral appointment with Charlene Zara, or Caz as she insisted on being called, recognising the same powerful rage she'd once had, the total rejection of help, the glint of desperation that all the outwardly-hostile behaviour failed to conceal. Although instinctively recoiling from the threatening teenager, she'd determined there and then to try to uncover the sadness at the root of her hostility and help in whatever way she could.

On the first occasion she did little more than to listen to the abuse directed at her. The second occasion was no better, nor the third, nor fourth, but gradually, over the next few weeks and months, she'd persevered and very slowly Caz got used to the environment. To Anna, it was a wonder she actually turned up at all, but there was something that kept her coming back.

Over the years, Caz had spoken about her day-to-day life, her scraps with the other girls in care, the uncontrollable rage she felt at the injustice of being punished when she believed she had done nothing wrong. How she could steal without being caught, how the weed that she smoked took away her cares, how attentive the paramedics, doctors and nurses had been on the various occasions she'd been rushed to hospital.

She'd never spoken about her obvious loneliness and feelings of rejection; the reasons she fought, stole or took drugs. Nor had she ever spoken about her descent into hard drugs and the reasons for her hospital admissions, the deep emotional needs that had fuelled the self-mutilation.

Caz's circumstances had changed with time. At eighteen, the care system relinquished its responsibilities and spat her into the world outside to make room for the next itinerant, rootless child. Caz was left to make her own way and with no particular friends, except one slightly younger girl, Ayeisha, she was quickly sucked into the world of crack cocaine and prostitution. Friends came and went; some murdered, some imprisoned and some dead from overdoses. Anna listened, but inside she wept at her inability to do anything other than wait... and hope.

With the arrival of Razor, even Anna's optimism was almost extinguished. Caz belonged to Razor and Razor controlled everything she did. Emotionally, however, she did seem more stable. She now had a central figure in her life and Anna was forced to concede that, although the lifestyle was depressingly familiar, Razor did at least provide Caz with a concrete, though questionable, form of security. Caz idolised Razor, working the streets and making her body available for him whenever he chose, and in return Razor gave her board, lodgings and drugs, needing her in his own way, as much as she needed him, albeit only for money and sex. Even when she turned up with visible marks of violence, Caz would defend Razor blindly.

It had been difficult to watch, but Anna knew that if she was to help Caz, she would have to keep her trust and be patient. She knew too, from personal experience, that Caz would reach a crisis point, a time when she would have to decide which way she wanted her life to go. It had been at this point in Anna's own life when she had been supported by a mentor and it was what she intended to do for Caz when that time came. The payments from the council had stopped when Caz had reached eighteen, but Anna had been determined to continue unpaid. The chance to do for Caz, what her mentor had done for her, was worth more than money. It was the opportunity to rebuild a life, just as hers had been rebuilt.

Now though, as Anna regarded Caz's adolescent body, ravaged by her lifestyle, she wished, once again, that she could give her the 'happy ever after' the young hooker craved.

As she watched, Caz shifted, stretching out both arms and pushing away the blanket. She pulled at her jacket, releasing the top button and unzipping it. With one hand she reached inside, clutching at a small, scruffy black bag secreted within. Anna had seen her with it before but had never seen its contents. It didn't appear to be materially valuable, but to the young prostitute it was obviously of vital importance and worth guarding jealously. She unclipped the opening and held it close to her body, her hand roaming sleepily inside. Anna watched transfixed as her fingers moved through the contents, a handful of condoms, various items of make-up and a plastic container full of needles until it found the item she sought.

Tucked beneath was a soiled and dirty ragdoll, its hollow body testament to the years she had clearly carried it. Caz's hand wrapped itself around the doll, her grubby fingers moving gently against the frayed material. Her other hand returned to her mouth, her lips sucking rhythmically on her thumb. An expression of extreme sadness swept across her face as if a shadow had blotted any last remaining light from her life and Anna recognised at once the rejected child she remembered so well from their first meeting.

Very gently she shook Caz by the shoulders, willing her to wake up and reach out to her. She had never seen the young prostitute looking so vulnerable before. As Caz stretched her legs out slowly and extracted her thumb from her mouth, Anna prayed that today Caz would begin the process of eradicating the demons from her past.

Chapter 12

Charlie held her breath as the mortuary assistant pulled out the tray on which their victim lay. The unidentified girl had been pronounced dead on arrival at King's College Hospital and had been taken straight to the council mortuary at Greenwich, a small section of which was kept aside for the use of police dealing with suspicious deaths.

The crime scene was yet to be forensically examined, but visually it had yielded nothing more than a large coagulated pool of blood and a pile of sodden ambulance dressings lying in an area of desolation and filth. It had been a clump of hair fanning out across the grey concrete that had sparked Charlie's curiosity. Until their arrival on scene, the hair had simply been described as long and dark, as it had appeared in the gloom of the night. With the first rays of sun peeping over the rooftops at sunrise, however, it became apparent that each strand shone with an autumnal intensity. If their victim was a prostitute, as her appearance suggested, then she had long red hair, not dark hair... and there was only one prostitute that Charlie knew who fitted that description. She just had to confirm it.

The body on the tray was partially clothed and still wrapped in a bright red ambulance blanket. There was little to see of her face other than a bloody mess. Charlie stepped forward and, with gloved hands, peeled some of the coverings back so she could get a better overall view of the young girl's head and body.

In the fluorescent strip lights she was clearly a redhead, her hair, or what was left of it, being nearer to ginger than auburn. Some of her hair looked to have been tugged out from the roots, while other parts appeared to have been cut or sliced off, but while this detail had been described, the specific hair colouring had been omitted. A fuller description might have assisted identification a little earlier, but it couldn't be helped. It had been dark; the accompanying officer was young in service and the girl's head wet with blood.

Now as Charlie eyed the body, she recognised the height and proportions of the only prostitute that worked the Lambeth streets who had ginger hair. While she couldn't distinguish the facial features, everything else fitted. The victim had to be Redz and Redz was Grace Flaherty, a nineteen-year-old girl, with the flame-red hair colouring synonymous with the Southern Irish and an accent that had never diminished over the years she'd lived in London. Charlie knew her well. She knew the majority of the prostitutes, pimps and street dealers in Brixton Town Centre and the surrounding borough having made it her mission since being posted from Charing Cross to Lambeth Borough nine years previously to get in amongst them, talking to them, searching them and, where necessary, arresting them. More recently, in the Community Support Unit, she, Hunter and the rest of the team dealt with the prostitutes as victims of domestic abuse, their vulnerability to violence in every form bringing them to regular notice. Charlie spoke with the girls in a respectful way, knowing how their histories had shaped them and continued to dictate their actions... and they, in turn, gave Charlie a heads-up on any serious threats or retaliations likely on the streets of Lambeth; from the sleepy backstreets of Streatham, to the bustling diverse town centre in Brixton, the throbbing LGBT clubs of Vauxhall and the tourist hotspots of Waterloo and the London Eye.

What the girls would never do, however, was commit any information to paper and Charlie and Hunter knew this. Everything they heard remained strictly off the record. As Charlie stared down at the dead girl with the ginger hair, she wondered what rumours would already be circulating.

'It's Grace Flaherty,' she turned to Hunter and Paul who stood next to her. 'Redz. I'm as sure as I can be, but we could do a check on her PNC record. She's bound to have some marks or scars that will match. She's one of Razor's girls.'

Paul pulled out his phone and tapped in a number, spelling out the girl's name and age to the control-room staff.

Hunter shook his head. 'If it is Redz, then Razor will be in the thick of it. I know him of old and he's a really nasty bastard. He's done quite a bit of time for violence; in fact, he revels in it. He gets his street name from carving up his enemies with razor blades.'

'Which would fit in nicely with her hair being cut off.' Charlie could feel the adrenalin starting to build. Everything was making sense. 'Shit, guv. Do you remember Caz? She was the prostitute who was good friends with Tanisha Fleming, the girl who was murdered a while ago? Caz was the one who helped us find Cornell Miller, remember?'

Hunter nodded, looking slightly bemused.

'Well, Caz is one of Razor's girls too, along with another girl called Dutch. Coincidentally, I saw Caz this morning when I dropped Ben off at Anna's for his counselling session. Anna is her shrink too. She was sitting on Anna's doorstep freezing and looked absolutely awful, like something had happened. If she'd just heard that another of her closest mates had been killed, then no wonder she was traumatised. Word gets round the streets quicker than it ever gets to us. She would have known straight away if it was Redz. She might even know who had done it, whether it was one of Redz' punters...'

'Or whether it was Razor.' Hunter's eyes were alight. 'And, I can tell you now, my money would be on him.'

'That's if it is Redz, or Grace Flaherty, or whatever she's called,' Paul interrupted. 'Right, if you can fold back her left sleeve, Charlie, Grace Flaherty is shown as having a triquetra symbol, whatever that is, on the inside of her left arm, just above her wrist.' He googled the name and they all peered down as Charlie carefully lifted the sleeve on the young girl's jacket and they saw a symbol that appeared like three interlinking ovals, tattooed in black ink on her pale skin. Paul held out his phone and the same symbol filled the screen. He squinted down and read out its meaning. 'It's a Celtic symbol, also known as the Trinity Knot or the Celtic Triangle. Triquetra just means "three-cornered". It has represented various threesomes throughout time: the Father, Son and Holy Ghost; mind, body and soul; past, present and future.' He paused, sighing heavily. 'Apparently it also symbolises equality and eternity.'

They stood in silence, knowing that, without doubt, they had the correct identity for their victim, before Charlie pulled the blanket back over the young girl's bloody face and sighed.

'Neither of which apply to Grace Flaherty, unless you count nineteen years living this sort of existence as an eternity.'

Chapter 13

The Punter opened his eyes and stared at the prostitute's blood and hair spread throughout his car, as the full implications of his night of violence became clear. The heady exhilaration of the night before was gone, replaced with a growing realisation that he was in deep shit.

He'd completely lost control. Now he needed a way out. He switched the car radio on and listened to the first crackly news reports of the body of a prostitute having been found in the backstreets of Streatham. The death was being treated as suspicious.

He closed his eyes and swore silently. Shit, the whore was dead. He'd killed her. He really had gone too far. As he tried to concentrate, flashes of the night before kept coming to him – the blood and thrashing of the first slag, her face pulped and fleshy, her screams goading him. Then the second, pressed against the fence, struggling, with his hand across her mouth while he'd thrust, hard and deep. It had been the best climax of his life and it would be repeated. It had to be... but not yet.

There were people about now; he could see them out with their dogs, walking their kids to school, going about their normal lives. Little did they know what horrors lay hidden within his vehicle, parked in the furthest corner of the car park. He was safe though; nobody need come close, there were plenty of spaces. He checked his watch. It was nearly eight-thirty. His wife would be wondering where he was, worrying, as she followed the morning routine in their quiet, respectable suburban home, with their enchanting twins. Everything would be arranged: doctor's appointments, shopping trips, family visits, games with the children. Even his marriage had been arranged. Everything in his life was bloody well arranged.

Out on business for the night and too late to return. The lie formed easily in his mind. He picked up his mobile and phoned his wife, speaking the words in his head, daring her to question him. She didn't. She never would.

'Yes I love you too, babe. See you later.' He finished with the obligatory words, his jaw clenching as he spoke. It made him angry that he was forced to speak untruths, that he was trapped in a joyless marriage. She didn't excite him, like the paid hookers did. She would never give him the violent sex that he craved.

His finger hovered over his lip, feeling the slight swelling from the whore's bite. The dead whore. It was sore to the touch, which served to concentrate his mind on what needed to be done. His main consideration was the car and its contents.

He started up the engine, waiting while the windscreen cleared and the heater started to warm. He was gambling on the fact his registration number had not been taken. It had been extremely dark in the alleyway, the main opportunity to see the index plate therefore being fleetingly as he left. At the speed and instance of turning, and in only the red lights from the brakes, however, he estimated the chances would be negligible. After that he'd stuck to the backstreets, away from the High Road, aware these were normally free from CCTV cameras, getting far enough away from the area before he risked the main roads to King's Cross. It was only as he'd left the second hooker gasping for breath that he realised the necessity of disposing of the car, but he also understood that to do so on the same night as the attack might provoke suspicions. A day later, in a different area and hopefully the connection would not be made.

He started to drive off slowly as a plan began to solidify.

A short distance away he found a secluded spot, in a quiet street, masked by overhanging trees and remote from driveways and house fronts. He parked the vehicle correctly against the kerb and went to the boot, taking out a picnic blanket and newspaper and spreading them over the front passenger seat and dashboard. He cleared the car of any personal items, gathered up his belongings and locked the doors. Lastly, he took off his long black leather coat and stashed it in the boot, before checking his hands and face to make sure there were no blood spots obvious to an observer.

That done, he walked off; knowing that his next move would bring even greater risk.

The police station was half a mile away. As he entered the foyer, his pulse quickened. With a click, the waiting room door opened and he was called to the desk by a uniformed station receptionist. A small group of police officers filed into the office behind where she worked and stood booking in property and filing reports. The Punter stared at their uniforms, listening as their radios sparked into life. He thrust his hand into his trouser pocket, feeling his growing erection, and then turned and nodded towards the female station officer.

'Good morning, officer,' he said confidently. 'I'd like to report that my car has been stolen.'

*

Razor woke from a fitful sleep to the sound of the news headlines blaring out from his TV. He'd achieved nothing on his return from Viv's. Caz was not there and Dutch had been too spaced out on crack to make sense of anything. He stretched and swung his legs off the sofa, flipping a cigarette into his mouth and inhaling deeply on his first draw of nicotine. Christ, he needed that.

The presenter changed to the usual pretty Asian woman who introduced the news in the South East. The scene switched to an alleyway he recognised only too well. A fresh-faced young reporter with an earnest expression stood to the side of a uniformed policeman and read from an autocue.

'The body of a young woman was found last night in this alleyway at the rear of a block of flats in Streatham Hill. The woman, who has yet to be named, was discovered after a nearby resident reported hearing screams. She was rushed to hospital with severe head injuries but was pronounced dead on arrival.'

Razor ran his hands over his shaven head, the stubble feeling coarse and rough against his fingers, and watched as contact numbers appeared on the screen. So Viv had been right. The girl was dead. Beaten to death. And it was Redz' alleyway. It couldn't be anyone else. He inhaled again on his cigarette, allowing the smoke to fill his mouth, before angrily switching the TV off.

He looked around at the squalor of his flat and tried to concentrate. A small wooden table glistened with the dried remains of spilt beer and a stinking ashtray leaked ash out on to the tarnished surface. The remnants of last night's hits – metal spoons, kitchen knives, aluminium foil and scraps of cling film – covered the remaining space. Dutch had clearly been scoring hard.

He went to the window, pulled back the makeshift curtain and peered out through the grime. He didn't know exactly what he was looking for, but he had the distinct feeling someone was coming after him. For a minute he stared down from his fourth-floor window, surveying the concrete walkways of the Poets Estate, each tenement block grandly named after an English poet, even though there was nothing remotely poetic in the concrete towers of run-down housing.

He let the sheet fall back over the daylight and walked carefully across the room. Nobody was about outside and the flat was silent. Where the fuck was Dutch or Caz? He needed to prepare an alibi, and it had to be sorted now.

The door to the smallest bedroom hung open. It was where Caz kept her stuff. Shoes, bags, make-up and a few other personal belongings lay around, but there was no sign of Caz.

Razor swore again, moving along the corridor to the end bedroom. Dutch was lying across the double bed in exactly the same position as when he'd last seen her a few hours earlier. Her arms were outstretched in the shape of a cross, one leg on the bed, the other hanging down towards the floor. Her skirt was hitched up across her thighs, showing the dark shadow of her pubic hair. Her shoulder-length straightened black hair stuck out from underneath a large afro hairpiece, which had slipped from its position half on to the pillow beside her. It was her ostentatious alter-ego when she walked the streets and one that gave her the confidence she required.

Razor reached down and shook her. 'Dutch, get up I need to speak to you... Wake up, you lazy bitch... Dutch.'

He brought his arm back and unleashed it towards the girl's sleeping face, hitting her hard with the back of his hand. The large ring on his middle finger caught the skin of her cheek, gouging a deep graze from which blood began to surface. Nothing. Dutch lay immobile, her chest being the only part of her body to move even slightly, her rib cage barely registering each breath. Razor grabbed hold of her hair and lifted her head up from the pillow, panicking slightly. He slapped her twice more across the face hard, the impact jerking her head from side to side. As he released her hair, her head dropped heavily back down on the bed.

'Dutch, wake the fuck up, will you?'

A thin smile appeared on Dutch's face, her rouged red lips opening slightly. Her eyelids flickered, opening to reveal glazed, glassy pupils.

'What do you want, Razor? I'm trying to sleep.' She wasn't with it.

'It's about Redz.'

'What about her?'

'I need to talk to you. The cops will be round soon.'

Dutch closed her eyes and smiled again. 'Fuck off,' she said, turning away from him and pulling her legs up into her chest.

Razor swore loudly as her breathing slowed again, before grabbing his jacket and car keys and slamming out of the door. There was no way he was going to get any sense out of her in this condition. He needed to find Caz, wherever she was, and get his story straight.

Chapter 14

A carrier of officers was sitting in the yard at Lambeth HQ when Charlie, Paul and Hunter returned from the mortuary.

'Ready when you are,' the uniformed sergeant called out. 'And we can be at your beck and call all day if you need us for anything else. We've already been briefed about the job on the brothel by your girls upstairs and have our instructions.' He grinned. 'It's like home from home.'

'Tell me about it,' Hunter raised his eyebrows. 'With the exception of Paul here, I'm pretty much surrounded by women.'

'You know you love it.' Charlie smiled and dipped her head towards Paul. 'Anyway, he's a bit of an old woman, as well.'

'Oi, I'm not an old woman.' Paul put on his campest voice and feigned affront. 'I'm an old queen!'

They all laughed, Charlie feeling her positivity growing. After the sights they'd witnessed in the morgue, a bit of humour was what was needed and Paul's self-effacing comments were always guaranteed to make them smile. He was gay and proud... and respected as such by them all.

'Cheers, Sarge,' she called across. 'In that case, we'd better go and be given our orders too. We'll be with you shortly.'

Naz, Sabira and Bet were waiting as they entered the office. Not only had they got the intelligence and the warrant for the brothel, they had also mobilised a few other detectives to do some early research on Redz and her pimp, Razor. Depending on how the warrant went, Hunter had made it clear an early visit to Razor wouldn't go amiss.

'Excellent work, team,' Hunter effused. 'I'll update the DCI on our progress and be back with you in a minute.' He disappeared, leaving Naz and Sabira to go through with them what intelligence was known around both crimes.

Naz flicked through the briefing notes on the brothel. 'We don't have much intel' on the brothel, but what we do have is interesting,' she began. 'Several neighbours have reported an increase in visitors to the venue, predominantly men. At first, the neighbourhood policing team thought there might be a new drug dealer starting up, but the locals have seen men of all ages and classes, some on foot and some in quite upmarket cars, turning up. They stay for longer than would be the case if it was just nipping in to buy drugs, sometimes several hours.'

'And at all times of the day and night,' Sabira added. 'But it's busiest in the late evening and early hours of the morning. The policing team have detailed what's known on a report and were beginning to suspect it to be a brothel. But the information from the DSU has confirmed their suspicions nicely, so we've had no trouble getting a warrant.'

'There seems to be two guys running it.' Naz peered at the notes again. 'One is a white guy, mid-thirties, very large build, but muscular, not fat. We think he's probably the security, but we've no idea of his identity. The other is also white, slimmer but still muscular and shaven-headed. He's probably the Russian guy, Dimitri, who Angie has mentioned, but we can't confirm that for definite either. A few girls have been seen inside the premises and they can be heard on occasions, but it appears that these two keep them pretty much under lock and key.'

Charlie grabbed her kitbag and hauled it up on to her shoulder, just as Hunter returned. 'OK. Let's go,' she said. 'I know it's a bit of a long shot, but in the absence of anything else, it's worth a try. Right area, right trade and the right motivation for ending an unplanned pregnancy.'

She headed towards the door, beckoning the others to follow on. 'And if they are connected to our dead baby, then I, for one, want to find out quick.'

Caz opened her eyes, squinting as the harsh lights of Anna's office struck her pupils.

'Can't you turn these bleeding lights off?' She covered her face with her hands, suddenly embarrassed as she became aware of the wetness of her thumb against her forehead. Sucking her thumb was a habit that had stayed with her since childhood, but these days it only surfaced at times of trauma, as did the ragdoll.

'How are you today, Caz?' Anna asked softly, moving towards the light switch. 'You've been asleep a long time.'

'I'd be bleedin' better if you weren't tryin' to blind me.' Caz squinted through her fingers, watching as Anna turned the main light back off, leaving just the table lamp on her desk still lit. She took the opportunity to hide the doll back inside her jacket as Anna pulled the blinds shut and the office descended into half-light.

'Are you well?' Anna tried again.

'As well as I can be on an eighty-quid-a-day habit,' she replied sarcastically.

'OK. Are you keeping yourself safe then?'

Caz knew what she really meant. *Are you using condoms? Are you using clean needles? Are you watching the amount of gear you take?* Anna rarely gave an opinion, but on those subjects she was frequently lectured and it still irritated her.

'Yeah, I know what I'm doin', 'right?'

'So how are you then?' Anna repeated the question for a third time, gathering her pen and pad and sitting down next to her.

Caz didn't answer immediately, instead letting her thoughts run back over the events of the previous night. The question lingered in the air.

'Redz has been murdered,' she blurted out suddenly. 'I heard it from Mand, one of the other girls, a few hours after it happened. I can't fuckin' believe it. She was only goin' to pull a few tricks. Then we was both of us goin' to head down the Hill to a party.'

Anna stayed quiet while Caz continued.

'We was out together, Redz and me, by her normal spot. Razor was hangin' out round the corner lookin' out for us, but after 'bout an hour he disappeared to buy some more gear. Anyway, I got a punter quick. I stung 'im for a hundred quid, which meant I was done for the night. I got 'im to drop me off near our flat an' downed half a bottle of Smirnoff while I waited for Redz.

'When she didn't come back I went out to find 'er, but Mand said she'd bin picked up by some huge Asian punter in a long black leather coat. He's bin around a few times, givin' some of the other girls trouble. Not paying up and getting nasty. They didn't think too much of it until the feds started arrivin', and then an ambulance. Mand said she went to see what was 'appening and reckoned she saw Redz bein' worked on, an' blood everywhere.'

Caz shifted on the couch, straightening her T-shirt and pulling her skirt down a little further over her pasty legs.

'Anyway right, I didn't feel like goin' on to the party. I sort of just knew she was dead. I've been wanderin' round all night since. Scored some gear with a dealer from round the Hatridge Estate. He said word on the street was that one of Razor's girls had bin topped. After hearin' that, I knew for definite it must be Redz, so I came 'ere. I've just been hangin' around on the common 'til you arrived. So, any chance of a brew?' She licked her dry lips. 'I'm parched.'

Anna nodded and moved across to the corner of the room, switching the kettle on.

'Milk and three sugars, please,' Caz called over, staring at Anna's short, dark hair brushed neatly on her jacket collar. Her shrink was always so smart and elegant. Although Caz knew her to be in her forties, she had the slim, petite figure of a twenty-year-old and a voice that exuded calmness, rarely changing in pitch or volume. Today she was wearing one of her usual, casually stylish well-tailored trouser suits with a soft woollen cashmere jumper.

Caz was in awe of her, even now unable to understand quite why Anna had put up with her initial behaviour and why she still entertained her. She felt herself drawn to Anna's kind brown eyes and soft features, detecting in her a genuine desire to help. Not since she was a young child looking up into her mother's eyes had she felt this acceptance.

The water was reaching boiling point, a steady jet of steam coursing from the spout of the kettle.

'Here you are,' Anna smiled a minute later, placing a mug on the edge of the table next to her, before going back to collect her own. 'One mug of very hot, sweet tea.'

Caz glanced over towards the drink, her eyes roaming across the laptop and desk diary towards the two large mahogany framed portraits in pride of place at the rear of the desk. Anna smiled out from the larger photo, standing adjacent to a handsome fair-haired man, one of his arms slung loosely around her shoulders. In the crook of his other arm lay a tiny, sleeping baby dressed in blue, with a shock of straight, dark, unruly hair. A little girl Caz estimated at about three-years-old clung round Anna's neck, her head thrown back in laughter. Her long wavy hair hung down her back and a pink bow clung perilously on the front, keeping the blonde curls from encroaching on her smiling face.

The other picture showed the same two children, but a couple of years later. The boy was wearing blue shorts and a blue and white striped, short-sleeved shirt and was sitting on a large cream cushion. His hair, still dark and excitable, was combed down with a side parting, although large strands were still stubbornly doing as they pleased. The girl was leaning towards him, her arm protectively around his shoulder. Her blonde hair, longer now, was tied loosely behind her head and draped freely over her shoulder. Ringlets fell, like a waterfall, cascading down each side of her pretty face into a maelstrom of pink and white frills, as her dress swept downwards to the soft cushioning beneath her. Both looked up in the direction of the camera, their faces a mixture of awe and delight, their innocence shining out from the stark frame.

Caz tore her gaze away from the portraits, feeling her mind drifting back towards her own childhood, the familiar stirrings of envy and regret starting to bubble to the surface. Dark shadows began to encircle her, all of a sudden bringing images of death, fast and hard. Visions of her dead mother exploded all around, the memories dragging her down into a bottomless abyss. She felt her arms flailing; trying to grasp at the slippery sides of the chasm, but she continued to fall.

'Caz, Caz.' She heard a voice calling her from afar. Subconsciously, she reached into her jacket, pulling out the ragdoll, stroking it across her cheeks, allowing the familiar odours and textures of the old material to calm her. 'Caz, you're all right,' the voice confirmed. 'You're safe. Wake up.'

She opened her eyes and looked up into Anna's worried face. Anna was holding her arm, shaking her gently, and she suddenly felt the need to be held; held tightly and never released. She allowed a tear to escape from the corner of her eye and wiped it away with the grubby doll. Perhaps now was the time to start telling Anna some of the secrets of her childhood, secrets that she'd kept locked away her whole life. Anna had waited so patiently, never pushing but always there. Perhaps Redz' death had affected her more than she cared to admit.

'I was thinkin' 'bout my mum. I really miss her.' She wiped her nose on her sleeve and sniffed. 'If she hadn't gone, everything'd be all right. I wouldn't be walkin' the streets on my own, or dealin' with dirty perverts, or feelin' like this.'

'Do you want to tell me about your mum?' Anna asked quietly.

'She was the best mum in the world.' Caz started to cry properly. 'I loved her to bits. There was nothin' she wouldn't get for us or do for me and my brothers. Then she changed, got on the booze an' started bringin' back men, boyfriends. They got 'er on weed, sittin' around smokin' joints all day. I wanted it to be like it was. Just me, my mum and my brothers.'

She paused, taking a sip of the hot, sweet tea.

'What happened to your mum?'

'She died. That's what fuckin' happened.' Caz snapped back to the present. She'd said enough, more in fact than she'd ever said before. She swallowed down the remains of the tea quickly and placed the scrawny doll back in her bag, swinging her legs round and rising shakily. 'Now, if I don't get goin' I'll be fuckin' dead too. Razor'll kill me.'

Anna stood up too and reached over, gently touching Caz on the hand. 'Come any time you want. You don't need to worry about making an appointment. Please come though.'

'OK, I'll try. See ya,' she said, pulling her jacket tight and nodding towards Anna. She would come again. Perhaps she'd even begin to tell Anna more, but as that notion ran through her head, her thoughts returned to Razor. He might sometimes treat her roughly. He might sometimes cause her pain, but he was still her man, her protector. Redz was dead and there was only her and Dutch left. He would need her now, more than ever.

She descended the stairs and opened the door, stepping out into the cold winter morning. The sun was shining through the trees opposite, throwing down abstract shapes that swayed and danced across the pavement. She let the final thought run through her mind, repeating itself again and again as the seed began to grow and suddenly she felt positive.

Razor *needed* her. Razor needed *her*.

*

Anna watched Caz as the brightness of the sun enveloped her and carried her away on a wave of optimism. She felt elated. Today she had witnessed something of a breakthrough. Never before had the young prostitute spoken of her love for her mother; only anger, hatred and hostility towards her time in care and a general mistrust of life.

Something about Redz' death had clearly prompted her first ever outpouring of grief. She wondered what specifically the trigger had been. Redz was as close to being a sister as was possible. Perhaps losing her was like losing one of her own siblings. Caz certainly seemed more exposed today. Anna had never seen her sucking her thumb or clutching a doll in any of their previous sessions and this glimpse of Caz's vulnerability affected her deeply. Her heart went out to the prostitute, having to deal with life, with no mother to guide her through the ups and downs.

Her thoughts returned to her own daughter. They still made time to chat, to share shopping trips and to watch their favourite TV programmes together. Caz had known a mother's love, but in her case only for a short time before it seemed to have been cruelly snatched away. Maybe this was worse than never having known it at all.

Slowly Anna turned and shut the door, climbing the stairs back up to her office. The wood panelling on the walls made the hallway seem austere, and the certificates showcasing her qualifications, more formal. As she stared at the proof of her achievements, the realisation dawned that helping Caz could throw her professional reputation into jeopardy. This time she needed to keep her head and not allow her heart to dictate her actions. She'd made the mistake once before, becoming too emotionally involved with a clinically depressed boy of fifteen... and the guilt was as raw now as when they'd cut his body down from the tree. Only time had helped her rationalise the decisions she'd made, but the experience had hardened her resolve to never again get so personally involved with any of her clients... and up until now she'd succeeded.

Caz was different though and the opportunity to right the wrongs of her own life, through the young prostitute, was a possibility too compelling to miss.

Anna ran the thought through her head as she sauntered across to the window, focussing on the figure in the distance. Caz was nearly out of sight, but as she watched, she saw a small dark car pull up next to her. Caz leant towards the passenger window, before climbing into the rear and pulling the door shut. Anna squinted towards the vehicle, anxious as to whether the driver was a friend or some anonymous stranger chancing his luck by the side of the common. She imagined her own daughter sliding in beside an unfamiliar male, the mere thought filling her with pure, unadulterated terror.

Closing her eyes, she visualised Redz' last sights, smells and sensations as the blows rained down, quickly reopening them as her mind was fleetingly drawn back into the sheer horror of what she herself had experienced. Caz's plight was leading her into dangerous waters, of that there was no doubt, but she knew deep down that she couldn't stand idly by as her client had her life stolen from her. Just as she'd been saved, so Anna instinctively knew it would become her mission to rescue Caz. The young woman needed one person who wouldn't let her down, one constant in her life... and if that meant she had to cross the line to free Caz from her present hellish life, so be it.

Chapter 15

The frontage of the brothel was gloomy, with the curtains still drawn and no lights on inside when Charlie and the team parked up. Hunter dispatched Paul to the rear of the premises with a couple of uniformed officers to check whether it was secure, before deciding whether to go in hard, or with a knock at the door. They were looking for people, rather than property, so there wasn't the need to get into the premises quite so speedily. The back door was unlocked.

Charlie walked round with the warrant to join Paul, feeling immediately despondent. Now she was here, she had the distinct impression they were too late. Her despondency was well founded as she pushed through the door and moved from room to room. The decor and some of the abandoned paraphernalia suggested that the house had been used for sexual activities, but every area bore signs of an exit hurriedly executed, devoid of people and personal items, with wardrobes doors hanging ajar and drawers left open and half empty. Her shoes sounded loud against the bare wooden floors as she stared at the stripped mattresses and the mishmash of remaining clothing sacrificed to the emergency move.

She climbed the stairs until finally reaching a bedroom at the top of the house. The air smelt of disinfectant here and the space was clearer than the others, all the bedding removed and little left of the occupant's personal effects. The surfaces too appeared to have been wiped down. A number of random items of clothing and correspondence were laid out across the centre of a large bed. She went across to the window and pulled the curtains open, looking out across the rooftops of the houses in the adjacent road.

Hunter entered, walking breathlessly across to join her.

'Well, it looks like Angie's source was right and that the place was being used as a brothel,' he commented, looking out in the same direction. 'I've sent Naz and Sabira round to do house-to-house enquiries to see if we can find out when the occupants were last seen.'

'It doesn't really matter when,' Charlie shook her head. 'We've missed them anyway. What we do need to know is *why* they've disappeared... and what made them leave in such a hurry.'

Idly, Charlie moved across and leant over the property on the bed, conscious that they needed to try and identify the occupant of each room. Perhaps there would be something to name this particular occupier. She pulled at several magazines, uncovering a large wet patch on the mattress. The stench of bleach wafted into the air, but around the edges of the patch was a dark red stain. She bent down further to closer examine the mark, suddenly excited. It was clear that attempts had been made to eradicate it from the material.

'Look at this, guv. It's blood and someone's tried to get rid of it. Do you think our forensic guys will be able to get enough of a sample from this to extract DNA? Someone was trying to hide it for a reason. Perhaps it's linked to why they disappeared?'

'And why they chose to leave in the dead of the night,' Naz pushed the door open and joined them. 'The man next door heard the sound of a van being driven in and out a few times during the night; the last time being at just gone 5 a.m. when he also heard voices. He was going to have a word, but then decided it was too cold for him to get out of bed, so we haven't any details of the van. That was the last he heard of them. It must have been when they finally left.'

Sabira came in half way through and nodded. 'I heard pretty much the same from another neighbour. The two guys that we knew about were here most of the time, Russians or Eastern Europeans, she thinks. She says they were always very pleasant, but kept themselves to themselves. Occasionally there were disturbances, mostly at night; and if there were, the two guys would always be most apologetic afterwards. The neighbour didn't really know what was going on inside and didn't really care as long as it didn't affect her. She did say she would recognise both the men though and she also said that they regularly changed their vehicles, usually driving rental vans. She heard some noise last night but pretty much just ignored it.'

Hunter pulled his handkerchief from his pocket and wiped it across his brow. 'So we'd have missed them even if we hadn't been called to the other crime scene.'

The thought had already crossed Charlie's mind, but as she stared down at the bloodstain, her brain was still racing. Something was telling her that this house was connected to the abandoned baby, although there was nothing concrete, as such, to confirm this suspicion. But the baby's body had been found two days before, and Dr Finch had estimated she had been dumped several days before that... so why the panic now? What had happened to make them vacate the house so suddenly just a few hours before?

<u>Chapter 16</u>

Razor had almost given up searching for Caz when he remembered her shrink, but as he watched her solitary figure walking towards him he didn't know whether to be relieved or angry. Not for the first time, he found himself irritated by her insistence on speaking to this stuck-up bitch.

The passenger seat was covered in shit, so he told Caz to get in the back, watching as she slumped against the rear, her clothes dishevelled and her make-up smeared across her face. She looked as if she'd been on the street all night.

'Where the hell have you been?' He revved the car angrily.

'I was just comin' to find you actually,' Caz sniffed. 'But I'm glad you're here. Mand told me what 'appened to Redz and it freaked me out.'

'What've you heard then?'

Caz repeated the same story as she'd told Anna about The Punter, adding that the money she'd earned earlier in the evening was safely stashed at the flat. He grunted with relief at this information. He still owed DK for the gear he'd got off him earlier.

'Was it definitely the same punter as before?' He didn't like the sound of the guy. Rumours had been circulating about this particular bloke over the last few months, but until this morning he'd not really taken too much notice. Now, it was very much his business. 'What do you know 'bout him?'

'Yeah, Mand said it was the same punter as before… and I ain't heard nuffin' more than you already know. Big bloke, Asian-looking, wears lots of jewellery and a long black leather coat. 'E even looks evil, apparently. Hope the cops get him quick 'cause I sure as hell don't want to meet him on a dark night.'

'Well *I* want to meet him and when I do, I'll fuckin' kill him,' Razor growled. 'He won't be worried about no cops when I get hold of him. He'll be crying like a baby for their help.'

He drove straight to his estate, still brooding on what he would do to The Punter when he found him. The bastard would wish he'd never set foot on Redz' patch. As he pulled into their garages, Razor's attention shifted to his other problem.

'Caz, I need you to say you was with me last night after I left to find DK.' He turned towards her and gripped her around the arm. 'I went to Viv's place after I saw all the cops swarming round the alleyway so that bit is OK. I just need you to cover for me up 'til then, right? The cops are bound to pick me up sooner or later.'

Caz winced as his fingers dug into her flesh. 'Don't worry 'bout that, babe. As far as I'm concerned, I was with you. I'll tell them we was both in the flat together shootin' up and that you dropped me off outside Viv's later when you went in.'

Razor released his hold on Caz, relieved that at least his alibi was sorted. Heaving himself up, he slammed the door shut, making no move to lock it and stomped off towards his flat. No one round here would dare mess with his car.

Dutch was lying as he'd left her, still sleeping off the effects of the night before, a fact that didn't fail to wind him up, but as he stood in the doorway, he was suddenly aware of Caz's hot breath on the back of his neck. There was one last thing he needed to do. Beckoning for her to follow, he strode into her room, stood by the bed and started to unzip his fly, removing the package of crack from where it was tucked and placing it on the bedside table. She tailed him obediently, not saying a word as he pushed her on to the bed and pulled her T-shirt up to expose her teenage breasts. He lowered himself down, his huge frame pinning her thin body underneath him, forcing her breath up in short pants as she gasped for air.

He could feel himself harden as Caz squirmed against him. Bringing his knee up into her groin, he forced her legs apart and entered her. She was unprepared, but he didn't care. Thrusting slowly at first, he revelled in the feeling of resistance, knowing she could do nothing to stop him. As his pleasure grew, he pushed harder and harder into her young body, his breathing becoming laboured, his body taut and rigid, until finally exploding within her.

The tension from the last few hours evaporated immediately, the tightness in his chest released as the last few shudders of his climax were expelled. He slumped against Caz's body, unusually feeling her arms holding his body close as she clung to him, either in gratitude or desperation, he didn't know which.

After a few minutes, he prised her arms apart, now irritated at this unwanted show of affection, watching as Caz curled up next to him, a peculiar expression across her face. He rolled himself a joint, passing it to Caz when he'd had enough.

'Got any spare gear?' she asked, putting the joint to her lips and looking towards the table where he'd discarded the package of crack earlier. 'It's been a hell of a night.'

Razor passed her a small creamy rock, viewing with satisfaction the trembling of her fingers as she prepared the hit. He was pleased at how things were progressing. Redz might be dead but Caz and Dutch were under his control. There was only one thing left to be done.

He closed his eyes, visualising with relish the path of his razor blade as it sliced through the skin of The Punter's face.

Chapter 17

Charlie watched as the Scenes of Crime Officer arrived, with a small team of forensic staff. There were plenty of possible samples to be gleaned from the other rooms, but it was the top room that was of the most interest to them. With the surfaces wiped clean and the presence of bleach and disinfectant to obliterate fingerprints and DNA it was clear that somebody wanted the identity of its occupant to remain anonymous, but with the traces of blood on the mattress and the departure from the premises being conducted in such a rush, the chances that some evidence had been left was high. Charlie was banking on a speedy identification, if for no other reason than to confirm or negate her hunch.

So far, all the enquiries at local hospitals, walk-in clinics and surgeries had been negative. If luck was on their side and they could establish that the blood stains on the mattress were from the same woman as the blood on the baby's head, they would at least know they were on the right track, even if they had no match providing identification on the DNA database. The brothel would almost certainly re-emerge in a different location. How hard could it be to track down the whereabouts of up to five young women forced into prostitution by two Eastern European men, one of whom was called Dimitri? She pulled her phone out of her pocket and dialled Angie's number. They'd do their own research of course, but hopefully her source might be able to help again.

'I'll get straight back on to it,' Angie was direct, after hearing Charlie's news. 'And I'll also try to find out why they moved out in such a rush. Something must have spooked them.'

'Thanks, Angie.'

Charlie put the phone away and sighed heavily. It would take a while for the SOCO to retrieve any possible forensic evidence from this new scene, and Hunter was keen to pay a visit to Razor while they waited for any news from Angie's DSU. Minutes were turning into hours and hours were becoming days. As she walked away from the disinfected bedroom, Charlie knew that with every minute that passed, time could be running out for the woman whose blood had been spilt across the mattress... if it hadn't run out already.

*

Bet clicked on to a custody photo of Razor, Grace Flaherty's pimp, along with his actual name. ROBERTS:

Clinton,   James/18:03:1960/Male/Non-white/Born: Jamaica.

Charlie recognised the heavy angular set of his jaw immediately as she walked back into the office. It was one that was not easily forgotten. She watched as Bet turned to the front

page of his record, illuminated in red flashing words: WEAPONS/VIOLENT/DRUGS/ ASSAULTS POLICE.

Nineteen pages followed, detailing forty-eight previous convictions all neatly set out in rows containing the exact date, the court, the offence and the sentence.

Charlie let her eyes run through the catalogue of crimes. It bore the same depressing similarity that she'd seen on so many other records of adults in the borough. Once entrenched, each young life-victim seemed destined to carry on the cycle; rarely could any agency intervene to change behaviours.

From his first juvenile convictions detailing street robbery, stealing cars, criminal damage, burglary and minor drugs offences, Razor had surely and steadily worked his way up the ladder. Possession of drugs with intent to supply, assault on police and carrying offensive weapons followed, culminating in armed robbery, GBH with intent and wounding. Terms of imprisonment were meted out for some of the more violent crimes, but these just served to have made him more selective in his choice of victim. Assaulting prostitutes seemed to be his preference now; he could beat them up with impunity, knowing they would never give evidence against him for fear of reprisals and the British justice system wouldn't care.

Charlie was well aware that the majority of murders in England were domestically related. If the victim was also a sex worker, and the suspect their pimp, then the risk was further heightened. Even the lure of money could not guarantee the violence was controlled.

She glanced at a printout of Redz, letting her gaze fall on a photo of Grace Flaherty as she had appeared before her face had been rendered unrecognisable. As if reading Charlie's mind, Bet nodded at the photo.

'She went downhill rapidly. Have a look at her intel', especially from when she met Razor.'

Charlie scanned through the record sadly. From the moment their first sightings were reported, his influence was clear... and it wasn't positive.

'Tragic isn't it?' Bet shook her head as Charlie finished the last page and threw the record on to the desk in front of her. She paused and pushed the paperwork to one side. 'This might help us though.' Bet slotted a DVD into the hard drive. 'I've been searching CCTV.' She navigated through several screens to a clip labelled 'STREATHAM HILL CCTV – 00.30 to 02.00'.

Hunter joined them and they both leant in as the screen filled with a grainy shot of Streatham Hill. Charlie knew the area well and could easily make out the three lanes of traffic running from south to north along the carriageway. The shot was of the west carriageway from which the side roads leading to Redz' alleyway were situated and, even though the image was dark and flickered intermittently, the registration numbers of vehicles travelling into view could be seen.

Bet fast-forwarded until she reached the frame showing 00.42 in the bottom right corner of the recording and pointed to a black Vauxhall Astra coming from the direction of Brixton and turning right, across the carriageway into Telford Avenue. She zoomed in on the registration number.

'That car belongs to Razor,' Bet said. 'It enters the road at 00.42 with apparently only the driver in it, and then look.' She fast-forwarded until the clock showed 01.05. Charlie squinted as the same black Vauxhall Astra was driven at speed from one of the side roads, barely slowing down for any oncoming traffic. As if to confirm what she was seeing, Bet freeze-framed the vehicle on the screen. 'It's Razor's car again and it's leaving the area within five minutes of Maria Simpson's call for an ambulance.'

'And at speed,' Charlie commented.

Hunter shot up straight. 'Good work, Bet.' He looked round towards them all. 'Right, troops. That's all the suspicion I need. Razor's record speaks for itself and now we have him at the scene, we have more than enough to bring him in. Be ready to move out in fifteen minutes.'

The trough of disappointment from earlier lifted and they were launched on to a wave of optimism. If they couldn't solve the first crime immediately, they could at least have a fighting chance with the second.

Chapter 18

Caz pressed her body up against Razor and let her arm drape loosely across his chest, her fingers stroking the thick black hair. He was deeply asleep, his face relaxed, his mouth open slightly and a wave of emotion swept over her. For once she was happy; happy to have Razor in her arms, happy to provide his alibi, happy that he wanted her.

The drugs had taken effect, the weed relaxing her, the crack heightening the sense of elation seeping through her body. It was not an emotion Caz experienced often, but for now she was luxuriating in the feeling.

Razor needed her. Razor *needed* her. Razor needed *her*.

She repeated the sentence in her head, savouring every word. She felt like singing, dancing, flying. Gone was the ever-present fear, the niggling apprehension that saying or doing the wrong thing would unleash a torrent of abuse or punches. She didn't care that he treated her roughly or that she was not the only woman he slept with. All she cared about at that moment was the desire in both of them for each other. Not since she had lain in her mother's arms, so many years ago, had she felt so contented, so secure.

Closing her eyes, Caz drifted into a troubled sleep. Visions of her mother faded in and out of her consciousness, mingling with dreams of Razor smiling at her, holding her, his arm encircling her protectively. The crack made her dreams vivid and realistic, taking her to an imaginary place where her life was perfect and she was surrounded by everything she had always longed for.

Through her picture-postcard world, she heard a muffled thud, followed by another and another. She felt Razor leap up and thrust what remained of the cling film of crack into her hand. As the door crashed open, she stashed the precious wrap in her mouth, pushing it to the side of her cheek with her tongue. Through heavy eyes she saw a number of boiler-suited figures, their heads encased in dark helmets, the visors down, thick gloves covering their hands. All around her was noise. The figures were shouting, bellowing out their instructions.

'Police, Police. Stay where you are. Don't move.'

Doors crashed open as the other rooms in the flat were also forcibly entered.

The figures were swarming all over Razor. They had him on the floor, his hands behind his back, all the time shouting, shouting at him to stay still. It all seemed so surreal that Caz fought back the urge to laugh. He'd said this was going to happen and now it was. The figures were blurry, out of focus. She tried to concentrate. One was bending over her now. She stared up at it, willing herself to see its features. No matter how hard she tried though, it still remained suspended in a fog.

Razor was struggling to get to her, his hands secured tightly behind him. He was also shouting.

'Caz, Caz. Tell them where I was when Redz was done, babe.'

'He was with me, right,' she slurred, recognising the moment for which they'd planned. 'He was here in this room, right here, while I was shootin' up, weren't you?'

'Right, that's right, we was. Just tell them that, right.'

She watched as Razor was jerked backwards away from her. She could hear Dutch calling out to him, swearing and shouting from a distant place. Her voice grew louder and she appeared, framed in the doorway, a figure on both sides holding her still.

'What the fuck's goin' on, Razor?' Dutch tried to pull away, but as she did so, the gloved hands that held her tightened and clamped round each elbow, moving her arms out in front and locking metal restraints in place. Through clouded eyes, Caz saw her propelled forward towards the bed on which she was lying.

'Sit down and be quiet,' the faceless figure was instructing.

Razor was taken from the room, leaving Caz and Dutch together, surrounded by the boiler suits.

Caz still couldn't concentrate properly on her surroundings, but the euphoria was starting to fade and her vision was at last beginning to focus on the strange figures. She recognised them to be police. She felt no fear or anxiety, just a strange feeling of déjà vu and inevitability.

Dutch whispered urgently to her. 'Caz, what's happened? What's Razor done this time?'

'Nothin',' she replied indignantly. 'Redz got herself bleedin' murdered last night. Razor never done it, I swear. The cops are takin' him in though. He said they would, but he's got nothin' to worry 'bout.' She put a finger to her mouth, winked towards Dutch and whispered. 'I'm coverin' for him.'

The words coming from her mouth still seemed indistinct and unfamiliar, but as she spoke, the reality of what she said was starting to dawn on her properly. Razor was leaving her, going to a place where she couldn't follow. She was on her own again, the bubble of euphoria deflating, as quickly as it had come. His arrest was purely routine, but this knowledge still did nothing to raise the gloom settling on her shoulders.

Dutch was sitting in silence, looking shell-shocked, her face frozen in a mask of horror. The fact that she'd lain in a drug-induced sleep while her best friend, Redz, was fighting for her life was clearly hard to bear.

The boiler-suited figures were becoming more human. Their helmets were now removed and two pairs of tightly fitted rubber gloves replaced the thick leather ones. She recognised a woman in normal clothes walking towards her.

'Hello again, Caz,' the woman said, indicating for the boiler-suited person next to her to move away. 'Are you all right now? It's me.'

Everything still felt bizarre. 'Well, if it's not DC Charlie Stafford,' she grinned. 'We can't keep meeting like this.'

'And you've warmed up and are feeling better? I wondered whether you would be here.'

'Where else would I be?' Caz kept the wrap pressed firmly against the side of her cheek, hoping that the slight difference in her speech would not be noticed.

'You're going to have to be somewhere else in a few minutes,' Charlie's boss came across to join them. 'DI Hunter,' he introduced himself. 'Is there somewhere you can both stay while this flat is searched?' He wasn't officious; in fact, on the few occasions they'd met, he had always been fair. That was all she ever asked for; to be cut a bit of slack every now and again. She nodded. She was used to this sort of shit and he wasn't saying anything that she didn't already know. She and Dutch could crash out at DK's place until the cops had finished.

'We can stay wiv a mate nearby. He won't mind. As long as we pay our way.'

'Is it far?' Charlie was asking. 'We could help you move your stuff if need be.'

Caz shook her head. Charlie Stafford was all right too. It was Charlie that had got her working with Angie and Von, passing on what she saw and heard on the streets, as well as what her mates Ayeisha and Mand told her. Money talked and the small amount of cash coming in from putting away another dealer or identifying a robber helped her to buy a few extra bits to wear and a little rest from her day job. Not that she could ever admit it. She couldn't even tell Charlie, although she had given her a few clues. *Keep yer gob shut* was what Angie had said. *Don't tell no one that you are working with us.* Angie was right though. Dead right. So right in fact that her life might actually depend on it.

'No, it ain't far.' She indicated towards Dutch, still sitting silently next to her. 'We'll be all right. I don't think my mate would appreciate you lot turnin' up on his doorstep wiv or wivout me.' She fixed a smile on her face. 'Suppose you lot will want to search us both first though.'

Charlie nodded. 'You can probably guess why Razor has been nicked, and it's not for drugs this time, but we'll still have to check you haven't got anything on you connected with what he's been arrested for.'

Caz snorted and turned to Dutch. 'He's bin nicked for murdering Redz, like 'e said 'e would.' She turned to DI

Hunter. 'But I can vouch that it weren't 'im, like I've already told your lot.' She was happy to go to court for Razor's alibi, but she'd keep news of The Punter for Angie or Von; that way, she might earn out of it. She lifted up her arms and spread her legs. 'OK, let's get this search over wiv, then we can go.'

Hunter moved away. 'I'll send Naz and Sab in to help. Search them both quickly. I'm not interested in drugs paraphernalia. We need to get going with Razor. The clock's already ticking.'

He left the room and was quickly replaced by two female officers. Caz stripped off indifferently, being used to total strangers seeing her body. Dutch too, both volunteering to be searched in the same room. Neither of them cared. The police officers were more embarrassed than they were, and anyway, she had nothing that they would find. Cops weren't allowed to search 'intimate' places, and mouths were off limits, though at one point she thought she saw Charlie staring towards her cheek, but the officer said nothing, and after a few minutes they were on their way, with only a small holdall each containing their worldly belongings.

They passed through the garage area on their way out of the estate, standing to watch as a pick-up lorry lifted Razor's Vauxhall Astra up in the air, dumping it unceremoniously down on the trailer.

'Bastards!' Caz muttered. 'Why'd they have to take his bleedin' car? He'll be fucked off when he finds out.'

Dutch nodded silently, still lost in her own thoughts.

They rounded a bend and Caz saw the familiar figure of her friend Ayeisha ambling along the concrete walkway towards them. They had met in a children's home and had been firm friends for some years now, even though Ayeisha was younger than she. When she'd moved in with Razor, they'd remained friends, with Ayeisha regularly visiting them and occasionally staying when she couldn't be bothered to return to the home. Redz and Dutch were counted amongst her friends now, though Razor still seemed to frighten her, much to Caz's amusement. If he was about, Ayeisha would usually make herself scarce, but tonight they could all relax. Caz grinned as they greeted each other. It would be good to hear her news.

The door to DK's flat was ajar, so they pushed it open and entered, waving towards several users who were watching a war film on the TV. They moved straight through to the kitchen, where a half-empty bottle of Smirnoff stood on the draining board. Caz indicated towards the bottle, but Ayeisha declined, instead pouring herself a beer from a four-pack she was carrying. As Caz poured out two neat glasses of vodka, Dutch eventually broke her silence.

'Caz, tell me what happened to Redz.'

Caz drained her glass and refilled it, before repeating the story, while Dutch and Ayeisha listened quietly. Dutch's hairpiece had slipped to one side during the earlier raid and wisps of her own hair, normally straightened carefully, were curling and frizzy.

Nearing the end of the account, Dutch sat down heavily. 'I've always said it's too dangerous in London. It should be made safer. This sort of thing don't happen in Amsterdam 'cause it's all legal and the punters are screened better. There's too many bleedin' pervs here.'

Caz gulped down half the glass, pulling up a seat and sitting opposite her friend. Dutch was her mentor, the one she had always looked up to. At twenty-one she had seen and done plenty in her life. She had been raised in the slums of Birmingham by her immigrant parents, but whilst her siblings had studied hard, Dutch had preferred to spend her time hanging around on the streets, gaining a reputation for being an easy lay with the boys. She had accompanied them eagerly on a lad's weekend to Amsterdam and what she saw whilst there appealed to her. When the boys returned, satisfied with their fill of cannabis cafes and casual sex, Dutch had stayed, finding work in the sleazy strip joints and pole-dancing clubs of Amsterdam's red-light district.

The men and the money, however, failed to fill the void in her life and, missing her parents and family, she returned to Birmingham only to find they'd disowned her. In despair, she travelled to London to seek work in the clubs and bars of Soho, quickly gaining her street name and a somewhat flamboyant reputation. She rapidly succumbed to crack and heroin and soon became

Razor's first working girl. Behind the brash exterior, Caz knew that Dutch was frightened; frightened of the punters and petrified of working the streets, preferring the safety of Amsterdam's regulated brothels, but she had no choice.

She watched as Dutch, still clearly stricken, searched for any more leftover booze, feeling a mix of sympathy, envy and camaraderie towards her older flatmate. Dutch was tall, black and willowy, with high cheekbones, full lips and an extrovert personality that kept Razor enchanted. She was his favourite choice for sex, offering games and experiences learned from her time in Holland. Sometimes Caz would lie listening to Dutch and Razor, jealously wishing she'd been chosen in the place of her friend. Although Razor could be rough and inconsiderate, it was a victory of sorts to sleep with him rather than the total strangers of the streets.

Ayeisha moved across and put an arm around Dutch's shoulder, calming her slightly. She turned towards Caz, her face still pinched and drawn. 'So do you think it's The Punter that Mand described who done Redz then?'

'It looks like it, don't it?' Caz downed the last dregs from her glass and pushed the empty glass across the table. 'Fuck knows what Razor'll do if he gets hold of him before the Old Bill does.'

'He'll do time inside,' Dutch spoke with conviction. 'Razor's not one to let things lie. He won't sleep 'til he gets his revenge on whoever's done this.'

Caz nodded, her gaze moving between her two friends. Dutch was right. She'd heard him say as much.

Chapter 19

'You've been arrested in connection with the murder of Grace Flaherty, or Redz as you know her. What were you doing last night?' Charlie came straight to the point. There was no benefit in playing softly-softly with someone who knew the score.

Razor leant back in his chair, his legs spread wide and his arms folded in front of him. He stared from Charlie to Hunter, his lip curling in a sneer.

'No comment.'

His solicitor slid a piece of paper across the desk towards Charlie. After half an hour in consultation before the interview commenced, saying nothing was clearly going to be their strategy. She picked it up and read out aloud the words that were written on it.

'This is a prepared statement: I, Clinton James Roberts, did not murder Grace Flaherty, also known as Redz, and I had no involvement in her death. I spent the night she died with my girlfriend Charlene Philips, before going straight to a bar in Brixton, where I was seen by many people, including a barmaid I have known for many years called Viv. I have nothing further to add.'

She placed the piece of paper on top of her own notes despondently.

'How did you get to the bar?' The statement he'd given would have to be probed.

'No comment.'

'Were you driving your car?'

'No comment.'

'If so, were you on your own?'

'No comment.'

The terms of Razor's interrogation were set. He had provided two alibis and was saying nothing more. Even when she brought up the CCTV footage, he refused to answer. There was nothing more she could do, other than pose the questions and wait for his two-word reply, but he had to be given the chance to answer the accusation, to give his first defence. If she didn't ask, he'd have a get-out-of-jail-free card when he got to court.

Charlie was positively seething with frustration. After the initial elation of the CCTV and his arrest, it now appeared that the impetus had slowed. Few witnesses could be found and forensics were still awaited on the alleyway and now on Razor's flat and car, though officers at the car pound had revealed that a quantity of dried blood and some hair could be clearly seen by the front passenger seat and footwell. Charlie was encouraged by this news, desperately hoping that it would belong to Redz, but until DNA had been extracted and an identification provided, it was not even worth a mention in Razor's interview. Why give him prior warning until they had the actual proof?

It would have to wait, until next time.

As she concluded the interview and turned off the recording, Razor propelled himself towards her, so close she could almost taste the stench of stale cannabis and tobacco on his breath.

'Was that all right, officer? Or do you want a piece of me too? Like my girls do.' He leant back, his hands moving across his groin. 'You know I'd be only too happy to oblige.'

Hunter shot up, the vein on his forehead bulging prominently, his voice tight. 'Your girls don't want a piece of you. You treat them like shit.' He bent over, mirroring Razor's previous pose, his face directly in front of their suspect. 'What they really want is peace away from you... and that's exactly what we aim to give them when we get you locked away for life.'

Chapter 20

'Are you nearly finished, love, only we're closing up soon?'

The Punter's thoughts were interrupted by the waitress, middle-aged, overweight and with a mouth missing half her teeth. She lifted the menu, sticking a yellow-coated tongue through a gap in her front incisors and wiped the table over with a grubby dishcloth.

He had no choice, even though he was sorely tempted to stay put. Standing up, he fished in his pocket and threw the money he owed on to the table in front of him before stalking out. He hated being forced into action by someone, particularly a female, and particularly one who was ugly and inferior, but today he dared not cause a scene.

'Thanks, love,' the waitress called out sarcastically, further increasing his ire.

A cool breeze swirled about the emptying shops, calming him back to his charming, persuasive persona. It was almost dark, the nights closing in by late afternoon in December. Christmas was his favourite time of the year; cold enough that his clients would be ensconced in their houses to listen to his patter, but too engrossed in preparations for the forthcoming festivities to fully consider any financial advice, signing almost anything he recommended in order to get rid of him. His commission figures always went up at Christmas.

His reflection stared back at him from the window of the shop he passed, darkly handsome, with closely cropped hair, a clear complexion and large, brown eyes framed with long, curling lashes. His facial features were as striking as his strong, muscular body and he exuded good health and a strong sense of well-being. His looks, added to his successful business acumen, had at least enabled his parents to choose one of the more striking girls from his community for him to marry. Or she was, before childbirth.

The crowds were thinning, and as he watched their exodus, he had nothing but contempt for them, caught up in their humdrum existences. He was superior to the masses, destined for greatness; his elderly parents had told him so. The younger generation would aspire to be like him, to emulate his lifestyle. People would know his name and be full of admiration.

He came to a small garage and purchased a petrol can, chatting amiably with the cashier. He filled it with fuel and paid, also selecting a pack of screwdrivers, a box of cigars and a packet of matches.

The car was as he'd left it and the street was empty. He let himself in and pulled the picnic blanket off the dashboard, exposing wisps of hair glued to the facia by the dried blood. Although the sight excited him immediately, he knew he had to concentrate on what had to be done.

He turned the ignition and pulled away, keenly aware that he was now driving a *stolen* car, and one that was covered in a murder victim's blood. The sounds of sirens seemed to be everywhere, each wail growing louder and louder as emergency vehicles appeared, fading as they disappeared through the traffic. With each diminishing tail-light, his confidence grew. He wouldn't be caught. He was too good.

The car park on Battersea Common had a few cars parked randomly about, but on the whole it was quiet and dark. He would have to be careful. He drove to the far end, where a small gate allowed access to the common for council vehicles. The gate had been knocked askew by a tipper truck several months previously and still hung open on its hinges. The Punter drove through and continued along the rutted pathway. Nearing the end of the track, he turned sharply left into a secluded clearing. It was empty now; too late for the clandestine trysts of work colleagues, but too early for the late-night hormonal fumblings of teenagers.

The moon was not yet up and the trees guarding the clearing were dark and menacing. He switched his lights off and sat in the car for a few minutes, his eyes acclimatising to the blackness, listening intently to the slightest sound that would signify another's presence.

There was nothing.

He unscrewed the lid of the petrol can and started emptying its contents all over the bloody interior. He took his leather coat from the boot and threw it across the back seats, spilling petrol out across its blood-splattered sleeves, careful to ensure every incriminating spot would be eliminated.

Finally, taking the screwdriver from his pocket, he forced it into the ignition barrel, twisting the lock beyond recognition and throwing the bent screwdriver into the footwell. Carefully, he withdrew to the cover of the trees, took out the matches and again listened.

Still nothing.

The noise from the tiny detonation of the match seemed to echo around the clearing and its light flared like a beacon, spotlighting the grisly scene. The Punter moved silently over to the car and opened the passenger door. He threw the lighted match into its rear and watched breathlessly as the back seat exploded into flames. Swiftly, he struck another match and threw it down on the petrol-sodden picnic blanket, admiring the ferocity with which it caught fire. He slammed the door and moved back into the shadowy security of the trees, staring mesmerised as the whole interior of the car lit up and blazed in a mass of white-hot flames.

As the first of the windows splintered outwards into the clearing, he retreated into the woods, picking his way carefully back towards the roadway at the edge of the common before turning casually to look back.

A mass of smoke and flames stretched up from the clearing into the black sky, the bright fingers of fire pointing upwards in a sign of defiance. Already the wail of sirens was getting closer.

The Punter smiled a satisfied smile. His stolen vehicle and everything in it would be burnt beyond recognition, any incriminating evidence from the previous night's activities converted perfectly to ash.

Lighting a cigar, he turned and started making his way home to his sweet, compliant wife.

Chapter 21

Razor screwed up his bail form and stuffed it into his jacket pocket as he walked away from the station. He was being released – much to the annoyance of the two cops who had interviewed him – on condition he lived and slept at DK's flat and returned for a possible ID parade if necessary. They couldn't keep him any longer. They had nothing on him and, apart from his alibis, he'd left them nothing to pick over.

He smiled wryly at the irony of it. There had been so many times, during a lifetime of crime, when he had been guilty but got away with it. On this occasion though, when he was actually innocent, he had been forced to remain on bail. Still, the less said, the better... and apart from seizing his car and keeping him from his flat temporarily, which was bloody annoying, it seemed to be working.

He now had one week of freedom before he had to return. One week to track down The Punter... and one week to get Caz and Dutch properly in line. They'd both have to work extra hard to make up for the loss of Redz' income.

He pulled out his tobacco and rolled a cigarette, lighting it in the protection of a shop doorway. Tonight was relatively mild and dry for this time of the year, which meant greater numbers of Christmas partygoers would be out and about. Thursdays were the new Saturdays. In a couple of hours, the clubs would pull down their shutters and the hordes of testosterone-fuelled young men would be out on the streets vying for the attention of any available girl. The thought brought his dilemma sharply into focus. His two girls needed to be out earning double.

Finishing the last of his roll-up, he threw the glowing dog-end down on to the concrete and turned into an alleyway behind the shops. Rooting around inside a nearby skip, he found a length of discarded metal and a rock.

Five minutes later, he was sitting in the driver's seat of an old Fiesta, listening as the engine spluttered into life. The car looked to belong to a young mother, toys and sweet wrappers were strewn around a child seat in the rear and a pair of high-heeled shoes lay across the passenger foot-well, but he cared nothing for the owner's inconvenience. His need was greater.

There was no trace of either Caz or Dutch in their usual patches, so he made his way to DK's flat, his anger spiking. Maybe DK would know where the hell they were. As he neared his mate's front door, he heard the sound of laughter coming from within. The door was ajar so he pushed it open and strode into the lounge to see Caz, Dutch and Ayeisha arranged comfortably across a sofa, giggling. DK sat opposite, obviously enjoying the spectacle. Empty cans littered the floor, along with freshly blackened foil and the remnants of cling-film wraps.

Before he could say anything, Caz and Dutch let out a cheer and, with squeals of laughter, jumped up from their seats and lurched in his direction. As they wrapped their legs around him from each side, Razor felt a hand slip down the front of his trousers, any trace of anger disappearing as his senses took precedent.

Forgetting Redz and The Punter, he unzipped his trousers and lay back. Tonight they would celebrate his release from custody. Tomorrow he would get down to business.

*

The Punter roused at the ring of the doorbell. His wife stirred next to him, turning over and murmuring sleepily. The sound came again and suddenly he was awake as a wave of panic engulfed him.

His wife was up now, heading towards the window. 'It's the police,' she whispered, spinning round towards him. 'What could they want at this time of night?'

He didn't know. The clock was showing ten minutes past midnight. What if someone had seen him after all?

What if they were there to arrest him for the whore's murder? His body refused to move, his mouth was dry and as he ran his shaking fingers over his head, he rewound through his movements, thinking through every eventuality, covering every question.

A cold blast of air from the open window brought his imaginings sharply into focus as his wife leant out, speaking to the officers at the front door. She pulled the window shut.

'Did they say what they wanted, babe?' He still couldn't think straight.

'No. Just that they wanted to speak to you.'

'It must be about the car being stolen,' he suddenly remembered his plan, hoping it had worked. His wife looked terrified. He stared at her pretty face, suddenly nervous himself. Although she'd lost something of her initial lustre, she was still so pure, so natural, so exquisitely beautiful. Now, he might be bringing shame on her and her family. 'Go down and let them in. Tell them I'll be down in a minute,' he said, smiling towards her and buying a little more time.

She rushed off downstairs obediently, her eagerness to please him immediately stirring his anger. It was all her fault. She did nothing for him. Her looks might be perfect, but they didn't physically attract him. She was boring and mundane, as was his life, and because of her banality he was now at risk of losing everything. He'd told her about the car, and she'd accepted every word.

He'd blamed his swollen lip on walking into a pillar, and she'd shown him pity. He could say anything and she would believe him. There was no challenge, no excitement.

The crackle of the police radios brought him to his senses. He could hear the officers moving into the living room as she offered them a cup of tea. The silly bitch! Hopefully they would refuse. The sooner they were out of his house the better.

Pulling a dressing gown on, he checked himself in the mirror, frowning at the face that stared back. He looked rough; sleep lines still etched into his cheeks and his chin peppered with two days' dark stubble. He descended the stairs, knowing that before he'd even set eyes on them, he was the underdog, ill-prepared and at a disadvantage.

'What can I do for you, officers?' The Punter entered the room, full of charm.

The police officers straightened, one pulling his notebook out from his trouser pocket and leafing through it to the last page of writing. 'I do apologise for waking you at this hour, but we like to come in person in these circumstances.'

He held his breath.

'Did you report your car as being stolen, yesterday morning?' The officer read out the registration number.

'Yes I did. I left it outside a client's house while I was offering financial advice and when I came out it had been stolen. Have you found it?' He tried to stay as casual as possible.

'Well yes, we have, but unfortunately it's been burnt out. From what I gather, there's nothing much left of it.'

'Oh no. What a bloody nuisance, excuse my language.' He feigned shock. 'I need my car for work. Have you any idea who might have done this.'

'Probably joyriders,' the second officer piped up. 'They think nothing of torching a car once they've finished with it. Perhaps they got up to something in it before setting it on fire. We'll have to see if anything gets flagged up later.'

The Punter relaxed. So clearly nothing had stood out so far.

'Would you know whether any of my belongings have survived?' He had to know for sure that all the incriminating evidence was gone. 'There were a few items of clothing, you know, designer stuff in the rear. Cost a fair bit.'

'Sorry, sir. The information I've received is that it's a blackened shell. The fire has destroyed all your property and any available forensics.' The first officer was speaking again. 'We'll mark up the crime report that you've been informed, but unless anything else comes to light, there's not much more we can do.'

The Punter shook his head in mock dismay, but underneath he wanted to laugh. He was in the clear. There was no reason he shouldn't get a full insurance payout and buy a better car, a bigger one that would make people's heads turn; a classy motor that would overtly display his success. He swallowed hard, thinking of the other benefits that would follow. With a new car he'd be free to go out cruising the streets again.

The first officer snapped his notebook shut and eased it back into his pocket. 'Check with your insurance company though. If you're lucky they might cover the extras.'

'Thank you, officers,' he replied, showing them to the door and ushering them out. 'I'll do that.'

Chapter 22

Dimitri's wallet was thin. It was not the way he liked it to be, but at least it wasn't locked into the property store of a police station. They had been lucky by all accounts. Bloody lucky. His girl from the care home had phoned to ask where he was, reporting back that she'd been to the house and there were police crawling all over it. She was worried something had happened, that he'd been arrested, that the girls had all been taken into detention. Her voice had sounded panicky, desperate even, and that had pleased him. It wouldn't be that much longer before she would give herself to him fully, her defences were falling, he could tell.

The information that had been disclosed, however, was displeasing. What had caused the police to come so quickly? Surely they could not have found Tatjana's body yet; and even if they had, how would it have led them to the house? Or the baby; maybe the baby's body had been discovered, but why would it bring police straight to him? There should be no link, even if DNA or fingerprints had been found.

In fact, the very existence of the brothel should have been unknown to police. The girls were kept within its walls and no one had ever been stopped, searched or arrested, Albertas and himself included. He pulled out a pack of Ziganov cigarettes and lit one, inhaling its strength, bringing with it the vague memory of a distant bar in St Petersburg, the air dense with smoke, and girls, young and innocent, gyrating nakedly on individual plinths.

No, it had to be the neighbours. There could be nothing and no one else; just nosy, interfering busybodies who campaigned for prostitution to be legalised but not if it meant on their own doorsteps. It was just pure bad luck, but now he had to be extra careful. Now the authorities were aware of the set-up, they might try to establish the identity of some of the girls, or Albertas, from past misdemeanours. Not him though. He would be safe because he was known only as Dimitri in this country. No one knew his true identity. He would just create a new one if necessary, and move on, again and again.

The new house was almost ready. It had been prepared for just this eventuality. He always liked to be one step ahead. It would open its doors the following night and his girls would have to be ready. A two-day break was enough for them to have become idle and restless. They needed to be put back to work. They were asking questions. Why had they moved so suddenly? Where was Tatjana? Why was she not with them?

He had explained that he'd taken her to hospital, where she had stated her wish to return to Russia after discharge. The authorities would help. She was not coming back. Hanna had disbelieved his words, but she would say nothing. Still, he would have to watch her closely, ensure she was not getting too influential amongst the other girls. She would be put to work hard, kept from Albertas and his familiarity, made to service the new men who would arrive, the risky ones who would try their luck, the ones who liked to dominate. She would keep her mouth shut or it would be shut for her. All the girls had to know who was in charge. There could be no dissent.

He took another drag on his cigarette and checked the padlock on the back door. It was securely in place. The house smelt perfumed; incense sticks wafting oriental aromas around the hallway, stairs and communal areas. Each girl had chosen her favourite scent for the privacy of her space. He could identify each one by their lingering fragrance. He pulled out his mobile phone, changed the SIM card and typed out a message:

> Your wish is our command. Doors open tomorrow night. Phone Dimitri.

He pressed 'send to all'. It was not too obvious but his regular customers would recognise his name. They would know to save the new number. He had made a habit of changing both his address and number regularly and he never moved too far. They would travel. They always did.

Now though, he had to plan. There were two rooms empty that required filling. His contact in Eastern Europe was working on it. A new young piece of Russian meat, or Lithuanian, or Slovakian would do nicely; a vulnerable girl, with few family members requiring cash, but enough whose safety could be threatened if she refused to comply. He felt his erection stir at the thought. The nubile young girl would be his at first, to do with as he pleased. She had to learn who was boss... and he looked forward to teaching her.

It would only be a matter of days before a foreign replacement would be on her way. They were poor, desperate and two a penny. His journey to France would be solitary, but his return trip to the new address in Lewisham would be accompanied. He loved the EU; free movement of girls from East to West, with or without their consent. Passports were irrelevant if they were stamped with the EU emblem. Nobody checked. Two people in a car or on a shuttle were waved through without a second glance and if the young, excitable female companion was destined to become a young prostitute, well, who knew... and who cared?

He stamped his cigarette out in an ashtray and picked up the van keys. There were lots of things that had to be done: a replacement van was required, a new house needed to be chosen and prepared, just in case they had to move on again, and a new set of ID papers created. You couldn't survive in this business without being organised and he was no fool. And, later on, as the evening approached, he would be waiting outside the large house in Norbury where his care home girl lived. A few more gifts and a little more persuasion and she would be occupying the last room.

He liked to give his customers a choice of home or away.

Chapter 23

Charlie parked outside the mortuary, with Hunter silent beside her. Her day was well and truly mapped out for her and it wasn't one that she was looking forward to. The post-mortems of both Redz and the baby were to take place. They needed to get as much information as was possible before the weekend. As she walked towards the entrance, the thought of seeing the tiny body laid out for examination made her feel physically sick. Every part of the sight she would soon be witnessing was wrong.

Dr Reggie Crane was also subdued on their arrival, his usual enthusiasm to establish the cause of death and obtain evidence as to how it had come about curtailed by the smallness of the body on the vast stainless-steel examination tray.

They shook hands and nodded seriously. There was no need for small talk. They all knew what had to be done.

The nameless baby girl's body was already prepared. Her weight had been recorded at just under 2lbs and she measured fourteen inches in length. With no placenta available, Dr Crane examined the cord and took blood and tissue samples, before painstakingly checking the exterior of her body and examining the internal organs for any signs of why the baby had died.

'She's about twenty-six weeks in gestation, so her death will be classified as a stillbirth,' Dr Crane explained. 'We'll have to wait for the results of blood and tissue samples to be checked, but at present, I can see no clear reason why the baby was miscarried. There are no deformities or signs of infection, nor are there any obvious puncture marks or contusions, but then at this stage of development she would have been well protected within the amniotic sac. It is unlikely that any blow to the mother would penetrate through to the baby. She seems to have been developing as she should and, as far as I can see, would have been born a perfectly healthy baby.'

It was as Charlie had expected. At the back of her mind she had hoped the PM might have thrown up a valid medical or natural reason for the loss, but the truth confirmed everything she'd feared. Although not absolutely conclusive, it appeared that the baby's early birth was likely to have been caused by force.

At the conclusion, a cloth was placed over the body. At over twenty-four weeks the baby was past the stage of legal viability and would require a burial or cremation, but it would remain to be seen if her existence would ever be acknowledged by a parent or whether her tiny form would be disposed of anonymously, with no tears shed for her loss.

The body of Grace Flaherty was brought out next and the mood, although still sombre, took on a different feel. This was an adult, and there was no doubt the woman had been murdered, therefore, they could view the requirement for evidence on a professional, rather than purely emotional level.

Whilst they awaited the formal identification, Charlie's thoughts turned to the investigation. Redz was dead and they had a suspect for her murder, a good suspect, but one who they'd frustratingly had to release. Clinton Roberts, Razor, fitted the bill and had been close to the scene. He was a man who regularly used violence to maintain control over his girls, but had he gone too far this time, lost control, beaten Redz too hard and for too long until there was no going back? They needed more... and after his last taunts, Charlie and the team were determined to find it.

To that end, while she and Hunter were at the mortuary, Naz and Sabira were arranging an identification parade for Maria Simpson and two other witnesses who had been found. With the darkness and distances involved, the chances of a positive ID were improbable, but they had to try.

Bet and Paul were scanning further CCTV, as well as researching the two alibis. Caz was unlikely to be deemed a credible witness, but could still cast some doubt on the prosecution evidence, but what would Viv say? Would she assist Razor, or help them?

Charlie herself wanted to speak to Caz, as well as Dutch and some of the other sex workers. If Razor was involved, by now the rumours would be flying, but would anybody be willing to put their words into writing? Apart from Caz, it was doubtful. What the team needed was good hard evidence and forensics was therefore likely to be their best hope.

Her thoughts were disturbed by the entry of the young cop who'd travelled with Redz to the hospital. He came in, looking ashen-faced and confirmed for continuity purposes that the body was indeed the same girl he'd accompanied from the murder scene. As he gazed at the waxy, blood-spattered remains, his cheeks paled and he bolted from the room.

Charlie watched sympathetically as the door slammed shut behind him. It was never easy seeing a young person lying dead on a tray and Redz was probably an equivalent age to a sister or girlfriend.

'I remember doing that myself the first time I saw a dead body,' Dr Crane chuckled, his eyes following the fleeing officer. 'After dealing with several thousand of them by now, it's just as well I'm used to it. Poor guy looked like he'd seen a ghost.'

'He looked like he'd almost become one,' Hunter added. 'Judging by the colour he went.'

The atmosphere had lightened slightly and they got ready to start. Dr Crane moved around the table measuring, combing, scraping and swabbing every inch of Redz' naked body. He spoke into a Dictaphone, detailing verbally every birthmark, blemish, tattoo, scar or visible injury, painstakingly working his way from head to toe, while Charlie assisted with the sealing, recording and labelling of every item and exhibit. The process took several hours and Charlie was appalled by the sheer quantity of injuries, both recent and old, added to the list.

After the external examination came the internals. Blood samples were taken to be analysed for the presence of legal or illegal drugs and alcohol. Swabs were taken from inside the mouth, nose and ears, cuttings and scrapings from the fingernails and swabs from the vaginal and anal areas. As she labelled the exhibits, Charlie wondered despairingly how many different DNA samples would be found on – or in – her body.

Finally Dr Crane was ready to investigate the methodology and the time and cause of death. He moved up towards Redz' head, bending down to concentrate.

'I mentioned when conducting my initial observations that our victim had injuries to her scalp and some of her hair was missing.'

'We're told she had long hair before the attack.' Charlie bent forward too, explaining, 'Her nickname was Redz because she had long red hair.'

Dr Crane moved his fingers through her hair, separating it into strands. Some of the strands were still long and untouched, but others were short, lying in untidy clumps of varying lengths. Dr Crane pointed to an area on the side of Redz' head.

'This area is devoid of hair, and the skin is inflamed, as if her hair has been pulled out by the roots.' He pointed to a different area. 'But in this area the hair is short, with the roots still attached to the scalp. In other words, the hair looks to have been cut off.'

'With a sharp implement, such as a razor?' Hunter clearly had their suspect in mind.

'Could be,' Reggie Crane confirmed. 'Or anything sharp.' He bent further forward until his face was almost touching Redz' head and gazed at the end of the hair through a magnifying glass. 'Yes,' he confirmed. 'The remaining ends of the short hairs look to have been clean-cut very recently. There are no rounded or split ends as you would expect if they had been cut a while ago and left to grow like the longer strands.'

'So whoever has done this has pulled some of her hair out, but also cut some off?' Charlie queried.

'It's pretty hard to pull hair out by the roots,' Dr Crane stood back up. 'You can pull small clumps out, but if you were after a large amount, especially if you wanted it quick, you'd have to cut it.'

'But why would anyone want to cut off a prostitute's hair?' Charlie was perplexed.

'Perhaps to take as a memento?' Dr Crane raised his eyebrows. 'Many people keep locks of hair from their babies or loved ones as mementoes. Hair evokes memories... but there are also plenty of people out there with hair fetishes. People love hairpieces, hair extensions and wigs. Hair is big business.'

Hunter was still staring down at Redz. 'Or, as a means of punishment, especially to a woman who loves her long hair. Cutting it off would be an extremely callous way of stamping your authority over someone.'

Charlie had to smile at the obvious slant of Hunter's words, but she had to admit things were stacking up against Razor. Some hair had been found in his car, after all.

'It seems you have someone in mind then?' Dr Crane had clearly understood her boss's comments. He turned back to the body. 'Right, let's get down to the cause of death.'

Carefully he examined Redz' face, looking for dirt, debris or fragments from any hard surfaces or other implements with which her face might have impacted. Layer by layer, he delved deeper into the massive injury to her skull, clearing the blood and tissue to allow for better access.

'The trauma to her skull and brain is extensive,' he said, carefully removing a piece of shattered bone with tweezers and turning towards Charlie and Hunter. 'She wouldn't have survived with these injuries, though I don't know as yet whether the head injury is the main cause of death.' He continued to examine her skull, speaking out loud as he did so. 'The frontal bone has been fractured in several places, as have both eye orbits, causing fragments of bone to be pushed into the frontal lobe of the brain. Likewise, with the nasal bone, nasal septum and maxilla, which have also been shattered by whatever has impacted with her face. Her four upper incisors have been either broken or knocked out completely and her mandible has also been fractured.' He stopped and stood up straight, stretching out his back. 'I'll check her lungs and stomach contents shortly as she would have swallowed or inhaled a large quantity of blood during the attack. My assessment at present is that she probably died from the combined effect of the head injury and asphyxiation from inhaling blood. I will confirm that when I open her up and will send the full report on to you.'

'Would she have died quickly?' Charlie wanted to know.

'Well, she would have died at the time of the attack, but how quickly I'm not sure. There is no possibility of surviving these injuries. I suppose it depends on how hard the first few impacts were as to how long she would have been conscious.'

Charlie nodded, recalling the fact that the witness Maria Simpson had heard screams. Redz had obviously fought for her life, at least for a short time.

'Are you able to say if a weapon was used? And if so, what type?' Hunter asked.

Dr Crane pursed his lips and looked down at the body, shaking his head. 'Sorry, but I can't be certain, I'm afraid. The injuries are consistent with blunt trauma, but because of their severity, I doubt I will be able to establish whether this is from a blunt instrument or from her head being forced against a solid surface, or both.' He sighed heavily and turned to face them. 'What I can say though is that the attack on this girl was brutal and sustained. I would suggest whoever did this totally lost control.'

*

Dr Crane's last words were still ringing in her head as Charlie climbed the stairs to the office at Lambeth HQ. Hunter had just received word that the forensic examinations on the brothel, as well as all three crime scenes connected with Redz' murder, had been concluded. The alleyway had been reopened and Razor was to be allowed back into his flat. Only the car was likely to remain with them, its recovery being unlikely due to it being untaxed, uninsured and without an MOT.

For now though they would have to wait for tests to be conducted on all the samples collected at each of the crime scenes and, with the weekend ahead, progress would slow.

What worried Charlie more was the fact she would shortly be informing Razor that with the crime scenes closed he could return to his flat, and that meant that Caz and Dutch would no doubt join him. Could they inadvertently be putting the two vulnerable women back into danger, especially if Razor was under further pressure from the arrest? Might he lose control again? But what could they do to prevent it? Razor had bail conditions to live at an approved address, and to report to a police station daily, but Caz and Dutch were adults, free to do whatever they wished. There was no way to restrict their movements. If the two women wished to return to his flat they could.

She pulled her phone out and keyed in Caz's number, Razor's phone having been seized as part of the investigation. It rang for what seemed an age before Caz came on the line, her voice slurred and hesitant.

'Caz, is that you? It's Charlie Stafford here. Are you with Razor? I need to pass him a message.'

'Yeah, it's me.' The phone line became muffled, as if Caz had placed her hand over the mouthpiece and was moving about. 'I can't see 'im, Charlie. What's the message?'

'Can you tell him we've finished at his registered flat and he's allowed back. That'll be his bail address, so he must sleep there every night.'

'Ah, thank fuck for that. He'll be well chuffed with that news.'

Charlie hesitated, thinking of what she wanted to say. 'Caz, you know *you* don't have to go back there though. Or Dutch. In fact, it would be much safer for you not to return.'

Caz let out a squeal of laughter. 'You 'ave no idea, do you? He'd kill us if we stayed put where we are an' didn't go back wiv 'im. Believe me, Charlie, we'd be much safer to return.' She continued to laugh before quietening suddenly. 'Besides, 'e's my man. I ain't got no one else.'

Charlie closed her eyes. It was as she feared. 'Please, Caz,' she said one last time. 'Don't go back. You know you have people that can help you.'

'I know that,' Caz spoke with deliberation. 'But I've got things sorted. I'll let 'im know, and don't worry, I'll be all right. I promise yer.'

The line went dead. Caz had rung off.

Charlie checked her watch. Friday was nearly over and she would be spending the evening with Ben and her family in the safety of her family home. As she walked out into the chill December air, and gazed out at the

Christmas lights twinkling brightly in houses across the city, she thought of Caz and Dutch and the unknown mother of the dead baby... and tried to imagine what it must be like to be constantly living in fear.

Chapter 24

Caz pushed her phone into her pocket and sat down heavily on the bed next to where Dutch lay comatose. News of Redz' murder seemed to have heightened her friend's already obsessive safety fears. A carving knife had been carefully stowed under the pillow and some scissors under the mattress. With Dutch preferring the safety of a flat and Razor wanting her out working the streets, they were heading for a showdown... and there was no doubt in Caz's mind who would win.

The greenish glow from the digital clock display showed 5.18 p.m. It would be good to get away from DK's flat and back home. She reached down and tugged Dutch up to a sitting position. Her friend was sleepy but responded, hanging on to her tightly as they stood and lurched towards the door.

'Where's Ayeisha?' Dutch strained her head from side to side as she stumbled forward.

Caz slammed DK's door shut behind them, shuddering as the freezing wind bit at her bare legs and ankles. 'She went earlier.'

'She's a good girl,' Dutch slipped as she spoke, grabbing at some railings. 'She shouldn't be wiv us.'

Caz knew she should agree; Ayeisha was young and deserved better, but she was also a carbon copy of how she herself had once been – reticent to experiment with drugs or sex – and in a macabre kind of way Caz wanted to see whether her friend would succumb to temptation as she had. Besides, Ayeisha knew about things that Caz did not... things that Caz needed for her secret job.

'Leave 'er be,' she said instead. 'We don't make 'er come. She comes 'cause she wants to and she enjoys being wiv us.'

Razor's flat was in sight when she heard the sound of a car horn, followed by a shout. Caz looked over the railings and saw a car entering the nearby parking area. It flashed at her and hooted again several more times. She didn't recognise the car, but as the window was wound down she saw Razor grinning up at them.

'Caz, get in,' he shouted, leaning out and shouting up at her. 'Let's go for a ride.'

She waved down and indicated for him to wait, pulling Dutch towards the flat and opening the door. The place was a shithole; no effort had been made by the police to return it to even its previous poor state, but as she lowered Dutch down on to her filthy bed, she knew it would have to do for now. Razor was calling and he couldn't be kept waiting.

Her pimp was in high spirits when she joined him.

'What we doin' now then?' she asked, looking around at the child seat and guessing immediately the car was stolen.

Razor chuckled. 'Thought we'd go an' turn over a few punters. We need some cash.'

Caz glanced across at Razor. He looked slightly manic, his whole persona crackling with danger, but the sight was intoxicating, and he wanted her with him.

Razor drove to a small car park adjacent to Tooting Bec Common and gave her instructions. She was to entice the punters to the car park either on foot or in their motors and he would do the rest. They would be relieved of their property at knifepoint and were unlikely ever to report the crime to police for fear of their indiscretions becoming public. It was risky but potentially very rewarding.

She nodded mutely, light-headed with fear and desire. At that moment, she'd do anything for Razor.

An hour later, they were counting their spoils in some underground garages nearby. He had been brutal in the execution of the robberies, his menace magnified tenfold.

'Two hundred and eighty fuckin' quid, credit cards, a gold watch and chain and a virtually new laptop. Not bad for a night's work,' Razor whooped, pocketing the cash and throwing the empty wallet and briefcase into a wheelie bin. 'I'll sell the rest of the stuff in the morning, but for now, let's get some fresh gear and go an' fuckin' party.'

Caz gazed across at Razor, his brooding presence lighting the touchpaper to her emotions. Razor was everything she wanted, and at the moment she seemed to be enough for him. Redz' death had undoubtedly brought them closer. She reached across, her hand straying from his chest towards the belt buckle on his jeans, and her thoughts straying across the common to a small office, with wood-panelled walls and a light that shone out even now.

Perhaps it was time to let Anna into the secrets of her childhood? It couldn't do any harm and she had already started the ball rolling. Anna was her friend. She had promised to listen. More importantly, she would be there in case the situation changed.

*

Anna put down Caz's file, chewing on the lunchtime sandwich that had not, until that moment, been touched.

With Caz in mind, she'd worked late into Friday evening. There was one last thing she had wanted to set in motion. Scribbled on a piece of paper was the address of a compact but tidy bedsit, which her friend, Maggie Owen, in the housing department of the local council had offered. It had been the culmination of a promise to assist with any urgent safeguarding issues, in exchange for Anna's help with a suicidal friend of her daughter's.

It didn't matter whether their agreement was fair or ethical; the important thing was that neither had any illusions as to the significance of their actions. Anna had literally talked Maggie's young acquaintance out of taking her own life. Now Maggie would be helping to potentially save Caz. Removing the restrictions of government red tape could salvage two young vulnerable lives.

The bedsit was situated in a small block of council flats on the Streatham/Norbury border, as far south in Lambeth as was possible. In Anna's opinion it was still too close for comfort to Razor's flat in SW2, but it was the best they could do and hopefully would be far enough away to at least put some distance between Caz and her pimp.

The room itself sounded ideal. Neat and manageable, with an open-plan kitchen/diner expanding into a reasonably-sized living area equipped with a pull-down bed and several cupboards for storage. The flat had lain empty for some time, but an audit of council properties had brought it back to the attention of housing officers and its redecoration had just been completed. The room was ready now and the key was to be left for collection.

Anna felt energised as she stared at the address on the email from Maggie. The room could be the lifeline her young client needed. Once she'd collected the key the next day, she could get the room furnished and ready. Caz would have the chance to start afresh and build a new life for herself. This was the first step.

She read the address out loud. It had a certain ring to it and Anna entered the information on a memo and attached it to the front page of the file before slotting it into the cabinet and locking it shut.

It was time to go home.

With any luck, Caz would return soon, to continue the journey into her childhood. A boundary had been crossed on her last visit and Anna was in no doubt there would be further revelations to come, but she had to be careful. She needed to pick the right moment… and until that time came, news of the room would have to wait.

Chapter 25

The Punter stretched out across his bed, his hands held firmly over his ears. The children were screaming downstairs and his wife was cooking dinner. It was monotonous shit and he wanted none of it.

Friday evening was his favourite night to go out, but tonight he would have to remain indoors. He had no car and, in any case, it was better to lay low. News of the murder might still be relatively fresh in people's minds, and though it seemed there had been no witnesses, there was no point in taking the risk.

There had been no further contact from the police, apart from a recorded message providing a crime reference. His car had clearly not come to light, and as each hour passed, so his confidence grew. Even the local papers had reported little. The death of a prostitute did not justify much publicity, and even less concern from the residents who had to put up with the filth and immorality left daily by the dirty whores.

The murder, in any case, was not newsworthy. It had merely been a *misunderstanding*, which should now be forgotten. The prostitute had brought it on herself and he had been fully justified in treating her the way he had.

Another shout sounded from below. The twins were arguing again. They were always fighting. Why couldn't his wife keep control? He rose from where he lay, irritated, and stood in front of the mirror, surveying his body from every angle.

Tomorrow he would purchase a leather jacket, matt black and smelling of money. It would demonstrate his ability to take charge of his own destiny, kowtowing to no one.

Tomorrow he would also buy a new motor. A few phone calls to his insurance company had secured him a preliminary verbal settlement and Health and Safety requirements had ensured that his burnt-out car had been efficiently removed from the public common and taken to the dump to be crushed. There was nothing left to show for his night of debauchery.

Come the morning he would choose a convertible that was cool, clean and sexy, epitomising his ongoing accomplishments at work. Promotion to managerial status was on the cards, promised but not quite delivered. He would soon be in charge of the South East Regional team of financial advisors.

He sucked in his stomach, turning again to admire his physique in the mirror. Appearance was everything. People's perceptions were what mattered. It was essential that, at least for now, he continued his mundane lifestyle; the perfect family man, doing everything required to earn his promised promotion. But as soon as it was safe, he would return to the streets, seeking out another dirty filthy whore, deserving of his wrath.

And as he shut his ears to the shouts of his children below, he knew without doubt that it wouldn't be long.

Chapter 26

Charlie picked the statement up and started to read. Even though it was the weekend, the whole team were in, happy to work the extra hours. The squad would be contacting every station, police service and agency that dealt with human trafficking in a bid to track down the new location of the brothel, before that trail went cold.

And they still had plenty to do on Redz' case. There was Razor's ID parade, which she would shortly be attending, and a raft of other enquiries to complete.

Hunter sauntered over and peered at the handwritten pages over her shoulder.

'You'd have loved Viv, boss.' Sabira chortled towards Hunter. 'She was a salt of the earth sort.'

'Yep, proper old-school barmaid, not unlike Bet Lynch from the Rover's Return,' Naz chipped in, grinning. 'And not afraid to keep you boys in order too.'

'There's not too many of us old dinosaurs around these days,' Hunter acknowledged. 'Or at least that's what Mrs H calls me, when she's bemoaning my lack of help with the housework.'

'You need to be a metrosexual these days,' Paul swivelled round on his chair and winked at Hunter, who opened his mouth as if to speak but then clamped it back shut. 'Don't ask,' Paul laughed instead.

'I don't think I dare.' Hunter grinned in return, looking totally perplexed. He changed the subject quickly. 'So, what did our Viv have to say?'

'Well,' Sabira took up the thread. 'She remembered the night well. She recalled speaking to Razor and that he complained that Redz had been causing him trouble and *needed sorting out.*'

'Nice,' Paul shook his head.

'She said that she specifically remembered telling Razor to go easy on Redz because she was only young.'

'Probably too late by then,' Bet joined in. 'But a good motive, albeit that he might only have meant to teach her a lesson, rather than actually kill her.'

'It would still be murder even if he only intended to cause her GBH, and he clearly meant to give her a good beating, judging by those words, and the massive injuries she sustained.' Hunter tutted loudly. 'And he'd be only too aware of the necessity to cultivate an alibi, when he realised what he'd done.'

Charlie had to agree with Hunter's analysis. Razor had been very quick to provide the two names; in fact, they had been the only thing to come from the interview. She turned towards Sabira. 'What about the timings?'

Sabira smiled. 'She remembers looking at her watch at around 1.15 a.m. when she first spoke to Razor and he said he'd had a shit day. She can't say whether he had been in the bar before then.'

'So Viv only really assists with what happened after Maria Simpson's call.' Charlie's interest spiked. 'Unless Caz says otherwise, it's quite possible that Razor was on his own at the actual time of Redz' death.'

Naz indicated the statement that Charlie held in her hands. 'And you'll like this bit too,' she pointed at a paragraph further down the page. 'It's Razor's reaction when Viv told him the rumours of what had happened.'

'Go on,' Charlie was all ears.

'Well,' Naz looked animated. 'She'd heard a girl had been badly beaten and left for dead at the back of the shops in Streatham. And she suddenly realised it might be Redz. But as she told Razor all this, she remembers being quite shocked at how calm he was – *almost as if he was expecting the news.*'

*

Charlie stepped inside Maria Simpson's flat, marvelling at how the sights and smells of the old lady's home were so similar to that of her own grandparents: the worn, patterned mat in the centre of the entrance hall, the exposed lino around its edge, the wax furniture polish and the wooden coat stand with the trilby hat perched to one side.

'Sorry to have kept you waiting. I'm nearly ready.' Maria Simpson shuffled out to the hallway and took a coat from the stand, tilting her head to peer towards the hat briefly. 'That was my Reg's. He passed away fifteen years ago but I can't bear to take it down.'

'It's like he never left.' Charlie understood exactly. The old maroon sofa at the family home, the sailor teddy she kept at her flat and the familiar songs repeated each night when sleep proved elusive, all reminded her of Jamie.

'Exactly,' Maria paused briefly and for a second their eyes connected. 'Before we leave, do you want to see where I saw that poor girl from?' She pushed open the door to the living room and pointed towards the window.

Charlie walked across the threadbare rug and squinted down on the miniature cars and people in the alleyway below. From six floors up, the lines and index number of their own unmarked police minibus were blurry and indistinct. Even in the daylight, it was hard to make out the shape of Hunter, sitting in the passenger seat, never mind identify him.

'I know what you're thinking,' Maria Simpson said, as if reading her mind. 'But when the interior light came on I saw him as plain as day. I have absolutely no doubt that he was a big man and that he wore jewellery on his right hand; it glinted in the light.'

Charlie remembered the large golden signet ring that Razor kept on the middle finger of his right hand, but she also knew that the participants in the line-up would be told to remove jewellery or keep their hands concealed.

Razor's solicitor had insisted on an ID parade, as was their right. Two other nearby residents had been identified as possible witnesses by the house-to-house enquiries and required to attend, but both had protested their vision was obscured by the darkness. Given the likelihood of failure, Hunter would rather have not bothered. He knew it would assist the defence more than it would benefit the prosecution, but the defence had requested it, so the prosecution had to comply. As she turned from the window, Charlie too felt the weight of defeat.

They made their way slowly down to the minibus, where she introduced Maria Simpson to Hunter, then went off to collect the other witnesses. They all had to be given the opportunity to pick out the suspect.

Eddie Burrows did not want the opportunity to pick out the suspect. He looked furious at being called on at all and made his view known as soon as he was able.

Mia Lo, a softly-spoken thirty-five-year-old Chinese woman, looked quietly petrified, also expressing her wish that she would rather not have been required.

As soon as Charlie started the engine, the volume of dissent amongst the witnesses in the rear grew louder.

'I don't know why I'm here. It's a total waste of time.' Eddie Burrows fired first.

'He won't be able to see us, will he?' Mia Lo enquired. 'I've got a young child and I'm frightened.'

'No, no. You're quite safe,' Charlie countered, explaining the ID viewing deck had one-way glass and they'd be kept securely away from the suspect at all times.

Mia's expression changed to one of relief briefly. 'I still wish I didn't have to do this. You just have to read the papers to see stories of what happens to witnesses.'

'Yeah,' Eddie Burrows added. 'I wish I'd never bothered speaking to you lot. In fact, I wish I'd never bothered getting up and looking out of the window in the first place.'

'Well, I wish I'd done more,' Maria Simpson said quietly. 'A young girl was murdered right in front of our eyes and I, for one, am ashamed to admit I was more interested in what was on my TV.'

*

Anna stood at the window, gazing out across the common. Her morning had been successfully spent collecting the key to the bedsit and starting the process of making it habitable. By the time she had finished, the

181

little room was looking cosy and welcoming. She was now using a spare hour to pop into the office to write up some notes.

As she watched the antics of a group of drunks sitting on a bench, she saw a familiar figure walking along the pavement towards her office. Her heart gave an involuntary leap as she realised it was Caz.

Caz seemed to be walking straighter and more upright than the hunched miserable figure from a few days earlier. Things could certainly change quickly in her life.

A few minutes later and Anna opened the door to be greeted by an exuberant Caz.

'Hi Anna, can I come in? I've got so much to tell you,' she bubbled. 'Razor an' me are on the up. We might even settle down, proper like.'

It was not at all what Anna wanted to hear. She groaned inwardly as Caz almost bounced up the stairs. Her eyes were still glassy and the same damp mustiness clung to her hair, but her face was scrubbed clean and her clothes were tidy and fitting well.

'Do you like my new clothes? Razor bought 'em for me,' she said, gesturing up and down over her outfit. 'He's gone to the nick now for an ID parade, so I thought I'd see if you was in.'

'They're very nice.' Anna tried to sound positive.

Caz swept into the office and pulled herself up on to the couch.

'Any chance of a brew? Razor only ever gets beer. Bleedin' idiot. As if everyone wants beer for breakfast. 'E says it costs less than coffee an' if I want bleedin' coffee I'd have to go and nick some for myself.' She threw her head back and laughed raucously. ''E also says that me an' him is the only thing that matters at the moment. He says that Dutch is useless, always out of her skull on the gear.' She stopped briefly and whispered across towards Anna, 'she's been shootin' up on brown, an' buying it from another dealer. Razor don't know that but 'e's still not happy. She's costin' him an arm an' a leg and not bringin' anything in.'

Anna spooned in three sugars and passed a mug of tea to Caz, frowning. Heroin, or brown, although euphoric, regularly caused respiratory depression. Half the time, addicts were so sedated that they barely knew what they were injecting into their bodies. As a result, overdoses were commonplace.

'Razor's gonna be havin' words, but it ain't all her fault. She's frightened of goin' out on the streets, but if she don't go soon, Razor'll fuckin' force her out. Mind you, it's made 'im appreciate me more, like. We've bin out cruisin' and 'aving a laugh. He's lookin' after me. I think I love him.'

Anna felt deflated. It was unlikely Caz would open up more about her past now she was happier, but perhaps it was worth her delving.

'Caz, I'm glad it's working out and you love Razor. Maybe now you're more secure you'd like to talk more about your mother and how much you loved her too?'

Anna held her breath, knowing that she was taking a gamble on how Caz would react to such a direct question. To her surprise though, Caz nodded.

'Yeah. Why not?', she closed her eyes and laid back.

For a while she was silent, her face betraying the pleasure and pain of her memories.

'My mum was real special,' she started at last. 'Being the only girl, after three boys, it was just me and 'er. When we was shoppin', she would always treat me to somethin' nice. She loved to dress me up, like. Real pretty. She was pretty too. Always smilin'. She had beautiful brown eyes and lovely long shiny hair. Sometimes I would sit on her lap and pull her hair round in front of me so as I was hidden behind it. She would put her hand through an' tickle me round the neck. Then she would laugh. We would both laugh. I really miss her when I think of those times.'

She paused and her expression darkened.

'I never knew me Dad. Mum says he used to come round when he wanted her and then piss off for days or weeks at a time. After me, he just pissed off altogether. Mum said it didn't matter though 'cause I was her special girl.' Her face lit up and she smiled towards Anna. 'One day we was out shoppin' in this big toy shop. That's where I found Goldilocks, my doll. She was beautiful; long blonde hair and so soft. I wouldn't put 'er down an' started cryin' and screamin' to keep 'er. In the end, me mum shelled out. Said not to tell me brothers or else they'd want somethin'. She said that as long as I always had that doll, I'd remember our day together. I've kept Goldilocks ever since. She's a bit dirty now, but she's always wiv me.'

Caz stopped talking and opened her eyes. Reaching for her bag, she took out the old ragdoll and held it close to her face, smiling awkwardly.

'She sounds like a lovely mother and you were obviously very happy together.'

Caz lay silent again, as if weighing up whether to continue.

'How did you get on with your brothers?' Anna changed the emphasis of the conversation. She didn't want the moment to end now they had got this far.

Caz turned to one side and took several gulps of the hot, sweet tea, before grinning broadly. 'They were bleedin' gits most the time, always fightin' an' bundlin' in the house. Mum used to go mad at them. She would shout at 'em to stop, but they would just laugh at 'er and carry on. But she never really minded. Always said they was good boys. Sometimes they would get into scrapes with other boys who would tease us all 'cause we was poor. Joey, my oldest brother, would fight anyone who said anything bad 'bout me mum. One day he got into a fight with this other boy and broke his nose. Anyway, this boy's dad came round to have a word. Mum tried to stick up for Joey, but she started cryin'. I never saw her cry before. Anyway, this man put his arm round me mum and they started talkin'. Kept talkin' all night and was still there in the mornin'. That was when everything changed.

'He moved in and they started goin' off down the pub. Me brothers looked after me 'cause I was only seven, but they was only young 'emselves; Joey was fourteen an' Mickey an' Ed, were thirteen an' ten. Me mum and 'im would come back late from the pub, stinkin' of booze. After a while, they just started drinkin' at home.

'She never done nothin' for us after that. I wanted me old mum back. Like she was when he weren't there. Fuckin' bastard, his name was Tommy. I'll never forgive him for takin' me mum away from us.'

Caz's expression was set hard.

'I'm not saying nothin' more now. He was the bastard that destroyed our family and I hate him. I hate him. He took me mum away from me, away from us. I don't think he cared a fuck 'bout anything, not even me mum. He just used her and us.'

Caz sat up, rubbing her eyes, and Anna knew the conversation was over. As quickly as Caz had opened up, so the shutters had now come down.

Anna, however, was elated. To have been gifted with this glimpse into Caz's life was more than she could have hoped. It was a time when Caz had known true contentment, and this was what she was trying to rediscover; a life where she was wanted, loved and secure and, above all, where she was happy. Anna now understood exactly what Caz wanted from Razor. It was what she too had constantly longed for; the all-encompassing love of another, the quest to return to a state of idyllic acceptance.

Anna watched transfixed as Caz tenderly tucked Goldilocks away in her bag. This doll, so dirty, so ravaged, was the mirror image of Caz, a beautiful child broken by her upbringing. Anna longed to reach out to Caz, take hold of both her and the doll and clean them, mend them and replenish them. But as clearly as she now understood the raw desperation that drove Caz to idolise Razor blindly above all others, so too did she know with awful clarity that Razor would never be able to provide the security and love which Caz yearned for.

It might yet be up to her to step in and save Caz from herself.

Chapter 27

Razor entered the communal doorway of Covington House and listened. He could hear the chatter of the usual addicts as the meeting place began to fill. It was nearing 3 p.m. and within a few minutes, a mobile phone would shrill with the location of that day's dealer. Razor knew the routine.

A few of the users were looking out from the window in the stairwell, a particularly mean-looking pimp called M keeping an eye out for any police. As Razor climbed towards them he recognised three of the regular girls sitting on a stair, beer cans in hand and arms draped around each other. Mand was in the middle, being supported by two of her mates, Jugs and Marcia. They had been friends for years and looked out for one another.

Jugs lived up to her name. She had the most enormous tits he'd ever seen and was not afraid to flaunt them. Age had brought with it desperation and Jugs was rumoured to do pretty much anything for cash these days. Marcia was a popular addition to any gathering, with an infectious laugh that would brighten the gloomiest crack house… and an infectious rash that she saved solely for her punters.

As he approached, Razor heard a screech and Mand launched herself at him. 'Razor, how are you? I heard the cops took you in for questioning.'

Razor laughed. Mand was a good girl. At twenty-eight years old, she'd worked the streets for over half her life. 'I'm fine. I knew they would, but they ain't got nothin' on me.' He pulled her close, his hand roaming down to her buttocks. 'Anyway, more importantly, when can you come and work for me, Mand? I've got a spare room now.'

Mand squealed and jumped to one side, laughing. 'You know I can't, much as I'd like to. DK would do his nut. He's got himself a piece now and he's just waitin' for the chance to use it, so if you don't fancy a bullet in your arse, you'd better get your hand off mine.'

The waiting crowd all grunted their appreciation.

'Don't you go thinkin' your arse is worth takin' a bullet for,' Razor chuckled. 'And anyway I respect DK, but if he ever turfed you out…' He gave Mand a playful wink before becoming serious. 'I do need to get my shit sorted though.' He offered round a packet of cigarettes. 'Firstly, I need to know who's givin' Dutch extra gear. She's obviously takin' more than just my white.'

He flicked his lighter and the girls leant in, sucking at the flame before Marcia spoke. 'I was told there's a new dealer called Turbo up your way, offerin' freebies to get people on board. I heard Dutch is gettin' her extras from 'im.'

'Sounds like he needs to be put in his place,' M growled. Muscling in on another's patch was against the dealers' code of conduct. This Turbo needed to be squared up.

'Watch it though, Razor,' Marcia blew out a mouthful of smoke. 'Word is he's carrying a piece too, and he ain't afraid to use it, neither.'

Razor swore silently to himself. Perhaps his blades needed an upgrade after all.

'He won't 'ave time to reach for it, never mind use it when I find 'im.' He had to show strength, but he could really have done without this distraction. Turbo was an irrelevance, but Dutch needed to be brought into line speedily. Tonight she'd be out on the streets earning, whether she liked it or not. At least Caz was back on track, seemingly taking as much pleasure in their night-time activities as he. She was acting a little weird though, but at least she was doing what she was told.

The sound of Mand's mobile phone ringing focussed his mind on his second priority just as the group got ready to leave. DK was doing that afternoon's drugs run.

'Before you go.' Razor put his arm across the stairwell to prevent them leaving. 'Tell me all you know about The Punter who you think has done Redz.'

They silenced and Mand turned towards him.

'He picked me up once. The minute we got to my normal spot he started to cut up rough, callin' me a fuckin' slag and threatenin' to kill me. He beat me an' raped me and kept saying I deserved it. I thought I was goin' to die. Then he just pushed me out of the car and drove off. Never gave me a second glance.

'I was goin' to tell the cops, but what's the point! So I just warned the other girls 'bout 'im.' She stopped and shook her head. 'I've seen 'im around since though, in his little black car an' I saw him near Redz' area the night she got done.'

She ran through his description again. Tall, heavily built Asian man, always wearing a long black leather coat and chunky jewellery.

'I need to teach this bastard a lesson that he won't ever forget.' Razor pulled a blade out from the edge of his wallet and whipped it through the air. 'Pass my number on to the other girls. If any of you see him, tell 'em to bell me straight away, right?'

The group nodded solemnly. No girl was safe with this punter still on the loose.

M reached out to shake his hand. 'If you need any help when you find him, let me know. I'd be only too glad to help you fuck 'im up.'

Razor took a last drag on his cigarette and threw it down, grinding it hard into the concrete. He would enjoy slicing this big man up good and proper.

'He's all mine,' he replied grimly, exhaling the smoke so it hung in a haze around their heads. 'But I'll let you know when I've finished with 'im and you're more than welcome to add a few more words of yer own.'

Chapter 28

'We're on our way,' Charlie swung the car round and pushed her foot hard on the accelerator. After the frustration of the negative ID parade, she was desperate for something to go their way on either case.

The rental company where they were heading to, in Tulse Hill, was less than a fifteen minute drive away.

'Give me the details.' Hunter pulled out a pad as Charlie drove. Bet's voice was clear over the mobile.

'The van you're looking for is a white Ford Transit 125ps LWB Luton Tail lift.' She read out the registration number. 'I was going through CCTV for Streatham High Road looking for vans like the neighbours had described entering or exiting any of the side roads that lead to the brothel. At 00.51 a large white Luton van comes out of one and turns left, heading towards Brixton. It gets to the lights by Streatham Hill railway station and turns left towards Tooting Bec Common and Balham before going out of sight.

'It then returns about forty minutes later at 01.29,' Bet continued. 'I got Paul to check the CCTV for Balham High Road for around that time, but there's no trace, so it must have turned off somewhere between Streatham and Balham. Interestingly, there were a lot of police cars around the area at that time. There were blue lights everywhere on the CCTV.'

'That was the same time as the incident with Redz, and only half a mile away.' Charlie tilted her head towards Hunter. 'If it's the van from the brothel, I wonder if that's what could have spooked them into leaving.'

'It could have been,' Bet agreed. 'After that, it left again about half an hour later, at pretty much spot on 02.00, before returning just over an hour later at 03.11. The last time I saw the van, it was at 03.35 when it left the area of the brothel and didn't return. On both of these last two occasions it headed north towards Central London.'

'That's interesting.' Hunter pulled an A to Z from behind the seat and flipped it to the front page showing the whole area of Greater London. 'Let's suppose the driver *was* spooked on his initial journey and decided to move out. Traffic would have been light at that time of night but they would still have had to take, let's say, a minimum of ten to fifteen minutes to unpack wherever they'd relocated, in order for him to return for the last few bits. So...' he drew an imaginary semicircle with his finger north from Streatham.

Charlie glanced across at the map. 'Not too far then? Maybe the Camberwell, Battersea or Lewisham areas?

And he wouldn't have wanted to drive fast and draw attention to the van, loaded up with all his girls and their belongings, so the new brothel must be within half an hour's drive of the Streatham one.'

The van rental company was now within view. With any luck it would be Dimitri, their Russian suspect, who had hired the van and they would have documentary and photographic evidence. If they were really lucky, the Russian would still be driving it, or have swapped it for a new vehicle, the details of which they would be able to circulate. Vehicles were much easier to track than people, particularly with the use of CCTV and automated number plate readers. Charlie navigated the one-way system at Tulse Hill and coasted to a halt outside the yard. They needed some answers and they needed them quickly.

*

'You've just missed him, officer,' the words struck Charlie as forcefully as a fist to the stomach. 'The van was brought back half an hour ago and the man who returned it unusually hasn't rented another.'

Charlie turned away, gutted. Yet again it seemed what progress they were making had been halted. Running the two cases together meant that they were permanently playing catch-up, but she was too personally invested with each to give either up. They all were. The death of the baby needed resolution and friends and relatives of Redz needed justice.

Hunter had already disappeared to the yard. The van would need to be recovered intact for a full forensic examination. It was at least fortunate they had arrived prior to it being made ready for its next hiring. They might have been too late to catch the driver, but there would be a lot to assist in the investigation.

Swallowing her frustration, she turned back to the assistant. There was still a job to be done.

'You intimated the hirer would usually rent out a new vehicle when he returns one?'

The assistant nodded. 'Dimitri has been coming here for six months and up until today has always re-rented another vehicle; sometimes a van, sometimes a car, occasionally both. He is a good customer.'

'And you have his driving licence and bank account details?'

The assistant went to a filing cabinet and pulled out a file. 'Yes, we have a photocopy of his driving licence but no bank details. He always pays cash. Even the deposits are paid with cash.'

Charlie eyed the grainy photograph on the photocopy. The address of the old brothel was printed underneath, along with the name Dimitri Ivanov and a driver number showing his date of birth. The driving licence looked legitimate, but without the original it was hard to tell.

She scanned the small office, noting the presence of a CCTV camera in the corner, trained down at the door. The assistant read her gaze and beckoned for her to join him at the other side of the desk. He pressed a few buttons on a computer hard drive and rewound a black and white recording, checking his watch and stopping it, just thirty-five minutes earlier. Charlie watched as he pressed play and the figure of a well-built man appeared on a monitor, walking into the office. His hood was up and his face was partially obscured as he moved about the desk area for a full eight minutes, returning keys, signing paperwork and counting the returned cash deposit. He appeared nervous in the way he moved, keeping his eyes averted and continually glancing at his watch, but as she watched, Charlie had no doubt that, should they check the footage from his previous visits, they would find a good facial image of the man who earned a living from the misery of others.

It was unlikely he had been so discreet on earlier business transactions at the rental office, but whether his name was actually Dimitri Ivanov would be another thing.

Chapter 29

Caz heard a scrabbling sound as she entered the flat and saw Dutch dart into her bedroom. Nothing had been cleared since she'd left that morning to visit Anna and the whole place looked shambolic. She called out to Dutch, waiting for her friend to re-emerge.

'Thank God it's you. I thought it was Razor. Where is he?' Dutch peeped around the door, her relief evident.

'He dropped me off after we was shopping. He was goin' to the barbers and then he had to go to the nick for an ID parade. Why are you so worried?'

''Cause he told me to get the place tidied up, but I got scared and went an' got some brown from that new dealer, Turbo. If Razor finds out he'll kill me... an' him.'

She showed Caz five small silver wraps of heroin and retreated back into the bedroom, with Caz close behind.

'Shit, Dutch. What the hell do you think you're playin' at?' Caz stared at the mess. The room was filthy. Until now her friend had kept it reasonably clean for the purpose of entertaining, but with nothing tidied since the police search, it was now virtually uninhabitable.

In addition to the disarray, the room stank of stale urine. Dutch was clearly unable to locate the bathroom, although seemingly capable of finding her new dealer. Christ knew how she was paying Turbo. Razor would be incensed if there was a debt owing.

Dutch collapsed down on to her bed and her expression crumpled. Caz watched as her friend's body was wracked with long shuddering sobs and a fresh stream of tears picked its way through crusty rivers of dried spittle on her cheeks.

'I don't know what to do, Caz. I can't cope. I can't do it anymore. I'm too fuckin' scared to go back out. Shit. It might be me or you next.' Dutch looked up at Caz, her eyes pleading. 'Caz, you gotta help me. That's why I'm takin' so much gear.'

She pulled her sleeves up and held out her arms towards Caz. Huge angry boils festered on the lower part of each arm and infection had set into the crook of one elbow, her favourite for injecting. The track marks glowed a poisonous white. Pulling off her boots, Caz could see the veins around her ankles were the same.

'Dutch, you can't carry on mixin' both. The brown'll kill you. You know it will. You've gotta clean up an' get back out to work. Razor's gettin' pissed off. He wants you bringin' in some cash.'

'I know he does, but I just can't. I just start shakin' an' cryin' so I take some more gear until I forget. I can't go on like this, Caz, I'm so tired.'

Caz sat down next to her flatmate on the bed. Never before had she seen Dutch like this. Dutch was always the strong confident one. Something had to be done. For every day that Dutch was comatose, she and Razor would have to cover for her and they couldn't go on robbing punters. It wasn't popular with the other street girls. It gave the area a bad reputation.

'You've gotta pull yourself together, Dutch, and for fuck's sake don't let 'im see that brown. I'll try an' help you when he gets back.'

As if on cue, Caz heard the sound of Razor slamming through the door. Dutch pushed the heroin wraps up her sleeve, shrinking back against the wall.

'Caz, Dutch. Where are you?' Razor shouted, striding down the hallway towards them. His head was freshly shaved and the previous thick coating of stubble on his chin was styled into a fine track, mirrored by thin lines shaved into his eyebrows. A new shirt, leather belt and shoes completed his powerful aura, a quality that wasn't lost on Caz. To her, he positively oozed masculinity. His mood had slumped since the high spirits of their early-morning shopping trip, and the set of his brow made his disposition difficult to gauge.

Caz leant towards him as he neared and the smell of cologne hit her nostrils. 'You're lookin' and smellin' good, babe. How did you get on?'

Razor pulled his shoulders back, his shirt tightening across his muscular chest. 'Sweet! I weren't picked out by none of 'em. It's just a pisser the cops 'ave kept me on bail and I 'ave to go back. I got other things more pressin' to do.' He pulled a snap bag from his pocket and started to roll a joint. 'I've just bin speaking to Mand.'

'She tell you what she saw with Redz?'

'Yep, and a few other things.' He frowned, pulling out ten rocks of crack from the front of his trousers and throwing them on to the bed. 'There you go. I got some more gear from DK for you.'

Caz reached towards them and stuffed them into her bra, watching as his expression darkened on seeing Dutch cowering against the wall behind her.

'It's nice to see you awake for once,' he snarled. 'I've been hearing all about what you're gettin' up to. Isn't it about time you started earnin', you lazy bitch, instead of makin' me look like a prize prick in front of everyone?'

Dutch made no reply. She didn't need to. Her eyes said everything Razor needed to know, widening in fear as she burrowed deeper against the wall.

'Did you hear what I just said?' He moved towards her and grabbed her roughly under the chin, pulling her off the bed and lifting her head so she was on tiptoes. 'I asked you a question, bitch.'

'Please, Razor, don't make me. I can't do it. I'm too fuckin' scared.'

Razor took a step back and released his grip, his expression as dark as Caz had ever seen it. She held her breath, watching the scene play out in slow motion.

'You're too fuckin' scared?' He lunged towards her, picking her up by the shoulders and shaking her. Dutch tried to break away, but he was too strong. 'Are you tryin' to say I don't protect you? 'Cause if you are, you'd better watch your tongue. No one says I don't do my job right an' gets away with it.'

'Please, Razor, please let me go. I didn't mean nothin'. It's not you. It's me. I just don't feel right.'

Dutch was crying, her voice little more than a high-pitched whimper, which seemed to antagonise Razor further.

Lifting her up, so that her face was square with his, he spoke slowly and calmly, the coldness and clarity of his words sending a shiver down Caz's spine.

'If you're not out later tonight then I will personally drag you out, and if you still don't want to play, you'll feel my bleedin' fist in your face, or worse. Do you understand?'

Dutch nodded. Razor kept his face close.

'And when you've finished servicin' the punters, you can service me. It's about time you an' I played our little games.'

He kissed her, biting hard on her bottom lip, before throwing her roughly against the bed. Her head bounced against the mattress and she flung her arms out to regain her balance, but as she did so Caz watched with horror as the wraps of heroin shot out from inside her sleeve and landed on the floor at Razor's feet. Time seemed to stand still as he slowly bent down to pick them up. Caz was frozen with fear and Dutch dragged herself as far from him as possible, her body held flat against the wall with her legs pulled up defensively in front.

'Please, Razor. Please don't,' Dutch begged.

He unfolded one carefully and as traces of brown powder became visible, he threw the wraps down and brought his arm up to strike Dutch's tear-stained face.

There was only one thing to be done. Launching herself towards him, Caz grabbed his outstretched arm and clung to it, hanging on grimly, knowing that it would be turned against her for daring to intervene if she let go.

'Razor, stop, stop,' she cried. 'Don't do this now. Let me try an' sort Dutch out. You go and find the guy who done Redz in.'

He remained static, his muscles tensed for what seemed ages, before relaxing all of a sudden and dropping his arm. Staring directly at Dutch, he pulled his head back and spat at her. The spittle hit her in the face and across the top of her knees, but she sat motionless, allowing it to run down her chin on to her hands.

'Mark my words, you lazy bitch. You'd better be ready to do what I say when I get back. Or else!'

With the threat still hanging in the air, Razor turned and strode out of the flat, slamming the door behind him.

Caz stayed still, listening as his footsteps died away. Only when she was sure he was gone did she dare move across and pick the five heroin wraps up, shoving them deep into her pocket.

'I'd better take these and get them back to Turbo. At least Razor might relax a bit if he knows he don't owe nothing!'

Dutch nodded miserably. 'Thanks Caz. You saved me from a real beatin'. In fact, you probably saved my life.' She rubbed her mouth, her fingers tracing the indentations left by Razor's teeth.

The two girls moved into the front room, bringing with them the rocks of crack left by Razor and prepared their own hits, Dutch taking two for the one that Caz prepared. The remaining rocks were put under the flowerpot in the corner.

'What're you goin' to do then, Dutch? You'll have to go back out. There ain't no other way.'

'I don't know.' Dutch tightened a tourniquet around her leg, waiting for the vein to bulge before sinking the needle into her ankle. 'I just don't think I can. I can't go on like this for much longer. Look at me; I look twice my age and I feel like shit all the time.'

Caz watched as Dutch lay back against the settee and closed her eyes, drifting seamlessly into a different world. Her hairpiece was back in position and she seemed more peaceful now, but it would only be short-lived. Razor would do exactly as he'd warned.

Caz thought of their morning shopping trip, just her and Razor, doing the ordinary, everyday things that couples did, and a pang of jealousy caught her off guard at the image of Razor and Dutch fucking.

She got up and wandered through to the kitchen aimlessly, remembering Ayeisha's promise to come round later. The crack she'd just prepared would have to wait until after they'd spoken. There were other important things to be done first. The fridge was empty. She switched the light on and went to the windowsill, helping herself to a few quid from the pot where Razor kept his stash. They needed booze and food.

Returning to the lounge, she knelt down next to Dutch and shook her gently. 'I'm goin' out in a minute, Dutch,' she whispered. 'But I'll get everythin' sorted for you. You don't need to worry about nothin'.' Dutch lay silent and unresponsive. Every now and again, her lips and brows twitched, her eyelids fluttering faster as a small sob broke the silence. She would be like this for some time.

Caz stayed for a while, stroking her friend's hand as an unexpected wave of optimism peaked. She would help Dutch overcome her problems and, when that was done, everything would be all right. She would show Razor that she was all he needed. Then, in a few days' time, when his case was dropped, they would be together, forever.

Chapter 30

Soft music throbbed throughout the confines of the new house. The lighting was dimmed and tinged pink for a more subtle effect and the rooms were perfumed with sensual fragrances. Dimitri moved from room to room, checking that all was in order, but his girls had done him proud. After initial differences of opinion when they had first arrived in the country they quickly learnt what *he* expected, even though it wasn't as *they* had expected.

Over time, they had grown used to the routine. He looked after them well, didn't he? Keeping them warm, fed and watered, allowing them to send a small percentage of their takings to family back home. While some might say their lives remained restricted, he liked to think they had enough; probably more than in their homelands... they just needed to work hard and show him gratitude. A particularly grateful twenty-year-old Lithuanian woman, rescued from a life toiling in the fields, sidled across as he entered her room. A see-through negligee hung loosely from her shoulders, only partially covering a bright red basque, fishnet stockings and high stiletto heels. She smiled as he moved his hand over her stockings, his fingers lingering at the bare flesh at her thigh.

'You should come to work for Dimitri also,' she nodded towards a young girl, standing silently watching from behind. 'He will treat you well and pay you good.'

'She's thinking about it, aren't you, my beautiful sexy girl?' he transferred his hand from the Lithuanian to stroke the young girl's silky black hair instead. 'But first I must get you home.'

He took a step backwards and the girl grasped his arm. 'Can't I stay tonight?'

He shook his head. It wouldn't do to let her have her way just yet, even though she was as good as his. 'Unfortunately, there are lots of things to be done and I will not be able to pay you the attention you deserve.' His expression was soft, at odds with the stirring in his groin. In the next few days, he would have her adolescent body, over and over, but tonight she would have to wait.

The sound of an argument stirred him from his reverie. The voice was Hanna's, loud and insistent.

'Go back to the car and wait for me,' he instructed the young girl. 'I will be with you in a minute.'

She did as ordered, even though he could tell she did not want to go. She was clearly ready to take up his last spot, primed, willing and obedient. He waited until she was out of sight before closing the door on the Lithuanian woman and ascending the stairs to Hanna's room. Hanna stood wrapped in a dressing gown, her arms folded tight across her body, arguing with Albertas. She quietened as he entered, but her expression remained mutinous. Dimitri said nothing as he took the two steps towards her and ripped the dressing gown from her shoulders. He waited while Albertas closed the door behind them, allowing his eyes to roam over Hanna's naked body.

'I have had enough of you and your loud mouth.' From his jacket pocket, he pulled a knife, pressing the catch and watching as the blade flicked out into position. He aimed it towards Hanna, smirking with glee as she shrank away from the razor-sharp metal, her hands clutched across her breasts and crotch in an attempt to cover herself. 'If you do not want to end up as Tatjana did, you will shut your mouth and do as I say.' He took a step closer and pushed the point of the knife against her stomach, tracing the line from her belly button downwards. 'Do you understand?'

Hanna opened her mouth and then closed it again without speaking, but her eyes remained defiant.

He put an arm around her shoulder and lifted the knife so that the blade pressed against her neck, swivelling it slightly so that her skin strained against the tip. 'I said, do you understand?' He gave the knife a jolt, so that the tip pierced her flesh, bringing a drop of blood rushing to the surface of her skin.

Hanna closed her eyes tightly, nodding silently as a tear pooled at the corner of her eye.

'Good.' He snapped the knife shut triumphantly. 'The first man to enter this house tonight will have you... and I will tell him that he can do anything he wants. Now, get yourself ready. I do not want to hear your stupid voice again.'

*

Dimitri Ivanov was known to police, but the photograph on the police custody imaging computer records did not match the portrait on either the photocopied driving licence or CCTV. Nor did the portrait on the photocopied licence match up with the photograph on the DVLA records. In other words, the driving licence ID card was a forgery. The man in the image, whoever he was, had stolen the identity of Dimitri Ivanov, with or without his knowledge. To any officer stopping him on the street, the licence card would have seemed genuine enough. It was a full licence, with a photo of the person they had stopped correctly shown, and with no access to custody imaging or the DVLA records on the streets, it would almost certainly have seemed credible. No wonder the hire company had been fooled.

Even close scrutiny of the genuine and fake Ivanov would have thrown up more questions than answers;

both men were very similar in appearance. Whoever had made up the forgery, had selected well.

Charlie stared at the man's face on the photocopy, taking in every feature. Even though they were still awaiting the forensic results, she knew without doubt, he was responsible for the baby girl's death. He had dead eyes. He was soulless, without conscience, and he was mocking her. But who the hell was he?

'Go home, team. It's been a long day,' Hunter shouted through from his office. Charlie wanted to add the word 'fruitless', but it seemed too harsh. They'd all been working non-stop, but it felt like for every step they took forward, they were knocked back twice as far. She shut down the computer and picked up her phone, waving as the others filtered out – Paul up town to a bar, Sabira to her new partner Preet, Bet and Naz home to their families.

She dialled Ben's number, listening as the line clicked in. Perhaps a good long run with him and Casper would lift her spirits. There was nothing like sprinting through the dark streets of London, with the freezing night air filling her lungs and limbs, followed by a hot, milky chocolate drink with extra sprinkles of cocoa and warm marshmallows, and all while curled up on the sofa with your best mate. Maybe more partner than mate soon, she was sure Ben was planning something special for Christmas. Or at least she hoped he was.

Hunter appeared, doing up the buttons of his old donkey jacket and pulling his tweed cap down over his ears. He pulled the door to his office shut and she heard him sigh heavily. With the post mortem completed, Redz was to be repatriated back to Ireland, and tomorrow they would be flying to her home town in readiness for the funeral. Until then though Hunter would apparently be spending the rest of his Saturday evening watching the finale of *Strictly*, with Mrs H, whether he wanted to or not. Mrs H had recorded it ready.

His ever-present radio sparked into life, just as Ben answered her call and voiced an enthusiastic greeting.

'Hi Ben,' she said, stopping abruptly as she heard a familiar address given out over the airwaves. Hunter recognised it too and they both stood stock-still as the rest of the details followed. Any plans for the next few hours were forgotten in an instant.

Another body had been found.

*

Charlie and Hunter raced to 59 Milton House, Poets Estate, SW2, with more information flooding in over the radio every minute. The body was that of a young female. It was believed to be an overdose. The informant who had found the body was also a young female, and she was now in with the neighbours at 58.

211

All Charlie's fears were coming back to haunt her. Could the body be that of Caz? Had they sent her to her death when they'd bailed out Razor and allowed her to return to his flat. Perhaps she should have broken her code of silence with the source unit and spoken to Angie of her worries, but then what could Angie have done? Any covert enquiries to try to assist would blow their informant's cover sky-high. Assistance had to be offered overtly, through the normal channels, and Caz had turned it down. There was nothing more they could have done. Still, until she saw the body with her own eyes she couldn't help worrying.

A paramedic and a uniformed police officer stood chatting at the front door when they arrived. On seeing their warrant cards, the paramedic spoke bluntly. 'She's in the front room and appears to have been dead some time. Looks like an overdose. We won't be taking her.'

'Do we have an ID yet?' Charlie asked straight away.

The police officer shook his head. 'Not yet, but my colleague is in with the informant next door.'

Charlie nodded and headed straight through, closely followed by Hunter. Nothing else mattered for that moment other than establishing whether the body was that of Caz.

To her relief it wasn't, but almost instantaneously the guilt kicked in as she recognised Dutch. The girl was lying along the sofa on her side, with her head resting on a pillow and her left arm tucked underneath her body.

One leg stuck out in front of her, stiffly held in place by the other, and a hairpiece, slightly askew, was combed out on to the cushion behind her. Flung out across the back of the settee, her right hand still gripped a syringe, the needle of which stuck up into the air. She looked to be sleeping, her eyes and mouth closed, her expression serene, almost angelic, the contrast with her life as a prostitute stark.

Charlie leant forward, her fingers brushing the girl's bare arm, recoiling instantly at the cool, waxy, model-like texture. She could never get used to the feel of death.

Hunter pointed towards the table littered with drug paraphernalia. 'Looks like a straightforward drugs overdose to me, like the paramedic said, but she'll still need to be checked thoroughly for injuries.' He turned towards the uniformed officer who had joined them. 'Have a good look for any suicide notes and bag up any items of value you might find in the rest of the flat, but leave this area intact. I'll arrange for a photographer and SOCO to attend ASAP to get some pictures of the syringe in her hand and to get it removed and packaged safely. Likewise, with any wraps or remnants of drugs; leave them to SOCO and hopefully we might get some DNA or fingerprints off them to identify her dealer, though I've a pretty good idea who it's likely to be.' He turned to Charlie angrily. 'Another young woman dead, no doubt from the amount of shit, dealers like Razor, mix in with their gear these days.'

They picked their way out and headed for the neighbours. The door to number 58 was slightly ajar and the buzz of people chatting could be heard from within. Charlie rapped succinctly on the wood and an elderly man appeared.

'Come in, come in. The poor young girl who found her is in here. She hasn't stopped crying since we sat her down.'

The flat was neat and tidy, with a dark, patterned carpet and embossed wallpaper. An umbrella stand stood near to the front door.

As she entered the lounge, Charlie saw a teenage girl sitting on the sofa, clutching a porcelain cup in her hands, her cheeks shiny with tears. Next to her sat an elderly woman, her hand lying on the young girl's knee, patting it gently. Both looked up as she and Hunter walked through, and at the sight of the police officers, the girl placed the cup down and started to sob.

'Don't worry lovie,' the old lady said kindly. 'They're here to help.' Turning towards them, she explained, 'Her name's Ayeisha. She found the girl, just now. We called the ambulance. She's been telling me all about her other friend too. It must be awful for her, poor thing.'

Charlie sat down in the armchair opposite and looked at the sobbing girl.

'Ayeisha. Can you tell me what happened?'

'It was like the lady said. I was coming up to see my friend Caz. When I got here, there was no answer so I went in.' She put her hands out as if in demonstration. 'I normally just go in if there's no reply. I was going to watch telly until Caz came back. Her flatmate, Dutch, was lying on the settee. At first, I thought she was just asleep but she looked different. When I tried to wake her, she didn't move and she was all cold. I got frightened and ran straight here.' The girl stared down at the floor. 'She's dead, ain't she?'

'Yes, I'm sorry, she is,' Charlie spoke softly. 'The paramedics think she probably died some time ago.'

'I knew it.' Ayeisha scrunched up the tissue and sniffed, as a fresh bout of tears threatened. 'What's going to happen now?'

'Well, we'll arrange for Dutch's body to be taken away, but in the meantime, if you're OK to talk to me now we need to find out what happened.'

Ayeisha nodded and the old lady patted her on the knee again. Charlie nodded her appreciation to the elderly couple. It was good that Ayeisha, as a juvenile was accompanied, even though they had only just become acquainted.

She turned back to the young girl. 'How well did you know Dutch?'

'I didn't know her that well, but she was nice, funny. She lived here with Caz and Razor. I know Caz had been worried about her since Redz got killed. She said Dutch had been taking heroin, as well as her usual crack.'

'Do you think she might have done this on purpose?' Charlie had planned to speak to Dutch about her flatmate's murder and Razor's movements. Perhaps she had known more than she should? Had she been living in fear of violent retribution and it had all got too much? With both cases ongoing, Charlie had simply run out of time, but now she was kicking herself that the opportunity had been lost.

'I don't know. I never heard her say she wanted to kill herself but maybe she did...'

Her words were drowned out by a piercing scream from the entrance lobby. Rushing out, Charlie saw the uniformed officer struggling to restrain a hysterical Caz.

'She says that she lives here. She pushed past me and got into the flat,' he shouted. 'She saw the body in the front room before I could get her out.'

As he spoke, Ayeisha burst out from behind them, flinging herself at the older girl. 'She's dead, Caz. Dutch is dead,' she sobbed.

Charlie watched as Caz calmed slightly, trying to console the teenager through her own grief. The young prostitute was clearly no stranger to tragedy, her experience in dealing with death evident. She stared at the two girls locked tightly together, watching as Caz shifted slightly. What would happen to her now? Her situation was even grimmer, the dangers made far worse by Razor's earning ability having been slashed still further. Two of her closest friends were dead, one possibly at the hands of their shared pimp and the other perhaps fearful of becoming a second victim.

As she stood wishing there was more she could do, Hunter emerged from the flat, his hand clasped over the speaker of his radio, muting the sound of a disturbance in the background.

'Get the two girls back to the station to make witness statements as soon as you can,' he whispered to Charlie. 'Razor's just turned up downstairs and he's not happy.'

*

Razor was in a rage as he stepped out across the road into the path of a passing minicab. The driver hooted long and hard, slewing the car to a standstill, before winding down the window and gesticulating wildly.

A group of lads turned to stare at the commotion from a bench, adding their laughter to his humiliation.

With a roar, Razor launched himself towards the cabbie, in no mood to take further abuse. Not only had the cops refused him entry to his own flat, they had also informed him why, and that they might need to speak to him about it at some stage; but they could go to hell. There was no way he would be assisting them and he'd said that in as many words. Still, there was not a damn thing he could do except walk away into the estate, knowing that another slag had made a laughing stock out of him. Two of his girls were now dead, two means of income gone. What the fuck was happening?

The taxi driver had almost managed to shut the window of the car as he reached it, so his fists slammed painfully against the freezing glass. The driver was leaning away from him even within the safety of the interior, desperate to put space between them. Razor grabbed the door handle, wrenching at it with all his force, but the door was locked. He screamed his fury towards the driver again, punching the wing mirror clean off before aiming his boot at the door panel. The cabbie slammed the car into gear and, with tyres screeching, pressed his foot down hard on the accelerator. In this neighbourhood, it was safer to drop it than force the issue. There was no way he was going to stay and argue with this madman, however blameless he had been.

Razor shouted as the engine started to whine, aiming a last kick at the car as it moved out of his reach, skidding away up the road. He turned towards the group of boys and took a few steps towards them, his hand moving slowly towards his belt. He might not have a gun in his waistband, but they wouldn't risk the possibility.

'Was there something you wanted to say?' he growled, watching in amusement as the group rose, as one, and backed away.

He stood watching them slink into the shadows, grateful for even this mild demonstration of respect, but at the resurgence of sirens, his rage returned. Caz would have to do the work of all three of his girls from now on.

And as for The Punter who had caused all this... he would be a dead man.

Chapter 31

Caz stumbled out into the cold night air anxious to get away from the claustrophobic atmosphere of the police station. The bars and takeaway restaurants had eventually closed and the town centre was subdued, only the last remaining nocturnal dealers and rough sleepers inhabiting the shop doorways. Up above, the angels mounted on the four corners of the red-brick and white stone tower of Lambeth Town Hall watched moodily as the clock at their feet chimed 04.45. All she wanted was to get home, though quite what she'd find when she got there was anyone's guess. Dutch was dead. Perhaps the police were still on scene, or Razor? It had certainly been a night that she wouldn't easily be able to forget.

Her mind focussed briefly on Razor. There were several things that needed to be done and two of them concerned her man. She had to ensure his freedom and the timing had seemed perfect to get her alibi statement for Redz' murder down on paper. After speaking first about Dutch, it had been Charlie Stafford herself who had brought up the subject, though seemingly unimpressed with her version of events. Yes, Razor had been with her all evening, only leaving her when he'd parked outside Viv's and gone in. Yes, she had been with him in the flat earlier that evening and then in the car when he searched for Redz, but couldn't find her, and if she couldn't be seen on CCTV it must have been because she had been tired and was lying down on the back seat trying to sleep. So, it couldn't be him, could it?

The detective hadn't looked particularly happy and her continual warnings that the truth needed to be told had proved tiresome, but she had stuck to her story. Razor was her partner and she would stand by him whether the detective liked it or not. Anyway, Razor would be eternally grateful for her loyalty and it would be down to the cops to prove she wasn't telling the whole truth.

The second thing required a quick call. Caz pulled her phone out and keyed in the number, waiting for the voice of her handler.

'Angie,' Caz asked carefully. 'Sorry to bother you at this time of night, but I thought I'd let you know something I've 'eard.'

'All right, mate, but it had better be good,' Angie sounded bleary and slightly irritated at having been woken. 'What you got?'

'Well, it's about Redz, you know, my flatmate who was murdered. I know who killed 'er.'

'Go on.'

'Well, I don't know his name, but 'e's a punter who's been around before.' She gave a full description. 'All the girls are talkin' about 'im and what 'e's done. I did hear it a couple of days ago but wanted to be sure before I passed it on to yer so I asked again earlier tonight. Everyone is sayin' it must be 'im.'

'Did you hear this from anyone in particular, and do you think they'd be willing to be a witness?'

'One of the girls saw 'im pick Redz up. I'm not namin' names 'cause she'd never want to stand up in court and she wouldn't be 'appy at bein' asked neither.'

'OK, mate. I'll pass it on, but keep an ear out and if you find out his details or the car he drives, or anything else, come straight back to me.'

'Will do, Angie. I got more good stuff too, but I'm still workin' on it. I'll bell you in the mornin' about it.'

She smiled to herself and ended the call. While waiting together in the interview room for their statements to be taken, Ayeisha had told her all about her evening's activities, culminating in the discovery of Dutch. Her friend had seemed different though, quiet and depressed. Perhaps seeing Dutch dead had affected her, but the conversation had been interesting, and exactly what Angie was after. It would need an update though before she passed it on, and to that end she'd have to wait for Ayeisha's phone call in the morning.

She put the phone away and thought about her new job. She was happy to go to court officially for Razor, as his alibi, but if she could earn some cash for them both by pointing police towards The Punter, then even better. Angie was doing a great job getting her a few quid for her information these days and even Charlie Stafford was proving to be a useful ally, steering her through the legal procedures involved in composing her statements. She couldn't lose.

As she walked up the main road, she was vaguely aware that a Royal Mail van had passed her a couple of times. The driver slowed as he approached for a third time and she beckoned him over. There were two things with which he could assist; a first-class transportation home service and cash-on-delivery. She checked in her bag and felt the presence of a couple of condoms safely stowed away next to her Goldilocks and agreed a price.

Ten minutes later and the postman was speeding off into the night, twenty pounds lighter, de-stressed and joking about this having been one of his more enjoyable deliveries. Caz too was pleased as she quickly exchanged the postie's cash for a new rock of crack from a local dealer. She'd chucked the one she'd prepared earlier on her trip to the police station. Now she was in her estate, warmer, contented and with some gear for her next fix tucked away. She didn't mind that kind of punter.

As she turned the corner of the block, her gaze shifted to the open rear doors of a private ambulance. The light was hypnotic, shining out against the darkness of the night, and she could see the silhouette of a man inside.

Two more men, smartly dressed in dark suits, appeared from the entrance to Milton House. They pushed a trolley, upon which lay a body zipped up in a black bag. They moved towards the light, as did Caz, walking silently round the edge of the block. The trolley was lifted on to the ramp at the back of the ambulance and the shadowy figure inside shuffled towards it.

'What's this one like then, Bill? Young or old?' he asked.

His hand moved towards the top of the zip and pulled it down, revealing the head and shoulders of Dutch. Although West Indian by nationality, her face had lost some of the darker pigmentation in death. It was now blotchy and her cheeks were sunken and faded. Her eyes were staring upwards, lifeless and dull, and her mouth hung open. Her wig had fallen off and was stuffed into the top of the bag to one side and her real hair was exposed, cropped short and spiky.

'Quite a young one then,' the same shadowy figure remarked, zipping the bag back up. 'Just another sad junkie. What a waste!'

Caz froze at the words, her legs trembling so violently that she stumbled backwards, falling against a gate. The man peered out in the direction of the metallic clunk before cursing.

The next thing she knew, she was running. Running through the walkways, down the stairs, along the concrete footways on and on, through the estate. *Just another sad junkie. Just another sad junkie.* The expression repeated in her head and the vision of Dutch's dead body hung hazily in her sights.

On and on, and out along the roadway. The intermittent car headlights blinded her as she ran and she threw her hands up over her face to shield her retinas against the brightness. *Just another sad junkie.* Down past the High Road and away into the quiet side streets until she came to the common. Only then did she stop running, squatting under a small tree, her breath expelled hard and fast, melting the frost on its frozen leaves.

Just another sad junkie who needed to score again. Dawn was just beginning to break with a faint glow. It combined with a street lamp opposite, shining through the branches to provide enough meagre light for Caz to shakily assemble her next fix. As she inhaled, the ghostly faces of Redz and Dutch faded in and out of her consciousness, neutralising any benefits from the crack. Fatigue and despair were enticing her to sleep on the frozen earth, but somewhere at the back of her mind a warning sounded. If she allowed her body to succumb to the temptation, she'd be dead within hours from hypothermia, but she need not stay where she was. Her subconscious had directed her feet to the only place where she felt safe. Climbing out from beneath the frozen branches, she walked falteringly towards Anna's office at the edge of the common.

The building was shrouded in darkness; only the glint from the nearby streetlight reflecting off the bronze plaque and glass panels in the door. A vague waft of leather and furniture polish drifted into her nostrils as she pushed the letter box open and stared up the gloomy staircase ahead. Almost absent-mindedly she expected to see Anna walking down the stairs towards her, but then she realised it was Sunday morning and the office would remain shut all day.

Caz cursed softly and wrapped her arms round her torso, imagining the occupants of the nearby houses tucked snugly into warm beds. She couldn't remain where she was, or she would freeze. Looking around, she found a broken piece of brick and an old newspaper discarded in the gutter. She wrapped the paper around her hand and thrust the brick at the small panes in the door, smashing the glass and splintering it inwards. Carefully she leant through the jagged hole and reached down towards the door handle, manoeuvring herself carefully and releasing the catch.

The empty office swaddled her in its warmth as she climbed the stairs and curled up on the couch like a newborn, but before she capitulated to the overpowering effect of the drug, she reached into her bag and found Goldilocks, positioning the grubby doll in her favourite spot against her cheek. Her thumb rose automatically to her mouth as she did so and as she began to suck rhythmically and instinctively, her mind cleared and she drifted into warm, secure nothingness.

*

Anna was woken from her sleep by a loud ringing at exactly six-thirty a.m. It took several attempts at the snooze button on her alarm clock before she registered it was her phone. She pushed herself up on to one arm, listening groggily to the police officer's words.

A prostitute claiming to be one of her clients had broken into her office and was saying that Anna herself would not mind. She had damaged the door and had been found asleep on her couch after a call from neighbours. He was sorry to wake her, but apparently the woman was insisting she be called before being arrested for burglary and taken to the station. The woman's name? Yes, she was calling herself Caz.

Anna dissected the information, trying to make sense of it. Why on earth would Caz be at her office now? She must know that Anna wouldn't be there at this time on a Sunday, therefore she must be in trouble and to break into her office must mean she was desperate.

The police officer apologised again, explaining that he needed to know whether she wanted to take action, or not.

'No, no. Leave her. She is one of my clients. I'll make my way straight there.'

She thought she could detect a slight disappointment in the officer's voice. It couldn't be that often a person was actually caught bang to rights, but still, Caz obviously needed help not incarceration.

It was still early, but her husband would understand. Anna threw some clothes on, brushed her teeth and tiptoed down the stairs, her hope building. Perhaps Caz had reached crisis point and could finally be let into the secret of the near-complete flat.

The car heater had barely warmed before she was pulling up outside her office, slightly surprised and a little apprehensive at the absence of any police. A few splinters of broken glass glistened on the pavement, but as she opened the door, she noticed some larger shards on the mat inside. Gingerly, she climbed the stairs and pushed open the office door, peering into the gloom. She could just make out the shape of a figure on the couch and for a second she was scared. What if the woman had been lying?

Switching the light on, however, she breathed a sigh of relief as she looked down at a sleeping Caz. Her pose was a carbon-copy of how she had appeared when Redz was murdered; thumb in mouth, doll clutched to her face. Something must have happened.

Very gently she took Caz's hand and bent close.

'Caz, Caz. It's me, Anna. Wake up. Are you all right?'

Caz sat up quickly, pulling away, her head turning from side to side as if searching for a point of anchor. As she focussed on the psychologist, Anna saw her expression relax and the tension begin to leave her face.

'Oh, it's you. I was scared fuckin' shitless. I dreamt I was lying on a cold slab in a bag and a faceless man was pulling the zip up over me. I couldn't move or stop 'im an' I couldn't breathe. An' it was gettin' blacker and blacker.'

Anna reached out and took her hand again, eliciting a sudden cry from Caz.

'Dutch is dead. It was *her* body they was takin' out in the bag, *her* body that'll be lyin' on a cold slab.'

'What happened?' Anna gasped audibly. First Redz, now Dutch. No wonder the girl was so distressed.

'I dunno. She took a hit; only she took twice as much as normal. I went out shoppin'. When I got back like, there was this cop standin' outside the flat. I knew somethin' must 'ave happened. I pushed past 'im and saw Dutch. She was lyin' exactly where I'd left her. Then Ayeisha came runnin' out of the next-door flat in a right state, sayin' Dutch was dead. An' then the cops said the same and that it looked like she'd OD'd.'

Caz spoke fast, her words tripping out almost automatically. Anna shook her head, still in shock. 'Do you think she meant to overdose?'

'I don't know. There was some other gear that Razor had brought back that she might 'ave used, but I don't think she really knew what she was doin' or what she wanted.'

Caz paused, as if deep in thought. Anna gazed at her young client and her heart went out to her. She knew only too well the dangers the girl faced on a daily basis. How was such a young woman supposed to deal with so much death? And what if Caz was next? Her life certainly seemed more precarious than ever. What if she never got the chance to reach out and be saved, grab the lifeline that was being offered? The time was surely coming when Caz's very existence would hang in the balance.

Caz shifted on the couch. 'I hope you don't mind me comin' 'ere and breakin' your glass. I didn't know where else to go an' I couldn't go back to the flat after seein' Dutch.'

'Don't worry, Caz. You know you can always come to me if you need help.'

Anna moved away to make a hot drink for them both. When she returned, Caz had swung her legs round and was sitting up on the couch. She took the mug offered and sat quietly staring as the ripples spread out from the centre of the liquid.

'People around me always seem to die,' she said eventually.

Anna looked at her, unsure whether she was referring to her childhood or the more recent events, but she seemed to want to talk and Anna was not going to let this chance slip away.

'Who else died, Caz?'

'The bastard who took my mum away from me. He died. I didn't mind that though. He deserved it.' She paused as if deciding whether to continue. 'I told you what he did, Tommy, didn't I? He took me mum away from us all, forever. Then he started to let 'is drunken mates come round to our house and they'd all get pissed. Sometimes some of the men would make me sit on their laps. They put their filthy hands all over me, touchin' me while Tommy and me mum would just laugh. Tommy 'specially. He would stare at me with a strange look on his face. Me mum was always sorry when she sobered up. She said that she loved me an' it wouldn't happen again, but it always did.

'Me brothers an' I all told me mum to get rid of 'im and she said lots of times that she would… but she never did. She would always bleedin' have him back and in the end it was me brothers who all left. I don't even know where they are now.'

Caz started to cry, silent tears that slid from the corners of her eyes.

'That's when he started on me, like. Just a little at first. He would make me sit on his lap when his mates was round an' then he started to touch me. Sometimes he would take the piss out of how small my tits was. He would pull my T-shirt up so as everyone could see and they would all laugh. Even me mum laughed. She would tell 'im to leave me alone, but she never did anything to stop 'im. When he thought he could get away with it, he would do worse stuff. I could feel 'im underneath me gettin' turned on, then I would make an excuse an' pull away from 'im and run upstairs to my room.

'One night though he followed me up. Mum was so pissed she'd passed out on the settee. He came over to my bed and put 'is hands under the covers and started tryin' to touch me. His breath stunk of cigarettes and booze. He kept telling me that he loved me and wanted me. He said that my mum didn't care about 'im anymore and that 'e didn't find her attractive like 'e had. He started tryin' to kiss me. I tried to pull away from 'im, but he was too strong. His mouth was all over mine. I wanted to be sick with the smell and taste of him.

'I tried shoutin' out for me mum, but he put his hand over my mouth. He was laughin' and sayin' that my mum would be pleased 'cause he wouldn't be botherin' her. That she wouldn't mind. Then he ripped my clothes off and raped me, in me own bed, with me mum downstairs. It hurt so much, but he wouldn't stop. It went on for ages and ages. I hated him so much at that moment.

'When he finished, he rolled over and told me how good I was. He warned me that if I said anything to me mum 'bout what had happened, he would tell 'er that I'd led 'im on and been the one to start it. That I had loved every moment.

'When he left the room I just cried an' cried. There was blood all over my sheet an' I rolled it up and threw

232

it away. I couldn't let me mum see it. I couldn't say anything to her 'cause I knew he would tell her it was all my fault.'

Tears were coursing down Caz's cheeks as she spoke. Anna longed to put an arm around her but sensed it would be unwelcome.

'After that he would come into my room whenever me mum was out of it. I tried to hide her booze and spliffs so as she wouldn't get pissed, but he would always make sure she had enough. I hated 'im. I hated everything about 'im. His smug look, his stinkin' breath, his dirty, filthy hands.

'One night, I heard him comin' up the stairs, pissed. He tripped up and was swearin' out loud. I knew he was comin' for me again. He came into my room and just stood by the door smilin'. He started tellin' me to take my clothes off and that he was goin' to fuck me. I just knew I had to get out. I couldn't take no more. As he came towards me, I managed to push him out of the way and I locked myself in the toilet. He was bangin' on the door, sayin' that he knew I wanted 'im and that I was an ungrateful little bitch. I'd never heard 'im as bad as that before.

'I was pushin' against the door so as he couldn't get in an' after a while I heard 'im move away. I thought he'd given up. Then a few minutes later, I heard 'im out on the landing again, laughin'. He said he had Goldilocks and that he was goin' to rip her to pieces.'

Caz lifted the ragdoll up and placed her on her lap, her hands gently caressing the dirty material.

'She was the only thing I had to remind me of me mum and that shoppin' trip. I couldn't let 'im destroy my last memory of the good times, so I opened the door an' I pleaded with 'im to give her back to me, but he just fuckin' laughed, laughed in my face. He said if I wanted 'er back I knew what I had to do an' he unzipped his trousers. I felt sick.

'He was standin' on the landing next to the stairs, holdin' Goldilocks out in his hands, swayin' about. Then he lost his balance. I'll never forget the look of panic on his face as he started grabbin' at the banisters, tryin' to get his balance, but he couldn't. He fell right down to the bottom of the stairs and his head hit a cupboard. There was blood everywhere. I looked down at him an' his stupid, pathetic, panic-stricken face an' I just remember feelin' happy.

'I went down an' took Goldilocks from out of his hand. I knew he was dead an' I was glad. Glad that he'd never be able to touch me again. Glad that he couldn't beat me mum up anymore. Glad that he was gone forever. Then I went back up to my room an' left him there. I wanted to make absolutely sure he was dead. After about an hour I checked and 'e was still in the same place, his disgusting eyes staring up at me. I knew then for sure that I was safe.

'I stepped over him and went to find me mum. She was still out of it, but I managed to wake her up. She called an ambulance but it was too late.'

Caz wiped angrily at her eyes.

'I never cried a single tear for that bastard at his funeral. I was glad he was fuckin' dead. I never told me mum what he had done to me neither. I was frightened she wouldn't believe me and that she would think it'd been my fault. You're the only one I've ever told 'bout what happened.'

Caz looked towards her for reassurance. It was clear it had taken every ounce of her courage and concentration to relive this awful part of her childhood.

'Caz, I believe you.' Anna made eye contact. 'I believe that Tommy raped you, and I also believe that you have been extremely brave to tell me this.'

She put her arm around Caz and held her tightly, gently stroking the young woman's hair as Caz clutched Goldilocks to her cheek. Neither spoke. Gently, Anna eased her down so she could sleep further. Caz lay silently for a while, before turning and smiling up at Anna, her face alight with an intensity she'd not seen before.

'You know what though? My mum got better after Tommy died. It was like he'd never been there. She cut down on 'er boozin' and refused to let Tommy's mates into the house. She started givin' me more attention and we even went out a few times, like we'd done in the past.

235

I think she felt guilty 'bout how she'd treated me. She kept tellin' me she loved me and that she was glad it was just me an' her again. An' I loved it. An' I loved her again. An' it was like Tommy had never come between us.

'For a few months it was the best time of my life. Just me and me mum. I wanted it to stay like that forever.'

As quickly as Caz's face had lit up, so the look was lost, replaced instead by one of intense pain. The spell was broken and Anna knew Caz would say nothing further.

She pulled a blanket from the cupboard and drew it around Caz's bare shoulders, wondering whether there could be yet more traumas buried deep. It was hard to believe any could be worse than the outpouring she had just heard.

As Anna waited for Caz to succumb to sleep, she knew that the day was quickly approaching when Caz would face the final choice; reach out and take the help on offer, or stay with Razor and risk becoming the next fatality. As yet though, it was anybody's guess which path Caz would choose.

Chapter 32

'I've got a description of a punter who picked up Redz before she was killed.'

Charlie rubbed her eyes and groaned. If it hadn't been Angie's name flashing on the phone screen she wouldn't have picked up. Her clock was showing 11.24, still less than five hours since she'd finished dealing with the overdose. She rolled over and pulled out a pen and paper from her bedside cabinet, jotting down the description as Angie gave it.

'That's all we need when we've got Razor on bail for murdering her.'

'I know, but I have to pass it on. It is only word on the street though. Nothing specific.'

'Suppose so.' Charlie was relieved for that crumb of comfort. All intelligence was graded according to the reliability of the informant and whether it was actually witnessed by them or heard from other sources. 'Word on the street' was a low grading that could be written off against actual evidence, but it could still muddy the waters, and they would have to do extra work to prove or disprove its validity. Added to Caz's alibi statement, they would now be facing an uphill struggle to convince the CPS to bring charges. She sighed wearily. 'Anything else, Angie? I really need something to make me get out of bed.'

'Well,' Angie sounded upbeat, 'as far as the brothel is concerned, Dimitri is working with a guy called Albertas. I still don't know why they relocated so suddenly, but they have now set up in the Lewisham area. Dimitri is sending out texts offering their services, so lots of people will know this. I'm pretty sure I'll have the actual address and his mobile number in the next day or so.'

Charlie swung her legs out of bed and sat up. 'That would be brilliant. Thanks, Angie. Bet identified a white van that we think was being used to move the girls from the brothel and it was rented by a male giving the name Dimitri, although that appears to be a false name. So, your source was spot on with that one and will hopefully be just as good with the rest. We'll start researching Albertas and putting out feelers in the Lewisham area.' She grinned to herself. 'If you could get his mobile number though...'

'I know,' Angie chuckled. 'You can trace it. And you might need to, if you want to catch him in the act.' She paused. 'Charlie, I've got more info that might help you do just that, but there are only a handful of people who know what I'm about to tell you, so you'll need to act extremely carefully.'

'You know I always do.' Charlie understood exactly what Angie meant. The fewer people who knew any information, the more danger a CHIS could be in. Careless talk could literally cost lives.

'Yes, I know, Charlie, but people involved in human trafficking don't mess about. This Dimitri, or whoever he turns out to be, must never suspect somebody told us what I'm about to tell you.' She paused again and Charlie felt her pulse quicken. 'Right, Dimitri has an accomplice in Eastern Europe who is arranging for another girl to be brought across. Dimitri will be travelling to Europe in two days' time to collect her and bring her back. If you want to get him bang to rights, then you'll have to stop him in transit on their way back, with the girl and with all their fake passport and ID documents still on them, before he has a chance to dump them.'

'Otherwise he'll just claim he was one of the clients, if his DNA or fingerprints are found at the brothel.' Charlie was thinking out loud. 'This way, we can prove he was the main person recruiting the girls, sorting out the fake IDs and organising the whole set-up.'

'Exactly,' Angie agreed. 'I'll make sure I get his mobile number and any updates I can ASAP, Charlie. He needs to be put away for life if he's got anything to do with that dead baby girl.'

'Or her poor mother.' Charlie stood up and started towards the bathroom, her mind in overdrive. 'What worries me now though Angie, is… why does he need a replacement? Unless he has a space to fill.'

*

'It's a positive match!' Bet jumped up as Charlie entered the office and rushed towards her, grinning broadly. Paul, Naz and Sabira turned to watch, smiling at Bet's enthusiasm. It was rare to see Bet move that quickly, what with her bad back and aching limbs.

'What is?' Charlie frowned uncertainly but returned the grin, caught up in her colleague's fervour.

'The blood sample from the bed in the brothel matches the sample of the mother's blood found on the baby's head. That baby was definitely miscarried there. You were right. Dimitri, or whoever he is, has got to be involved.'

Charlie let out a whoop of delight and put an arm around Bet's shoulder, squeezing it fondly. The two of them were determined to resolve this particular case together and this confirmation was essential. Even though she'd been certain in her own mind that the two were linked, it was still a relief to know that there was solid evidence to back up her hunch.

'Hunter spoke to the DCI when he got in and the DCI made a phone call to the lab insisting we had this result.' Naz looked at her curiously. It wasn't often they were able to get results from the skeleton staff that worked at the lab at the weekend.

'Any more joy with an identity for the mother then?' Charlie swung round to face Bet, who gave a small shake of her head.

'Unfortunately not. The blood on the bed is identical to the blood on the baby's head and there were fingerprints and other samples with the same DNA from that top bedroom, but the DNA is not known on our system. Our mother has never come to notice in the UK.'

'Damn it. So we still don't know who she is.'

'Or what condition she's in.' Naz pulled a face.

'But at least we know we're definitely on the right track now with Dimitri and the brothel.' Charlie looked up as the door to Hunter's office swung open and he emerged.

'Which is just as well,' Hunter strode through. 'Because there was no way the DCI would sanction us running around the South of England on a full-scale man hunt, if we didn't at least have confirmation that our suspect was actually the right one.'

'Sounds intriguing,' Sabira came across to join them.

'Angie phoned me earlier.' Charlie looked towards Hunter for approval to explain. 'She has a CHIS who is very close to Dimitri, so close that they would be in serious danger if he found out we knew this bit of information.'

'So, what we're about to tell you does not leave this room until either I or the DCI give the word.' Hunter took over, dropping his voice so that they all gathered round. 'Dimitri will be heading to France to pick up a new young victim in two days' time, and we will be waiting to stop him on totally fictitious grounds when he returns. Charlie and I have to travel to Ireland for Redz' funeral this evening and the DCI will be in charge, so, while we're gone, work out a reason to stop Dimitri and make sure it's bombproof. He cannot find out how we got this information and we cannot afford to fail.'

Chapter 33

The store detective wasn't watching as Caz moved around the shop, placing scented candles, food and drinks conspicuously into a wire basket and slipping other items straight into the top of a carrier bag, held loosely over her arm. She moved fast, trying to avoid making the surreptitious moves that would bring attention. At the checkouts, she paid for the items in the wire basket and left the store speedily, jumping on to a waiting bus and relaxing properly only as the doors closed and the bus moved away. Not all shopping need be paid for; cleaning equipment should always be free.

By the time she got to the flat, Caz was in high spirits. Nothing could dampen her enthusiasm. A future she craved was within her grasp. Just as hope had returned after Tommy's death, so could life now return after the deaths of Redz and Dutch... and that life was with Razor.

She switched on the light, moving quickly into the lounge area. It was too quiet and the memory of Dutch's dead body filled her with unease. She switched on the TV and turned the volume up, letting the sports commentators drown out the voices in her head. A can of lager lay unopened on the table. She pulled the ring tab and swallowed some of it down gratefully, assessing what was required. Razor's flat was to be turned into their home.

For several hours, Caz frenziedly worked her way round the flat, fuelled by her anticipation of their future together, now there was just the two of them. It was only the second time in her young life that she had felt hope, and it was a feeling that she was savouring with every minute she cleaned. Bin bags were filled, covers smoothed and cushions plumped up. Furniture was rearranged and their shared bedroom made ready. Razor was her man and would soon be made welcome to a flat he would be proud of, a dwelling they would make their own. She would make herself available to him in every way and in time he would love her properly as she had always dreamed.

When she'd finished, she turned the taps on in the bathroom and surveyed her work with satisfaction. Nothing was perfect, but at least it was tidy. Water cascaded into the bath, sweet-smelling and fresh from moisturising salts she'd found in Dutch's room, where the bulging rubbish sacks were now stashed, alongside her dead flatmate's belongings.

Finally, luxuriating in the warmth of the fragrant water, Caz ran her hands over her emaciated body. The bones of her skeleton pressed through her skin in places;

hip bones, ribs and shoulder blades all sticking out prominently. Her arms and legs felt stick-thin, tender spots and bruises emphasising the existence of past injuries. She slid down under the water, letting the soapsuds encase her, her skin imbuing the richness of the aromas. Her hair spread out across the surface of the water and, as she lathered it up, she thought about her earlier meeting with Anna.

Not many people would have accepted the cost of repairing the broken glass in the door out of their own pocket, but Anna had. She was different from the rest and the bond between them was growing with each visit. She was the best counsellor she'd ever had, the one woman who listened to her every word and made no judgements.

Anna had provided food, drink and compassion... she'd also provided her personal mobile phone number, *in case of an emergency,* writing the number on a piece of paper and tucking it into a side pocket of her handbag, next to Goldilocks.

'Do you think Razor will be there for you, when you need him?' she'd asked finally, staring deeply into her eyes, as if completely recognising her predicament.

Caz hoped he would – she really hoped he would – but life had a way of kicking her feet out from underneath her, just as it had with her mother. For the time being though that memory would remain buried; she preferred to remember the good times, the few months after Tommy died when her expectation for a happy ever after was achievable, just like it was now, with Razor.

A small stream of cold water filtered out from the tap, on to her foot, breaking her solace. The suds had died down and a thin film of grease lay across the surface of the water. She moved her hands, swilling the dirty residue back beneath the soapy membrane, splashing deep within the water so that the bubbles reappeared. Things looked good on the surface, but things were never as they seemed.

She rose from the soapsuds, feeling clean, refreshed and reborn, the chance for a new life stretching out brightly before her. All she needed now was Razor. When last he'd been heard, his rage had been all-pervading, his voice sounding loud and furious over the police officer's radio. Dutch was dead and he was barred from his own flat... again. His reaction was totally understandable. Now though he should be chilled. The cause of his most recent worries had overdosed and with only the two of them left, they would have more than enough cash from his drug dealing and her secret work on which to live. No longer would she have to work the streets.

She dressed scantily, the way Razor liked, moving excitedly around the flat, lighting the candles.

Perfectly on cue, she heard the door opening.

'Caz,' Razor shouted, striding into the hallway. 'What the fuck happened with Dutch? You was supposed to be sortin' her out, not lettin' the lazy bitch top herself.'

She ran towards him, immediately recognising the veiled threat in his voice. 'Razor, I'm sorry. I tried to talk to her.' She pressed herself against him. 'She must have scored some more gear when I was shoppin'. I thought I'd taken it all off her. I found out she'd been gettin' it from that new dealer, Turbo.'

'I 'eard that too. Been out lookin' for 'im meself all day, but the bastard's gone missing. Out country, buyin' some more gear, but I heard he should be back tonight.'

She took his hand and led him through to the lounge, anxious to calm his temper further. The candles flickered moodily, casting shadows across the walls and lighting up her labours.

'Let's not worry about Dutch now. Look what I've done for you.'

Razor looked puzzled. 'What's this all in aid of then, babe?'

'Just tryin' to make things right. An', on that note, I 'ad to go down the station with that copper Charlie Stafford, after they found Dutch, so while I was there I did your alibi statement, just like we agreed; said that I'd been with you until you went into Viv's. She tried to say there was only you in the car, so I made out I was sleepin' in the back. She weren't very pleased.'

247

She laughed, before disappearing into the kitchen and re-emerging with a can of cold beer and a sandwich from the shop. Razor sat on the settee and ate while Caz slipped down next to him, sitting on the floor by his leg.

When he finished eating, he leant into the cushions and unbuttoned his shirt. 'You're a good girl, Caz.'

She looked up at him, giddy with joy, musing happily about their future together. Rarely had he ever spoken to her like this before.

This was it, the moment had come and this time it would be real. Turning round towards him, she knelt between his spread legs, rubbing her hands slowly up the inside of his thighs and unzipping his trousers. She felt him respond immediately, elation flooding through her. He wanted her just as much as she wanted him and as they moved rhythmically together on the same settee that Dutch had lain dead on just a few hours before, she felt closer to him than she'd ever felt before.

'I love you, babe,' she whispered. 'I love you.'

She felt Razor pause momentarily, before he climaxed noisily. Experience had taught her not to keep going for her own gratification when he finished, so she stopped moving, clinging to him for several more minutes as his breathing returned to normal. Losing Dutch seemed to have unleashed a hidden passion in them both, and the same thing had happened after Redz' murder. Death obviously brought them together, but for how long?

Every time happiness was within her grasp, it was snatched away.

As if reading her mind, Razor rose, buttoning his shirt and zipping up his fly. Hazily she watched as he checked through his wallet and slipped a flick knife down between his buttocks.

'Don't go out, babe. Stay with me,' she called over to him. 'I love you.'

Razor swivelled round and stared at her icily for a few moments.

'Please don't leave me,' Caz pleaded again, desperate to keep a hold of her dream.

'Shut the fuck up,' Razor growled. He let his eyes roam up and down her naked body, before striding towards the door. 'I've got business to sort right now, but when I get back, be dressed and ready to do some work.'

*

Razor knew exactly what he had to do.

Turbo had to be taught a lesson that he wouldn't forget… and he was looking forward to being the teacher. There was nothing like the feel of cold hard metal against the soft, tender skin of a throat to engender a bit of respect. Turbo would regret going behind his back. Caz, too, needed to be reminded of her place. She'd been in a strange mood and he wasn't sure how to handle it. What the fuck were all the proclamations of love and begging him not to go? He frowned. He'd enjoyed his welcome home but who did she think she was, trying to tell him what he could or couldn't do? For now though, she would have to wait, he had bigger fish to fry.

As he walked, his mind ran through the information on Turbo. The boy was muscling in on other dealers' customers and not giving a shit. He was also allegedly in possession of a 9mm handgun, though nobody had actually seen it. Consequently, word on the street was that Turbo was all mouth. In their world, if you had a burner, you well and truly flaunted it. Still, the boy was obviously useful enough to have scared off a few of his adversaries. He worked from the Sackville Estate, a smaller one with little vehicular access, which suited his preference for slinking, unseen, between the walkways, away from the perimeter roads where the cops patrolled.

On nearing the estate, Razor slipped his trademark razor blades out from his wallet and repositioned the knife from his trousers to a more accessible place in his jacket pocket. It gave him an adrenalin rush just knowing his weapons were close at hand. The jumped-up kid wouldn't know what had hit him.

He walked slowly into the estate, looking round at the dimly-lit blocks. Turbo apparently liked to deal from the first-floor stairwells; it gave him time to swallow or plug any gear should the cops be on to him.

Razor heard the sound of footsteps from nearby and moved back into the shadows to watch. A skinny young female approached a nearby block and, after glancing around, went into a doorway. Two minutes later she was back out and walking away in the direction from which she had first appeared. A deal had obviously gone down.

Razor watched the block silently and saw a slight movement on the first floor. This was it. Turbo was there. He pushed his hand into his jacket pocket and gripped the knife, positioning his finger over the catch in preparation. As he entered the communal door, he heard a slight scuffle from above and then silence. Eagerly he climbed the first set of stairs, stepped slowly out on to the landing and stopped, waiting.

After a few seconds, a figure emerged from the shadows.

'What do you want?' the figure said coldly.

'You must be Turbo?' Razor asked equally frostily.

'Yeah I am. Who's asking?'

The man facing him was young, only around twenty years of age, Hispanic in appearance, short in height and with shoulder-length black, wavy hair. Exactly as Turbo had been described; though with his slight build and baby face, Razor thought with amusement that he looked more like a girl. This boy would be no match for him. He relaxed slightly. Turbo was going down.

'I'm Razor and I suggest you talk to me with a bit more respect if you know what's good for you.'

'Ah, Razor. I've heard all about you, and from what I hear you should be the one speakin' nice to me. Word is you're a spent force. All washed up. Can't even keep your own girls in line.' Turbo looked him up and down and smiled contemptuously. 'Never mind, old man. Fuck off out of here and we'll pretend this little conversation never took place.'

Razor stood his ground. How dare the boy talk this shit!

'You need to learn some manners,' He pulled the knife from his pocket and pressed the catch, thrusting the serrated blade towards the boy.

Quick as a flash, Turbo reacted, kicking Razor's knife straight from his hand, sending it clattering across the stairwell and down the steps out of reach. At the same time, the boy caught him off balance, swinging him round and pushing the barrel of a gun hard against the side of his head.

'I think it is you who needs to learn some manners. Now, say sorry, old man.'

Razor clenched his teeth but said nothing. How the fuck had this boy reduced him to this position with such ease?

'I said apologise, old man, or I'll blow you're fuckin' brains out.'

Razor winced as the barrel drilled harder against his temple. After all he'd fought for in his life, he was going to die, right here, alone on an isolated, freezing stairwell at the hands of a kid.

'I'm sorry,' he mumbled quietly.

'Say it louder, old man, I can't hear you.'

'I'm sorry,' he repeated louder.

'That's better.' Turbo laughed loudly. 'I don't like people mumbling. It makes me think they're not showing me the proper respect.' He pushed Razor away, sending him sprawling out on the concrete walkway before taking aim at Razor's buttocks. 'Now get out of here before I change my mind and put a bullet in your sorry arse.'

Razor dragged himself to his feet and stumbled away down the stairs, his footsteps pounding in time with Turbo's mocking tones. As he neared the bottom step, he spotted his knife and picked it up, the temptation to issue another challenge almost luring him back up the stairs, but this time Razor knew better. He had been beaten fair and square by a younger, better-equipped adversary and could not win.

Folding the blade safely into its handle, he slunk off, like a wounded animal into the darkness. A knife was no match for a 9mm. He would find Caz. He needed an easier victim.

*

The Punter could stand the monotony no longer. He had to get out. This particular weekend had been torture.

Now he had a car, a shiny nearly new Silver Audi A5 TFSI Convertible, with lavish integral gadgets and an electric roof that purred open at the touch of a button. His shopping trip, as well as being the only thing of interest that weekend, had been a great success and he was the proud owner of a smart new brown leather jacket, brown brogues and a chunky gold signet ring. Christmas had come early for him. The timely estimate from the insurance company on his burnt-out car and the imminent promotion at work provided all the means required to afford the extra borrowing on a loan. Tuesday morning would bring the confirmation of promotion. It was already in the bag, but he couldn't wait.

He flexed his fingers, staring down at the ring with pleasure. Jewellery demonstrated the trappings of wealth better than any other possession. Everyone had a car, everyone had clothes, but few people had enough spare income to waste on gold. It wasn't a necessity, it wasn't even customary, but there was nothing like it for promoting his image… and image was everything.

'Can't you two just be quiet?', he snapped at the twins, earning a withering glance from his wife.

'Leave them be, can't you? They're just excited.'

Her rebuke was the final straw. He wanted excitement too and there was none to be had here, with his family.

Rising from his chair, he strode to the hallway, hauled his jacket on and slammed out of the house, ignoring the cries from his wife and children for daddy to stay.

The new car was everything he desired, sleek, sexy and sophisticated, and as the engine growled into life, he relaxed. The engine responded to the tiniest of pressure as he manoeuvred along the backstreets until he reached Lambeth. This was better. This gave him the thrill he craved. His heart was pumping as he cruised slowly around his favourite places, the corners where the dirty whores frequented, the dark shadows where they practised their filthy rituals, the alleyways where they received their punishment. He knew them all.

A girl stepped out from behind a tree and stared towards his car. She wanted him to stop. She wanted him to pick her up. He could tell from the way she was dressed and how she held herself, and the knowledge turned him on. He was mesmerised by her presence, the anger and desire building within his head and groin. The filthy bitch was messing with his mind. She needed to be chastised for the way she made him act.

A slight movement in the nearby bushes caught his attention. He flicked his headlights on to main beam, watching closely as the whore shielded her face and turned towards the shrubs. He focussed on the greenery, catching the glint of metal and the movement of a solidly-built man dressed all in black. The bitch had protection. Her pimp was at her side, waiting to pounce on any man letting his dick rule his brain, too stupid to take care. But they wouldn't trick him. He was far, far too clever. The bitches would all learn he was not to be fucked with. Nobody even suspected what he'd done just a few days before. It had been far too easy covering his tracks.

He accelerated away, glorying in the surge of power from his new car. The Audi would not be recognised. He would not be recognised. He could come and go as he pleased... and he would.

Chapter 34

The phone call came in the early hours when Dimitri was least expecting it. Business was slow at the Lewisham house, but this was to be anticipated. Details of its new location had to filter out amongst their regulars and the locals were still to be cultivated. The area was ripe for a thriving business though, many of its population having left wives and families in distant lands in order to establish a base in London. The trickle of customers through the back doors would soon become a torrent.

Dimitri prided himself on doing his research well. He also delighted in maintaining control; even Hanna was complying with his every command. Things were going well.

He pulled the phone from his jacket pocket and answered the call. The reception on the line from Europe was crackle-free and the instructions of his Russian counterpart clear and coherent. There could be no mistakes.

'It is all confirmed,' the voice said. 'I have your girl now. She is young and keen and ready to leave her parents and come to you. Her documents are prepared and we will start the journey tomorrow. Meet me at the usual place at 16.00 hours on Tuesday and I will introduce you. Then she is all yours.'

Chapter 35

The funeral service was to be held in a large Catholic Church in South Dublin within view of Dublin Castle. Charlie and Hunter were up in plenty of time, choosing a position at the rear of the church in order to oversee the mourners. As prominent members of the Murder Investigation Team, they had been selected to represent the Metropolitan Police; attending the service and wake in order to glean any snippets of background information that might assist the investigation. Where a suspect, or suspects, might sometimes be expected to attend, today this would be unlikely. They would be there predominantly to show respect to the victim and her family.

At 11 a.m. precisely, the procession arrived. Redz' coffin was carried slowly and reverently up the aisle with her two brothers assisting the undertakers to bear the load.

The coffin was laid at the front of the church, adorned with a large wreath of red roses and white lilies. As the first organ notes rang out, Gerald Flaherty, Redz' father, stepped forward and carefully placed a large bronze frame on top of the casket. Charlie's eyes were drawn immediately to the photograph of a young, flame-haired girl smiling coyly from behind a tree trunk, her auburn locks blowing freely in the breeze. With a shock, she realised the same young girl, so innocent and pure, had transitioned into the woman whose life had been beaten from her in a filthy alleyway in London.

Charlie had read all about Redz' history, extensively detailed by the Family Liaison Officers, and the details had been harrowing. Grace had been sent by her parents, Gerald and Ann, to stay with Gerald's sister in London as a child, to continue her education. At first, her life had been good, but after a while allegations started to surface that the aunt's boyfriend had been sexually abusing her. Grace's strict Catholic parents were kept fully informed of the allegations, but rather than rock the family boat, they decided instead to ignore the accusations, closing their minds and hearts to any inherent disgrace. Their daughter didn't say a word either; probably being too worried or ashamed of their reaction. Grace, or Redz as she was now known, told her parents only that she'd moved on and was living cosily with her boyfriend, Clinton Roberts... and they chose to believe her. Her slow decline into drugs and prostitution had begun.

If Gerald and Ann Flaherty had chosen not to believe the distressing allegations earlier, however, the truth was now abundantly clear, principally because the aunt had declined to attend the funeral. The truth was to be buried, alongside their daughter; even her siblings unaware of the whole truth about Redz' lifestyle. Gerald Flaherty was a broken man, believing his daughter's death to be entirely his fault for sending Grace to live with his sister in the first place.

Charlie had listened to his voice cracking with emotion, as he spoke of the young girl who had never returned. He couldn't even bring himself to repeat her nickname. Redz had no place in his memory. Grace would always be Grace and would remain pure and untarnished in his eyes.

The priest who conducted the full Catholic funeral mass concentrated only on the Grace Flaherty in the photo too, making little mention of her life and death in London. Prayers were said for the souls of both Grace and the person who had taken her life, and the family was held up for supplication. Charlie scanned the congregation as the service progressed with growing sadness. The family spread out across the front pews. As the youngest of five daughters and two sons, Redz had been the last in a long line of red-headed children. Most of the siblings were easily recognisable, their similarities astounding and their grief at losing their little sister heartbreaking. As they filed out at the end of the service, the brothers and sisters held hands, as if by standing in unity, the strength of their bond would somehow ward off evil.

Gerald Flaherty glanced towards Charlie and Hunter as he followed on behind the coffin, acknowledging their presence and nodding his thanks for attending. For Charlie, any frustration at not being with the team to assist with the preparations for hunting Dimitri was swept away on the wave of the family's gratitude. It was important that they show their solidarity of purpose and for her it was also a way of connecting the body on the slab with Grace, a living, breathing daughter and sister. Redz might have been regarded by some as human refuse on the streets of Lambeth, but here, in Ireland, she was lauded for the beautiful child she had once been.

The burial was to take place in the graveyard of a small fisherman's church overlooking Dublin Bay. The River Liffey snaked through the city and reached the sea at this point, stretching out across the sandbanks and escaping the confines of the city. The gentle breeze brought with it a crisp saltiness that masked the urban aromas. To the south, the Wicklow Mountains stood guard, further incarcerating the growing sprawl in an area, which was already too small for its population.

Charlie and Hunter followed the cortège to the nearby site. Opting for a burial rather than a cremation had helped to speed up the release of Redz' body, internment at least allowing the police the opportunity to re-examine the body, should extreme circumstances necessitate. As Charlie entered the gates to the graveyard, the noise and bustle of the city became hushed. A peace and tranquillity suffused the whole area and she was struck by its deep silence and beauty. Gulls and terns flew high above, circling the shallows, their cries wafted in with the wind, the only noise to break through the silence.

The family was already clustered around a freshly dug plot, facing towards the sea as Charlie and Hunter made their way to the rear of the group. Charlie felt as if she was intruding, but at the same time, she knew how important it was to Gerald Flaherty that they should understand the family's grief. As the pallbearers carried the light oak coffin containing Grace Flaherty's broken body towards the waiting mourners, she looked towards Redz' father. His eyes held an expression of terror, as if permanently imagining the horrors perpetrated on his youngest daughter. In the few days since hearing of his daughter's murder, his cheeks had become sunken and gaunt, his hair speckled grey and his frame frail, grief and anger having literally sucked the life from him.

Next to him stood his wife, Ann, Redz' mother, a short, ruddy-faced woman still with a full head of vivid orange hair, whose looks most of the children had inherited. She appeared the sturdier of the two, although tears constantly glistened in her red-rimmed eyes.

The priest walked in front of the coffin, reading out passages from the Bible, the crunch of the gravel getting louder as he approached. He finished his reading and as the undertakers stepped on to the grass, the squawking of the gulls faded into the distance, and the waves became still. Everything slowed as the coffin was lowered carefully down into the depths of the cold earth, the silence overwhelming. Charlie held her breath as Gerald Flaherty sunk to his knees on the damp grass, his face convulsed in torment. As the priest sprinkled holy water on to the casket and red petals rained down from the hands of those above, Redz' father threw his hands up over his face and a low guttural moan escaped from his lips.

'Please forgive me, Grace,' he cried out. 'I should never have let you go.'

Chapter 36

Little had changed for Caz. She'd thought it would, she'd even dared to hope that it might, but two days on from Dutch's death she was standing at the entrance to the alleyway where her friend Redz had met her end, exposed to the elements and subject to the same dangers as before.

She pulled her handbag closer, the security of her crack pipe and ragdoll providing her succour. Razor's disposition was the only thing to have changed. If anything, he was even meaner and moodier than usual. Every word or action annoyed him, every silence or inaction increased his rage.

Something had clearly happened, but for now, Caz had no idea what. It couldn't be the police case, surely? She'd provided his alibi and planted the seeds of doubt with Angie's information about The Punter... but that seemingly wasn't enough. Nothing she did was enough.

The night before, he'd brought her here. It was to be her new permanent patch and she was to get used to it. She was to wait at the entrance for the passing trade and entice the clients into its darkened recesses. There was no scope for arguing. It was as if he'd got the future all figured out in his brain, and this location was where their fate was destined to be played out.

Right now, he was watching her every move, waiting in the shadows in case of trouble. She wanted to believe it was because he loved her and couldn't bear for anything bad to happen to her, but realistically she knew it was because he dare not risk another dealer poaching his last girl, or a punter harming her in any way. Still, at least it was just the two of them against the world.

Monday evenings were traditionally quiet on the streets. With any luck, after one or two tricks, Razor would give her a break and they could return to the relative warmth of his flat for the night.

Her phone vibrated within the leg of her boot and she bent down, seeing Ayeisha's name appear on the screen. It was only a shitty old iPhone, reconditioned several times in the local tobacconists, but it was her lifeline to the outside world. She pulled it out and answered the call, aware of the risk she was taking. Razor didn't like her socialising when she was supposed to be at work, and he would be watching and listening. The conversation would have to be kept short.

Ayeisha spoke fast, her mood today upbeat, her shock from finding Dutch clearly forgotten now. It was the news that Caz had been awaiting, but she couldn't talk now, not within Razor's hearing. This was secret and needed to be passed on secretly.

'Come round first thing in the morning and tell me all about it,' Caz enthused, keeping her tone normal. 'It sounds exciting.'

Before she could return the phone to her boot, another number pulsed on to the screen. This one was even more risky, but just as necessary. This one could potentially earn her enough cash to pay for a reprieve from the streets, at least for a while, and the chance to show Razor there was no necessity for her to return.

She glanced around and saw Razor glaring at her from behind a gate in the shadowy recess of a nearby garden. This would have to be quick.

Pressing the button, she tried to keep her voice as natural as possible, composing a greeting to give the correct message. 'Hi, there. I'm just at work at the moment, and it's likely to be busy tomorrow,' she said evenly. 'But I'll phone you in the morning for a proper chat.'

'All right mate, I understand,' Angie answered. 'So it's going ahead tomorrow?'

'Yes.'

'Do you have what we need?'

'Yes,' Caz replied, ending the call and smiling as she replaced the phone in her boot. *Or at least I will have*, she thought.

*

Charlie punched the air as she put the phone down from Angie.

'That was Angie and it looks like tomorrow is a goer,' she shouted. 'We should get everything we need in the morning.'

Hunter gave a thumbs up and headed towards the door. 'I'll let the DCI know.'

The pair had just returned on a late flight from Ireland and the news was just what was required to perk up an otherwise flagging team. Charlie pushed the button on the kettle, searching the room for empty mugs. If anything could be gleaned from the expressions of her friends, it was that a shot of caffeine would clearly not go amiss.

Within a minute, the water was churning and the team were sipping gratefully on steaming mugs of hot, strong coffee.

Hunter turned towards Bet. 'You look as though you've all been busy while we've been gone. What do we need to know?'

Bet pulled a printout from a file on her lap and passed it around. 'Paul and I have gone back over the CCTV at the hire car company and this is the best image we could find of Dimitri, or whoever he really is.'

Charlie stared at the printout. The image they now had clearly showed a muscular, shaven-headed white man with a large scar running across his face. Whatever his true identity, he was certainly a man well used to giving and receiving violence.

'*Dimitri* had been a regular customer for six months and changed his vehicle every fortnight approximately, always using the same fake driving licence,' Bet continued. 'He was usually unaccompanied, but on one occasion, he was with another man, presumably Albertas, the security guy that Angie's CHIS mentioned.'

Charlie turned the paper over and gazed at the new image, scanning each feature to memorise the man's features. He had the appearance of a prize fighter; extremely stocky, with a pockmarked face and a nose that appeared to have been broken on more than one occasion.

'We're still waiting for the forensics to come back on the brothel, but to be honest, there're likely to be dozens of DNA profiles, so we haven't been able to make a start on trying to identify either of these two yet, but at least we have images. I've had both photos sent out to be put on the daily briefings at all surrounding stations in the Met and Angie has passed them around to other DSUs in case other CHIS know them.'

'And I've sent them to the other forces and agencies we've been liaising with on human trafficking,' Paul added. 'But so far, nothing's come back.' He pulled his own file open. 'I've checked the registration numbers for the different vehicles hired by Dimitri against the ANPR cameras for the times he had them, but there's no real pattern. The vehicles ping up a lot all over Lambeth and South London, particularly around the area of the brothel in Streatham and further south on the main road towards Norbury.'

'Any idea why he goes there?' Hunter looked quizzical.

'Not as yet.' Paul shook his head. 'The ANPR cameras only pick up the number plates, but I've checked the council CCTV cameras for the times the vehicles have tripped the ANPR and have spotted them several times. I would hazard a guess he's picking someone up. When he heads south, he's usually alone, but when he returns it appears there is a passenger, and vice versa, though the shots are far too grainy and distant to even tell whether it's a male or female.'

Charlie grimaced. 'What about the night the baby was dumped?'

Bet shook her head. 'No, nothing. That was the first thing we checked. On the date Dr Crane estimates the baby died, Dimitri had possession of the Luton van that we know about, but there's no trace of it near to Ramilles Close, where the body was found. It moves around as normal, but nothing unusual.'

'So, if it was him, he was probably on foot,' Charlie interjected. 'Ramilles Close is not that far from the brothel. It's easily within walking distance, especially if he's switched on to the possibility of cameras, as seems likely, looking at his last visit to the hire company.'

'That's what we thought.' Bet shook her head again. 'We've also tried all the local hospitals for the Luton van, in case Dimitri did drop the mother off, but managed to dupe hospital staff into believing there was nothing wrong, and therefore nothing to report to police.' Bet chewed on her bottom lip and turned towards Charlie. 'But there was no trace of the van. So we still don't know who the mother is.'

'Or where she is.' Charlie's thoughts immediately flipped to Angie's information about the forthcoming trip. 'Or why Dimitri is looking for a replacement.'

The room silenced momentarily at the comment, before Hunter stood up. 'Well, we don't know for certain that he is. Let's hope it was all planned and that they just have a bigger house and therefore more space.' He sat down again heavily.

'I did find a photograph of a girl who was with Dimitri on an earlier trip.' Paul tried to be upbeat. 'You never know. It could be our missing mother.'

He passed around a further printout and Charlie stared down into the eyes of a teenager, younger even than her own two half-sisters, Lucy and Beth.

'When I was checking the ANPR for the previously hired vehicles, there was one journey that went further afield than London and that was when it travelled to Folkestone, about three months ago. Interestingly, it was a car rather than a van,' Paul explained.

'Go on,' Charlie caught his optimism.

271

'I phoned the Border Force, as it seemed too much of a coincidence, knowing what we know about his activities. They checked the manifests for the vehicle and found it shown travelling on the Eurotunnel to Calais, with Dimitri Ivanov as the named driver. The outbound ticket was a single, not a return.'

'But he did come back in the same car, later the same day, so maybe he was trying to hide the fact it was a quick turnaround,' Bet interrupted. 'Because, on his return journey, he had a female with him.'

'So he went and collected a girl from Europe?' Charlie tilted her head.

'Well, yes, and we were really excited as we managed to get some CCTV from Folkestone which showed the car going straight into a petrol station at the port on its return.' Paul pointed to the photo that Charlie held in her hand. 'Dimitri filled the car up and then they both went into the shop. They're pretty clear images.'

Bet sighed heavily and turned to another page. 'But we still don't know their real identities. The details on Dimitri's ticket were exactly the same as he'd given at the car hire; same name, same date of birth et cetera, so we had to assume that the passport he used at the time was also probably fake.'

'And it was. We contacted the Passport Office and they sent across a scan of both Dimitri and the female's genuine passports.' Paul took over again. 'And, like we thought, Dimitri's genuine passport showed the same photo as the genuine Dimitri Ivanov on his DVLA driving licence, not the one on the fake driving licence photocopy we seized at the car hire or on the CCTV.'

'And the girl's passport is the same.' Bet shook her head disbelievingly. 'It's a very professional set-up. The fakes that are being produced are of a very high quality. They select genuine people with genuine passports and driving licences, but then make identical fake identity documents with the photos of the people they want inserted in them instead. Someone sitting on passport control at a port or in a car hire office would never spot they're fake.'

'The girl's details are genuine and match a girl living in Ukraine, but when we did some further checks at the Ukrainian Embassy, we found the same story as with Dimitri. The photo on the genuine passport is the same as the image of the girl in their records and identity papers, but it's not the same girl as in our garage photo, or probably on the passport that she used to gain entry.'

'So do you think she could be our mother?' Naz asked. She and Sabira had been sitting silently listening, having been working instead on Redz' murder case. 'Or could she just be another poor girl who has been trafficked in for Dimitri's pleasure?'

Charlie shrugged. She didn't know and she was trying desperately to be optimistic. They didn't have much, but they did have something. Dimitri would be heading to Europe the next day. He would probably have a car, rather than a van, and he would probably go from Folkestone to Calais using the Tunnel... but there was no doubt they were going to struggle.

Charlie stared back down at the photo of the girl, her youthful exuberance not yet dulled by the reality of her new life. She imagined the fear, hope and excitement the girl must have felt, travelling to a new land to make money to help her family back home, catapulted into a city, worlds apart from the humble existence she probably knew. Little would she have comprehended the nightmare in which she'd find herself, especially if she was indeed the baby's mother. The comparison between the girl's plight and Charlie's sisters' cosy existence was almost more than she could bear.

If they were to nail Dimitri, they had to catch him red-handed. Angie and her CHIS would have to come up with a mobile number, to give them the means to track him through his phone. They then would have to sort out the rest. Numerous reports and requests for authority would be required, as well as a surveillance team and backup officers to follow him to the site of the new brothel and get him stopped with the girl, in possession of the fake documents... and all without him suspecting the reason they knew his movements.

A new sense of urgency was infecting them all. Tomorrow morning could see the culmination of their enquiry and they all knew the stakes were high. Lives could literally be saved or lost. They had the manpower on standby, but what they didn't yet have was the information. They needed more and they needed it now. Failure was not an option.

Chapter 37

The Punter pulled into his allotted parking space and watched as the electric aerial retreated smoothly into the bodywork and the automatic rain sensor front wipers turned themselves off. How he loved the luxury of his new car.

It was early and there were only a handful of vehicles already in their designated positions, but he couldn't help scanning the office windows to check if he'd been seen. Carefully, he lifted his leather briefcase from the passenger seat and climbed out, noting the presence of his boss's car tucked into its usual bay.

Confirmation of his promotion was due this morning and within the next hour he expected it to be delivered. The pay rise would provide the extra funds he required to cover the monthly loan repayments for the car and keep his wife from moaning. She'd already lambasted his choice of motor. It wasn't a sensible, economical family car; it was an extravagance, but then he wasn't a sensible practical family man. Work gave him the chance to be leader of the pack and if he used a small percentage of his wages to pay for his own indulgences, then so be it. Nothing and no one would stop him.

He walked into the building, waved a greeting to the receptionist and stepped into the lift, emerging into the shiny chrome and beech interior of his company office. A couple of other early birds turned to watch as he strutted towards his workstation, his gait upright, nodding a greeting regally as he passed. Organisation was the key to his success and he always arrived ahead of time to look through his list of appointments and make any necessary adjustments. He was the employee with the largest client base and the fact that many of his work colleagues resented his success did not bother him. They were just losers.

An email flashed on to his screen as he fired up his computer. It was a request from his boss asking for a meeting upon his arrival at work. This was it then. The rumours and speculation were true. The next time he left the building it would be as the South East Regional Manager; he would be taking charge of the bottom rung of financial advisors, the position where, until now, he had been trapped. Never again would he be forced to bow to ignorant clients or take humiliating lectures from his equally stupid bosses.

He checked his tie and rose, aware of the eyes of his colleagues watching his every step, before knocking smartly on the door to his boss's office.

'Come in,' a voice called.

As he entered, his boss, Malcolm Ferrier, rose and indicated the seat across from him.

'Good morning Malcolm,' The Punter said. 'How are you?'

'I'm fine thank you. Take a seat,' his boss replied.

Malcolm Ferrier was a middle-aged, middle-income personnel manager. A shock of pure white hair gave him the air of a suave actor, but it masked a steely determination to make the right staffing judgments and not be swayed from his decision.

'Firstly, may I congratulate you on your personal achievements this year. Your work is faultless and your determination is commendable.' He paused. 'Secondly, may I also congratulate you on the financial results you have achieved for the company. Your client base has grown substantially this year, but the way you also maintain relationships with existing clients has been noted. In light of this, the management feel that you deserve a reward for all your hard work.'

It was coming now. The Punter held his breath, barely able to keep the grin of satisfaction from his lips.

'And we would like to offer you a bonus of £2,000 which will be paid directly into your account this month. Well done!' Malcolm Ferrier rose and leant forward, offering his hand to shake. The Punter stayed seated, ignoring the offer. Two thousand pounds? Was this some kind of joke? This was absolutely not what he had expected.

'But I thought I was going to be offered promotion,' he spluttered, unable to keep his composure.

'It was a hard decision, which is why we thought we should offer an incentive for the runner-up. We wanted to keep the pair of you chasing new business because that's the area where you both excel. You only narrowly missed selection.'

'So who did get it?'

'Well, after careful consideration, I decided that Kavya should be given it. She has also built up a very impressive client base, but in addition to that, she has the necessary personnel management skills to lead the workforce effectively. I told her late last night as she was leaving. It was a very close decision though.'

He knew the last sentence was supposed to assuage his disappointment but it had the opposite effect. In his head he heard the voice of reason. It should make no difference. They lived in a modern society of gender equality where both sexes had the same opportunities. Deep down in his gut though, he knew it was wrong. It couldn't be happening. Culturally it just wasn't right. Yes, Kavya was good. She was almost as good as he. But she was a woman; and an Asian woman at that. It was humiliating. Her place was at home, not in business... and certainly not beating him to promotion.

'What personnel management skills does she have, that I don't?' he asked, a little too forcefully. 'I would easily command the respect of my staff.'

'I think that's the trouble.' Malcolm Ferrier paused, fixing him with a stare. 'You would command it, but you wouldn't necessarily earn it.'

'Well, I think you're making a big mistake.' He rose to his feet, his voice icy with rage. The man was an idiot. What did he know? With that he turned and slammed out of the office, without waiting for a reply.

He ignored the half-smiles playing on the lips of his colleagues as he strode straight through the main office and he turned his head away from Kavya, anxious to avoid any false sympathy that might be forthcoming. Climbing into his car, he screeched out of the car park, accelerating through the nearby streets, now filling with early-morning rush-hour traffic and children preparing for the last few days at school before Christmas.

Kavya was a bitch! A scheming fucking bitch! All women were!

Chapter 38

The phone call when it arrived provided almost everything that Charlie could have hoped for and the relief amongst the team was tangible.

Angie relayed the approximate time Dimitri would be leaving London, confirmation that he would be driving towards Folkestone and crossing to Calais on the Eurotunnel and the fact that he would be returning later that evening with a new girl. The clincher though was Dimitri's mobile phone number.

Everything would, however, hinge on them identifying the car by the time he and the new girl returned, but with a phone number this should not be an issue. They would be able to get the phone cell-sited and follow the course of his journey. By establishing when his mobile left the country they should easily be able to see which Eurotunnel train he had used and take a look at the manifest. Any Russian-sounding names could be noted and, with the number of possible vehicles narrowed down, checks could then establish those that were hire cars, and enquiries made with individual hire companies. A quick scan of the driving licence tendered by the hirer would confirm whether it was their suspect, and the name he was using. For ease of memory they were continuing to call him Dimitri, until they established his correct identity.

The process should be relatively easy. The vehicle would then be tracked, both by cell-siting and the surveillance team, straight to the new brothel in Lewisham, the exact location of which was still unfortunately not forthcoming. Only then would they strike. They couldn't risk intercepting him earlier and losing the opportunity to free his previous captives. All in all, they had enough to at least get them started.

'That's brilliant, Angie,' Charlie enthused. 'Any chance you could keep us updated throughout the day if anything changes? We could really do with a vehicle, or the address of the brothel.'

'Mate, I'm hoping so, but don't forget the information is tight. There are very, very few people who will know these details, so don't slip up. A traffic stop, a drugs stop, anything to throw our man Dimitri off the scent of how he's landed on the police radar. Even when you have him, you'll still have to be careful; let on too much and he'll know someone's been talking.' Her voice tailed off. Angie was clearly as nervous as Charlie that the job be handled correctly.

'I understand, Angie. And don't worry. I promise to deal with the information as sensitively as if your CHIS was my own relative.'

If her suspicions were correct and Caz was indeed Angie's informant, they would really have to be extra careful. Caz was already at risk from Razor. If she had knowledge of Dimitri, either personally or through a contact, then both she and the contact would face added danger. Both were dicing with death, literally. Razor and Dimitri were brutal men who would think nothing of crushing Caz or anyone close to her if they got in their way and it was now Charlie's responsibility to make sure that did not happen.

She finished the call and closed her eyes, her imagination taking her to two crime scenes, both bloody and shocking in their own ways.

If she didn't do this right, she would risk causing another.

*

'He's on his way,' Hunter shouted out, just under an hour later. 'The phone's on the move. The first masts have it on the M20 now, about twenty miles from Folkestone. It won't be too long before it merges into the queues of traffic waiting for the shuttles.'

Having completed the paperwork to get cell-site authorisation in record time, Charlie had hoped they'd be quick enough to establish the address in Lewisham from which Dimitri was leaving. If they could place exactly where the brothel was before he got going, it would take the pressure off having to follow his every move.

She checked her watch and swore under her breath. They were already playing catch-up. Dimitri had clearly made an early start, before even their information had arrived. She glanced at her colleagues, all the team having turned up for work early. Like Charlie, the impetus to catch Dimitri and identify the baby's mother had prevented each of them getting a solid night's rest.

A surveillance team was already out on the ground, one half remaining in the vicinity of Lewisham and the other half travelling towards Folkestone. An armed Trojan unit also waited in the wings, the DCI having arranged for its presence the night previously. There was no direct intelligence that Dimitri was carrying a weapon, but they had to be prepared for every eventuality. Organised crime groups involved in human trafficking didn't mess about.

Charlie, Paul, Naz, Sabira and a couple of other detectives were to form an arrest squad, split between two vehicles, taking their orders directly from Hunter. Initially assisting with enquiries in the office, they would be on hand to move out and make the arrests once the location of the brothel was identified, unless it transpired that Dimitri was armed, in which case the Trojan unit would clear the way first.

Bet, as usual, was to be in the communications cell. Everyone knew she had the safest pair of hands when it came to liaising with each unit and keeping everyone abreast of the situation. She was also to have a direct link with a member of the Border Force; there was no time to be wasted in identifying the car in which their suspect would return with his newest victim.

Charlie checked the calendar on her desk, suddenly feeling uneasy. It was 19th December and with less than a week until Christmas Day the whole of Folkestone was likely to be rammed, with hundreds of day trippers heading for the Christmas markets.

There was an awful lot that could still go wrong.

*

Dimitri pulled into the Eurotunnel terminal at Folkestone and parked the car up. He had an hour and a half to wait until his train was due to leave and with the queues long and tedious he knew there would be no chance of jumping on an earlier one.

'Let's go and find a restaurant,' he said. 'We'll have something to eat before I go.'

'Please let me come with you,' the girl said. 'I promise to help and it would be fun.'

Dimitri clenched his teeth. Half an hour into the journey he'd known it had been a mistake to bring the girl. She was young and annoying and was spoiling his anticipation of the new foreign woman he would soon be collecting. But it had to be done. The care-home girl was just as crucial to his plans as the Slovakian and she was on the brink of offering her own nubile body to fill the final space.

He felt the girl's hand on his knee, her fingers lightly caressing his leg, each touch spidery and unsure. He placed his hand over hers, stopping the movement, even though her touch was having an effect. She had to really want to be his, to yearn to do as he demanded, to beg for his attention. Unlike his other workers from foreign lands, this girl would have to remain living at her present address. He couldn't risk the authorities being alerted to her new circumstances. She would have to come to him willingly and keep her mouth shut, but it wouldn't be long before he could start her training in earnest, and he was looking forward to doing just that.

'I'd love to be able to take you with me, my darling, but you know I can't. You would need a passport and you don't have one. And I need you to look after the car and everything in it.'

He thought about the knife and the small paper bag containing several vials of GHB hidden in the glove compartment; the drugs to keep the Slovakian girl quiet if she quarrelled and the knife to reinforce his threat. He would have preferred to have the knife with him, being more secure when armed, but he didn't envisage any problems and besides, the sortie into France would only take an hour at most.

The girl was pouting sulkily. 'Why do you want another girl, when you could have me?'

He lifted her hand from his leg and kissed it, letting his lips linger against her skin. She smelt good. 'It is just business. The girl I am collecting will go straight to work for me. She is ready.' He slid one of her fingers into his mouth and sucked on it gently. 'You know I want you, but you are still young and inexperienced.'

'But you could teach me.' 'And I will, but at the moment I am busy. I want the chance to spend more time with you, but because of the move I have none. That is why I have brought you along today, to keep me company and so that I can be with you.' He smiled and let her hand drop, kissing his own fingers and blowing the ends toward her. 'So let's go and find a nice restaurant and I will treat you to whatever your heart desires.'

The girl perked up at the idea, although her expression remained morose. Dimitri switched the engine off and watched as the girl gathered her belongings together. She was easily bought. A ride in an exquisitely expensive car, a meal of her choice, a few items from the duty-free shop to keep her occupied while he was gone was all it took. He turned away from her knowing that she was his. In a couple more days he would make her his own.

*

'The phone signal has disappeared. He must have boarded the shuttle.' Hunter passed on what the lab technicians were telling him.'

'So, we have to assume that he is probably on the 13.50 or possibly the 14.16 departure.' Charlie had the timetable set out on the screen in front of her. 'I'll get Bet to phone her Ports contact and arrange for the passenger lists for both shuttle services.'

The wait was excruciating, especially knowing the journey to Calais took only thirty-five minutes. If Dimitri was on the 13.50 and his contact was ready and waiting in the terminal, he could potentially be returning with his new girl on the 14.50 and arriving back at Folkestone at 15.25. They might have less than an hour and a half. They had to hope that he would take longer, but they were still painfully aware they had no time to lose.

Nearly thirty minutes had already passed when the manifests eventually came through and the two lists seemed endless. Each passenger shuttle had the capacity to hold one hundred and twenty cars and twelve coaches and each one of these vehicles could potentially be carrying a full load. They had hundreds of names to look through. At this point they couldn't even be sure Dimitri was in a car. It was a possibility he was travelling across on foot and the car was parked up.

Charlie could feel the tension intensifying in the office as the list churned out of the printer. It had all seemed so simple until now. She dialled Angie's number again.

'Any updates?' she asked. 'We could really do with finding out what car Dimitri is driving, and whether he's definitely taken it across to France. The passenger lists are huge and we can't afford to miss him coming back.'

'I'll see what I can do mate, and get back to you.'

'Thanks, Angie.' She picked up the lists and divided them up, staring down at the reams of names on the printout. 'You might just be the person to save the day.'

Nothing stood out on the two lists. Charlie was working on the 13.50 time slot with Paul, while Naz and Sabira worked on the 14.16. Women's names were crossed through and the men's names analysed, but many were foreign-sounding and the team weren't even sure they knew from which nationality they derived. A third list containing any possible matches and the vehicles linked to them was being compiled and checks were then being completed on each number plate to try to establish which were on hire. So far there was at least eighteen, all of which were registered only to the head offices of each hire company. When they tried to contact the various head offices, many of the staff members with whom they spoke were not exactly helpful, if not downright obstructive, in revealing which local office loaned out the cars.

Time was slipping away and Charlie was at boiling point. They could not lose Dimitri, not now they were so close.

*

Dimitri stepped off the 14.50 shuttle in Calais and took a deep breath. The air always seemed different in France for some reason, even though it was just as full with the stench of diesel fumes as on the English side. Maybe it was because France was part of the same landmass as Russia, and Russia was home. Perhaps just having this connection was all it took to make it feel familiar.

He pulled his phone from his pocket and switched it back on, waiting for the new French network provider to take over the service. He'd switched it off while in the restaurant with the girl. There were no updates from his contact and the girl was being difficult, asking why he only had a cheap phone and wanting to use it to play 'Snake' while he was gone. Her whining had irritated him. She already had her own phone and use of the sound system in his car, his decision to leave the vehicle at Folkestone on this occasion being a good choice. The shuttles were so busy at this time of the year and it only took one breakdown to slow his progress, however quick the port authorities were at dragging the faulty cars to one side.

No, today his trip was to be short. He had only to collect the Slovakian girl from the usual cafe in the terminal at Calais and return. Her belongings were apparently sparse, fitting comfortably into two small bags, the promise of being kitted out with uniform and clothes by her new employer, allowing her to keep her own belongings to a minimum. He smiled as a seagull screeched overhead, swooping low to cast its beady eye across the arrivals. The *uniform* she would be required to wear would not be of the sort she would be expecting, but he would enjoy seeing her reaction when produced.

He checked his watch and started to make his way slowly towards the cafe. There was half an hour to kill before he would meet the girl, but he always liked to secrete himself at the rear of the seating area and try to guess the correct one. He was normally right. They were the young, vulnerable ones with fresh faces, ruddy cheeks, eyes alight with hope and adolescent bodies still plump and rounded.

He ordered himself an espresso and sat down to wait. At ten minutes to four a text message pinged into his phone, informing him that his contact was on time and asking for confirmation that he was there. He answered the query and then scanned the car park, watching as a black Lada Largus Cross 4 x 4 pulled into the entrance. He recognised the girl immediately as she stepped down from the passenger seat and pulled her bags close. She had all the virginal qualities he had come to expect and he would enjoy teaching her what was required. At 16.05 he took her bags and held out his hand, taking her small pale fingers in his.

'Hello,' he said, speaking slowly so that she understood. 'You must be Michaela? My name is

Dimitri. I am your new employer and I will look after you.' She smiled up at him coyly, before dipping her head to him in respect.

The next shuttle was due to leave at 16.20 and they would be on it.

*

'The phone's on the move again, and it's back in England.' Hunter shouted the update across to the team.

'Dammit,' Charlie checked her watch. It was only just gone 5 p.m. and as yet they hadn't been able to identify the car Dimitri and his new girl were in. Now it seemed he was already on his way. The surveillance team and armed Trojan units would be left idle, waiting for their orders and they would be no nearer to catching Dimitri red-handed or locating the brothel.

'We could get the passenger lists for the last few inward-bound shuttles and see if we can find any names that reappear from the earlier outward-bound?' Paul frowned.

'That's assuming he took his car to France,' Charlie closed her eyes. 'Besides, it'll take too long to manually check all the names on each list. We only have paper printouts don't forget. He'll be home by the time we find a match.'

'We still have the cell siting.' The vein on Hunter's forehead was prominent. 'Carry on working on the enquiries we have on the possible hire cars and in the meantime I'll get the Folkestone surveillance team back up here. Maybe if we can track which roads he's using when his phone pings up at each mast, we can get both teams plotted up at junctions into Lewisham and they might just be able to spot him.'

Charlie opened her eyes again and stared around at the blank faces of her friends. They all knew that the chances of the surveillance teams being able to peer into every car moving past them on a busy main road into London, and recognise a total stranger was negligible and cell siting always ran behind time. A phone had to pass a mast before a signal was read and by that time whatever vehicle the phone was in would again be one step ahead. Dimitri and his precious female cargo could be hidden away in the brothel and their chance to prove his full culpability would be gone.

Charlie suddenly felt the weight of the investigation on her shoulders. It had been her idea to go to the DSU. Her initial hunch had proved right, but now the operation seemed doomed to failure. Even with the teams' joint efforts, they had failed to identify a vehicle. There was only one person who could provide the information they so desperately needed.

Charlie picked up her phone and tapped in Angie's number again, suddenly anxious. Had something happened to prevent Angie's CHIS passing on the necessary information. Perhaps providing this final piece of the jigsaw had been one risk too many.

Chapter 39

Caz shifted sleepily on the settee and tried to open her eyes, but they remained firmly glued shut. She forced a dry tongue from her mouth in a vain attempt to lick moisture back into her chafed lips, but all she could feel was the skin cracking painfully at each movement. The ringtone of her phone sounded somewhere in the background, its noise becoming louder and more insistent as she concentrated.

She pulled herself upright and listened for its location. All her limbs ached and she was aware of a dull pain at the base of her spine, where her final punter from the previous evening had shoved her hard against a wall. Razor had put an end to his violence swiftly, but she was still smarting at having been forced out on to the street at all. There was no need.

When Ayeisha had finally left her that morning after excitedly recounting her likely activities for the day, Caz had fulfilled her responsibility to Angie. The information had been passed across and was Angie's to do with as she wanted. It was time to allow her body to finally rest and if she needed half a bottle of Smirnoff to help her sleep, well, so be it.

The phone stopped ringing but restarted almost immediately, the sound vibrating out from under a cushion. Somebody was clearly keen to speak. Locating the handset, she stared at the screen, noting the numerous missed calls from both Angie and Ayeisha. Shit! Could she have slept through the chance to earn more cash legitimately? Angie's name was flashing again now. Her handler would not be happy.

'Where have you been, mate?' Angie's voice was clipped. 'I've been trying to get hold of you for hours.'

'I'm sorry, Angie,' Caz stammered, her head clearing at the rebuke. 'I 'ad an awful night last night an' crashed out after we spoke this mornin'. I gave you all I 'ad and didn't think you'd need nothin' more.'

Angie's voice softened. 'Sorry to hear that, mate. I hope you're all right?' She didn't wait for an answer. 'What you gave us earlier was great, but we really need Dimitri's vehicle. Any chance you can get it?'

Caz concentrated, trying to recall her friend's earlier conversation. Ayeisha had said she'd pop round when she got back and she wasn't there yet, which meant she must still be with Dimitri. 'I dunno,' she said. 'It's too risky.'

She heard the sharp intake of breath and could almost sense Angie's disappointment down the line. The vision of a large wad of cash slipped into her mind, before, note by note, it started to disappear... along with her chance of a life off the streets with Razor, at least for a short while. She glanced down at her phone, desperately trying to think of an excuse to phone her friend. Along with the missed calls from Ayeisha were texts and photo images.

'Hang on, Angie,' she almost shouted, putting the call on to speaker. 'I might 'ave something.'

Quickly she read through the texts. Ayeisha was bored. She was on her own. Dimitri had left her in his car. She was pissed off. A number of photos downloaded. They were all of Ayeisha, selfies of her friend pouting and posing, reclining against cream leather upholstery, lying across the back seat of an expensive-looking car, seated in front of an open window with a sign saying *Welcome to Folkestone* clear against a cloudy backdrop. The last two photos were taken outside in the open air. The first showed Ayeisha lying across the bonnet of a sleek silver Mercedes, clearly the vehicle in which she was travelling. Caz held her breath as she opened the last image.

'Bingo,' she screamed in delight, as a selfie of her friend crouching down at the front of the same silver car appeared on the screen, with lips pouting and one finger pointing at the registration plate of the brand new Mercedes. 'You got a pen and paper, Angie?'

*

Dimitri pulled up around the corner from the care home and stalked across to the passenger side. He pulled the door open and indicated for the girl to get out. Having her with him had not gone to plan. Rather than being friendly towards his Slovakian guest, she had remained sulky and steadfastly refused to swap places with her or join her in the rear to make her feel welcome. The return journey had therefore lapsed into long periods of awkward silence. In one respect this was good as it signalled the girl's growing affection for him and her jealousy at the prospect of his interest in another. On the other hand, it also pointed to prospective difficulties; jealousy was not an emotion that was to be encouraged. It made a house full of females far more difficult to manage.

'Why can't I come back with you?' the girl's tone was petulant, even though she did at least do as bid and climb out. He swallowed his irritation at her neediness. She would still be a welcome addition to his group in due course, but would clearly need to be handled firmly.

'I've told you.' He tried to keep his tone soothing. 'Michaela is experienced. She will fit in straight away.'

'She doesn't look experienced to me. She looks more like a child from the countryside, who knows nothing.' The girl was right. Michaela was an innocent and it would make his job moulding her that much more pleasurable; in fact, just the thought of what he would shortly be doing was already making him light-headed.

'I want to give you more of my time,' he reverted to his previous platitudes. 'I will come for you in a couple of days and then I will be all yours.' He cupped her face between his hands and leant forward to kiss her.

'But I can't wait that long,' the girl's voice was whiny now.

'Well you'll just have to,' he snapped, before quickly calming. 'But I promise I'll come for you soon.' He closed the passenger door and started to walk back round to the driver's side, glad to have a few days' peace away from her demands.

'You might want this?'

He turned at the tone of her statement and saw she hadn't moved. In her hand, she held his knife. She pressed the catch on the handle and the blade shot out. His temper flared at the sight. How dare she delve around in his property! He took a few steps towards her, his arm raised in anger. She flinched and ducked away, her expression fearful, allowing the knife to clatter to the ground. The noise brought him back to his senses. The Slovakian girl could be watching and there was an old man shuffling along the pavement opposite who might also report the disturbance. Quickly, he placed his body between the girl's outstretched hand and the car, shielding any view of the weapon from Michaela, before bending down to pick it up. For a few seconds he held the knife towards the girl, its blade still open, before slowly folding it away. She was quiet now, all hostility and fight having subsided.

He turned away and opened the door, tucking the knife back in the glove compartment behind the paper bag of GHB. At least she hadn't touched the drugs.

The girl was still standing to the side of the car. He pushed the door closed and leant towards her.

'Why did you try to steal my knife?' he whispered, knowing his question would prompt her to put her defences up.

'I wasn't going to steal it,' the girl looked panicked. 'I was just going to ask why you had it.' She cast her eyes down at her feet. 'I'm sorry.'

He stared at her for what seemed like ages, until she finally raised her head, watching sullenly as he ushered Michaela into the front seat.

'No matter,' he said, smiling casually. 'I will come for you in a few days.'

*

'We have eyeball on the vehicle, heading north on Streatham High Road. Two occupants, believed to be a male driving and a female front-seat passenger. Standby for confirmation the driver is our target.'

The team stood as one, open-mouthed, hardly daring to breathe. You could hear a pin drop in the office. Cell siting had placed Dimitri heading towards the same area of Norbury that he had come and gone from on previous occasions. Although the reasons for his visits to that area were unknown, Hunter had taken the calculated decision that at some point he would then travel towards Lewisham and the new brothel. The surveillance teams were therefore plotted up on the main road between Norbury and Lewisham. They just had to hope he hadn't dumped anything off that would be of value to the investigation. It was the best they could do.

'Positive ID on male known as Dimitri,' a second voice said across the radio.

'All received,' Hunter clapped his hand over the radio handset as Charlie and the rest of the team let out a loud cheer. The relief was palpable. 'Right let's go,' he shouted across to her. 'We haven't got time to relax just yet. There's work to be done.'

Within minutes they were on their way, Charlie driving an unmarked car with Hunter and Paul, closely followed by Naz driving a second, crewed by Sabira and the two detectives from earlier. The armed Trojan team were to follow on but remain nearby as backup, no information having being received that Dimitri was actually armed. After hours of frustration, they were at last out of the office and on the right track.

The surveillance teams were in full flow, their directions clear and fluid.

The Mercedes was easy to track. It stood out in the queues of commercial vehicles, family cars and hatchbacks, its sleek silver livery reflecting the twinkling coloured lights and flashing Christmas displays as it passed through each high street. The traffic moved slowly, but with rush hour now almost over, the queues were dwindling and the previously static lines of vehicles were gradually dispersing. Charlie was easily able to move across South London with blue lights flashing and sirens wailing to skirt around to Lewisham, where Dimitri was clearly heading. As Charlie neared the area, she switched off the twos and blues and slowed, taking streets that ran parallel to the Mercedes, her mind instead concentrating on how to actually play the stop. They couldn't afford to let Dimitri realise they already knew the trade in which he was involved and that the documents he carried would inevitably be forged. They had to play it cool. She didn't know how close Angie's CHIS was to Dimitri and, if it was Caz, her life could literally depend on their actions.

'Remember, we're dealing with this as a traffic stop,' she repeated the team's plan. 'And we have to stick to that story, even if it gets difficult.'

'Target vehicle now passing Lewisham Hospital, still on A21. Slowing down now and indicating left, left, left into Ladywell Road.' There was a slight pause on the radio before it sparked up again. 'Now right, right into Algernon Road.'

'I've got it on the map,' Paul confirmed. 'Algernon Road doesn't really lead anywhere, except to a few residential streets so he must be getting close to his destination.'

Charlie could feel her pulse quickening. They would be waiting just around the corner for the go-ahead.

'Turning right, right, into Marsella Road and slowing.'

Hunter put the radio to his mouth. 'All units, I repeat my previous instructions. Stay close, but do not attempt to stop this car or any of the occupants until we can identify the actual venue where he's heading.'

They just had to hope that this time their luck would hold.

Chapter 40

'Go, Go, Go.' The voice of the surveillance officer was clear. 'Target male parked up outside number thirty-two and at the front door to the building now.'

Hunter indicated with his hand for Charlie to move forward. Initially it would only be them. Naz and her crew were waiting around the corner, as were the armed Trojan units, and further local units could be summoned if necessary. Who knew what they might face inside the building.

Charlie drove slowly, not wanting to spook Dimitri with screeching tyres or excessive speed. This was just a routine stop. As she pulled level to the Mercedes, she saw two large men stepping out from the front of number thirty-two towards the roadway. There was no mistaking the figures of Dimitri and his minder Albertas, or whoever they actually were from the CCTV at the hire company. The two men hesitated as Charlie and her colleagues climbed out of their car, clearly recognising them as police, even though none wore uniforms. A word was said between them and Albertas backed away into the house, shutting the door firmly.

Dimitri continued to walk towards them, his manner calm.

'Do you realise you're parked on double yellow lines?' Charlie asked, holding out her warrant card towards the man and indicating parallel yellow stripes that were fortuitously running alongside the kerb. She could hear Hunter whispering orders to Naz for them to deploy on foot and keep watch on the house. Subconsciously, her hand moved to check her ASP and CS spray were safely stowed within her jacket. The situation bristled with danger and having to act casually was against everything her head and nerves were communicating.

'I'm sorry, officer. I'll only be here a few minutes. I'm just dropping off a friend.' He pointed towards a young girl sat in the passenger seat of the car. The girl made no move to get out.

'Is this your vehicle?' Charlie engaged him.

'Well, it's a hire car, if that's what you mean, officer?' Dimitri replied, smiling confidently. 'I hired it a day or so ago. I have all the documents if you need to check.'

He reached into his inside jacket pocket and carefully pulled out a wallet containing a wad of documents, leafing through them until he found the hire agreement. He passed it across and Charlie stared down at the name Leo Markin, momentarily wondering if she could have passed over it on the list of passengers. It didn't sound that Russian.

'Is this you?' she pointed at the words. 'Leo Markin?'

Dimitri was nodding his head. 'Yes, ma'am, that's me. I have my driving licence if you wish to see it.' He rooted through the wallet again and passed across a driving licence ID card. Charlie stared down at it in the gloom. It was a UK licence with the name Leo Markin and a photo of the same man as was standing in front of her. A check would no doubt reveal, just as his last licence had, that there was a genuine male named Leo Markin who had a British licence. It wouldn't be Dimitri though, or whoever the hell this man in front of her was. Lifting it up towards the light, she could see a hologram across the front of the photo. It was an excellent forgery and she knew he would suspect something was up if she questioned its validity. He'd probably been stopped many times before with similar licences and got away with it.

She needed to come up with something quickly, because at the moment all his documents were in order and apart from the fact that he had parked on yellow lines there was nothing that she could use to keep him or arrest him that wouldn't risk immediately giving the game away.

'I'll just do a few checks,' she said, desperate to buy time. She'd made a promise to Angie.

She ran the driving licence through the computer and it was as she thought. It would take hours to circumnavigate Data Protection and get a photo of the real Leo Markin sent through from the DVLA. She checked on the name he had given and there was no trace of any previous convictions, so there was no existing custody photo that he could be compared against.

Dimitri stood patiently to one side, his expression appearing almost cocky.

Paul sidled over from where he had been standing next to the girl, still seated in the car. She was claiming to speak no English, so there was nothing he could suggest from any conversation that would help, but Charlie couldn't allow Dimitri to think he had the upper hand.

'I'll just run a check on the car,' she said, reading out the registration number over her radio. An initial check when Angie had first phoned it in had revealed it as correctly registered to a nearby hire car company, with nothing further of note, but it would give her a further few seconds of precious thinking time. At the moment she had three options. Arrest him on suspicion of running a brothel and for his possible involvement in the death of the baby, but to do so would ri compromising the safety of their informant. Make up fictitious reason to arrest him, which would no do later come out in disclosure and might then potentially identify their informant, as well as leadi a complaint for abuse of process.

Or let him go... and that was unthinkable.

'Are you free to speak?' The question came back across the radio.

Charlie perked up. The control room only usually asked this if they had sensitive information that a police officer might not want a suspect to hear. But then there had been nothing of note earlier. She nodded to Paul and stepped away, giving the go-ahead.

'Your vehicle should be a silver Mercedes C class saloon registered to a hire company in Forest Hill. It was involved in a disturbance with a female half an hour ago in the Norbury area,' a voice said over the radio. 'Information from a passer-by states that the male driver ʾas seen to threaten a female with a knife.'

*

oticed the body language of the woman officer
he spoke into the radio. It was subtle, but he
ꞯ these types of things. Her stance was
her expression more assured as she

ꞵ
a
ubt
still
ng to

ᴵ information that the male driver of
in a disturbance a short time ago in
ꞏfe was seen.'
hell could she know this? He
ꞓmembering the old man
It must have been him,
ꞛsn't wanted, but it was

all the girl's fault. If she hadn't touched his belongings he would be on his way. The stupid little cow had caused all this. His mind was racing fast. He knew what would happen now.

'My name's DC Charlie Stafford,' the officer said, taking a step towards him. 'And I'm going to search you and your car for weapons.' She took hold of his arm.

Suddenly he knew what he had to do. He jerked it from her grasp. There was no way this bitch was going to search him. She lunged towards him again, grabbing his sleeve, and again he pulled away, struggling violently to escape. Three bodies flew against him, pushing him back against the bonnet of the car. He tossed and turned, freeing an arm and pushing his body on to one side. He could see Michaela's face tear-stained and petrified, staring out from the interior of the car. As he was twisted round and pushed face down against the Mercedes' smart silver bonnet, his eyes found hers and he held them, not breaking the connection until he was hauled to his feet. Through the melee, his warning was delivered plain and unambiguous. It was the same message he gave to all his girls: *Open your mouth just one single time and your family will die.*

*

Charlie stepped to one side as a van screeched to a halt and a couple of uniformed officers jumped out, taking control of Dimitri. Hunter, having summoned extra help, was now barking commands down the radio, ensuring Naz had the house surrounded and secure and requesting Sabira join them to speak to the girl. Dimitri was handcuffed and detained for the purposes of a search. Quite clearly he had something to hide – or at least she hoped he did. They still needed an obvious substantive offence to secure his arrest and allow them access to the house. She let Paul do the honours, watching as he went through each pocket thoroughly, patting him down as much as he could to check for hidden items.

The man had regained his composure now, looking almost smug as each pocket was cleared.

'Who was the man you were with just now?' Charlie asked.

'He is my friend. I run errands for him.'

'He's not a very good friend if he's not come back out to check you're all right.'

'Why would he come out? He can see you are police and he doesn't like police.' His eyes narrowed. 'Nobody likes police.'

'Only if they have something to hide.' She'd had enough of Dimitri's taunts. Leaving the uniformed officers to hold him, she and Paul moved across to the Mercedes. The young girl was with Sabira now, seated comfortably in the rear of their police car whilst her colleague tried to persuade the girl to talk. So far, she

310

had said nothing, other than to give her name as Michaela and the fact she was from Slovakia.

The interior of the hire car smelt new and, apart from two small bags stowed in the boot, looked to have little in it. Charlie took the passenger side whilst Paul searched the driver's. The first thing she saw when she opened the glove compartment was a brown paper bag. She opened it and immediately recognised the clear fluid contained in six vials as illegal drugs, almost certainly GHB. She'd come across similar on a few occasions recently. Behind the paper bag was a flick knife. Relief flooded through her as she reached in and carefully placed the weapon straight into an exhibit tube. The two items were all she could have hoped for.

Dimitri was watching as she walked across to him with the exhibits. It didn't seem to worry him as she told him he was under arrest for possession of the knife and possession of the drugs with intent to supply. He shrugged as she said the words of the caution.

'The knife is not mine,' he said, pointing towards the weapon tube she was holding. 'It belongs to a girl I was trying to help. I took it off her for her own safety and was going to dispose of it.' He nodded towards the paper bag. 'And I know nothing about whatever is in there. I have never seen it before. It must also belong to the girl who had the knife.' He paused and smiled nastily towards where the Slovakian girl sat. 'Or maybe it is hers. Perhaps she put it there while you were all concentrating on me.'

Chapter 41

The front door was sturdier than it looked and Albertas was refusing to open it without seeing a warrant. Charlie had attempted to persuade him through the letter box that they didn't require one, but with no movement after the first explanation, her patience had run out. Dimitri had been seen coming from the address and the drugs offence for which he'd been arrested gave them the power to enter without one. Finding the GHB had been the perfect result.

Several hefty thumps with the enforcer later revealed the reason, as the multi-lock door and a reinforced bar padlocked on to the doorframe eventually gave way. They entered swiftly, spreading out through the whole building until every room had a police officer standing guard. Albertas was detained, handcuffs preventing his movement, but they all knew the possibility of finding any more drugs was remote. He had been in the house far too long to imagine any illegal substances would not already have been flushed down the toilet. But it didn't matter. It wasn't drugs they were looking for. Charlie's main concern was tracking down the mother of the dead baby and it was on this job she now concentrated.

The house was a Victorian terraced town house spread across three levels, with high ceilings and ornate coving. On entering the ground floor, a stairway lay straight ahead leading up to the first floor. Several doors off the hallway opened through to a kitchen, a utility area and an integral garage. This was evidently where both Albertas and Dimitri slept as the space had been converted into a twin-bedded room, with two single beds and a range of male toiletries and clothing on display.

Climbing the stairs, Charlie could see that the whole first floor was one large open-plan living space with a central candelabrum, several wall lamps and an old cast-iron fireplace. This space had been split into three, by the use of wooden partitions, each area having little more than a small double bed positioned in the centre and a chest of drawers. The whole room was dimly lit, but each space was decorated with a cream rug, lush bedding and fragranced candles. Pictures of nudes dotted the walls and an array of oils and sex toys were arranged on the top of the drawers. She had to admit that the attention to detail was remarkable for the time they'd had to relocate. The operation must have been very well organised.

In the last area she walked through sat three scantily-clad women, clinging to one another in silence, placed together by their police guards in a vain attempt to dispel their fear.

She nodded towards where they sat. 'Don't be frightened,' she spoke gently. 'We won't hurt you. We're here to help.'

The girls said nothing, but their grips on each other loosened slightly.

'I'll be back in a minute,' she said, climbing the stairs to the second and final floor. This floor was divided into three purpose-built bedrooms and a family-sized bathroom. A fourth girl sat in one of the rooms, guarded by a police officer, but the other two were empty, one clearly having been made ready for Michaela. It was warm and inviting, and it too had a candle flickering in one corner.

The girl got to her feet as Charlie read the name 'Hanna' out loud from the officer's notes. She stood with one hand on her hip and an expression that seemed both feisty and defeated at the same time.

'Why are you here?' she asked hesitantly.

Charlie stuck to the safe reply. 'Because we stopped a man outside and he had a knife and drugs on him. We're here to search for more drugs.'

'Is that *all* you're here for?' The girl's stare was so intense that Charlie felt instantly uncomfortable. 'Is the man outside called Dimitri?'

Without thinking Charlie nodded, before hastily correcting herself. 'He's given the name Leo. He's been arrested.'

The girl flinched at her nod, turning to gaze instead out the window. 'So what's going to happen to us?'

'Hanna,' she tried to appeal to the girl directly, 'we can see what this house is being used for. We're going to take you to a place where you can talk to us safely.'

The girl spun round, her eyebrows pinched together, the same angry, defeated look in her eyes. 'You do not understand,' she spat. 'If we talk to you, we and our families will never be safe.'

*

It was almost 2 a.m. when Charlie finally pushed through the revolving doors of Lambeth HQ into the night. The team had been released to rest, but in a few short hours they would begin the task of interviewing each young woman from the brothel, all of whom had been found safe accommodation for the night. Although the day had ended well, there was so much more to be done. Neither case, against Dimitri or Razor, was clear-cut; both suspects having far too much wriggle room. Moreover, she couldn't get Hanna's words out of her head. Caz too, although professing her love for Razor, had spoken, just a few days before, of being safe only if she and Dutch returned to his flat and followed his commands. It was clear that both girls were petrified of the men close to them, possibly too frightened even to speak the truth. The success or failure of both investigations would be dependent on getting the correct testimony from highly vulnerable witnesses.

Charlie looked across the road and saw Ben waiting under his usual lamp post with Casper. One phone call, half an hour earlier, had ensured his arrival. She walked across to join them, slipping her arm through his and returning Casper's eager greeting with a gentle slap on his hindquarters. Something was pulling her in the opposite direction from her home, instead taking her towards the river. Ben fell into step with her and within a few minutes she was standing on the walkway next to the Thames. The tide was out and the muddy shoreline, peppered with stones and discarded plastic, stretched out at the foot of a set of damp, slippery steps. Gingerly she released her grip on Ben's arm, indicating for him to wait, and descended on to the riverbank, her feet sinking into the silt.

As she walked slowly towards the water, her head started to spin at the sight of the black eddies, swirling and twisting, sucking everything down below the surface. She was immediately catapulted through time, back to her childhood, with her brother Jamie struggling to breathe as he thrashed impotently at the stormy sea, each wave dragging him downwards to his watery grave. She remembered again his fingers clawing at the seawater, and the desperation in his eyes as he sunk into the void. She remembered too her own desperation at being unable to save him. She forced herself to stare into the water, for once letting the memory of her brother's death have free rein and allowing her whole body to fill with fear. She needed to know again what real debilitating terror felt like.

For a few seconds she froze, before she threw her hand over her mouth to prevent a scream escaping, staggering slightly backwards until a pair of strong hands took hold of her. Ben's touch alone had the power to banish her alarm and make her feel safe. She stood still allowing his strength to flow into her bones, knowing now what had to be done. Somehow she had to demonstrate to Caz, Hanna and the other girls from the brothel that she too was a safe pair of hands in which to trust. Somehow she had to give them the strength to take control. It was the only way she could get the men who had terrorised them for so long, locked away for life. It was the only way that they would ever be free.

Chapter 42

'Any joy?' Charlie emerged from the lounge at The Haven, holding the phone tightly to her ear. Each of the girls from the brothel had been taken to a specialist examination suite, examined by a doctor and each had voluntarily given their fingerprints and a DNA sample for elimination against those found at the crime scenes. Now they were at separate Haven sites around London being sensitively debriefed about their situations. It was almost midday, but so far they'd made little or no progress. Leaving Hanna with a colleague and an interpreter, she pushed through the door of the sanctuary and out into a flurry of snow.

'No, nothing,' Naz's voice came on the line. 'Same with Sab. They're all too terrified to speak out.'

Charlie closed her eyes. This was not at all what she wanted to hear.

'Keep trying,' was all she could say, ending the call and immediately dialling Paul's number.

'How's it going your end?' The team had split: Hunter and Paul in charge of interviews with Dimitri and Albertas, while she, Naz and Sabira, being experienced at dealing with domestic crime and victims of sexual offences, were speaking with Hanna, Michaela and the other girls rescued from the brothel. So far though not an ill word had been voiced against the two men, never mind written down in a statement.

'Albertas is making no comment, but Dimitri is at least talking,' Paul responded. 'But so far he's coming up with a good defence.'

'What's he saying?' The team were continuing to refer to their man as Dimitri, even though his fingerprints and DNA had now positively identified him as a male of Russian origin called Viktor Egorov. As well as the names Dimitri Ivanov and Leo Markin, Egorov had at least nine other aliases known to police forces across Europe. He had entered the UK illegally, using one of his pseudonyms, and disappeared into the murky criminal underworld, operating the black economy and vice trade in the backstreets of London. Never having been arrested in the UK until now, he had remained unknown to police in England, but a trawl through Interpol records had shown him to be a well-known player in a number of foreign OCNs or organised crime networks.

'He knows his fingerprints and DNA will be found at both brothels, so he's saying that he has frequented both locations regularly as a client. He claims to be allowed to live there in return for running errands for some *acquaintances*.' Paul emphasised the word. 'He can't, or won't, name these people or say anything further about checked on the name he had given and there was no trace of any previous convictions, so there was no existing custody photo that he could be compared against.

Dimitri stood patiently to one side, his expression appearing almost cocky.

Paul sidled over from where he had been standing next to the girl, still seated in the car. She was claiming to speak no English, so there was nothing he could suggest from any conversation that would help, but Charlie couldn't allow Dimitri to think he had the upper hand.

'I'll just run a check on the car,' she said, reading out the registration number over her radio. An initial check when Angie had first phoned it in had revealed it as correctly registered to a nearby hire car company, with nothing further of note, but it would give her a further few seconds of precious thinking time. At the moment she had three options. Arrest him on suspicion of running a brothel and for his possible involvement in the death of the baby, but to do so would risk compromising the safety of their informant. Make up a fictitious reason to arrest him, which would no doubt later come out in disclosure and might then still potentially identify their informant, as well as leading to a complaint for abuse of process.

Or let him go… and that was unthinkable.

'Are you free to speak?' The question came back across the radio.

Charlie perked up. The control room only usually asked this if they had sensitive information that a police officer might not want a suspect to hear. But then there had been nothing of note earlier. She nodded to Paul and stepped away, giving the go-ahead.

'Your vehicle should be a silver Mercedes C class saloon registered to a hire company in Forest Hill. It was involved in a disturbance with a female half an hour ago in the Norbury area,' a voice said over the radio. 'Information from a passer-by states that the male driver was seen to threaten a female with a knife.'

*

Dimitri noticed the body language of the woman officer change as she spoke into the radio. It was subtle, but he picked up on these types of things. Her stance was straighter and her expression more assured as she stepped closer.

'I've just received information that the male driver of this car was involved in a disturbance a short time ago in the Norbury area. A knife was seen.'

He bristled. How the hell could she know this? He thought back quickly, remembering the old man shuffling along the street. It must have been him, sticking his nose in where it wasn't wanted, but it was them, other than to assert he is frightened of them as they sometimes turn up armed with firearms and so he doesn't ask questions. He accepts that the documents found in his possession were false but reiterates that he was given them to use by the main guy and, being an illegal immigrant, he was scared that he would be kicked out on to the streets if he refused to do what was instructed.'

'So basically he's saying that he's acting under duress and that there are other people out there who are pulling his strings and masterminding the whole operation... rather than it being him. That's pretty smart, especially if we can't get any of the girls to say otherwise.'

'Quite!' Paul agreed. 'We're even going to struggle to get him charged with the knife and drugs offences.'

'What do you mean?' She thought they at least had enough evidence to hold him in custody for those.

'Bet's contacted the elderly male passer-by who gave the info on the knife. He confirms Dimitri's account, in that he says that there was another girl who did actually have the knife first, before Dimitri got possession of it. She walked away when he drove off. In the eyes of the CPS he has a credible lawful excuse for having it. Plus, it was found in his car. It wasn't even on his person.

'As for the GHB, SOCO hasn't found any fingerprints on the vials and won't be able to get fingerprints off the paper bag, so we'll never be able to prove they belong to him. Especially if we don't know the other girl, and Michaela is staying silent and not denying they're hers.'

'Dammit. So, apart from being in this country as an illegal immigrant and a rather weak possession of false IDs, we have nothing to conclusively prove he was running the brothels or had anything to do with the baby's death. He'll probably be given a slap on the wrist and deported back to Russia in due course, if that's the case.'

'Yep. And then, he'll be released and come straight back using a different name.'

'Unless we can persuade one of the girls to testify.'

Charlie could feel her frustration growing as she ended the call and shoved her phone back in her pocket. Hanna's words came forcefully to mind. None of the reassurances they'd offered had been enough to assuage their fears. Each girl still believed she and her family were in danger, but, at the same time, how could they stay silent and let their captor get away scot-free. One of them could even be the mother of the dead baby, yet still none were willing to speak out. The thought prompted her to pick up her phone again. They couldn't afford to wait a minute longer.

The lab technician spoke clinically and without emotion. The DNA sample provided by each of the girls found at the Lewisham brothel had finally been compared against the DNA from the blood on the dead baby's head... and none of the samples matched. Charlie heard the words, struggling to remain unaffected as the full implication of the results sunk in.

'So, our baby's mother is still missing,' Charlie mumbled out loud down the phone to the unknown staff member. 'We know she gave birth at the brothel in Streatham, but she never arrived at Lewisham.' She let her arm drop, leaving the line still open, and voiced the question that was now her number one priority. 'So where the hell did she go?'

*

Viktor Egorov stared at DC Charlie Stafford as she entered the interview room, slipping in next to Detective Inspector Hunter. He was enjoying the chance to pit his wits against the famous Metropolitan Police, the Best of British, supposedly the best in the world. So far, he had run rings around them, confounding them with his every answer, agreeing with many of their premises but then giving credible explanations to throw them off track. It wouldn't do to deny any involvement. That would just show him to be a liar. No, he had to accept what they had, but find plausible reasons to explain their findings. And so far he had.

He'd read this woman officer before, noticed the slight change in stance when she thought she'd got one over on him, outside the house in Lewisham. Now she was here again, and she was staring directly at him. He stared back at her, their eyes connecting momentarily before he broke away, allowing his pupils to rove up and down dispassionately over her face, her neck, her body. It always made women feel insecure to be looked at in this way, their bodies analysed, graded and summarily used or dismissed. This woman was unremarkable physically, and she knew she was unremarkable, but there was something about her that made her stand out from the rest; she had an aura that he hadn't as yet figured out. And she didn't care what he thought of her.

'Good morning, Dimitri, or should I say Mr Viktor Egorov,' she spoke slowly. 'I'm going to call you Dimitri though because that is the name that everyone knows you by. I'm told you have an answer for everything?'

He smiled at her assessment. She was right.

'So, do you think these so-called "acquaintances" of yours will believe your answers?'

He stared towards her, satisfied that she knew his defence but awaiting a follow-up question. She lifted her head, staring him directly in the eyes.

'How will you explain to them that one of their girls has gone missing? How she was with you at Streatham but is no longer around. Might they not think you've set up a rival business and have poached her from them? What will you say, Dimitri?'

He grinned nastily. She could say what she wanted. 'I know nothing of any missing girls.'

'What about the girl from the top bedroom in Streatham? You know, Dimitri, the one whose blood you tried to hide? Where will you tell your bosses she's gone?'

He made no reply. The policewoman could prove nothing. She was still staring at him, unblinking, her pupils boring into his and, with a start, he recognised the nature of her aura. It was confidence, pure unadulterated self-belief. She was not frightened of him in any way, shape or form, unlike all the usual women around him, and he didn't know quite how to deal with her. He couldn't use his usual methods. He cleared his throat.

'There are no missing girls. All are accounted for.' He kept his voice even.

'Except one, Dimitri. Or are you forgetting her? Don't tell me you've misplaced her. That's just careless. What will your bosses say when they hear there's one less girl earning them money? Or did you somehow lose her in the transfer to Lewisham?'

The policewoman inched forward, her head propped up in her hands, her eyes still searching. He tried to ignore her persistence, the way she wouldn't let the issue drop, but as her questions probed, he was reminded of Tatjana's weight as he struggled with her body in the darkness, along the freezing railway track. His eyes narrowed at the memory of the task and he rubbed the scar on his head subconsciously.

The policewoman stood, backing towards the door to the interview room now, her unremarkable face lit up with a remarkable glow. 'Or did she fall out of the back of your van, Dimitri?'

She pulled the door open as he started to laugh, turning tail as his voice chased her from the interview room.

*

Charlie walked straight through the custody area and out into the yard, the sound of Dimitri's laughter still pounding in her temples. His body language had told her everything she needed to know. Now she had to get out of the station. It didn't matter where she was headed. Round and round the block for all she cared. Her mind moved forward with each step, as if evaluating every piece of the puzzle. She thought of the photo on the passport of the young girl travelling with Dimitri on his previous trip back from the continent three months before. The girl on that photo was not one of the girls they had rescued. Could she be the baby's mother as Paul had mooted? She thought of the photo of Dimitri on his fake driving licence and the van that he'd hired with it. The van and that last journey held the key, and his laughter showed that he knew it, and didn't care.

Suddenly she was running. The snow stung her face as she sprinted on, wetting her hair and freezing the tips of her fingers, but she couldn't stop now. As she ran, she knew without doubt that the forensic results on the van, when they arrived, would show that she was right and that the baby's mother had been transported in it. Something had spooked Dimitri into moving that fateful night when they'd watched his van coming and going from the Streatham brothel… and now she knew exactly what.

Chapter 43

The area between Streatham High Road and Balham High Road took in residential gardens, two school fields, half a dozen churchyards and the whole of Tooting Bec Common. A body could be hidden in any one of those places, but Charlie had no reservations. With his limited timescale and the prospect of being spotted, there was no question in her mind that the darkness and invisibility of the common would have made it Dimitri's location of choice.

Four dog units were quickly assembled, each taking a quarter of the common, their brief to concentrate mainly on the wooded areas and train lines criss-crossing the area. The electricity would be cut and the trains held stationary at the nearest stations for the duration of the search, but the railway embankments would still be cold, inaccessible and dangerous. There could be no postponing the moment though. It had to be done.

Charlie, Paul and Hunter waited nervously in a heated police car at the rendezvous point, conscious of the freezing conditions outside. In Charlie's mind, it would only be a matter of time before they would be trudging across a snow-covered field to witness a sight she had for so long dreaded.

The call came exactly thirty-six minutes later.

'Body found.'

The three of them climbed out of the car in silence, pulling winter coats and scarves tight around their warm bodies. They followed the directions given, across the grass, over a gap in the fence and along the side of the track, to a disused railway shed. The dog handler was waiting to one side, his German Shepherd playing happily with his reward for a job well done.

The handler passed Charlie a small maroon book sealed within an exhibits bag. The book was open and on its cover the word 'Diary' was embossed in gold lettering. At the top of the first page, the name Tatjana Pipenko was written by hand in ink, the writing perfectly formed and upright, with a smiley face added within its last letter.

'It was lying on the ground in front of the body with a few other personal belongings,' the officer said, shining a flashlight into the gloomy outbuilding to where a tarpaulin lay partially unravelled on the filthy concrete floor. The end of the cover was torn away, probably by a fox or other wild animal, revealing a single leg, sticking out from a large body-sized package, its bare foot stiff and white.

Charlie pulled her scarf up over her hair, blocking out the silent screaming in her head, counting each lifeless frozen toe. Her eyes moved along the roll, focussing on the thick fake fur cream rug in which the body of Tatjana Pipenko was wrapped, recognising it as one she'd seen several times before...

It was the same style rug she'd walked across so recently in the brothels of Streatham and Lewisham.

*

Hanna was still saying nothing when Charlie returned to The Haven. Charlie stamped her feet and rubbed her hands together as she entered, wishing she could remove the image of the girl's dead body from her memory as easily as the dirt and snow fell from her boots. Maybe a description of what she had just seen would prompt the girl to talk. It might also, however, confirm to her the danger of speaking out, but she had to try.

'Hanna,' she sat down beside the girl, taking the place of her colleague, 'was there a girl who left your house in Streatham recently?'

The interpreter repeated the question.

Hanna looked past her, staring out of the window.

'Please, Hanna. We've just found a girl who we think lived with you.'

Hanna's expression changed momentarily but she said nothing.

'We think her name was Tatjana.'

'You found Tatjana?' Hanna turned towards her, smiling suddenly. 'Is she all right?'

Charlie hesitated in her answer. She'd thought Hanna would know; that this was the reason for her fears, for all their collective silence.

Hanna was staring directly at her. Before Charlie could think of the words, the girl turned away, burying her head in her hands, her eyes filling with tears.

'You said *was*. We think her name *was* Tatjana.' She waved her hand towards the interpreter in dismissal. 'I know exactly what you mean. I had feared what you are saying, but I had still hoped.' Her face hardened as she spoke. She wiped her sleeve against her cheeks angrily, drying the tears, her eyes now becoming steely. 'All the time I believed Dimitri's promise, I knew I could not talk. None of us could. He fed us and kept clothes on our backs and even though we did not like what we had to do, we accepted it. This has changed things.'

She turned to face Charlie again, her expression set. 'You said we could talk to you safely, but tell us how this can be done? Dimitri knows everything about us, and our families. There is no guarantee he will not escape justice as he has done so many times before and come after us.'

'He will only escape justice if you keep quiet,' Charlie met Hanna's eyes. Gaining her trust was the only way she could get justice for the tiny baby and now her mother, but she would not make promises she could not keep. 'We need you to tell us who is in charge of the brothels, what you have been made to do, how you have been treated, the threats you have received and how you were brought into the country. We need to know everything. If it is Dimitri who has done this to you, then we can get him convicted of human trafficking for the purposes of sexual exploitation and other serious offences of that nature and we can ensure he is sent to prison for many years.'

Hanna pulled her gaze away, frowning and shaking her head. 'It still might not be enough. I have seen other men in this trade walk free after just a short time, only to hunt the girls down who betrayed them.'

She turned away, her shoulders slumping. Charlie felt the opportunity slipping away.

'You said things had changed when I mentioned Tatjana. That Dimitri had broken a promise. What promise was that, Hanna?'

'He promised that she had been taken to a hospital for treatment. He said that she would be all right and that she was to go back to her home country... but she still died.'

'Tatjana was never taken to a hospital. He might have told you that, but he lied.' Charlie spoke softly. 'I have come from where her body was found, just now. There were personal items with Tatjana's name nearby.' Charlie had brought with her the bag containing Tatjana's diary. Although still sealed, she had been able to open the book and read some of the entries. The last few pages were written in English, as if its author wanted her final thoughts easily recognised. 'These are the last words your friend wrote.' She lifted the diary to the light and read. '*Please help me. Dimitri has killed my baby and now he is killing me. Tell my mother I didn't know to what I was coming. Tell her I love her. Please tell her...*' The last word was written across two pages, the handwriting shaky, the last letter trailing off across the edge of the page. Charlie turned it towards Hanna so she could read the word.

'*Goodbye*,' Hanna whispered, her voice faltering.

Charlie pressed on, her own voice equally unsteady. She couldn't let this chance slip through her fingers. 'Tatjana was wrapped in the same style sheepskin rug as you all have, inside a tarpaulin and dumped in a freezing outhouse at the side of a railway line near to your house in Streatham.' She watched as the girl's shoulders slumped still further and her hand came up to her mouth. 'A few days before, the body of a baby girl was found, thrown out with the rubbish. She looked as fragile as a tiny broken doll. I have been searching for the baby's mother ever since and I believe it will be proved to be Tatjana. We contacted every hospital, every council, every possible place, that her mother might have sought assistance, but to no avail. Nobody had seen her. Nobody could help us.'

She turned to Hanna and took hold of her arm gently. 'Hanna, Dimitri didn't care about Tatjana or her baby. He treated them as human refuse. He threw them away with the rubbish... and if you or any of the others know anything about what happened, then you can help. We can't use Tatjana's diary because she is dead and her words are inadmissible, but we could use yours. If we have the evidence to get him charged with the manslaughter, or even the murder, of Tatjana and her baby, then we can ensure he is locked up for life and will never again harm you, or your families or any other young girl. If you won't do it for me, Hanna, then please do it for Tatjana.'

Hanna stood up silently, walking towards the window. For what seemed a lifetime, she stared through the glass, as large flakes continued to fall from the skies, coating the branches of the trees and the roofs of the houses in a layer of pure white snow. Charlie waited, watching as a myriad of different emotions passed across the girl's face, before she finally straightened, her shoulders lifting.

'Tell me what I must do,' she said, strongly and evenly. 'I owe it to Tatjana.'

*

Hanna's voice grew more passionate with every phrase. It was as if now the decision had been made, every

gave her the impetus to continue. She spoke
out how she and the other girls had been duped
travelling to London, on the promise of work and a
life.

ou think any of us would have come, had we
known?' Hanna looked stricken as she turned the
question on Charlie. 'Our families would be shamed if
they knew what we had to do for the small amount of
cash that Dimitri permitted us to send to them.' She
shook her head forcefully and walked across to the
window, staring out across the skyscape of London.
'Dimitri organised everything for us; our food, our
clothing, our lives. He knew all our families… and we
knew what he would do if we disobeyed. He had his
contacts in our countries, of course, but it was he that
forced us to do what we did, and it was he that we all
believed would carry out his threats.'

She didn't wait for Charlie to pass comment. Instead
she continued, the volume of her speech rising with each
word she spoke. 'Dimitri is evil. He raped me as soon as
I arrived in London and since then he has made me do
things that I could never have imagined in my worst
nightmares.' She closed her eyes, blinking away the
tears, her voice now simmering with anger. 'He has
allowed men to use me for their sick pleasures. He has
made me submit to them, even when my body ached
with pain and my head screamed to be allowed to return

home. I have been bruised and beaten, and Dimitri allowed it all to happen.'

She pulled up her sleeves and the hem of her skirt to show Charlie scarring across her wrists and thighs and the remains of a burn mark dragged across her stomach. 'Albertas was supposed to protect us, but by the time he stepped in, the worst of it had already happened.' She pulled her clothing back in place and sat down, hugging her arms around her body. 'And then he took his turn also.'

Charlie waited silently for Hanna to speak again, not wanting to interrupt the outpouring of anger and grief, or the steady flow of information, allowing Hanna to dictate when she next spoke and on what subject she wished to dwell. She was skimming over the notes, when the silence was broken by the sound of Hanna quietly sobbing, her hand held tightly across her mouth to try to stem the noise.

'I should have done more to help Tatjana,' Hanna could barely say the words, the strength of her previous statements having leeched away, replaced instead with little more than a whisper.

Charlie looked across at the girl, Hanna's raw emotion taking her breath away.

'I was allowed to roam around the house freely,' Hanna continued. 'As the oldest there, Dimitri wanted me to talk to the younger girls, encourage them.' She lapsed into silence again. 'That room, at the top of the house, where Tatjana was put…' She sobbed again. 'I saw what happened. I saw everything.'

Hanna hugged her body even tighter but lifted her chin to speak, allowing the tears to fall unabated. 'I was standing just outside the room when Dimitri found out about Tatjana's baby. I heard his anger when he saw how her belly had grown and realised that he had been deceived. He would never have brought her to London if he had known she was pregnant.' She paused, turning towards Charlie. 'It was morning and light outside, but in the room the curtains were still drawn. Tatjana didn't want to get up. She felt sick. Dimitri was in a rage. He pulled the curtains open, but Tatjana still wouldn't move, so he pulled the covers off her bed. It was then that he realised.'

Hanna was staring past Charlie now, her eyes vacant. 'Dimitri stamped on her. He was shouting abuse, calling her a whore and a liar. He stamped on her and as he did so he shouted that he wanted the baby dead… and gone. I should have stopped him.'

Charlie listened horrified, automatically reaching out and putting her hand on Hanna's arm. Nothing had prepared her for the starkness of the description and as she watched Hanna's pupils glaze over, she realised that nothing could ever have prepared the young girl sitting next to her now for what she had seen.

Hanna stopped crying. 'Later that evening, Tatjana went into labour. I will always remember her screams and the way Dimitri tried to silence her.' Charlie felt herself drawn into the room as Hanna spoke, recalling the bed, the blood, the smells of disinfectant. 'Dimitri wrapped Tatjana's baby girl up in a pink towel and shoved her tiny body into a bright orange carrier bag. He was laughing as she sobbed. He wouldn't let her hold her baby, he wouldn't let her even touch it. He took it away from her that night.'

Hanna stood suddenly, pulling away. 'He killed Tatjana that night, as surely as he killed her baby. There was no one else involved. She never recovered after that. I tried to persuade him to get help or take her to hospital. I could see my friend was getting weaker. He promised he would. Later on, he promised that he had, but she disappeared the night we went to the new house. I never saw her again. I knew he had lied, but I didn't want to believe it, until you told me... and I saw my friend's own words.'

'Now, I know what I must do and I will do it. And I must also seek out Tatjana's mother and tell her the truth.' Hanna spun around suddenly towards Charlie, taking both her hands in her own, her face passionate. Charlie was amazed at the potency of her grip and the intensity of her newly-found strength. Given the promise of justice, she had now embraced the power to succeed. 'And you must allow me to tell the other girls to speak out about what they too have seen. Dimitri must be stopped. He cannot go on taking young girls' lives.'

Charlie listened to Hanna's words, her thoughts now turning to Redz, another young girl whose life had been taken. Razor was due to return on bail the following morning. She watched the strength flowing back into every part of Hanna's body, and as she marvelled at the transformation, Charlie hoped that she too would understand what was required to achieve justice... and be gifted with the power to succeed.

Chapter 44

Charlie was in extra early the next morning. With all the ongoing developments in the trafficking case over the past few days, she hadn't had time to really bottom out the information from Angie in relation to Redz having been killed by a punter. Although Razor ticked all the boxes, the possibility they had jumped to the wrong conclusion was bothering her. A few more background checks were required.

Hunter, knowing Razor of old, was convinced he was their man and the rest of the team clearly acquiesced, but as was often the case, she had an itch that needed to be scratched. She fired up the computer logging on to the Crimint system. Criminal Intelligence from another borough was what might prove, or disprove, the existence of a predatory punter. Charlie selected those boroughs with red-light areas initially, carefully choosing a search thread and waiting as the system scanned every piece of intelligence entered over the last year. The results churned in and she watched in dismay as dozens of results started to appear. There were far too many to check each individually. She needed more detail

– a name, a registration number, anything to distinguish one suspect from another. She clicked on a few results, scanning through the reports, but nothing stood out. Concentrating only on those that flashed red for danger, she clicked on a few more, reading details on almost every report of the violence shown towards sex workers on the street. To Charlie it made the widely-held belief of many observers that somehow women choose prostitution as a credible occupation, laughable. Walking the streets was not a choice, as far as she was concerned, it was a necessity and one that brought with it the risk of death, or serious injury.

She was about to give up when she noticed a report entitled, 'Prostitute assaulted – believed serial attacker'. Pulling it up on the screen, she read the details.

Information given by anonymous sex workers in the King's Cross area state that there have been a number of violent attacks on prostitutes over the last six months. The description of the suspect involved is a male, Asian, over 6ft tall, large build, wearing distinctive chunky jewellery. The male is sometimes on foot and sometimes in a small dark car – no further details known.

She re-read the report, noting the similarities with the description given by Angie of Redz' attacker and turning on to the next page dealing with the action taken. The informant was anonymous, although shown as being a victim/witness. Reading between the lines, she guessed it would be a prostitute, who was happy to pass the description on but not to have it recorded formally as a crime. The description had been circulated to all vice units, for the purpose of warning other sex workers, and the report marked up finally as complete.

To Charlie it leant weight to Angie's information, although not adding any meat to the bones. The itch was still there, unable to be scratched and nullified, or its origin detected and formalised. She was no further forward. Redz could have come into contact with the same man. She may even have been picked up by him, but without anything further, it would remain just a rumour. All the actual evidence pointed to Razor.

She logged off, noticing that the rest of the team had filtered in, unbeknown to her, and were discussing the developments in Dimitri's case. Their delight at the continuing progress was obvious, but today was another day. It was Redz' day and in the next few hours they would all have to switch their concentration to the hazards faced daily by every sex worker on the streets of London… and the desolation of a graveyard on the banks of the Liffey.

*

The team fell silent as Charlie walked to the front of the office and pinned a copy of the same photo as had been displayed on Redz' coffin to the whiteboard for them all to see. Gerald Flaherty had been insistent.

'Wow, is that Redz?' Naz shook her head in disbelief. 'She was a beautiful child.'

'I'm sure she would have been a beautiful woman too, if drugs and the likes of Razor had not got to her.' Sabira came across and repositioned the photo next to one of Redz at the crime scene, the contrast bringing a collective lump to each of their throats. 'But it's not what's on the outside that matters.'

Charlie was about to agree when Hunter walked through, his eyes flicking over the photos of Redz and coming to rest instead on the custody image of Razor.

'Razor returns in an hour's time,' he said. 'Do we have enough to charge him, bail him again, or release him completely? Hopefully we're looking at the first option. Naz, Sab, is there anything else that's come in during the last few days while we were in Ireland?'

Naz jumped up first. 'Well, the phone data on Razor's mobile confirms his sightings on CCTV. He was using his phone within the area of the alleyway just before Maria Simpson's call to police and afterwards several masts show that he headed towards Brixton and Viv's bar. In fact, several of his earlier calls were made to Redz' number, but they were unanswered.'

'So he found her and beat her to death for ignoring his calls?' Hunter threw out the question. 'Anything more on the alibis?'

'Well, Viv's is as it is. She can only confirm Razor's presence after Redz was killed.' Sabira dipped her head to one side. 'And, of course, she gives a possible motive that Redz needed to be "sorted out" and her impression that Razor already knew what had happened.'

'Which is her opinion,' Charlie pursed her lips. 'It isn't exactly evidence.'

'But she also says he stayed in the bar for some time afterwards!' Bet came across and threw a pile of goodies down on to the table, a habit of hers when they all needed a boost. 'You'd have thought that he'd have been straight out looking for whoever had killed his girl.'

'He wasn't, because there wasn't anyone else! And he knew that. He was obviously just cultivating his alibi.' Hunter selected a packet of nuts and pulled the wrapping open, tipping a few out on to the table. 'How about Caz?'

'She says she was with him at the flat and then for a short time while they searched for Redz in his car, until he dropped her off and went into Viv's.' Charlie selected a Crunchie and ripped the top off the wrapper with her teeth.

'Even though CCTV shows only one occupant in the car?' Sabira ignored the temptation.

'I asked her about that. She said she was lying down on the back seat.'

'Well, she wasn't anywhere near Razor actually and we can prove it.' Sabira grinned. 'There was a robbery nearby around the same time and some vice officers dealing with it recognised Caz walking past them. We've checked CCTV and you can clearly see it's her, so her alibi for Razor is blown out the window.'

'I knew she wasn't telling the truth,' Charlie shook her head, sadly. 'But she's like Hanna and the other girls were yesterday; too terrified to risk the repercussions. She'd rather go to prison for perverting the course of justice instead. Still, at least it helps our case. We can prove Razor was on his own when Redz was killed.'

'And the other piece of good news is that the forensic results on Razor's Vauxhall Astra confirm what we were hoping.' Naz took a deep breath as if to keep them in suspense. 'The blood and hair samples taken from the front passenger seat came back to Redz.'

She passed a file to Hunter, who spread it out across the desk, enabling Charlie to also read its contents.

The report stated that, as Naz had said, the blood and hair samples did indeed belong to Grace Flaherty. The pattern of the blood corroborated the fact that her face had impacted with the dashboard facia on the passenger side of the vehicle, most of the spray pattern indicating her head was turned slightly towards the left-hand side, as if she had been looking away from her attacker positioned in the driver's seat.

Cracks and dents to the dashboard facia were consistent with a heavy object, such as her head having hit it, though, it was pointed out that the amount of damage was not overly extensive. Charlie knew that the defence would concentrate on whether the damage bore out the massive injuries Redz had sustained, but Dr Crane had suggested this was how her injuries had been caused... and this is what they had.

She scanned down to details of the hair samples. The report stated that most of the strands still had their roots attached and had therefore been pulled out forcibly.

'So we're missing the cut hair?' Charlie grimaced and turned to Naz. 'Not that that excludes Razor. He could have cut the hair off outside the car. Was any hair found at his flat?'

Naz shook her head. 'No hair. But there was a pair of jeans and a jacket with blood spots predominantly down the left-hand side. Razor's DNA is all over the clothing and the blood belongs to Redz. It'll be the clothing he was wearing when the bastard pulled her hair out and smashed her head against the dashboard.'

'Bloody animal,' Hunter joined in, standing up and walking towards the window.

'Anything further to confirm Dutch's cause of death?' Charlie noticed the smaller photos of both Dutch and Caz stuck underneath the ones of Redz on the whiteboard. 'The post-mortem results are in now, aren't they?'

'Drug overdose, like we thought.' Paul raised his eyebrows and frowned. 'She had no significant injuries, other than the normal for a user, and there was nothing suspicious of note. Dr Crane did some initial tests, which have come up positive for both opiates and cocaine. She'd taken a cocktail of cocaine and heroin. The full tox' report will tell us the exact amounts of each drug, but suffice to say, Dr Crane is happy that it was a straightforward OD.'

'I thought as much,' Charlie sighed heavily. 'It's a shame nobody could get Dutch away from Razor sooner. What a waste!'

The sight of Caz brought Angie's information to mind. If Caz was indeed her informant then it may well have been she who had passed on the description of the violent punter from the King's Cross girls. Word spread easily from one patch to another. Maybe she had hoped it would muddy the waters, and help Razor further, especially in light of the now discredited alibi statement.

'Oh, and this morning I checked out Angie's information about Redz being killed by a punter.' Charlie was careful not to mention the link with Caz. 'There is one report of a similar nature in King's Cross, with an almost identical description of the male, but it's anonymous and uncorroborated. It came in months ago, before Redz' murder, so it could be legitimate.' Charlie spelt out her thoughts. 'But our girls might have just repeated what they'd heard from the girls uptown. None of them is willing to put their name to the information so, as far as evidence goes, it's little more than a rumour and won't hold any weight at court. You'd think if there was a violent punter doing the rounds who has killed one of their mates, one of them might actually stand up and be counted.'

She ran her fingers through her hair, as a shiver of apprehension caught her off guard. Hadn't their experience in the last two days shown how hard it was for vulnerable women to make a stand, but at the same time, they had a solid amount of circumstantial evidence against Razor, backed up with some useful forensics.

For once though she didn't know if it was enough. She shrugged the feeling away at the memory of Razor's sneering words at the end of his last interview. *Do you want a piece of me too?* The thought repulsed her, yet very soon she would be listening to the same voice and staring into those same cold eyes. Whatever her doubts, Hunter had to be right. It had to be him. He had the eyes of a killer; they just had to get the CPS to agree...

The office had fallen silent, everyone staring, mesmerised, as Hunter returned to the table on which he'd tipped the peanuts. He positioned a ruler on its side halfway across the desk, mounted three of the nuts on to a small stack of books and flicked two of them in turn, watching triumphantly as they shot over the upturned ruler. 'Well done, team,' he said. 'Razor's going to have a hard time explaining all our evidence away, and with his long history of violence, we should be home and dry.' Charlie watched as he took aim and flicked the third nut, sending it flying over the ruler and out across the floor, before standing up and grinning towards them all. 'Game, set and match, as it were.'

*

Razor rolled himself a cigarette and stood idly watching the shoppers flitting from one shop to another. With Christmas now only a few days away, panic had set in, the rush to find the perfect presents negating all common sense. They would be easy pickings, with wallets hanging out of their back pockets, purses lying on top of shopping bags and handbags left open for ease of purchase.

He finished the last drag and threw the butt down angrily, grinding it into the paving with a heavy boot. There were far better things to be doing amongst the shopping arcades than wasting his time returning to the police station.

His solicitor was waiting for him, his hand outstretched. 'Remember,' the man said. 'Just make no comment to everything they throw at you. Stay calm and don't react to any of their questions. If anything awkward comes up, we'll request a further consultation.'

Razor nodded. This wouldn't take long. He would soon be waving the bastards goodbye and then he could get back out to play.

DC Charlie Stafford and DI Hunter were eager to start, ushering him into an interview room once the preliminaries were complete in the custody office.

Razor sat back in his seat, legs stretched out in front of him, knees wide apart, arms crossed. He looked across at the two detectives going through the well-versed preparations for the interview, assured and confident, and for no apparent reason he suddenly felt unnerved.

DC Stafford was to be the main interviewer, as before. She looked across at him. 'You have been arrested on suspicion of the murder of Grace Evelyn Flaherty, known to you as Redz,' she spoke calmly, enunciating every word of the caution clearly before getting started. 'We spoke about Redz last time. She worked as a prostitute around Streatham, didn't she?'

'No comment.'

'And you were her pimp? You protected and looked after her, didn't you?'

'No comment.'

'You controlled her? You told her what she should and shouldn't do?'

'No comment.'

'And you didn't like it if she didn't do what you told her, did you?'

'No comment.'

'You *really* didn't like it if she disrespected you, did you, Razor?' The woman officer stared straight at him.

'No comment,' he said the words with deliberation. The bitch was getting on his nerves.

'In fact, if she didn't do what you said, you hit her, didn't you?'

'No comment.'

'You hit her so hard that you made her bleed? You pulled her hair and assaulted her, didn't you?'

He shook his head. 'No comment.'

'So why are blood and hair samples belonging to Redz all over the dashboard and front passenger footwell of your vehicle?'

'No comment.'

Razor stiffened subconsciously. He tried to relax, fixing a smile on his lips. The woman detective leant towards him, her eyes drilling into his.

'They got there because you put them there. You smashed her head against the dashboard, didn't you? You beat Redz so badly that she died. That's why her blood is also all over the jacket and jeans we found at your address, your jacket and jeans. You killed her, Razor, didn't you?'

He swallowed hard as he suddenly remembered the events of the night before Redz' death.

The police officer was speaking again.

'Had Redz been a bit disobedient, Razor? Did you need to put her back in her place? Give her a bit of a slap? Sort her out? Did you lose your temper with Redz? Go a bit too far this time?'

The questions were coming thick and fast and he couldn't think. He heard her voice, talking to him, *at* him, asking him about Redz, and as he heard her name, repeated again and again, the same burning anger as always, raged through his head. He had to keep calm. He had to keep control, but all he could think about was the humiliation, how Redz had made him look foolish and weak in front of his competitors. And then the memory took over; how he'd grabbed her long red hair, dragging her from the crack house and down the path to his car. How she'd screamed as he'd opened the passenger door and shoved her in. How, when he'd smashed her face against the dashboard, her nose had erupted blood, all over the carpet and glove compartment. How he'd seen the clumps of hair in his hand and had wiped them against her as she leant as far from him as she could.

It was over as quickly as it started. By the time they'd reached his flat she had calmed and was full of apologies. It had happened before, and it would happen again. He'd thought no more about it. The blood and hair had dried and in the darkness and hubbub of the following night its existence had been totally forgotten.

Now though its presence was going to be harder to explain away. Damn Redz and her disrespect. He looked at the detectives as a bead of sweat formed on his top lip. A thin smile was playing on the lips of DC Stafford. She was a bitch. He longed to wipe the smugness from her face. The silence lengthened and his solicitor shifted in his seat, a frown flickering on his brow as he awaited an answer.

'No comment,' Razor said throatily, forcing a cough.

His solicitor took the hint, setting his pen down on the desk directly in line with his pad and talking stiffly. 'My client needs a drink of water and requests a further consultation with his solicitor.'

Razor coughed again. 'Yeah, that's right. I need what he says. I'm not feeling well.'

He watched as the two police officers glanced across at one another and the senior one nodded. Denying him what he requested could potentially render any further questioning inadmissible should the case ever go to court. They wouldn't risk it.

'Interview suspended at 11.36 hours for legal consultations and refreshments,' DC Stafford said through gritted teeth. She removed the two CDs, sealed one and left the room, followed closely by DI Hunter.

His solicitor turned towards him, his face ripe with displeasure. 'You'd better tell me everything you know about the circumstances surrounding Redz' murder, and I mean everything.'

'Damn it,' Charlie grumbled as the door swung shut. 'Just when we had him on the ropes.'

'Yes, I know,' Hunter pulled a pen from his top pocket and chewed on the end of it. 'But the look on his face was priceless. He looked like he'd seen a ghost.'

'Maybe he had... and it wouldn't have been a pretty sight.'

She turned away in frustration. As far as she was concerned, any person who exercised their right to silence had something to hide, and Razor was no exception. Right now he would be concocting an excuse for the presence of Redz' blood and hair in his car, knowing full well that a court could use his failure to answer as an inference of guilt. The more he lied and sought to hide the truth though, the more any doubts of her own were laid to rest.

It was half an hour before the interview recommenced, a fact that irritated her further. Before she could speak, Razor's solicitor placed a piece of paper on the desk in front of her, with barely legible writing scrawled across it. It was like déjà vu.

'My client would like to read out a prepared statement.' He sniffed and leant back in his chair. 'After that, he will be making no further comment.'

Razor picked up the sheet of paper and started to read, 'I am making this statement of my own free will and with advice from my solicitor. Redz was my girlfriend and has been in my car lots of times. The night before her murder, she was at a friend's house in Brixton. When I went to get her, she had been drinking and taking crack and was very excitable. She did not want to come with me, but I was concerned for her welfare. We argued and I admit that I forced her to leave as I did not want her to remain there in the state she was. She was unsteady on her feet and as she was getting into the car, she stumbled and fell forward, hitting her face on the dashboard. Her nose started to bleed and she became hysterical and started to thrash around. I took hold of her by the hair to stop her throwing her head back and hurting herself further. I had to hold her for a few minutes until she calmed and some of her hair must have come out.

'The next night Redz wanted to go out again. I dropped her off in Streatham Hill and spent the evening at home with Caz. I stayed in my flat until it was time to pick Redz up. She wasn't where we had arranged to meet. Then lots of police cars and an ambulance arrived and I decided to leave. Caz was with me and I drove straight to Viv's bar in Brixton and stayed there for a few hours, returning home at about 3 a.m. I thought that Redz would make her own way home or phone me if she needed picking up.

'I know nothing of Redz' murder and completely deny any involvement in it. Further to this I have spoken to some of the other girls in Streatham and they have told me that Redz was picked up by a large Asian man with lots of jewellery. He usually wears a long leather coat and drives a small car. I suggest that he is the man who killed Redz.'

With that Razor replaced the sheet of paper on the table in front of him and folded his arms decisively. It was clear he was saying nothing more.

Chapter 45

The Crown Prosecution Service representative wore the expression of a disgruntled parent at the end of the school holidays. He was a short, skinny man with beady eyes, a button nose and a set of pearly white dentures that barely fitted into his mouth. He greeted them with a thin smile, his lips stretched so tightly over his teeth that they became almost invisible. He ushered them across to two seats set together in the centre of the room. Pulling the door shut firmly, he circled round them and slipped silent and wolf-like behind his desk, eyeing them now with a mixture of pity and cruelty.

Charlie passed the updated report across the desk to him and waited while he devoured the details of the last interview and Razor's statement, the full case file for R v Clinton ROBERTS, aka Razor, having been sent across a few days earlier. As she waited, Charlie understood exactly the meaning of the phrase 'like a lamb to the slaughter'.

An hour later and it was all over; seven days of sixteen-hour shifts and a raft of promises all now broken and worthless, their work rubbished in five words spoken by the Senior Representative of the Crown.

'There's just not enough evidence.' He shook his head firmly to every argument levelled by them both.

Charlie scanned through his report, picking out the salient points. It was as she had feared. The motive was believable but not particularly strong. The CCTV was effective but it didn't cover the actual alleyway in which the murder had occurred and other cars had also been seen entering and exiting the nearby roads. With a negative ID parade, there was no definitive identification evidence. Most of the forensics could be explained away by the relationship between Clinton Roberts and Grace Flaherty and there was a fair chance a jury would accept Roberts's explanation for the presence of the victim's blood and hair in his vehicle and on his clothing. More importantly, none of the cut hair had been found. The extent of the victim's injuries was clear, but the amount of damage on Roberts's dashboard was such that it could not be proved, without doubt, that this was the weapon or surface that had caused all the injuries. The alibi statement given by Vivienne Bancroft contained opinions and did nothing to assist the prosecution and the disproved alibi statement from Charlene Philips, aka Caz, was helpful but the alibi would never have been assessed as reliable in any case. Roberts's previous history was comprehensive and did much to show 'bad character', however, many of the domestic allegations were inadmissible due to them being uncorroborated. Only Charlene Philips was still alive to assist the prosecution with this – and she was giving evidence instead for his defence.

Added to that, were the rumours of the large Asian punter, which, although unproven and with no substantive witnesses, might still provide an element of doubt.

All in all, Charlie had been right to be apprehensive. The evidence was good, but there were too many inconsistencies. A strong defence would crucify them.

They were back to square one. If Razor was not their man, then who was? If they did indeed have the correct suspect, then it was imperative they found the additional evidence to meet the criteria required for a charge. Charlie picked up her file and turned towards the door, the lawyer's last words, hanging like a weight around her neck: *'The recommendation is that no charges are brought in this case. Unless further evidence comes to light, Roberts should be released immediately.'*

*

Razor heard the key turn in the heavy grey cell door and it swung open.

'Your solicitor's waiting in custody for you,' a young gaoler said.

He was up on his feet within seconds, pushing past him and striding towards the custody area. 'About fuckin' time too. Why am I still here and why haven't you got me out yet?'

The solicitor was standing by the desk as he advanced. 'I have got you out,' he answered simply, smiling.

*

It was the confrontation Charlie had been dreading, but she was not facing it alone. Hunter, as always stood beside her. With only ten minutes to go before Razor's twenty-four-hour custody deadline expired, she had to get the paperwork for his release completed swiftly, but she would have given anything to keep him in for another twenty-four... and then another, and another. Every glimpse of the violent pimp made her feel sick to her stomach.

'This'll teach you, you lying bitch, for trying to fit me up,' he snarled, signing for his property in readiness to go. 'I'll be speaking to my solicitor about suing you for wrongful arrest and detention. You won't get away with this.'

Charlie said nothing. She didn't trust herself to speak. Hunter led him to the door, leaning in as Razor neared.

'We'll be seeing you again soon,' he whispered as their suspect brushed past. 'And next time you'll be banged up for good.'

'Yeah, right,' Razor laughed out loud, sauntering nonchalantly out into the grey streets of Brixton.

With the streetlight glinting off his heavy gold signet ring, Charlie and Hunter were forced to watch as he raised the middle finger of his right hand and strode off into the rush-hour gloom.

Chapter 46

The Punter was working late. Since being overlooked for promotion, he preferred to stay out of the office, visiting clients for as long as possible each day, only returning to catch up with the admin when many of his colleagues had left. Just the sight of Kavya reinforced his public humiliation. He wasn't immune to the whispered taunts and quiet sniggers. His workmates were thoroughly enjoying his discomfiture and he was fast becoming the butt of their jokes. For the first time in his life he hated coming to work.

Home was no better. The news that he wasn't, after all, to be offered a pay rise had been met with anguish – but not anguish for his disappointment. His wife was worried only for how they would pay the monthly instalments on his new car. Too late had she offered her sympathy. She had never agreed with his choice of motor, but to throw this back in his face now had been totally inappropriate and he resented her for it.

Today, even his clients were conspiring against him. Two appointments had been cancelled and a further two had turned him down flat, despite a full charm offensive.

Any hope of commission was gone. The day had been a complete waste of his time.

The office was silent as he sat brooding, all the other staff having already left. A screen saver from a solitary computer rotated its geometric pattern around the walls. He wandered across to it and switched it off, watching angrily as the screen, like his career ambitions, flickered and died.

From afar he heard the sound of rowdy singing. It was getting louder with every minute he listened. The words became audible. 'For she's a jolly good fellow' repeated, loud and slurred. A small gaggle of his drunken colleagues swung into the car park. In the centre of the group was Kavya, adorned in a festive flashing hat and swigging from a wine bottle.

'And so say all of us.'

As they completed the last line, Kavya held the bottle high in the air and they all cheered and clapped, swaying together in intoxicated unison. They stopped as one, next to his car, peering into its smart interior.

He slid behind the edge of the window, listening to their muffled voices. One of the younger men looked up towards the window where he hid.

'Well, I for one am glad you got the promotion, Kavya,' he pronounced each word loudly and distinctly, as if knowing he was there. 'There's no way I would have taken orders from that arrogant prick.'

The words were greeted with a chorus of agreement.

The Punter heard the laughter, embarrassment burning through him. Not only had he been passed over for promotion, he had been snubbed by his own colleagues and not invited out for a Christmas drink... and now they were publicly abusing him. The reception was filling with noise. He couldn't let them bask any further in his humiliation. He would have to return home and face his wife's criticism. There was no other option.

Grabbing his leather jacket, he ran through the fire exit and out into the night.

Chapter 47

Razor punched his fist against the steering wheel of the stolen car. His earlier victory was quickly turning sour. What was it with his girls? Caz was nowhere to be found. Turn your back on them for even a minute and they did their own thing. First Redz, now Caz, and it hadn't helped with Dutch topping herself. As for that young upstart, Turbo, he had to be taught a proper lesson. No one treated him like a fucking beggar. The bastard would have bragged to everyone how he'd felled the mighty Razor. He slammed his fists down against the wheel again. Fuck!

Mand was standing exactly where she should, a fact not lost on him.

'Hello, gorgeous,' He wound the window down and stared blatantly at her cleavage. 'Have you seen Caz?'

Mand bent low towards him. 'Don't look like your eyes are pointin' in the right direction to be searchin' for 'er at the moment. But yeah, I saw 'er earlier. She seemed pretty contented. Said you two was goin' to settle down together.'

'Like man and wife, eh?' Razor snorted. 'If she thinks she's enough for me, she'd better think again.' He reached forward and ran a finger over the flesh on display. 'You sure you're not free, Mand? I could look after yer.'

She slapped his hand away, good-humouredly, and stood up. 'Get on wiv yer. I've already told yer I'm taken, an' anyway...' She stopped abruptly. In the silence that followed, Razor let his imagination finish the sentence. *We all know that you're a spent force around here.* It was written right across her face. Word had clearly got out.

'DK wouldn't like it,' she finished weakly.

'Another time then,' he forced a smile, gripping the steering wheel tightly. 'An' don't forget to bell me if you see that Punter.' Spinning the wheels, he accelerated off, trying to quell the rage that was running through him like white hot magma. Actions would speak louder than words. Caz and The Punter would pay.

He drove straight to his flat and barrelled through the front door. What the hell was going on? The aroma of scented candles hit him as he entered, the light from the bare flames flickering amongst the shadows. Caz lounged on the settee, her T-shirt low, exposing a tempting amount of milky white breast.

'Razor, I wondered where you was. Come and join me. I've bought booze. We can celebrate you bustin' your case.' She smiled towards him. 'You did get off, didn't you?' He nodded in return and she patted her leg. 'I knew you would. I've bin waiting for this moment. Now come 'ere. I'll make it worth your while.'

The offer was appealing, but there was a lesson to be taught and Caz was refusing to learn. She had to understand she couldn't dictate his movements.

'Get up, you lazy bitch. When you've done a few tricks I might consider what you want, but until then...'

'Come on babe,' Caz lifted her skirt a little higher. 'Forget work. You can have me now.'

Razor stared at the bare pale flesh disappearing upwards to her crotch and was instantly aroused; the urge to fuck her almost overwhelming, but then the words of Turbo drifted back into his stalled thinking.

'I told you to get out and work, you lazy bitch.' He moved towards her. 'Now it's just you an' me you've got to work twice as hard. Redz and Dutch gave me grief and look what 'appened to them. Now get yerself out there before I really fuckin' lose it.'

He yanked her up from the settee and pushed her towards the front door, grinning nastily at the sight of her tears. Only when cold hard cash was in his hand would he take what was on offer, and only on his terms. He kicked a pair of shoes along the hallway and threw a thin jacket down, watching contentedly as she pulled the garment tightly around her skinny frame.

'Please, don't make me do this, Razor,' she whimpered, but he ignored her pleas, opening the door and shoving her out into the freezing air. She would do as he said or else he would break her...

A hundred quid later and he threw the passenger door open.

'Get in,' he ordered. 'You can fuck me now.'

Caz climbed slowly into the seat, bending her frozen body with care, as if it would snap. She sat silently, her face a blank mask, her body shaking more violently with every minute it thawed. Razor lit a joint, blowing the smoke in her direction but offering her none. He drove towards his flat, grinning callously as she hugged her arms around her rigid torso, until the shuddering gradually subsided and eventually she sat motionless.

She stayed subdued when he helped himself to her body in the candlelit bedroom, but he didn't care; in fact, he found it amusing. Rolling over, he traced a finger over her naked breast, up her neck and on to her lips, heaving himself up so that his face was directly in front of hers. 'Same again tomorrow,' he whispered.

*

The Punter turned the key in the lock and pushed the door open. For hours he had put the moment off, waiting until after the twins' bedtime, not wanting to face their seasonal excitement, but as he entered, he heard his daughter's plaintive call.

368

'I'll come and tuck you up in bed, in a minute,' he returned her plea sulkily. Being the perfect father was OK in front of onlookers, but tonight he wasn't in the mood. His wife got up to greet him.

'How was your day, darling? You're late.'

He didn't hear the question, just the accusation. Ignoring it, he poured himself a large brandy, gulping it down in one, before pouring another ready and heading upstairs. Better get his fatherly duties done. His daughter was half asleep when he slipped into her room. For a few seconds he sat on her bedside, peering down at her drowsy expression.

'Where have you been, Daddy?' she whispered lethargically, reaching out for his hand. 'We've been waiting for you.'

He tensed, automatically irritated. Did all females have to be on his case? Bending forward he kissed her, his fingers gently closing her eyelids, her skin warm to the touch. The feel of her body stirred his frustration still further. 'Working,' he replied. 'To keep you all happy.'

The unbidden impulse shocked him, prompting him to move swiftly from her room to where his son lay asleep. For a few minutes he stood, admiring his son's boyish good looks. He would be a strong, handsome man. Everybody commented on how alike they were.

'You need to learn to keep girls in their place, son,' he said with conviction, stroking a lock of hair from the boy's forehead. 'They want everything from you and are not willing to give you anything in return.'

He heard a muffled call from below.

'I've made you dinner,' his wife tried again.

He returned downstairs to the brandy he'd poured earlier. 'I'm not hungry,' he said sulkily. He could feel his wife surveying him but chose to read her concern as interrogation.

'I'm sorry if I was not understanding enough earlier this week, I was just worried. I didn't know what we would do.'

He remained silent, swilling his brandy round in the glass.

'You could have given me some support.' He swallowed down the brandy and poured himself another.

'I know and I'm sorry.' She came across to where he stood and leant gently against him, resting her head on his shoulders and caressing his chest.

He sipped the brandy slowly, not willing to completely forgive her past misdemeanours, but at the same time acknowledging she was at least making an effort.

'Why don't we have an early night? We haven't made love for a long time,' she whispered, her lips grazing his ear.

The Punter groaned inwardly. The overture was not unexpected, but the idea held no appeal. These days he performed intermittently only because marital relations demanded it, but at least it might dispel some of his frustrations until he could get back out on the street.

'Go and make yourself ready. I'll just have one more drink and then I'll be up.' He closed his eyes and took another sip of brandy, savouring the warm drowsiness it brought. Maybe it wouldn't be so bad after all.

Chapter 48

Caz sat alone in the half-light, only the glow from the candles keeping the darkness from fully swallowing her up. Was this as good as it was going to get? Ever since she'd first met Razor, he'd been her saviour, her knight in shining armour, the man she'd looked up to and loved. She'd been prepared to give up everything for him.

Now though she was cold, hungry and desperate; her dreams of happiness and contentment slowly eroded by Razor's desire for dominance; the camaraderie of their previous escapades replaced by cold hostility. Her optimism for a future with the man she loved had been more than matched by his disdain. Even the way in which she'd helped him to his freedom had failed to lift his spirits. Now he'd disappeared again, leaving her half-naked and bereft.

Her misery was temporarily put to one side at the sound of the door opening. Ayeisha entered with a bagful of beers and watery eyes.

'You all alone?' She smiled as Caz nodded and selected two cans, pulling the tab on one and sinking on to the seat next to Caz.

'What's up?' Caz had already guessed.

'Dimitri ain't phoned since Tuesday,' she sniffed hard. 'He said he'd bell me in a couple of days, but I ain't heard nothing.'

'I'm sure 'e will. Give 'im time.'

'No he won't and it's all my fault.'

'Why?' Caz was interested to hear her friend's side of the story. Angie had already filled her in on the story of Dimitri's arrest, but she felt slightly guilty at having to pretend that Dimitri would get back in touch, when she knew differently. Business was business though, and passing on Ayeisha's information would pay well.

''Cause I went through his car while I was waiting for him at Folkestone and found a knife and some drugs. He weren't happy. We had a bit of a fight in the street when he dropped me off an' we didn't make no actual arrangements to meet. Now his phone is switched off and he's not rung me back like he promised.' She wiped her sleeve across her face and sniffed again. 'And he said that I weren't experienced enough and that 'e would 'ave to teach me what he likes, so we could be together. He promised it wouldn't be long.'

Caz snorted as Ayeisha dabbed at her eyes. Dutch had been right; Ayeisha was far too young and innocent to be mixed up with the likes of Dimitri, especially if she still believed he would treat her any differently to how Razor treated them. He might pretend she was special, but that would change when she was under his control. Perhaps she'd saved her friend from finding out the hard way.

'Here's to 'im doin' what he promised, then.' Caz raised her can towards her friend, acknowledging for the first time the deadness in Ayeisha's eyes. The last few days had changed her friend's outlook. It was if the sun had set and she was finally seeing the world as it was. Darkness, defeat, death. She'd soon learn, if she hadn't already. It wouldn't be the first promise that would be broken.

*

They were still chatting when Caz heard footsteps in the hallway and Razor poked his head around the door. She froze, waiting for his demands, but instead he was all charm.

'Ladies, can I interest you in some good quality skunk?'

He reached into his pocket and pulled out several snap bags, rolled an extra-large joint and lit it, offering it to Ayeisha first.

'Here, try this. I think you'll like it,' he grinned, as she shrank away, before taking a deep breath and reaching forward to take it off him. 'Good girl.' He passed it across, winking at Caz as Ayeisha gingerly inhaled.

Caz relaxed. This was more like the Razor she loved. She could forgive him anything when he was in this mood. At her turn, she let the cannabis fill her mouth and throat, swallowing it down with several swigs of the beer, her mind hazy with well-being.

Ayeisha brightened too, chatting animatedly as the skunk took effect. Rather than her usual reticence in Razor's presence, she became giggly, swallowing the last can down in long gulps and laughing at the slightest thing.

'Caz, run to the shop and get some more beers,' Razor said after a while, upturning his can to show it was empty. 'Get a bottle of vodka too. I've got some gear. Let's have a good night.'

'Why can't Ay—' she stopped mid-sentence, recognising immediately the set of his jaw. There was no point spoiling his good mood. 'Give me some cash then,' she sighed instead, pocketing the notes that he offered.

A slight sleet was falling as she stepped out from the tepid smog of the flat and looked out across the hazy skyline. The top of the Shard was barely visible, and the lights on Canada Square and the Heron Tower in Canary Wharf blinked out intermittently from within the dark clouds. The landing was freezing, but nothing compared to the temperature outside the block. As she left the protection of its cover, the chill wind surrounded her, whistling along the walkways and throwing her off balance. It tore at her ruthlessly, whipping the hail around her bare legs and neck and penetrating her skimpy clothing. She pulled her coat close and struggled against the gusts towards the parade of shops.

The off-licence was crowded with folks on their way out to parties, and as she waited in the queue, Caz warmed in the midst of the scarves, woolly hats and good tidings. The shopkeeper was in good spirits too.

'Glad to see you're paying for this tonight, Caz?' he laughed, slipping her purchases into a carrier bag. Many a time he'd caught her secreting the odd can or bottle inside her jacket. It had become a running joke between them.

'Yep,' Caz held out the cash, smiling in return. 'It's your Christmas bonus, but don't count on it when I'm broke again in the New Year.'

Even the frozen rain couldn't dampen her spirits as she left the warmth of the store. Perhaps now Razor had calmed, they could have the relationship she so craved. She quickened her step as the feeling grew stronger.

The lounge door was partially closed when she returned, but she could hear Razor and Ayeisha moving about. All was well. Peering around the doorframe, she froze, stunned at the scene before her. Ayeisha was lying across the settee, her clothes in disarray, her breasts exposed. Razor was on top of her, his trousers down, his bare buttocks moving rhythmically.

With a shout, Caz kicked the door wide open, her hand flying automatically to her mouth. Razor turned to face her, flicking his tongue against his lips gleefully. Underneath him, Ayeisha struggled to cover her nakedness, her face a mask of guilt.

'Meet your new partner,' Razor gloated.

Caz looked at them both and saw only betrayal.

'You bastard,' she screamed at him. 'You cheating, evil bastard.' She turned towards Ayeisha, her voice cold. 'And you was supposed to be my friend. I took you under my wing and gave you a place to stay away from the children's home, yet you've chosen now, when all my dreams was about to come true, to get your first experience with my man. No wonder Dimitri don't want you. No one does. You deserve everything you get.'

She ran from the room towards the front door, with Ayeisha's cry of anguish ringing in her ears.

'Come back here, you fucking bitch, and do what I say,' Razor roared.

She continued to run, out on to the landing and down the stairs. Behind her she could hear Razor cursing and the sound of heavy footsteps clomping against the concrete. She couldn't stop. She daren't stop. The wind pummelled her as she left the block; lifting her up and speeding her round the corner towards the garages. She squeezed herself between two large wheelie bins and sank down into a dark corner, breathing hard as her head hit the metal handle of a disused amenities cupboard. Tears emptied themselves down her cheeks as she cursed her clumsiness, rubbing at her scalp to relieve the pain.

How could she have been so stupid to think she would ever have been enough for Razor. Yet his betrayal had still stunned her, and with her best friend too. Tonight, he had shown his true colours, contemptuous and cruel, just as her stepfather Tommy had been, all those years before.

The footsteps were getting closer. She pushed herself further into the darkness between the bins and held her breath, trying to calm the shaking in every part of her body, too petrified to expel her breath into the freezing air. She could see Razor's breath fanning out into the dimmed lighting as he moved about outside the garages; she could hear the rattle of his chest and she knew without doubt that he meant every word that he snarled.

'Come out now, you bitch. Come out now or when I find you I'll fucking kill you.'

*

As he climbed the stairs, The Punter could hear the gentle rasping sound of the twins asleep in their rooms. He crept quietly into the bedroom and saw his wife's shape under the duvet. She roused, smiling up at him sleepily as he stripped off and climbed into bed beside her. The bedroom smelt of lavender perfume and the cotton of her nightdress was crisp and cool to the touch.

The brandy was making his head muzzy, having stayed downstairs drinking for a few hours longer, but as she moved across the bed towards him, he wished he'd stayed away all night. He felt her kissing him gently and willed himself to respond but remained stubbornly limp. The more she tried, the less happened.

'Is anything the matter, darling?' she asked.

He thought he could detect the usual critical edge to her voice and his temper flared, shamed at his inability to get an erection. It was all her fault. The humiliation from earlier that evening returned, the toxic laughter, the sneering faces. He looked down at his spouse, so pretty, so submissive, so inanimate, and felt no passion. He needed a return to the filthy hookers and the intoxicating violence on which he was addicted.

Tugging off the duvet, he started to dress, desperate to get away; the guilt at his thoughts slowly transforming itself into fury. His wife was imploring him to stay, telling him not to worry, but that just served to increase his rage.

He heard his children stir as he stepped heavily down the stairs, their cries increasing his feelings of entrapment. Downing a last brandy, he stepped across the threshold of his middle-class, semi-detached residence and climbed into the driving seat.

The Punter knew in exactly which direction he was heading.

Caz stayed rooted to the darkened recess for what seemed like hours until Razor's footsteps gradually faded away. She remained hidden at the sound of Ayeisha calling out her name, not willing to place any further trust in her so-called friend, until her voice too became fainter and finally disappeared.

Only then did she make her way out from her hideaway and scan the area, listening for the slightest sound of their presence before quickly running to the main entrance and up the stairs to the flat. Outside the door she stopped, waiting and watching for any evidence they had returned, but all was quiet. As she entered the stillness of the flat, she knew, without doubt, she could never return. She grabbed her bag, briefly checking that Goldilocks was still safe within, and then gathered together a small quantity of clothes and other belongings. Stuffing them into a small holdall, she took a last look back at the flat that was to have been her forever home with Razor. Her dreams were shattered, her hopes dashed. She had been betrayed again, as she had so many times before.

With that, she walked out of the block and out through the Poets Estate for the last time, knowing she was lucky to have escaped with her life. In the side pocket of her handbag was the small scrap of paper on which Anna's phone number was written. She pulled it out, staring blankly at the number. It might be her only means of escape.

Somehow she had to get to Anna, before Razor got to her.

Chapter 49

Anna was just heading up to bed when her mobile phone vibrated. There was no name displayed on the screen and she was tempted not to answer, but a niggle in the back of her mind brought her finger to the button.

The operator's voice came on the line. 'Will you accept a reverse connect call? It's from a public call box in Streatham.'

'Yes, yes,' she replied, initially confused but realising quickly it must be Caz.

Seconds later her assumption was proved correct as Caz came on the line.

'Anna it's me.'

'What's happened?' She could sense the panic in the young girl's voice.

'I've run away from Razor. He's tryin' to find me an' if he does, he'll kill me. I know he will. I've got nowhere to go an' you said, like, to phone if I needed help.'

'Where are you now? I'll come and get you.'

'I'm in the phone box near the cinema, but I'll hide nearby 'til you get 'ere. I can't risk him seein' me, or I'm done for.'

'Stay there. I'm coming now.'

She explained the situation hastily to her husband, grabbed her bag and, against his strongest entreaties, ran to her car. Now was not the time to falter, though everything in her head knew him to be right. The whole situation screamed danger. She just had to hope Caz had not left her cry for help until it was too late, as Anna herself so nearly had.

It was only a short way, but every second counted. She had to get to Caz before Razor did. This was the chance she had been waiting for. It might be the only opportunity she would get.

The adrenalin was coursing through her body as she pulled up next to the cinema. What if Razor spotted them and attacked them both? Was she just being selfish, placing her own desires before that of her husband and her children?

Before she had the chance to change her mind, the passenger door opened and Caz jumped into the seat beside her, clutching her handbag to her chest and pushing a holdall through to the rear. She looked petrified.

Anna shrugged her reservations to the back of her mind and pulled away, checking in her mirrors that she wasn't being followed. Her office seemed the only option, being a neutral place where they could talk. There was nowhere else they could go. She couldn't bring danger to her family home and she couldn't yet risk telling Caz about the flat until she was sure she was ready. Better to wait and hear what had happened first. They didn't speak on the journey, as if fearful that the slightest sound would alert Razor to their whereabouts.

Entering the office, Anna wrapped Caz in the blanket that was fast becoming her own, switched on the heating and boiled the kettle. She could at least provide warmth for the freezing young girl. Caz wore an expression of complete bewilderment as she sat clinging to a lukewarm radiator.

'What's happened then?' Anna asked quietly. 'Things were going well the last time we spoke.'

'I don't know what the fuck happened, Anna,' Caz said miserably. 'One minute he was good as gold an' I really thought we 'ad a future together, but then it all changed. 'E didn't say nothin', but I 'eard some boy dealer made 'im look stupid and Dutch died. Since then 'e's bin forcin' me out on the streets every night and 'e won't give me no crack until I'm cluckin' for it. I've made 'is flat look nice, but nothings good enough for 'im.' She paused and looked directly at Anna. 'I would 'ave done anything for him. Anything, but 'e's betrayed me now an' I hate him.'

Anna heard the irrevocable finality of her client's last sentence, sensing the same steely determination as when Caz had spoken of Tommy's death. The girl was moving on. Her mind was set and Anna truly believed this could be the end of her relationship with Razor, but, before she let Caz into any secrets, she still needed to hear what had caused the change of heart and whether it was over between them for good.

'What did he do that was so bad?' she asked gently.

'My mate, Ayeisha, came round.' Caz smiled a sad, apologetic smile. 'We was all havin' a drink and smoke. He asked me to go an' get some more booze 'cause we'd run out an' when I got back he was screwing her. Right there in front of me. My best friend. An' he was laughin' at me. The fuckin' bastard was laughin' straight in my face.'

Anna watched as Caz's eyes welled up and the tears flowed unabated on to the floor beneath.

'I screamed at him. I called him a cheatin' evil bastard. Then I ran away. I had to get out. I could hear him comin' after me, so I hid behind the bins. I waited until they'd both gone, then I crept back up the stairs and got my things. I can't go back there now. 'E would kill me.' She paused, closed her eyes and leant her head against the radiator. 'Maybe that would be the best thing for me now. Go back an' let him finish me off, like Redz and Dutch. Nobody would fuckin' care. No one gives a damn what I do. Even my own mother didn't care. She betrayed me as well.

'She killed 'erself, right in front of my eyes. After Tommy died, like I said before, we got close again, Mum and I. Then one day I comes home from school an' she's pissed again. Says she can't cope no more an' she don't want to live no more. I tried to tell her she would be all right. That she had me. That I would always be with her an' look after her, but she said it was too late, that she'd already taken a load of tablets. I ran an' phoned the ambulance, but by the time I got back, she'd cut her wrists with a knife. Slit 'em right up, nearly to her elbows. There was blood spurtin' out of them everywhere. I tried to stop them bleedin', but they wouldn't stop, just kept pumpin' out all over me, all warm and sticky.'

She stopped speaking, rubbing her forearms and tracing the scars on her own wrists.

'I cradled her in my arms an' kept askin' why, why, but all she could say was that she was sorry. Just before she went unconscious she looked at me an' said she loved me, then she closed her eyes. She looked so sad. She never opened them again. I kept shakin' her, tryin' to wake her up, but I couldn't. Gradually the blood stopped pumpin' so hard and then it just stopped pumpin' altogether. By the time the ambulance arrived it was too late.'

She turned and looked up at Anna.

'So now you see. Everyone betrays me. Just when I thought my mum an' I was happy, she betrayed me an' left. Do you know what she said in a letter I found next to her? She said that she could never live up to my expectations and I'd be better off finding someone else to take 'er place. She said that she could never be enough for me… but she was. She was all I ever wanted.

'After her I thought I would never find another person who loved me, 'til Razor rescued me from the home. I loved him an' I thought he loved me too. Even when the other girls was givin' him grief, he always seemed to go easy on me. What a fuckin' stupid bitch I've been. 'E never really loved me at all. I was just there to bring him cash and give him sex when 'e wanted it. Well, I'm not goin' back. 'E can 'ave Ayeisha for all I care now, an' I hope they're happy together.'

Anna watched as Caz's stricken face became firm, resolute. A profound sadness swept through her body as she tried to imagine what it must have been like for Caz witnessing her mother's suicide and being powerless to prevent it happening. At least when her own parents had died it had been accidental, an awful tragedy that had orphaned her in a blink of an eye but had left her without guilt. Caz had been forced to watch as her mother and, to a lesser extent, Razor – both people she adored – betrayed her love, throwing it back in her face.

She reached across, taking Caz by the hand. The time was right to divulge the news of the flat. The girl had to be given a reason for optimism, a slim ray of hope on which to cling.

'Caz, I can help.'

As she spoke, a deafening noise echoed up from the stairwell below and Caz spun round towards the door.

'Anna. It's him. It's Razor.'

Anna could hear Razor's voice bellowing from the street below. Another crash and the door went in, smashing against the wall. She could hear his grunts of exertion as he took the steps two at a time. Grabbing the office phone, she dialled 999, just as he strode into the office. He lunged towards Caz, bringing the back of his hand down across her face and knocking her head hard against the wall, before taking her roughly by the arm and dragging her to her feet.

'That'll teach you to disobey me, you fuckin' bitch.'

He turned towards Anna, staring at the handset in her palm and with no further hesitation ripped the phone from its socket and smashed it on the floor. For a few moments Anna cowered before him, her arms thrown up in self-defence, frozen with fear as he raised his hand to strike, reliving the same debilitating terror she'd known throughout her childhood.

'And that'll teach you to keep your fuckin' nose out of my business.' He dropped his arm. 'Not so fuckin' brave now, are you?'

He turned away and pushed Caz out of the office, kicking her forcefully at the base of her spine so that she stumbled and fell down the stairs. Anna could hear Caz's screams of agony but was powerless to assist. Running to the window, she watched helplessly as Caz was bundled into a car and the door slammed shut behind her. She could just make out the number plate in the faint light of a nearby street lamp and jotted it down.

Shakily, she retrieved her mobile from the bottom of her handbag and dialled 999 again. As the operator came on the line, she saw Caz's terrified face pressed flat against the passenger window, before the vehicle screeched away and swiftly disappeared from view, knowing that she too had failed Caz. With growing horror, she realised it might be the last recollection she would have of her young client alive.

*

Caz touched her hand to her swollen face. The blow had caught her off guard and her right eye had borne the brunt; it was now swelling painfully and partially closed. Every part of her body hurt: her spine and limbs bruised from the kicking to the foot of the stairs, her knees grazed from being dragged forcefully along the pavement and her head aching from the impact of the strike against the wall. Her eyes had connected with Anna's before the car had whisked her away, taking her forever from the safety of the psychologist's office, and the only person with whom she'd ever shared her story.

Razor was still spitting out his vitriol within the confines of the stolen car, but she couldn't understand what he was saying. All she knew was that her destiny was now beyond her control. Her life was in the hands of this rabid man, she had until so recently loved.

The doors were locked. She was trapped and there could be no escape.

The car hurried onwards through the night. She watched the familiar streets rushing past her, blurring together into an ugly maze of dark alleyways and threatening crevices. Razor continued to shout, but his voice seemed far away, drifting in and out of her head, like waves breaking on a shore. Every now and then, she felt him tugging at her head, his fingers clamping into her cheeks as he bawled in rage, then the noise would recede into the background, ready for the next swell of abuse. The car stopped briefly while Razor bought some drugs from DK. He pointed towards her and laughed, shoving the small package of crack down the front of his trousers. Vaguely, she wondered whether she could escape while they talked, but the impossibility of outrunning either man in her condition forced a thin smile of resignation on to her lips. Then they were on the move again.

'Can I have a rock?' she asked dully. 'I need a fix now.'

Her voice sounded alien to her, as if a stranger was operating her mouth. She closed her eyes and tried to focus. Razor was laughing again, his malice filling every square inch of the car's interior.

'You'll have to fuckin' earn it.' She said nothing as he pulled her head roughly to face him. 'Do you understand?'

Mand was standing on her usual corner in the Hatridge Estate. Razor slowed down as he neared her and hooted, braking to a halt and reversing back when she beckoned him over. He wound the window down.

'Hey, Mand. How's business?'

'Good enough! Why? You interested?' She threw her head back and cackled with laughter.

Razor licked his lips slowly. 'You know I'm always interested.'

Caz watched her betrayer's flirting and a surge of pure hatred shuddered through her aching limbs. She pushed herself back in her seat, trying to maximise the distance between them.

'Hey, Caz. I didn't see you there. How're you doin'?' Mand looked past Razor. 'You don't look too good.'

'She's fine,' Razor snapped. 'Looking forward to doin' lots of work for me, aren't you babe?' He slapped her leg, pinching the skin hard between his fingers, and turned back to Mand. 'Anyway, what do you want me for? Can't stay chattin' all night. I'm out an' about tryin' to get my shit sorted, if you know what I mean.'

Mand nodded and flashed him a toothy grin. 'Well, you're in luck then. He's back, the Asian bastard. I was just about to give you a ring when you passed. He's got a flashy new silver sports car, but it was definitely him. I would recognise his fuckin' evil face a mile away.'

'Well, well, well. How's that for perfect timing?' Razor grew suddenly animated. 'Thanks Mand.' He wound the window up and pulled away sharply, heading in the direction of Streatham. 'Best we set the trap.'

A few minutes later, Razor nosed the car into the entrance to Redz' alleyway.

Caz stared out into the desolation as a feeling of dread burrowed deep into her psyche. 'Can't I go back to my normal patch?' she pleaded. 'Please Razor. Why here?'

'Because a murderer always returns to the scene of his crime. Why do you think I've been gettin' you used to workin' here?' Razor unlocked the door and leant across, pushing her out on to the frosty pavement. 'Now stand there, you lazy bitch, and let's see if this bastard wants a piece of you.'

She shivered violently as he slammed the door shut and unwound the window.

'And don't you dare fuck this up. I'll be watching your every move.' He made a V-shape with his fingers, pointing to both of his eyes before turning them to thrust directly through the open window towards her. 'And I've a feeling you won't have to wait too long.'

Chapter 50

'So much for the Christmas spirit,' Charlie shook her head glumly. 'Two glasses of non-alcoholic mulled wine and a Diet Coke.'

'Think yourself lucky,' Paul shoved his hands into his pockets. 'At least your wine was warm. You try drinking three pints of cold apple juice and then coming out into this.' He blew a lungful of breath out into the freezing air, watching as it swirled around his head and dissipated. 'I think I'm frozen from the inside out.' He shuffled from one foot to the other. 'And, I need a piss.'

Charlie laughed. After the disappointments of the day, it had been good to head out for a few drinks with the team, even if having their cars parked up in the yard had meant none of them could properly imbibe.

'Make sure you get a train in tomorrow all of you,' Hunter pulled his scarf tighter around his neck. 'It's the last Friday before Christmas and you deserve a glass of champagne after all your hard work on the Dimitri case.' He turned to Naz, Sabira and Bet. 'You've done a great job getting the girls' further statements today.'

'While I've been releasing Redz' murderer.' Charlie chewed on her lip. 'I'm dreading phoning Gerald Flaherty tomorrow to let him know.' She'd been putting it off since watching Razor walk away into the late-afternoon gloom. It wouldn't be the result any of the Flaherty family would be wishing for this Christmas. It wasn't the result she'd wanted either.

'Something will come up,' Paul squeezed her arm. 'It always does.'

She shook her head. Something had worried her about the investigation right from the start. Everything had seemed so simple, too simple. Razor ticked all the boxes, and they all knew, statistically, women were more likely to be killed by their partners, especially when the partner happened to be a violent pimp. Hunter and the team had always believed Redz' killer to be Razor, and she'd gone along with their fervour, her usual sixth sense not sending her in any other real direction this time. Razor had got away with his violent crimes in the past, he might even have got away with murder, but had he murdered Redz? She honestly didn't know, and it bothered her that she didn't.

A police car shot past her, its siren blasting a path through the queues of traffic around Waterloo. Groups of revellers turned their heads to watch as the blue lights mingled with the greens, reds and yellows of the street decorations. The officers on board would be dealing with the crimes, speaking to witnesses and collecting the clues. The evidence would be out there for them, just as the evidence against Redz' murderer was out there for her. She just had to find it.

'So are you offering to buy the champagne then, boss?' she pushed her doubts to one side and grinned towards Hunter as Lambeth HQ came into view. Paul was right. Something would come up. She offered her hand out towards her boss and he gripped it firmly, shaking his head at the same time as shaking her hand.

'You know me. I'll always put my hand in my pocket when I think you've earned it.'

'But I'm not sure that we have today.' Charlie tilted her head to one side thoughtfully. She looked at each of her colleagues in turn. 'I was going to suggest that when, and only when, we have our suspect for Redz' murder charged and banged up in the cells, you buy us champagne.' She shook his hand firmly, grinning outright at the expression on Naz's face as she remembered her recently championing of a nice glass of Moet et Chandon. 'But until then it's Prosecco all round.'

*

The Punter drove slowly round the streets.

The brandy was taking away his wariness, warming him, making him strong. The cops had nothing on him. They would have come for him already if they had. Now he was back and the knowledge of what was to come was making his skin tingle.

He passed a group of whores standing on a corner, their filthy bodies exposed, their voices screaming in a drunken show of debauchery. Their excesses disgusted him, but he knew that by the end of the night all the wrongs heaped on him by Kavya and his wife and every other female would be righted. Another dirty hooker would be humbled, made to obey his every command. One of them would pay.

He continued onwards, scanning each corner, searching each street for a solitary whore, finding himself indomitably drawn to the area in which his last prostitute had worked. The lure was addictive, irresistible, and as he turned into the road with the alleyway, the sight of a female, alone and vulnerable on the corner, validated his decision. Her pose was provocative, and at the sight of her miniskirt and open jacket, he was immediately aroused.

He pulled up next to the lone figure, lowered the window and waited for her to lean in, his eyes lingering on the soft skin of her breasts so invitingly close. This one showed signs of a beating already, her face battered and swollen. She clearly had not learnt the error of her ways.

'How much for a blow job, darling?' He would enjoy reinforcing the lesson.

'Thirty quid to you.'

He thought he saw a spark of recognition cross her face, but she said nothing to corroborate his notion. Instead, he nodded, watching as she slipped in next to him, the adrenalin beginning to surge through his body. The hunt was almost concluded, but the games were about to begin.

'Turn into the alleyway.' She indicated the entrance he recognised so well. 'It's nice and quiet here and we won't be disturbed.'

He couldn't believe his luck. Memories came flooding back as he aimed the car into the potholed driveway. His whole body was alive, drinking in the smell and sight of his willing hostage. He pulled in behind a garage and switched the engine off, plunging the car into darkness.

A lone street lamp shone a short distance away, casting a faint light across the surrounding area, revealing the ghostly shapes of several bouquets of dead flowers hanging from a nearby fence. The significance was not lost on him, the sight serving only to increase his anticipation.

'Can I have my money?' the whore was saying.

'Not before you give me what I want.'

'The money first or you get nothing,' she insisted.

Her ultimatum stirred the first delicious prickle of anger. How dare she make demands? He turned and grabbed her by the hair, pulling her face towards him. 'You'll get nothing until you do what I tell you.'

She tensed against his strong forearms and he wanted to laugh. She was a fighter and he was going to enjoy bringing her to heel.

He pulled her jacket open, exposing a low-cut T-shirt. The sight of more flesh sent his senses spinning. He unzipped his trousers and lunged towards her, his mouth clamping down on her unwilling lips, waiting for the anticipated struggle.

Was it his imagination or was she not fighting as much as he had anticipated? He'd expected the whore to fight him with every bit of her strength, just as had the last. He wanted to subdue her, to humiliate her, but instead she was barely resisting. The thought of his passive wife in her cotton nightgown came to mind and his anger spiked.

His hands were around her throat now, tightening with every breath. He drew back and watched as she struggled to take in enough air, but she still wasn't fighting hard enough. He released his grip slightly and she took a deep breath, letting out an ear-piercing scream, and started to thrash out. This was more like it. His pleasure was mounting with every strike attempted, every struggle to break free, bringing the moment of climax closer. He pressed down on her windpipe harder, each tiny increase in pressure bringing with it such exquisite gratification. Should he allow her to live or die? The power was all his and the dilemma spurred him on to a peak of pleasure.

He loosened his stranglehold again and waited for the next desperate scream, but this time she remained quiet. He pressed down against her windpipe and released his grip once more, but still she did not cry out. He felt his pleasure diminish. Why was she not screaming?

Taking hold of her with both hands, he squeezed hard against her neck, watching closely as her eyes started to bulge. He felt her trying to swallow, but still he kept the pressure exerted. She was staring straight past him now, a look of defeat on her face.

'Fight, you bitch, fight,' he screamed.

But she fought no more. Instead, her body became limp, her head floppy and her pupils rolled upwards into her skull.

A sudden noise distracted him as the door was flung open and a hand grabbed him by his shoulder. Cold, sharp metal sliced into his throat and he felt the flow of blood down his neck.

With a jerk, he was pulled backwards against the driver's seat. He tried to rear up against the force but stopped as the blade pierced the skin of his neck again. The reflection of a large, shaven-headed man loomed large in the centre mirror and he felt a vague sense of shock at what was happening. In that instant he realised the tables had turned and it was now he who was at the mercy of this stranger.

The man had one arm around his neck, with the knife in his other, held firmly to his throat. He felt himself dragged backwards out of his car and tried to cover himself, where his trousers lay undone.

'You're the bastard that murdered my girl, aren't you?' The knifeman laughed at his efforts. 'Now it looks like you're tryin' to kill another.' A punch knocked his head back against the concrete and he felt the blade of the knife pushing down on to his throat again. His assailant was on top of him, pinning him down, and he dared not move. 'Seems like I'm goin' to have to give you a taste of your own fuckin' medicine.'

'Please don't hurt me,' he sobbed out loud. For the first time in his life, he knew fear; real incapacitating terror. It held him immobile, gripped tightly in its icy claws. It threatened to strip away his respectability, and everything he had worked for so long to obtain. The shame he would bring to his family and community was immeasurable. He would be lucky to come away from the situation with any dignity intact.

More than that, though, as he looked up into his assailant's cold, merciless eyes he knew he would be lucky to escape with his life.

Chapter 51

Razor looked down into the face of his blubbering adversary and felt no pity; in fact he couldn't believe his luck. It had all been far too easy.

Ayeisha was now his. So what if Caz didn't like it; she would just have to get used to the idea... and she certainly wouldn't be going back to see her meddling shrink again, ever. God knows, it had been a mistake to allow her visits to continue in the first place.

The rest had been perfect. His hunch had been right. The Punter had literally driven into his trap, returning to his old stomping ground, even unwittingly helping him to teach Caz a further lesson. It had been sweet seeing the expression on her face as he'd allowed the beating to continue far longer than was necessary. Protection would only be forthcoming, if her obedience was guaranteed.

Redz' murder now required proper avenging. The razor blades had been prepared earlier in the evening, placed carefully for ease of access in his jacket pocket. Keeping the knife held to his captive's throat, Razor reached in and took one out, holding it directly over his victim's face.

'What are you going to do with that?' the man stammered, hypnotised as the blade moved slowly across his eyeline.

'I'm going to make fucking sure you never forget who I am.'

He pushed The Punter's head against the ground, exposing his left cheek, keeping the blade of the knife pressed hard against his chin. The bastard was shaking. It was fun to toy with him.

Placing the razor against the top of his cheek, he sliced vertically down to the corner of his mouth. The man tensed, whimpering softly as the blood sprang up from the wound, running darkly across his cheek towards his ear.

'That's for Redz,' Razor said, positioning the blade back on the uppermost point of his first incision.

The Punter was sobbing out loud now, either from pain or humiliation, he didn't care. Carefully he traced a semicircle to the centre of the vertical line, the blade slicing easily through the soft tissue.

'And that's for Caz.'

'Please stop,' his victim sobbed. 'You're hurting me.'

Razor stared down unsympathetically at his prey. It was surprising how easy it was to reduce a grown man to tears.

The blood was flowing freely now and it was difficult to see where the last incision would start from, but Razor was an expert. He'd left his initial etched proudly on the face of countless other challengers over the years. He bent forward towards The Punter, the razor hovering over his bloody cheek.

'And this one's for me...'

His concentration was shattered by the dazzle of headlights and the sound of vehicles screeching across the gravel towards him. He looked up, temporarily blinded as blue lights rotated across the garage tops and torchlight was shone directly into his eyes. He could hear shouting and registered the sight of people, some in uniforms running towards him.

'Police,' a voice shouted. 'Put your weapon down and let him go.'

But he wasn't finished yet. Placing the razor quickly down on his prey's cheek, he looked up, daring them to come any further.

As the full force of CS spray reacted with the insides of his eyes and lungs, he scored downwards in a last flourish, rounding the last stroke off across the man's cheek, before releasing his grip on both blades and falling backwards. Tears, mucous and phlegm poured from his eyes and nose as the chemical filled all his facial orifices. He brought his hands up to rub his burning eyes, coughing and retching as he struggled to breathe through the mist of CS. In one movement his arms were forced behind his back, handcuffs clamped around his wrists, and he felt himself lifted to his feet and his head held high into the night air. Through the shouting and confusion, the same female voice instructed him not to panic and to breathe normally. It was a voice he recognised well and for once he did what it said. As the crescendo of noise died away, he stared in the direction of the voice, the tears in his eyes making his vision blurred and distorted.

'I'm arresting you for GBH,' DC Charlie Stafford said evenly.

He started to focus and, as he did so, the way in which their roles were reversed was not lost on him. She was now the one with the upper hand.

'You should be fuckin' nicking him, not me,' Razor shouted, looking round blindly for the Punter.

Paramedics and police were swarming all around Caz and The Punter. He watched as Caz was lifted on to a stretcher and carried to the rear of an ambulance. She was still motionless and he wondered carelessly whether he had left it too late before intervening.

Another paramedic was tending to The Punter, placing dressings over his cheek and neck. As he watched, he saw them walk the bastard to another ambulance. A sudden flash of anger surged through his body as he watched the door of the ambulance close behind him. He lunged forward struggling violently, until his legs were kicked from under him and his face pushed down into the dirt and grit of the alleyway. He strained his head up, spitting out the filth and watched as two burly policemen climbed up into the ambulance behind The Punter.

'Don't let him get away,' he shouted, almost half-heartedly now as the anger drained away. Suddenly he didn't really care anymore. He'd given his adversary something to remember him by and he'd avenged Redz in the eyes of his community. That was all that really mattered. Hopefully now the cops would do their job.

As he was led to the police van, he turned to DC Stafford, speaking almost nonchalantly. 'He was the bastard who killed Redz... and he just nearly did the same to Caz.'

Chapter 52

Charlie slammed the cage door of the van and held her sleeve to her face. Her nose and eyes were also streaming from the effects of the CS spray but it had all been worthwhile when she'd realised who had borne the brunt of it.

'You OK?' Paul was at her side, pulling some man-size tissues from his pocket. He offered them to her. 'I think you might need these,' he said, chuckling, as Naz joined them.

'Yeah, I'm fine. Thanks, Paul.' She took a couple, blowing her nose gratefully. 'You were right when you said something would come up.'

She and the rest of the team had been just about to leave Lambeth HQ for the night when they'd heard the call over Hunter's radio. *Disturbance. Female screaming.* It was only when the name of the witness was given out that Charlie's ears had really pricked up though. Maria Simpson was the caller and the location was Redz' alleyway. It couldn't be happening again.

Grabbing her kit belt, Charlie had jumped into one of the cars about to leave the yard and got an express ride straight to the scene, arriving in the first wave of emergency vehicles. Paul, Hunter, Naz and Sabira had arrived soon afterwards, but she'd been so caught up dealing with Razor and the initial action, she'd not had time to find out the full circumstances. All she knew was that Caz was one of the casualties and a large Asian male was the other, and both looked to have sustained serious injuries.

The two ambulances loaded with their casualties were just about to leave, with Sabira accompanying Caz and a couple of hefty police minders with the Asian man. Both were to be taken to King's College Hospital, although they were to be kept separate. Hunter had ensured that neither casualty was to be released until they knew exactly what had been alleged. Neither was in any state to do so in any case.

'How is Caz?' Charlie wiped at her eyes as the ambulances headed off, with blue lights flashing. 'She was still unconscious when I last saw her and she didn't look good.'

Paul pursed his lips together, frowning. 'Well, she did regain consciousness before they left, but she's been beaten up pretty badly and wasn't able to talk.'

'I doubt Sab will be able to speak with her for a good few hours,' Naz added.

'Do we know yet what's happened?' Charlie stuffed the tissues into her pocket and blinked. 'Razor said that the guy he'd assaulted was the man who'd killed Redz.'

'He would say that,' Hunter joined them.

'He also claimed that the same guy had tried to kill Caz just now,' she added.

'Well it certainly looks like one of them did. But it'll remain to be seen if Caz says the same. Or the other guy for that matter. At the moment we only have Razor's side of the story.'

'There's some interesting information coming in about Razor.' Paul held his radio to his ear and repeated the latest information. 'Uniform found a Fiesta at the end of the alleyway. The engine was still warm and it was insecure and appeared to have been hotwired, so they did a check on it. Needless to say, it was reported stolen a few days ago, from just around the corner from the Poets Estate where Razor lives. Even more interestingly it also has a linked report on it from just under an hour ago.'

'Go on,' Charlie caught the smile on Paul's lips. 'Don't keep us hanging.'

'Well, the report states that a female by the name of Charlene Philips, Caz, had been abducted by a known male, assaulted and bundled into the vehicle in Tooting Bec Common. The male is her pimp and goes by the name Razor.'

'Does it say who the informant is?' Charlie knew that Anna Christophe's office was situated by the common. She checked her watch. Surely she wouldn't be there at that time of night.

Paul called up the control room to enquire and she listened, intrigued, as the reply confirmed the caller as the psychologist. Quickly she dialled Anna's number, listening as her friend repeated exactly what had happened.

'Anna claims that Caz called her earlier, desperate because Razor had threatened to kill her. She opened the office to give her refuge, but Razor found them. He smashed his way in, threatened her and assaulted Caz. Caz was in a right state. She really believed that Razor would kill her.'

'Well maybe that's the answer to our question then,' Hunter looked hard at Charlie. 'But it's very convenient to have someone else there to blame.'

*

'What's this man been arrested for?'

'He's been arrested for GBH with intent, Sarge,' Charlie replied, as she and Paul walked Razor into the custody office, still covered in blood and dirt from the alleyway. 'We caught him in the act of cutting his victim's face with a razor blade. He may also have other weapons secreted in his clothing.'

'In that case, take him straight to a cell and get him searched thoroughly. And bag up all his clothing. He can have one of our suits to wear.'

Paul nodded and selected a white overall and a pair of black plimsolls. There was nothing like a plain white tight-fitting onesie to bring a scowling prisoner down a peg or two.

While they were gone, Charlie took the opportunity to phone Maria Simpson. With any luck she could shed some light on who had attacked whom. The old lady was glad she had called but wasn't able to assist. At the first scream, she had dialled the operator and had still been on the line as the first blue lights flashed their entrance. She had seen nothing.

As Charlie put her phone back in her pocket, Paul re-emerged with Razor in tow. She stifled a laugh at the sight of their suspect in his regulation overall, still attempting to walk with a swagger as he neared them. His large frame filled it completely, each of the legs and sleeves being slightly too short, giving him a rather comedic appearance.

'We found this hidden down the front of his pants, Sarge,' Paul placed a property bag on the counter containing a small package. 'I counted approximately ten rocks of what I suspect to be crack cocaine in the package. He's been further arrested for possession of a controlled drug with intent to supply.'

Charlie brightened. The pendulum seemed to be swinging right back in their favour. The amount was probably not enough to elicit a charge of possession with intent to supply, rather than straight possession, but it was sufficient to allow them to search his address again. She sought the relevant authority and gathered a small group of officers together in readiness.

It would be good to have one last chance to look round his flat.

*

Charlie knew the way to Razor's flat like the back of her hand. She knew her way around the interior of the flat equally well. As they entered, she immediately noticed it was in better order than at their previous visit when the body of Dutch had lain dead on the settee. A number of scented candles were spread around the lounge and main bedroom and their fragrances still hung in the air, masking its normal dank stench.

She, Hunter and several uniformed officers would be conducting the search and for Charlie it was imperative they were as thorough as possible. This might be the last opportunity they'd have to get Razor put away, at least for something. She instructed the others to shout immediately if they found anything at all of interest. She would be searching the lounge.

She pulled on her latex gloves and decided where to start, working her way methodically round, uncovering and upending every item of furniture and examining every drawer and box thoroughly. Her gut was telling her there was something here. She just had to find it.

After half an hour's meticulous searching, she came to the final item of furniture. No shouts had been forthcoming from the other rooms and Charlie was beginning to acknowledge, with a slight sense of disappointment, that it might all have been a waste of time after all.

She opened the door to the wall unit, lifting it as it swung drunkenly on its only hinge. Several old envelopes and forgotten bills fell out on to the floor, freed from within a pile of paperwork. An old carrier bag was lying on a shelf, its handles folded around itself. Its weight surprised her as she lifted it carefully to one side. Flicking her torch on, she aimed the light down inside the bag, before staring uncomprehendingly at its contents.

As her brain processed what her eyes were seeing, her hands began to shake. She called out to Hunter, who joined her within seconds, staring down wordlessly at where she was pointing. Pulling out his radio, he barked out some instructions to the control room, before turning back to her.

'Great job, Charlie,' he rubbed his hands together and grinned. 'We've got the bastard at last.'

Chapter 53

Caz lay back on the hospital trolley and stared up at the ceiling. All around was noise and clamour but she felt at peace. She watched as the nurses came and went, checking temperatures, blood pressures, smiling and whispering words of encouragement. She watched as doctors frowned and gave orders, their pens scratching diagnoses and instructions across each patient's chart.

Caz knew she was lucky to be alive.

Her whole body hurt. A neck support kept her head from moving and every part of her body throbbed painfully. Dark, mottled bruising covered much of her limbs and face.

She thought back over the events of the night, her mind replaying the betrayal and fear, the escape and the capture, the fight and the surrender. Now, as her fingers gently brushed the swelling on her cheek, she knew without doubt that everything would turn out all right in the end.

She heard the sound of hushed voices outside her cubicle and then the curtain was pulled to one side and a nurse peered in.

'You've got a friend to see you,' she said as Anna's anxious face appeared over her shoulder.

'Thank God you're still alive,' her friend exclaimed, taking a step forward and squinting towards her. 'I thought we'd lost you. Can I come in?'

Caz tried to smile but her mouth was dry, her lips chafed, and the neck support kept her from nodding. She lifted her hand and waved.

Anna stepped forward, followed by the nurse and a policewoman, Sabira, who had accompanied her in the ambulance. She'd brought with her Caz's belongings – her handbag and holdall – left behind in the office just hours before.

The curtain was repositioned and Anna came closer, putting the bags down on the bed next to her and bending to examine her injuries. 'Ow,' she exclaimed. 'Looks like you came close.'

'She did.' The nurse lifted a chart up from the end of the bed and indicated in Anna's direction.

'She's my friend,' Caz croaked painfully. 'You can talk to her.'

The nurse nodded her understanding and read from the notes. 'In that case, you'll be pleased to know that even though you've got injuries over almost every inch of your body, there doesn't appear to be any that are too serious. You should make a full recovery. X-rays do show several small fractures around the orbital and nasal bones, and the soft tissue around your neck and throat is badly swollen and has internal bruising.' She scanned the chart again before turning to Anna. 'She's also been given painkillers and some diazepam to help her rest and to assist with any withdrawal symptoms and she'll be monitored and kept sedated until we can complete further tests.' The nurse hooked the chart back on to the end of the bed and took a step back. 'All in all, she has been very lucky.'

'I wouldn't put it quite that way. But I know what you mean. You'll put her back together physically.' Anna frowned and bent down next to Caz, wetting her lips with a small sponge. 'And I'll be here for you if you need help to be put back together mentally.'

Caz smiled, searching Anna's face as she spoke. She saw the tears glistening at the corners of her therapist's eyes and could sense her sincerity. It was a strange feeling, knowing that this comparative stranger was prepared to help her, but Anna had proved her trustworthiness.

'Could I have a quick word with Caz?' Anna was asking now.

Caz watched as the others trooped out, leaving her alone with her confidante.

'Caz,' Anna sat down next to her. 'Thank you for talking to me about your mother. Now I have a secret of my own to explain. I was about to tell you when Razor arrived and dragged you away.' She swallowed hard. 'I wasn't sure I'd get another chance, but thank God I have. Anyway, a friend of mine at the council has a small studio flat that has become available. She's kept it for you. It's ready now. You just have to sign the paperwork and it's yours.'

Caz couldn't quite believe what she was hearing. Not only had Anna helped her break free from Razor, she was now providing the means to make it permanent.

'But, it's only yours if you're prepared to work for it?' Anna sounded a note of caution. 'You'll have to stay away from Razor and all those people who are destructive influences in your life, the other dealers and even your friends. I can also help you get a place in rehab, but you'll have to make a fresh start. You can't go back. Do you understand what I'm asking of you? If you revert to your present lifestyle, you'll lose the flat.'

Caz looked at Anna as she spoke. Anna was strong and would be there to support her, unlike all the others who were weak and had let her down.

For a few seconds her life flashed before her; the twisted pleasure of her stepfather Tommy as he touched her young body, the abandonment as her mother closed her eyes for the last time, the derision on Razor's face as he screwed Ayeisha in full view and the knowledge that The Punter sitting beside her in his car was the same madman who'd attacked Redz. More than anything though, she remembered Razor standing at The Punter's shoulder, watching as the life was squeezed from her. The sight of his cold, remote eyes staring down at her from outside the car window would be etched forever in her psyche.

The decision came easily, the memories shaping her need to take back control. Not only did she want Razor out of *her* life. She wanted him sentenced to the rest of *his* in prison… and to understand on whose terms he was sent. And now she had the means. Things were turning out even better than she'd envisaged.

'I'll do whatever is needed,' she promised.

Anna left then, promising to collect her as soon as she was fit to be discharged.

Caz was left alone in the cubicle and she knew now exactly what had to be done. She rummaged in her handbag and found Goldilocks, stroking her gently over her face and noticing immediately the stench of the crack house. The precious memento of her mother looked even dirtier and more soiled in the sterility of the hospital.

Hoisting herself up painfully, she swung her legs round and eased herself slowly upright. Her head swam and she steadied herself against the trolley. Her whole body felt leaden, but gradually she managed to shuffle out of her cubicle and head towards the toilet and washroom. The policewoman was seated directly outside but nodded her understanding, and no nurses stopped her to ask unnecessary questions.

She closed the door and ran the hot tap, gently immersing Goldilocks in the steaming liquid and watching as her thin empty body yielded to the ripples on the surface. Carefully she lathered soap on to the threadbare material, the dirt and grime turning the water in the basin a murky brown. Time and time again she replaced the water until eventually it stayed clear.

When she was satisfied Goldilocks was clean, Caz lifted the sodden doll to her face, inhaling its new perfumed aroma and softness, all memories of Razor now gone, washed away forever from her life, just as he would be. She would start afresh, a new beginning, a new life, with just her precious, clean doll as a memento of her past.

Returning to her cubicle, she placed Goldilocks on the radiator to dry, climbed back up on to the trolley and pulled the blanket over her. It wouldn't be too long before her plans would be set into motion.

Chapter 54

'Hello, Caz. Are you up to speaking with me now?'

Caz smiled almost apologetically, as she recognised Charlie Stafford peeping around the curtain. She nodded. 'Hi Charlie. Yeah, I'll tell you everything that happened an' I need to tell you some other stuff an' all.'

Her throat was still sore and it hurt to talk, but she was determined to get started. The police officer was clearly pleased at her words. She'd be even more delighted when she'd heard her account of the evening's events.

Charlie pulled up a chair and beckoned her colleague in. 'I've just come from Razor's flat. I was going to ask Sabira to take your statement, but I wanted to see how you were myself. So, how are you?'

'Not so bad, seeing as that bastard tried to kill me,' she whispered.

She watched the officer's slight confusion as she pulled out a pen from her rucksack and opened a notebook.

'I've spoken to Anna and she's given me her account but just run through it from your point of view.'

She took a deep breath and started, telling Charlie about the previous week and how Razor's mood had changed after the deaths of both Redz and Dutch. She explained the events leading up to her escape from Razor that night, after finding him with Ayeisha and what had happened at Anna's office. She indicated her eye, which was still partially closed, the bruising an angry mauve. Charlie nodded and smiled as she went through it, taking the odd note but clearly pleased that her story matched with that of Anna.

'Anna is happy to make a statement about what happened,' Charlie confirmed. 'In fact, another colleague should be taking it now.'

Caz smiled. 'Yeah I guessed she would.'

'Anyway, carry on,' Charlie prompted.

'Yeah, right. After he dragged me from Anna's, he pushed me into a car and locked all the doors.'

'Do you know whose car it was?' interrupted Charlie.

'How the fuck should I know?', Caz replied quietly. 'He had to start this one with a screwdriver, so I expect it was nicked, but I couldn't do nothin' about it. Anyway, we drove round a bit, then he took me to Redz' old patch and pushed me out on to the street. I was freezin', like, but I got picked up by that big guy pretty quick. We agreed business an' he drove me to the garages where Redz was done. It freaked me out when I saw those dead flowers. Anyway, I asked The Punter for my cash upfront an' he said that he would pay me, but could we just talk for a bit first. Some of them is like that if they lose their bottle, but normally I can do some persuading pretty quick, if you know what I mean?'

She grinned, painfully. 'We was just talkin' an' The Punter was nearly ready when the door suddenly flew open an' there was Razor. He pulled the guy out, sayin' I'd had enough time an' where was the money? I said I hadn't got it yet an' he went fuckin' mad. He grabbed me round the throat and was just squeezin' an' squeezin'. He kept shoutin' that I was a useless bitch an' he'd have to teach me a lesson. I managed to scream a few times when I could, but he wouldn't let go. I could hear The Punter in the background telling him to stop, but Razor just told him to fuck off an' leave him to sort 'is business out. Said I deserved everything I got. The last thing I remember was seein' The Punter tryin' to pull him off me. Then I must have blacked out. I don't remember anything more. All I know is I'm bleedin' lucky to be alive.'

She stopped, watching Charlie who was scribbling furiously.

'I really thought I was a goner. I didn't know where I was when I woke up. It was only when Anna arrived that I gradually started to remember what 'ad 'appened. I know I'm fuckin' lucky. It could've been me this time.'

Charlie looked up and their eyes met. Caz held her gaze.

'Are you absolutely sure The Punter was trying to help you?' the police officer frowned. 'Only, we received information recently that a man fitting his description was responsible for Redz' death.'

'Probably just a rumour put out by friends of Razor.' She smiled. 'There was a punter a while ago that sounded a bit like this guy. We got warned about him by girls from a different patch. It's probably where the rumour came from. It's just a coincidence if they look similar. But this guy helped me. He didn't attack me.'

'And you're sure about that? Because Razor says that you were being attacked by The punter… not him?'

'Well he would say that, wouldn't he? That fuckin' bastard hunted me down, punched me, kicked me and then tried to throttle me. He's fuckin' mental. No, I'm lucky The Punter was there. It must have been him that saved me.'

'Are you willing to make a statement to that effect?' Charlie asked.

'Too right I am an' I also want to bleedin' take back what I said in that other statement I gave you.'

'What do you mean?'

'You know,' Caz persisted. 'That statement I made saying that Razor was with me on the night Redz got murdered. He weren't with me at the flat at all. He went out earlier with Redz an' I never saw him 'til the next day. He forced me to be 'is alibi, said I'd be fuckin' next if I didn't back him up. Said he'd enjoy watching me die, like he'd enjoyed watching Redz die, an' he nearly fuckin' did, the bastard.'

*

The Punter lay on his trolley in the hospital cubicle nearby and cursed his bad luck. None of this would now be happening if it weren't for bloody women.

His cheek and neck throbbed painfully. Although the main bleeding had been stemmed, a sticky pink fluid still seeped out from the wounds. Nurses came and went, changing and checking his dressings, but the cuts required stitching, and he was no longer a priority. As each new casualty arrived, so the wait increased, but he didn't mind. At least it was delaying the inevitable time when he would be taken to the police station.

Two bulky policemen stood guard outside his cubicle, watching him through the gap in the curtain, but the rigid metal handcuffs removed any notion of escape. He was under arrest for GBH on the whore, but she'd deserved it. Now he was being made to pay the price for her depravity.

Nobody as yet knew of his whereabouts; not even his wife having been informed. The longer the better though; she would likely treat him with contempt or, worse still, pity, but she'd have to understand it was her to blame. A wife could not treat her husband with disrespect as she had done earlier. It was her responsibility to cater for all his sexual needs and she had clearly failed.

Whichever way he looked at it, it wasn't his fault. His predicament was not of his own making, but at the same time, he could fathom no way out of the situation. When news of his activities became public, he would be ruined, all his hard work building up a professional profile within his community rubbished.

His thoughts were interrupted by the arrival of the doctor. Her cheery practicality did nothing to allay his sense of grievance towards the female gender. She peeled off the dressings, dealing first with the cuts to his neck, before concentrating on his cheek.

'Nasty old wound you've got here. How'd you manage to get this?' she asked, tilting his head over to get a better look at it.

He mumbled an explanation. A group of drunken youths had jumped him as he left a pub. He certainly wasn't going to tell this interfering bitch his business.

She prepared a syringe, injected a small amount of local anaesthetic around the edges of the wound. 'Still, it's neat.'

'Will I be left with a scar?' he ventured, already knowing the probable answer.

'Well yes, there will be a scar, but hopefully, if it heals well, it won't be too prominent. And there's always the option of plastic surgery.'

She bent over him, her perfume filling his nostrils as she stitched the skin together. Her hands brushed against his cheek. She was teasing him like all the rest.

'Do you realise it looks like a perfect letter "R"?'

He tensed at the question; the doctor's face being momentarily replaced by that of his assailant. *My name's Razor. Just giving you something to remember me by.*

So this was his attacker's mark; he'd been branded for life, but he had to admit to a grudging respect for the man. The scar would be perfect for ensuring his assailant's name was never forgotten and he'd forever be forced to explain it away.

The doctor tied off the last knot of the fine nylon suture and stepped back to admire her handiwork.

'Can I see it?' he asked.

'I don't have a mirror, but there's one by the washbasin at the end of the corridor.' She signed his discharge and stuck a dressing over the injury, leaving the upper edge open. Turning towards the police guards, she handed them two replacement dressings. 'I'm all finished now. You can take him away. Get him to seal the top edge of the dressing properly over the wound when he's seen it.'

The two police officers nodded, guiding him down the corridor and stopping at the mirror. Gingerly he peeled the pad down so it flapped open, staring in shock at his reflection. Stubble shadowed his chin and dried crimson blood showed darkly against his jacket collar. The letter 'R' stained his dusky skin, each stitch screaming his disgrace, the ugliness of the branding seared against his handsome features.

Pushing the dressing back in place, he stared in growing panic along the hospital corridor. Daylight was streaming in through the exit. A police van was positioned directly in his view, its rear doors open wide, giving its gloomy interior the appearance of a dark cavern, waiting to swallow him up into its depths.

As he stepped up into its unforgiving jaws and the engine growled into life, he knew there was no escape. He was finally beaten. Now he had to accept his fate.

Chapter 55

'Your other suspect is on his way back from the hospital. He'll be arriving in about half an hour.'

Charlie thanked the custody officer and shouted the information out across the office. It was the news they had been expecting and it focussed their minds on the job in hand. The whole team were still in, now working into their thirtieth hour, with red-rimmed, gritty eyes and mouths that tasted of caffeine. Apart from adrenalin, it was the only thing keeping them awake.

She picked up the office phone and crossed her fingers, as Hunter looked over.

'Wish me luck,' she said, dialling the number for the Crown Prosecution Service.

The same senior CPS representative with whom she'd previously disagreed came on the line. She closed her eyes with a sigh and started to explain the previous night's events, along with the new evidence in Redz' murder case. At least he knew the details of that investigation inside out. Hopefully this time it would go their way.

'I'll phone you back when I've made my decisions.' His voice gave nothing away.

'Well?' the whole team were looking towards her when she put the phone down.

'I don't know yet. He's thinking about it.'

'We have Caz's statements and the new exhibits that you found at Razor's.' Hunter pulled his handkerchief out and dabbed at his forehead. 'What is there to think about?'

Charlie glanced down at her précis of all the new evidence, completed on her return from the hospital and sent on to the CPS just prior to the phone conversation. Hunter had recommended which charges should be considered and which allegations should be dropped.

No charges were to be levelled at Caz for being in a stolen car. She was perhaps the most obvious victim in the whole course of events and was being kept in hospital for observation, leastways until the swelling to her throat was reduced. On discharge she would be taken to a new address arranged by Anna Christophe, who had been remarkable in Charlie's opinion, not only putting her neck on the line for her client, but being prepared to also tell her story in court.

Charlie walked across to the window, staring down at the busy streets below as her thoughts returned to Caz. Her assault in the alleyway was the only part of the previous night's incident that remained unverified. Apart from Maria Simpson, no other resident had phoned police, all no doubt choosing to close their ears to the screams on this occasion. There was nobody therefore to confirm which man was her attacker.

Razor claimed it was The Punter, but Caz was adamant it was Razor, somehow finding the inner strength to agree to having her words transcribed into writing from her hospital bed, whilst fully understanding the statement would be scrutinised by her violent pimp and his defence team.

It would be Caz's testimony against Razor's. She was playing a dangerous game if she was lying.

Charlie's mind switched to the man, soon to be returning. Bet had provided the information for the CPS but, with fatigue setting in, she hadn't really digested all the facts.

'Bet, can you run through what we know about the punter again before he gets here?'

'There's nothing much of any note,' Bet replied. 'His name is Rashid Kanthan. I've checked the PNC and he has no previous convictions and the voter's register shows him and his wife living at the address given. He appears to be a regular law-abiding bloke. We've got no photo, no intelligence, nothing.' She raised her eyebrows. 'From what I can gather from his guards at the hospital, he's hardly said a word. Still in shock probably and wondering what on earth possessed him to get involved with prostitutes in the first place.'

'We've seized his vehicle, haven't we? Anything on it?'

'No, nothing. Though it appears he's only recently bought it. It's not registered to him yet.'

'But,' Paul flicked to some notes, 'I found another car registered to his address.' He read out the registration number. 'It comes back to a black Vauxhall Corsa. Interestingly, it was reported as stolen on the afternoon of Thursday 14th December, the same day as Redz was murdered. It turned up on Battersea Common the next evening totally burnt out. I've checked the report. The whole car was gutted by fire. Nothing left but a shell, and that's now been removed by the local council and crushed.'

Charlie frowned. The niggle that had been in the back of her mind came to the forefront. 'What did Kanthan have to say about it, Paul?'

'Nothing much. He parked near a client's house and, when he left, the car had been stolen. It's a basic theft report. He was informed in person at his home address after the vehicle was found burnt out, albeit a few hours later, and was in bed, so no raised suspicions then either.'

'So, we have a large Asian male involved in a serious assault on a prostitute.' Charlie rubbed her lips anxiously, thinking of the previous intel' from King's Cross. 'And it turns out he used to drive a small dark car which was reported stolen the same day as Redz was killed, and then found burnt out the next day...'

Bet chipped back in. 'But I've run that registration plate through our list of vehicles seen in the vicinity of the crime scene on the night of Redz' murder and it didn't show up, although the vehicle was out and about that night. It does ping up on an ANPR camera further into Central London.'

'I know what you're getting at, Charlie.' Paul tilted his head to one side. 'So, let's say that uncorroborated report from King's Cross *was* accurate, it's still possible his car was spotted uptown and a warning relayed to our local girls, who have put two and two together?'

'And come up with five.' Hunter shook his head. 'And that's leaving aside the possibility that his description was leaked specifically to assist Razor.'

Charlie remembered Caz making exactly the same suggestion. 'But it's still a bit of a coincidence, and the CPS may well think the same.'

She stopped abruptly as the phone on her desk started to ring. Paul motioned towards it and they all watched as Charlie strode over and picked up the receiver. Any second now they'd know.

Chapter 56

Charlie looked into the rear cage of the police van as the doors opened. Slumped on the seat she saw the bulky figure of the punter. The man was looking down at his feet and only raised his head slightly to glance at her. Plastered across his cheek was a large dressing, the top edge peeling away slightly. There was another taped to his neck. Charlie took in his large frame, closely cropped hair and leather jacket, still with dried blood caked across the surface of the collar. It wasn't a long coat, but it was leather.

For a moment she wondered again whether there was any credence in Razor's assertions or the intel' reports of the violent punter, but then, they had the new evidence and Caz had made it quite clear she regarded this man as her saviour.

There was no point delaying further. Charlie had her instructions. She knew what she had to do.

'Rashid Kanthan?'

The man looked towards her as she said his name.

'Yes.'

'Rashid, you're free to go. The woman that was assaulted has made a statement, stating that it wasn't you that attacked her. In fact, she says that you probably saved her life.'

She watched the male closely, his expression changing from one of defeat, to surprise as her words registered.

'I'd like to take a statement detailing your account of the incident though, before you leave. I witnessed the other man assaulting you and arrested him, but to get him charged I will still need a victim statement from you.'

Now the surprise was replaced with a frown.

'I'd rather not,' the man said after a long pause. 'I feel deeply ashamed at being caught with a prostitute. If my wife found out, I would bring embarrassment to my whole family.'

'But you have serious injuries which may leave scars. Don't you want your attacker charged?' she persisted.

'No, I want nothing further done and I don't want to have to go to court and have it all dragged up there.'

'But we have the man responsible and police witnesses. Are you sure you won't change your mind?' Charlie felt exasperated. After seeing his brutality first hand, Razor was about to go unpunished.

'Yes, I'm quite sure. I am regarded with respect in my community and I don't wish that to change. I just want to go home to my family and try to forget it happened.'

'I'll need to take a statement from you withdrawing the GBH allegation then and I'll make arrangements for your car to be returned as soon as possible.'

She sighed and took out a blank form, scribbling out the words of a withdrawal statement. As she passed it towards the punter to sign, she realised the man was still handcuffed.

'Let me take those off,' she pulled out a key, staring mesmerised as Rashid Kanthan held out his hands. A row of heavy gold rings adorned his right hand, moving hypnotically as she removed the restraints and he signed the statement.

'Can I go now?' he reached up, scratching at the edge of the dressing. The padding folded down, exposing the large 'R' gouged across his cheek.

'At least your name begins with 'R',' she commented, still transfixed.

'Yes, handy, isn't it?' The man stretched languidly, sticking the dressing back over the stitches. 'Now can I go?'

She paused, as another wave of disquiet rolled down her spine. Slowly she stepped back, allowing Rashid Kanthan to climb down from the van. She indicated the way out and watched as the man walked slowly towards the exit. As he reached the street, he turned round, smiled and gave a slight nod.

Charlie felt the same wave of doubt surge, stronger now, every instinct telling her to go after the man, every signal pointing to his guilt... for something. But what? She had the right man locked away in the cells, hadn't she? Caz had said so and both Hunter and the senior CPS lawyer had agreed the course of action, but she still couldn't escape the feeling of unease that had settled upon her.

*

'Sarge, on the advice of the CPS, I've just de-arrested the hospital detainee, Mr Rashid Kanthan, and released him.' Charlie had set her doubts to one side and returned to the custody office. 'We have a victim statement from Miss Charlene Philips stating that her pimp, Clinton Roberts or Razor as we know him, and not Mr Kanthan, was responsible for her assault.' She paused and took a deep breath. 'And Mr Kanthan does not wish to pursue his own allegation of GBH against Roberts. He's just made a withdrawal statement to that effect.' She pushed a copy of his statement across the desk. 'I'll need to update Roberts fully on what's happening.'

Quickly she ran through the decisions made by the CPS lawyer during the course of their conversation.

The sergeant nodded his approval. 'I think it would be best if you speak to him through the wicket. I don't think he's going to like what you have to say.'

Razor was lying flat out on the blue plastic mattress looking up at the ceiling in the cell when Charlie opened the wicket. He sprang up and came straight over to the Perspex window, his expression turning to his familiar sneer.

'Have you come to admit you're wrong again and let me out?' he hissed.

Charlie stared directly into Razor's eyes, feeling her previous unease lifting as he tried to front her out. The man was an animal, an emotionless predator who preyed on weak defenceless young women. One who thought nothing of using violence to prove a point, a bully who had taken a young girl's life in response to her so-called insubordination and had come close to taking the life of another. He would now get everything he deserved.

'Razor, the allegation against you of GBH on the punter is being dropped. Luckily for you, he doesn't want to press charges.'

Razor snorted loudly, stepping away from the wicket. 'Well he would drop it, wouldn't he? He started it. Are you letting me go again now?'

'No, we're not letting you go,' Charlie was looking forward to this bit. 'In fact, Clinton Roberts, I'm further arresting you for the attempted murder of Charlene Philips, or Caz as you know her. You don't have to say anything, but it may harm your defence if you do not mention, when questioned, something you later rely on in court...'

Razor was at the cell door, his face contorted in fury. 'What do you mean?! I'm being fuckin' nicked for that. It weren't me! It was that Asian bastard, like I said.'

She ignored the slight prickle of unease at his words, concentrating instead on Razor's snarling face as he flung himself at the door, kicking, punching and swearing in such uncontrolled rage that for a few seconds Charlie could almost imagine the terror endured by both Redz and Caz.

The sound of a particularly vociferous threat drew her away from her imaginings at the realisation she, unlike his two young victims, was fully protected from his rage. Stepping forwards towards the heavy metal cell door, she pressed her face directly against the Perspex window.

'Listen to me, Mr Roberts,' she spoke formally and without fear, waiting for their suspect to quieten. 'As a result of new evidence that's come to light, I'm also further arresting you for the murder of Grace Flaherty, better known to you as Redz. You'll be charged later with both offences.'

Chapter 57

Charlie rubbed her eyes as she pushed the door open to the office. Although it was now gone midday and her body was functioning on autopilot, her mind was still racing. Alongside her was the SOCO that had been in attendance at Razor's flat on their last search. He carried with him a holdall containing the definitive evidence on which the whole case was now based.

The team had been told of the find. Now they were to be shown it.

Hunter came out from his office and joined them, the team all crowding around as the bag was laid out on the desk. Charlie opened the holdall and took out three property bags containing the contents of the carrier bag found in the wall unit at Razor's flat during the search. These were the clinchers; the crucial items that had convinced the CPS that Razor should now be further arrested and charged. They were the exhibits that Charlie hoped would lead to his conviction for the murder of Redz.

In the first one, contained in a long plastic tube, lay a hammer. Its wooden handle was stained red and dried blood and strands of hair covered its metal head.

In the second bag, also inside a plastic tube, lay a pair of scissors, the blades of which were also bloodstained and matted with hair.

In the third property bag was a mass of hair. Blood was congealed around it, but the crimson of the dried blood could not mask the redness of the hair itself.

Charlie had known instinctively that this belonged to Redz. The missing hair, cut from her head at the time of her murder, which had been so elusive from the start. They'd been unable to find it until now, only having possession of the hair pulled out at the roots, and much had been made of this fact. The CPS had come back to this discrepancy time and time again when airing their view that a jury would believe Razor's explanation of the fight the previous night.

This mass of hair had been deliberately cut from her head and no doubt shoved straight into the plastic bag. To prove her theory right, Charlie had asked the Scene of Crime Officer now standing next to her to do a preliminary examination of a strand of hair from the bag. He'd been able to conclude almost immediately that this new sample was cut and not plucked. This was obviously Redz' missing hair and the scissors used to remove it.

'I've just come from the lab,' the SOCO said, as if to confirm Charlie's thoughts. 'Both the hair and blood samples have been verified as belonging to Grace

Flaherty. A control sample of hair has also been examined under the microscope and none still have roots attached. The ends have all been cut, most likely with these scissors, but further tests should confirm this.'

'And the hammer?'

'Also has Grace Flaherty's blood, and some brain tissue on it and was almost certainly used in her murder.' The SOCO pre-empted Hunter's question.

Charlie had always thought that the cause of death cited on the post-mortem report was a touch ambiguous. The bloody dashboard in Razor's car could certainly have caused many of the major impact wounds, but both she and Hunter had had reservations that it alone could have caused all of Redz' injuries. She now felt sure that the hammer would be proved to have caused the fatal wound.

'We'll be conducting full forensic tests on the hammer, scissors and the bag they were in, but a couple of swabs have already been taken and matched with DNA belonging to Clinton Roberts.'

'Well, in that case, Razor's well and truly fucked,' Naz exclaimed.

Charlie had to laugh at her bluntness. Still, there was no doubting they had the right man. All their initial evidence had been convincing and the withdrawn alibi had assisted further. Redz' insubordination had provided the motive and now they had the means. The hammer, scissors and hair found in the bag in his flat were the icing on the cake.

'And that's without the second charge of attempted murder on Caz.'

Charlie recalled the paramedics carrying her broken body from the scene on a stretcher and the appalling injuries on almost every inch of skin. The young prostitute was indeed lucky to have survived. She deserved to see her attacker convicted and incarcerated.

The team started to pull on their coats, preparing to pit their tired bodies against the cold outside. It had been a hell of a week. Tonight they would sleep. Tomorrow they would return to tie up loose ends.

A fine haze was lying across the city, partially obscuring the view of some of Charlie's favourite buildings, but rising up above the vapour cloud, the top of the Shard stood magnificent in the afternoon sun. She stared at it, her eyes taking in its jagged form, her mind grasping its beauty and promise, just as she'd grabbed the shards of evidence that had unexpectedly surfaced from the mire of the investigation.

Suddenly she felt weary. Casting her gaze away from central London, she followed the building line outwards in a westerly direction, until the rooftops became sparser and the wavy, green hills filled the horizon. Out farther and farther, her mind roamed, across the Irish Sea until she reached Dublin and the small, peaceful graveyard on the Banks of the Liffey.

Slipping out unnoticed, she made her way along the corridor until she found an empty office. She sat down and dialled Gerald Flaherty's number, memories of his anguished cries echoing in her head.

'Hello Gerald,' she said as the line clicked in. 'I thought you'd like to know. We've got Grace's killer.'

Chapter 58

Caz watched the medical waste sack thrown into the trolley. The cleaner wheeled it off, humming nonchalantly on his way to the next ward. As it disappeared, she relaxed, knowing that the contents of her discarded holdall might have given rise to some uncomfortable questions. It was gone now and she was starting afresh. She had everything she needed. There was no point keeping more reminders of her previous life.

She heaved herself up and made her way to the bathroom, stripping off the hospital gown and looking down at her emaciated body, covered from head to foot with livid bruises and life scars. Her neck and throat were still tender, but the swelling around her windpipe had reduced and each breath came easier.

The water in the shower warmed quickly, running hot and steamy by the time she stepped in and allowed the jet to flow through her lank hair. Looking around, she found some soap and lathered it up in her hands, massaging her fingers into her scalp and letting strands of hair cover her face. Her mind strayed back to memories of sitting on her beloved mother's lap, hiding behind her glossy curtain of dark hair. She had always loved hair. Loved the feel, the texture, the colours. It was why she loved Goldilocks so much. Her long silky hair had reminded her of her mother, until Tommy had arrived.

She had never felt guilty for pushing him that night; never regretted watching as he toppled and fell, helplessly grasping for the stair rail, his pathetic face panicked as he stared upwards into her eyes for the last time. Goldilocks had fallen from his hands, just as surely as had the scissors. He shouldn't have cut her hair off. He shouldn't have. In one loud snip her beautiful doll, her treasured memento of the good times with her mother, had been defaced, violated by the same beast as had violated her.

She hadn't planned it, hadn't meant it to happen, but she'd been both surprised and delighted at the result. Her mother had returned to her, never guessing Tommy's death was anything but a tragic accident, an inevitable result of his heavy drinking. The years of abandonment melted away and for a few precious months she and her mother were reunited, thrown back together into the close intimate relationship of which she had always yearned.

Her skin was becoming softer as she caressed the dirt from her body, her movements smooth, the soap fragrant, remembering the good times. For a few minutes she luxuriated in the memories, massaged by the gentle jet. The water cascaded over her head, rinsing the soap from her hair, following the contours of her empty body. Her life was empty too, the lifeblood drained from her, just as surely as it had bled from her mother. Her mother had betrayed her, abandoned her to the loneliness of the children's home. The knowledge was still raw. It always would be.

She turned the shower off and found a towel. Wrapping it round her, she pulled it from one side to the other, harder and harder, dragging the coarse material savagely over her flesh, until the skin on her back became reddened and sore, reliving again every hurt from the care home; the solitude, the fights and the trips to the hospital, desperate for the love she craved.

And then Razor had entered her life. As she thought of him, she let the towel drop to the ground and stood naked, her eyes closed, her senses heightened. His encouraging words and ready smile had ensnared her. He'd been prepared to look after her when she was at her most vulnerable, her emotions exposed. He'd taken her in, fed her and, in his own way, loved her; and she had loved him, with every inch of her body, exclusively, desperately, jealously. She'd watched as the other girls had taken advantage, disrespected him, disobeyed him, laughed behind his back. She couldn't bear knowing he was losing his reputation.

Looking round, she found the fresh gown supplied by the nurse and slipped it over her shoulders, yanking at the thin straps and wrapping it snugly round her naked body. She sat down in the corner of the bathroom and drew her legs up in front of her, hugging them close. Tighter and tighter she held them, as if never wanting to let them go; recalling in an instant the realisation that Razor was paying her less and less attention. Redz and Dutch had come between her and Razor, just as Tommy had caused the gaping chasm between her and her mother.

Caz closed her eyes, letting her memory replay the scene when Razor dragged Redz from the dealer's house the night before her death. Even as he had forced her into his car, she had resisted and fought against him. She remembered the mocking laughter of the dealer and his other girls, taunting and mimicking her man. She knew then she would be willing to do anything to protect Razor from their jeering. Anything.

Killing Redz was easier than even she could have imagined. Nobody had seen her as she'd crouched down in the darkness of the alleyway, her head clear, knowing exactly what she had to do. She was doing this for Razor; for her and Razor. In the end, The Punter had nearly done the job for her. She couldn't believe her luck as she'd watched Redz forced forward time and time again, her head slamming against the dashboard, her blood flowing, until finally her semi-conscious body was pushed out of the car on to the ground almost at her feet.

She'd thought Redz might be dead as she lay motionless on the concrete, but then her flatmate had moved, gradually dragging herself up into a sitting position. The ending was easy. Redz was still dazed and didn't see Razor's hammer coming until it smashed into her skull with a sickening thud. It was all over in one go. Redz let out a groan and slumped sideways, face down in the dirt. Caz knew straight away she was dead. She was glad she was dead. She deserved to die for belittling her man. Replacing the hammer in the plastic bag, she'd quickly taken out the scissors. She'd only meant to take a few locks of Redz' wonderful auburn hair as a memento, but as the sharpened blades sliced through it easily and quickly she found herself cutting more and more away.

In less than a minute, she'd shoved the hair, scissors and hammer into the plastic bag, hidden it within her jacket and melted into the background, disappearing through the concrete walkways, into the road behind. Taking the backstreets, she'd walked to Razor's flat where she stashed the bag and its grisly contents into the amenities cupboard by the wheelie bins.

She wasn't surprised when Razor was arrested. She'd been expecting it. She knew that he was not guilty and would be let out and she wasn't wrong. Planting the seed of doubt about The Punter through Angie, her handler, had been perfect. Angie understood her not wanting to talk about the man she loved, but at the same time she expected something. It didn't matter that the information was non-specific and not entirely accurate. The Punter *had* been around the area; he *had* beaten Redz up; he just hadn't been *totally* responsible for Redz' death.

Angie was more than happy with her work. Dimitri had been identified and arrested as a result of what she'd established and a nice reward was waiting. It wasn't a problem that the information had come from Ayeisha, and that her former friend would not see a penny of it. Ayeisha was dead to her. She had committed the ultimate betrayal, stealing her future, and for that Caz would let her rot... unless of course, the girl could be of use again in the future.

Her thoughts returned to Razor, banishing the memory of Ayeisha to the back of her mind. She remembered Razor's reaction to Redz' death; how he'd turned to her in the following days, just like her mother had after Tommy's death. She smiled at the thought, releasing the grip on her legs and letting the blood flow back into her numb, oxygen-starved toes, feeling her body start to tingle and pulse, just as life with Razor had restarted with Redz gone.

The decision to kill Dutch had also been straightforward. Razor had wanted to fuck her that night and she couldn't let that happen. Not when she and Razor had become so close. Her friend had wanted to die anyway and she too was becoming burdensome. Injecting the additional wraps of heroin from Turbo into her body was easy. Dutch was out of her head anyway on the extra crack. Her intervention had just speeded up the inevitable, clearing the way for her future happiness with Razor. Nobody would ever know she'd been assisted to her death. *Just another sad junkie overdose.*

The fact that Dutch had also been given a haircut had escaped everyone's attention. Her black silky tresses were far too beautiful to ignore; so Caz had snipped them off, placing them in a separate carrier bag and carefully positioning Dutch's wig over the missing locks. Nobody knew any different; few people ever having seen her without the hairpiece and certainly not her estranged family who would identify her. The carrier bag containing her guilty secret had been hidden within the amenities cupboard too, until it was safe to be retrieved.

Caz had promised to get everything sorted out... and she had. Razor would be hers and he would love her, and she would love him, and they would live together happily ever after, like she had always dreamed.

Until...

She picked herself up off the floor and gathered up the wet towel, wishing she could stay cocooned in the warmth and tranquillity of the small room forever, but as she opened the door and shuffled painfully back to the ward, the day-to-day bustle of the hospital swept away the cosy humidity of the bathroom. Life was cruel. Just as the chill, starkness of the ward encompassed her, so the brutal reality of her life with Razor had hit her in the nights after Dutch's death. All her hopes and yearnings were torn apart at the sight of Razor's final betrayal, her best friend Ayeisha inflicting the fatal wound.

Caz climbed back into her bed and felt herself enveloped in the warmth and comfort of the covers. She pulled them up over her, breathing in the airless environment, feeling safe at last within its claustrophobic atmosphere.

She thought of Anna. The woman had thrown her a lifeline by making herself available. Here was someone who truly cared, someone who believed in her, someone who seemed even to love her. As her life turned into a nightmare Caz had known the only way out was to turn to her counsellor.

Squashed behind the wheelie bins, she'd remembered the plastic carrier bags and retrieved them, fearing for her very existence and hiding them back in the flat. What followed then was out of her control and she could do nothing to stop it. She was catapulted into a whirlpool of violence, torn and tossed around and spat out to die. She knew she was lucky to have survived.

Razor was finally gone. Charlie Stafford, DI Hunter and their team had written out his life sentence with her help. The only certain way to gain freedom from his hold was to have him locked away. He would never have let her go. Ultimately she'd have ended up dead, just like Redz and Dutch, their breath snuffed out by their forced lifestyle, the drugs supplied by their pimp, dictating their choices. Nobody lived long on the streets.

She was a survivor though. She knew that now.

Someone was outside her refuge, shaking her gently. She pulled the covers back and the brightness dazzled her. Standing in the intensity of the background light was Anna, almost saint-like in her appearance. She was smiling at her and stroking her hair. She was saving her.

'Are you ready to go?' her saviour enquired gently. 'I've brought you some clothes. Hurry and put them on. I can't wait to show you to your new life.'

Chapter 59

'Clinton James Roberts, you are charged that on Thursday 14th December 2017 you did murder Grace Flaherty. That is contrary to Common Law.'

Charlie watched as Razor spat and scowled from within his cell as the custody officer read out the words of the caution. Their suspect had refused food, refused legal representation and refused to come to the custody office. Hunter had been prepared to interview him one last time, on the advice of the CPS, to give him a chance to explain how Redz' hair and the murder weapons had come to be in his flat, but their suspect had stayed stubbornly lying on his mattress, alleging only that he had been fitted up. The time police were allowed to hold suspects after arrest had now elapsed and he had lost his opportunity. As the words of the charges were read out, it was apparent that he had also totally lost control.

'You are also further charged that on Thursday 21st December 2017 you attempted to murder Charlene Zara Philips. That is also contrary to Common Law.' The custody sergeant started the caution, but his words were drowned out as Razor threw himself at the cell door, kicking at it and shouting abuse as his eyes came to rest on Charlie.

'No reply then.' The custody officer shrugged.

'I don't think he likes me very much,' she shook her head and grimaced in good humour towards Paul, who was finishing off the last bits of paperwork in the custody office.

'That's because he knows he's guilty,' Paul picked up the case file. 'In my experience the only people to claim they've been fitted up are those who know they are absolutely banged to rights.'

'I agree,' the sergeant pressed a button on the base of a small Christmas tree squashed on to a shelf on the rear wall of the custody office. The boughs of the tree sprung into life, starting a medley of Christmas carols, with the sergeant grinning as he sang 'Away with the fairies' in place of 'Away in a manger'.

Charlie had to laugh, as Paul joined in, changing the words too as he sang along. Not for one minute could she imagine Razor laying down his sweet head in the hay.

'Right, Charlie we're all done. Let's go,' Paul stopped singing and headed for the door, signalling his thanks to the custody officer. 'Apparently we've got visitors.'

Charlie's interest was awakened, but Paul refused to expand. She followed him to a large interview room at the front of the station, where she could hear the sound of voices, mostly female, some with foreign accents.

Opening the door, she saw Hanna and Michaela standing chatting to Naz, Sabira and Bet. Hunter was on the periphery, obviously not quite sure of himself among so many young females. He looked up, relieved to see Paul as they went in.

'Charlie,' Hanna called out her name as she entered, rushing towards her with her hand outstretched.

'It's good to see you,' Charlie gripped her hand, genuinely pleased. 'How are you?'

'We are both well, thanks to you,' Hanna replied, as she was joined by the younger girl. 'We are flying back to our home countries tomorrow, just in time to be with our families for Christmas. We wanted to thank you. None of us thought we would ever get to see our families again, or at least not for a long time, but you have made it possible.'

'But it is all of you that have made it possible,' Charlie looked around at the whole team before focussing her attention back to Hanna and Michaela. 'If you two and the other girls hadn't been brave enough to speak out, then we wouldn't have had enough evidence to lock Dimitri away.'

Michaela took a step forward. 'Did you ever find out who the other young girl was, in the car with Dimitri?'

Charlie shook her head. 'Not yet. The knife that Dimitri was carrying has been sent off for examination, as has the car you were in. If any other DNA or fingerprints are found, we'll take a look.' She paused.

'But at least, with Dimitri in custody, she should now be safe.'

'What about Tatjana and her baby?' Hanna's eyes clouded. 'What will become of them now?'

Bet shuffled over, passing a sheet of paper to Charlie before putting an arm around Hanna's shoulder and offering the girl a tissue. Hanna took one, holding it to her eyes, while Charlie scanned through the report. A weight was lifting from her shoulders as she read it.

'I thought you'd want to tell Hanna and Michaela the news yourself,' Bet smiled warmly towards Charlie. 'I know I would have, if it had been me who had seen...' She broke off, clearly searching for the right words. 'If it had been me who had been driving the investigation,' she said instead. Charlie guessed exactly what was on Bet's mind. It was the same as was on hers.

'It's good news, or as good as it can be. Tatjana and her family will have justice,' she said, smiling gently towards the two girls. 'Dimitri is to be charged with murdering Tatjana. The post-mortem was carried out yesterday and concluded that the cause of death was from an infection aggravated by lack of treatment after a stillbirth, but the examination also showed severe bruising in the area of her pelvis. Usually the CPS would only advocate a charge of manslaughter in these circumstances, but as you were able to give evidence that the bruising was in all probability caused by Dimitri's assault on Tatjana, along with his outright refusal to obtain medical assistance, they have upgraded the charge to murder.' She paused. 'Working together, we will ensure Dimitri is convicted of his crimes. He will never be able to treat other girls in the same way that he treated you.'

Hanna was sobbing. 'I was too late to save Tatjana. I should have done more.'

'You did everything you could in the circumstances. Dimitri is an evil, violent man. He will also be charged with child destruction and various other serious offences relating to prostitution and human trafficking. Because of your courage in speaking out, he will be in prison for many years. Albertas too. He is to be charged with the same trafficking offences. They are part of a network operating throughout Eastern Europe, each member of which, will be identified and hunted down, and all because of your bravery.'

'And Tatjana's baby?' Hanna buried her face in the tissue.

'She and her baby are together now,' Bet said softly. 'I made some phone calls after we received the formal news of the charges. Their bodies will be buried together back in Russia where her family live. The coroner's officer has been liaising with them and has explained everything. Hanna, they want the baby girl to be named in honour of you, or Charlie.'

Charlie was taken aback. For a moment she was speechless, recalling the tiny baby lying amongst the rubbish, but then she shook her head.

'She must be called Hanna then. All I did was respond to a call and start something off. Without Hanna we would never have reached the conclusion that we have.' She waited as Hanna lifted her head, tears flowing freely down her cheeks. 'Besides,' she added, grinning sheepishly at each member of the team. 'You're always saying I'm a proper Charlie, so who'd want to saddle a beautiful Russian baby girl with that name.'

The tension was broken as the team laughed and Hanna brightened immediately, her eyes now shining with the recognition.

'I will be with Tatjana and baby Hanna when they are buried and after the service I will tell her family how brave they were, and how determined you all were to catch their killer.' She turned to Charlie. 'You will not be forgotten.'

'Neither will you, Hanna,' Charlie glanced around to see Bet smiling towards them both. 'And nor will Tatjana and her baby.' She knew she would never forget what she had seen, but, just as Bet had promised, she could now foresee a time when baby Hanna's murderer would be brought to justice and she could fully move on. 'Don't forget to come back though. We still need you to give evidence.'

'Don't worry, about that. We're used to doing what we're told, aren't we?' Hanna squeezed Michaela around the shoulder and laughed, a high tinkling sleigh bell of laughter.

'Here I have made something to thank you all.' She opened the bag she was carrying and took out a tin, carefully unwrapping its contents. 'It's Medovik, or honey cake, and it's a very popular delicacy in Russia. I made it myself from my mother's recipe. Here, try some.'

The smell of honey quickly filled the room as Charlie peered at a beautiful multi-layered cake, drizzled with cream and pre-cut into a dozen slices. Her hand moved towards it automatically, before glancing at Hunter, suddenly aware that they weren't really supposed to accept gifts.

'It's Christmas,' he said with a grin. 'How could we say no?'

*

The Camel and Artichoke was bursting at the seams with Christmas revellers. Saturday night had started early, every single occupant in the bar already tipsy with good cheer.

At each new entry, the air trapped within the confines of the bar escaped into the street with a loud gasp of relief. Even the rumble of the overhead trains from Waterloo seemed unusually subdued against the barrage of noise.

Hunter had gone ahead but was nowhere to be seen. Ben, resplendent in a bright green and red Christmas jumper, was waiting by the door to the garden, as arranged, welcoming each member of the team as they fought their way through. Angie, who had been invited to share in the team celebrations, had arrived early, and was watching Ben with amusement, already having downed two large glasses of Merlot. Bet greeted Ben with a chaste kiss, Naz and Sabira with slightly more enthusiastic kisses and Paul with a full-blown bear hug, leaving Charlie unsure of what was expected of her. She paused before she got to him, grinning in delight to see Hunter battling towards Ben from a different angle, holding up two bottles of Moet et Chandon in outstretched arms.

'Here, take these,' he shouted to Charlie as he got closer. She reached up over the top of a few revellers, taking hold of them, and turned to find Ben standing directly in front of her with a sprig of mistletoe held aloft in one hand.

'Hmmn, now that's what I call a welcome,' Ben laughed, wrapping his spare arm around her waist and jiggling the mistletoe above her. 'I've wanted to do this for some time.'

Charlie felt her cheeks colouring as the team gathered round, cheering and clapping. Paul reached up, rescuing the champagne and leaving her hands to fall empty on to Ben's shoulders. She twisted her head round in panic, still unsure of how she should be acting in front of her team and, more importantly, her boss.

'Well go on then,' Hunter prompted, winking towards her as he finally drew close. 'I promised champagne to celebrate if we got both our men. Now it looks like you've finally got yours.'

Charlie grinned at the analogy. Life was full of surprises; this week more than most. But she was also well aware that this new development could muddy the waters, just as things were becoming clearer. Ben was good at present, calm, sober and in control of his demons, but who knew whether it would last?

Paul was pouring the champagne now, toasting the team's success, Charlie's success, lifting the glass to toast her future with the man in whose arms she now stood.

She closed her eyes, pushing any doubts aside, and melted happily into Ben's strong embrace... before finally lifting her lips to his.

<u>Chapter 60</u>

Christmas Day 2017

Ayeisha stood thoughtfully by the murder scene. There had been no joy in staying at the children's home. She had never valued the friendship of the other residents, seeking out new thrills and older companions instead. Now, as she stood at the spot where Redz had died, and her best friend Caz had almost met her death, her loneliness was almost overwhelming.

Two bunches of dying flowers remained tied to a fence post, the heads hanging limply from each stem, their leaves brown and dead. The life had disappeared from their petals, just as it had faded from her friends. She wandered over to the first posy, picked up the discoloured card and read the message.

> *To Redz, our great friend,*
> *We'll always remember your wicked sense of humour.*
> *Love from all the girls xxx*

The other was attached to a small bunch of shrivelled red carnations and it read.

To a young child whose life was cut tragically short.
I wish I had done more. I'm so sorry.
Maria Simpson

A few dying stems and a handful of people was all there were to remember her friend, Redz. There was even less to remember Dutch. Dutch had died alone and lay alone now in a mortuary somewhere in London, Ayeisha knew not where. As for Dimitri, she had heard nothing from him in days; clearly having moved on to older, more experienced girls, like she had so wanted to become.

She laid the second card back against the fence and shook her head sadly at the thought. How could she ever have given her virginal body to Razor believing he would provide the experience she craved? How could she have believed his promise that her friend wouldn't mind? Caz had loved Razor, even though he was a man of violence, even though she might even have suspected what he'd done. And she had ridden roughshod over Caz's dreams, just as they were materialising. Now she had lost her only real friend and, worst of all, Caz had almost died because of her stupidity.

She pulled the tab on a can of extra-strong cider, before swigging down its contents and throwing the can to one side. It clattered against the concrete, coming to rest on a dark patch that stained the roadway. She closed her eyes tightly at the sight, knowing what the darkness denoted.

Bending down, she picked up the first card and started to walk; her mind numb, her feet moving automatically. She walked on and on, passing the block where Caz and Razor had once shared their lives with her. Razor's flat was boarded up now and Caz had vanished, taken from the hospital to a new home, a place of safety where she could not go.

On she went, ignoring the coloured lights, the holly wreaths, the flashing reindeer and the sounds and smells of festivities in full swing behind windows covered in condensation.

She came to a plain wooden door, with broken locks, a splintered frame and no decorations. As she approached, she heard a shout and saw the door open wide and a figure emerge, beckoning her to join him with a bony finger. For a moment she hesitated, reading again the words of camaraderie from the girls on the card, hoping afresh that Caz just might be inside. Hope was all she had. Her friend would turn up back at her old haunts, wouldn't she? She would forgive her and forget what had happened. The other street girls would become her family again, just as Caz and Dutch and Redz had been.

DK was grinning now as he held the door open and ushered her inside, his fingers brushing her buttocks lazily as she stepped forward into the vapid smoky air. She wafted her hand to better see who was there, scanning each and every one of the bodies lying comatose along the settee and against the filthy carpets, but Caz was not there.

Ayeisha stood silently staring, tears stinging the corner of her eyes, at the gradual realisation that this was to be her destiny. The room was full, but inside she was empty.

The door slammed shut behind her and an arm circled her waist, pulling her slightly off balance. The same bony finger as had beckoned her in was drawn through her hair, slipping steadily down inside the neck of her jacket. She heard the rasping of his breath, warm, stale air filling her nostrils as his lips grazed her bare shoulder.

'Happy Christmas, Ayeisha,' DK murmured. 'So glad you could join us.'

*

Ben sat at the head of the table, a paper hat clinging heroically to the side of his head. At his feet, Casper lay curled into a ball, sleeping soundly, his belly full with Christmas treats. To his side were Lucy and Beth, both red-cheeked and bright-eyed, singing along raucously to the words of 'White Christmas' on the compilation CD, their wine glasses already half empty.

Meg staggered through, weighed down with a tray laden with roast potatoes, roast parsnips, bread sauce and the obligatory Brussel sprouts. She slotted the various dishes into gaps spaced down the centre of the table before hurrying back out to the kitchen to gather more.

'Are you ready?' Meg shouted breathlessly to where Charlie stood gazing out across the still frosty lawn, over the frozen birdbath and naked trees, towards London. Charlie tore her eyes away, waiting for her thoughts to follow, before turning to prepare the turkey platter for its grand entrance. For a few seconds her mind was transported to a time long ago and the story of Christmas, a tiny baby swaddled in a manger surrounded by onlookers, its mother and father standing proudly to the side. The reality of life as she had seen it crowded in, trying to push away her imaginings, but this time she wouldn't allow the horrors to take precedence. There was evil in the world, but today she would be concentrating on the goodness in humanity, the Hannas, the Michaelas, the Maria Simpsons, the Annas, even the Cazs. Today she would be celebrating family, friends and the future.

She hoisted the serving tray up in readiness, pausing for a second to gaze at her mother's giant bronzed bird, resplendently displayed amongst the seasonal stuffing and pigs-in-blankets. It was a standing joke that Meg always chose the biggest turkey in the world for the Stafford Christmas dinner.

Taking a deep breath, Charlie pushed through the door into the dining room and was met with a loud cheer. Lucy and Beth stood to salute the entrance of the turkey, while Ben cleared a large space in front of him, clashing the carving knife and fork together in preparation for its first slice. Charlie edged around the table to where he sat, her eyes passing over the empty seat opposite her sisters that would forever remind them of their missing brother. Carefully she bent over, depositing the precious load on to the table in front of Ben, before moving to the seat between him and where Jamie should be.

Christmas Eve had brought her and Ben together for the first time, but not without the odd nightmare bringing her doubts to the fore. Was he really ready to throw himself into a relationship yet? She didn't know, but she had to give it a chance.

Ben was grinning from ear-to-ear as he leant forward and placed the knife against the turkey breast, but Charlie could still see the glimmer of a tear in his eye. His childhood had not been the happiest, and his adult life too had not been without pain. Suddenly she realised how much today would mean to him. Reaching under the table, she gave his knee a squeeze, leaving her hand resting against his leg. Automatically, he put the knife down and cupped her hand in his, tracing his fingers over each of hers. For once there was no sign of a reaction as his finger passed over the scar on her ring finger and drew the shape of a heart against the back of her hand.

'Come on, get on with it. We're all starving,' Beth shouted, bringing Ben's hand shooting out from below the table to grab the knife again, his cheeks burning red.

'Aw, poor boy,' Meg admonished, laughing. 'He'll wish he hadn't joined us all.'

'There's no chance of me ever feeling like that,' he smiled back at Meg, his face suddenly becoming serious. 'I know this isn't what a rufty-tufty old soldier is meant to say, but I really do appreciate you inviting me here. This is shaping up to be the best day of my life.'

He bent across to plant his normal reserved kiss on the top of Charlie's head, but this time she lifted her head and allowed herself to dream about the future. Christmas Day had brought the best present she could have wished for.

*

Caz leant back on the settee in her new apartment and looked at the recently unwrapped presents. A small hamper of Christmas food, several scented candles and a box of assorted smellies lay on the coffee table. Not since her mother had died had she been given gifts at Christmas and the sentiment had moved her deeply.

Anna had only recently left, promising to return later when the kids had fallen exhausted into their beds, full of turkey and chocolates. For the first time on Christmas Day, Caz would be on her own. This year though she didn't mind. This year was to be the start of her new life. The studio flat was everything she could have hoped for. In it she would find safety. In it she would find stability.

Her body felt rested and the doctor's prescription was holding her crack dependency at bay. She got up and slowly walked around the living space. A rug lay on the floor next to the bed and she curled her toes in the wool, feeling its softness and depth. The texture stirred a familiar feeling inside her. Her handbag lay on the bed. As she opened the zip, Anna's phone number fluttered down on to the covers. She smiled and placed it carefully on the bedside table.

Climbing up on to the thick duvet, she pulled Goldilocks tenderly from the bag. She came out with difficulty, the new stuffing filling the inner emptiness of her precious doll. She was clean and fresh now, but her short blonde hair would always be a stark reminder of Tommy and her mother; a time of her life that was gone, but never forgotten.

Caz held her breath and stroked Goldilocks across her face, revelling in the familiar texture and softness. She lay back against the pillow and closed her eyes, brushing

Goldilocks slowly against her cheek again. As she did so, she thought of Anna, her face smiling out from the confines of her family photograph. She thought of Anna's little daughter, her hair so beautifully long and curling, her arm draped protectively around her younger brother's shoulder. So many times when she'd lain on the couch in Anna's office, she'd stared at those photos, admired them and coveted the family bond.

She frowned. Something wasn't quite perfect. As she stroked her doll's plump body with her fingers, she felt something sharp and bristly. Looking down, she saw a few strands of the new stuffing sticking out from her doll's belly. She pulled at the strands, extricating them carefully from Goldilocks. Lifting them up to the light, she saw two hairs, one long, glossy and red, the other shorter, coarser and black.

People around me always seem to die. The warning had been given calmly and explicitly to Anna just a few days earlier.

Caz smiled as she released the two hairs, watching mesmerised as her two precious mementoes floated down on to the rug.

Anna was hers now... and nothing or no one would ever come between them.

Or else...

Acknowledgements

Sometimes an image stays with you for a lifetime. Sometimes you do nothing with it, allowing it to fade into the background, though it never quite disappears. Sometimes you try to forget it, but it rears up and reminds you of its potency, motivating you to write, or draw or just simply remember.

The image of a young girl, lying on a hospital trolley, has remained with me since around 1986, when I first started work at Streatham Police Station and became aware of her plight. I got to know her and her family over many years. I still remember her name. Her life is not one that I would want for myself, my family or indeed any girl on this planet and the memory of her decline comes to me on almost every occasion that street crime, drugs or prostitution is discussed on TV or in radio debates.

I do not know whether drugs or prostitution should or should not be legalised. I don't know whether legalising drugs would take away at least some of the dangers surrounding their purchase and use, or whether properly controlled brothels would afford women in that occupation at least a little more safety. What I do know is that both drugs and prostitution, to my mind, are dangerous and degrading and I say this only from my experience in working the streets of Lambeth, as a police officer for many years, and getting to know many of the women, and sometimes men, caught up in the vice and drugs trade. I make no judgement of the rights or wrongs because I have been lucky enough to avoid the pitfalls.

This young girl did her best, but without the support she required it wasn't enough to save her from a lifetime of drug dependency. For quite a few years, she tried to escape its clutches, but ultimately she was too damaged. I fully acknowledge her efforts and I wish I had been able to do something substantial to assist. She is regularly in my thoughts, however, and even though there was little I could do, that image has been a driving force in my quest to help people and seek justice.

I also would like to acknowledge my sister, Dee Yates. It was the fact that Dee had written a published novel that got me dreaming and it was she who encouraged me to set my early memories about the young girl into prose. She, more than anyone else, initiated my love of writing crime fiction and has encouraged and motivated me ever since. Dee herself writes beautiful historical family dramas and has recently seen her third book, *A Last Goodbye*, published. She remains my inspiration, and though we don't see each other often due to living at opposite ends of the UK, I love to talk to her and hear her news and we will regularly swap writing manuscripts for each other to critique. I have to also acknowledge her tenacity in doing this, as our subject matter and style is very different and I know she finds some of my storylines challenging to read. Perhaps I was a police officer in London for too long?!

I also would like to say a huge thank you to my friends and family for their faith in me and the encouragement and patience they continue to show. My partner Trish and daughters Suzie, Jen and Jackie are always on hand to offer their thoughts and cast their votes on my ideas for plotlines, straplines or titles.

My siblings, Rosie, Malc, Phil, Katie and Chris in particular are my greatest supporters, pushing my efforts onto their own friends and relatives in all parts of the UK and Australia, as well as to book clubs and anyone else they happen to meet. I thank you all very much.

Combined with my thanks, I also send my apologies to the above. When I have a deadline, I have to say that everything else gets set to one side and I disappear into the cavern of my study, grim-faced and demented, only reappearing every now and again to top up the mugs of tea – an action that I repeat quite liberally in my characters' lives.

And now, to my great agent Judith Murdoch and inspirational editor and publisher Caroline Ridding, whose job it is to keep me writing. A massive thank you for continuing to believe in me, and for your words of wisdom and advice in the editing and publishing processes, both of which are gradually becoming a little less daunting as time goes by. I believe you both go way over and above what would be expected and I cannot thank you enough.

Caroline, you are a legend. Thank you for your endless enthusiasm and sound judgement as well as your ability to see through my worries and get the best out of me, whatever the time of day or, certainly, late evening. Thank you too for heading the exceptionally close, enthusiastic team at Aria and Head of Zeus. The whole team is a joy to work with, providing boundless energy, endless updates and a huge amount of additional work

.

Extra thanks too go to Nick Walters and Rebecca Winfield who continue to work hard with Judith on my behalf in Europe, with *Mummy's Favourite*, *The Trophy Taker* and *Liar Liar* now being rolled out in Germany, Poland, the Czech Republic and Italy. I love seeing the new covers and translations of my books by Weltbild, Amber and Omega and continue to be amazed and excited at their popularity.

Finally, many, many thanks to every reader who takes the time to read, review and recommend my books. It makes a huge difference and I can't tell you the pleasure I feel at reading that someone has stayed up all night to finish my novel or couldn't put it down – although I'm not sure their family or boss would think the same. To all the bloggers who have been part of blog tours or have conducted a 'cover reveal', I send my heartfelt thanks. We authors would be nothing without those of you who give us your support or pass on the word. Thanks also to everyone at Goodreads, Amazon, Kobo, Netgalley, Sainsbury's, Facebook, Twitter and Bookbub for getting my name out there. Please continue to message or like my pages and I will continue to reply where and when I can.

Last, but by no means least, thank you to Lynda Kelly for your detailed reviews. I love your hugely positive comments about the content and will continue to concentrate on parts of the English language I struggle with – and I do mean that sincerely. Don't give up on me yet!

Thank you so much to everyone,
Sarah xx

HELLO FROM ARIA

We hope you enjoyed this book! Let us know, we'd love to hear from you.

We are Aria, a dynamic digital-first fiction imprint from award-winning independent publishers Head of Zeus. At heart, we're avid readers committed to publishing exactly the kind of books we love to read — from romance and sagas to crime, thrillers and historical adventures. Visit us online and discover a community of like-minded fiction fans!

We're also on the look out for tomorrow's superstar authors. So, if you're a budding writer looking for a publisher, we'd love to hear from you. You can submit your book online at ariafiction.com/we-want-read-your-book

You can find us at:
Email: aria@headofzeus.com
Website: www.ariafiction.com
Submissions: www.ariafiction.com/we-want-read-your-book
Facebook: @ariafiction
Twitter: @Aria_Fiction
Instagram: @ariafiction